"As gritty and shrewd as Chicago itself, *Coyote Loop* brilliantly probes the underbelly of our city's famed trading pits in the nadir of 2008, where brutality and grace collide in John Ganzi: South Sider, struggling dad, and a character I won't soon forget."

—Emily Gray Tedrowe,
author of The Talented Miss Farwell

"In John Ganzi, Fiore gives us a fast-talking, foul-mouthed, money grubbing options trader we would love to hate—if only we could. As he navigates fatherhood and friendship, and runs headlong into his own tragic flaws, he earns our hearts."

—Heather Newton,
author of Under The Mercy Trees

"Irreverent, funny, heartfelt...*Coyote Loop* drops us into a bull pit in Chicago at the peak of the '08 recession, guided by a trader's voice that seems the very eye to our human condition. Masterfully spun and deeply entertaining, Fiore has delivered us a literary grenade with the pin pulled."

—Owen Duffy,
author of One Summer on Cutthroat Lake

"Populated by wonderfully drawn characters and lighting prose, *Coyote Loop* is a hell of a joyride through Chicago's financial district right before the late 2000's crash and recession. This interesting cast of characters is lead by narrator, John Ganzi, a recently-divorced, wealthy options trader who is out of out shape, out of control, and whose life is transformed when his teenage daughter comes to live with him.

"Fiore paints this world with the practiced hand of a skilled writer as a man and a city are on the verge of change. Like all good fiction, *Coyote Loop* takes us to a place we hadn't expected, yet somehow entertains and informs at the same time. This is a novel you don't want to miss."

–Steve Cushman,
author of Hopscotch: a Novel

COYOTE LOOP

Coyote Loop

A novel
by

L.C. FIORE

Adelaide Books
New York / Lisbon
2021

COYOTE LOOP
A novel
By L.C. Fiore

Copyright © by L.C. Fiore
Cover design © 2021 Adelaide Books

Published by Adelaide Books, New York / Lisbon
adelaidebooks.org
Editor-in-Chief
Stevan V. Nikolic

For any information, please address Adelaide Books
at info@adelaidebooks.org
or write to:
Adelaide Books
244 Fifth Ave. Suite D27
New York, NY, 10001

ISBN: 978-1-954351-37-0

Printed in the United States of America

For Eloise, of course.

Woe to him who doesn't know how to wear his mask,
be he king or pope!

LUIGI PIRANDELLO, Henry IV

I wish I was ocean size.

PERRY FARRELL

Chapter 1

Mid-morning crush, up to my elbows in the pushy, sweaty gnarl of the trading pit. Markets are totally fucked, guys already talking about throwing themselves into the Chicago River, and it's not even 10:00 am. Also, somebody has passed gas, and it settles, slow and thick as honey. The fragrance hangs an impossibly long time, comes to rest in our nostrils and on our tongues. That strange way other people's farts sometimes smell like an invitation, on a primal level. How dogs sniff each other's asses to figure out if they're friend or foe.

"What would you do if you didn't have this, huh?" Pasternak, in his beige clerk's jacket, leers up at me from his place on the desk.

It's like he's read my mind. "Was I talking just now?"

I've been talking to myself a lot lately. I'm not the only one.

Every trader in my pit is in crisis mode, trying to figure out if now's the time to sell, or if we just need to sit tight and wait for the bounce. Days like this, when the VIX shoots way up and throws everybody else into frenzy, I like to get up on my little fucking footstool, breathe deep, and really take it in: the abject panic. The bloodshot eyes. The sweat stains turning blue traders' jackets nearly black. The way other traders slam their phones into the cradles; the way they jerk their ties back and forth because Jesus Christ, sometimes we forget to breathe. Not just my guys, but in all the other dozen pits along the trading floor. The louder people scream, the quieter it gets for me. The slower the ticker scrolls.

In the old days, when I was first starting out, back when ours was the only options exchange, when you literally could not trade options except through one of the brokers at CBOE, like myself, who owned a seat, or several seats, the trading floor was a stocked pond: you just cast your line in the water and caught something, no skill required, and you motored away feeling like you had the biggest cock on the lake. You'd go upstairs to the third floor and find half the Executive staff passed out at their desks, drunk from lunch.

Now that things are going electronic, customers no longer need to trade through a broker—they don't even need a seat on the Exchange. Yet those of us who own seats still wade into our pits every day, thrashing our arms and crying out until the veins in our necks bulge, knowing that not only are we expendable as human capital, but that the very trading pit we occupy is obsolete in today's fiber-optic world. Ignoring the empty pits around us, the void encroaching like an unknowable darkness; ceding more and more of our real estate each day to puissant tech-nerds programming tangles of circuitry and wires meant to do one thing and one thing only: outperform us.

It's me against the machines. Fucking John Henry and his silver fucking hammer.

Banks of monitors, six or eight high, loom over us. Our modern gods—only by their graces do we exist at all. And today, they're a sea of fucking red. Everything's down. Like a pointillist painting of a blood spill, tiny red dots in aggregate show everything trading at a loss.

"Pull your heads out of your asses," I shout. "We're going under eight."

I just lost my two best guys, kids I hired right out of college. The minute I staked them, I told them to save—save until it hurts. And they actually listened. Now they're millionaires at thirty. Both deciding to take time off, one to airbrush vistas in fucking Tibet, the other to start his own vineyard somewhere south, like real South, not south like Champaign, but Virginia. The state. Part of me envies them. But they're dead to me, leaving me short-staffed at year's end.

"*Sportscenter*," I say, then louder. "Somebody turn on some fucking *Sportscenter*."

I want to watch a ticker scroll past that I don't have millions of dollars invested in. I return to the wall of screens. Finally, one of the monitors clicks over to ESPN.

What would I do if I didn't have this? Maybe pick up a hobby, handball or squash—something lateral so I don't have to run too much. My blood pressure would be forty points lower, I tell you that. Maybe meet a member of the opposite sex, in the flesh.

The trading pit erupts—thirty dudes shouting and waving their hands. I look toward the screens. CNBC is on commercial; nothing special on the ticker. Then I notice *Sportscenter* is showing highlights from the Bulls' game. Our rookie point guard drained eighteen points, but turned the ball over five times.

"Fucking Rose!" somebody cries. Others shout him down. The pit, like the city, is divided on whether or not Derrick Rose is the future. We've seen the future before, in David Terrell or Mark Prior. It always ends the same. On the television, red jerseys like slips of ribbon weave down the hardwood, leaking out into the stands.

I was eighteen when I started out as a clerk, taking classes at Harold Washington part-time. Earned my degree, the whole time moving up. Millionaire at twenty-six. What would I do if I didn't have this? Get a tan, maybe. Drive an ambulance—do something fucking useful. What's happening now is unprecedented. Fannie Mae, Freddie Mac, Lehman Brothers. Most of the world's major economies are in full-blown recessions. Numbers whirl across the screens faster, almost, than a human eye can read them, but there's really only one number I care about.

The Dow Jones Industrial Average hasn't been below 8,000 since 2003. It's not even lunchtime, and we're down 300 points. Another quarter of that, we're below eight. And then? Welcome to the White House, president Obama. You've just inherited the worst economy since the Great Depression.

"JAG!"

Down here, we mostly go by our call-signs, which, to be honest, I like better than making up nicknames for fucking everyone, which would otherwise be the irritating biproduct of so many men spending so much time together, day in, day out. JAG stands for John Andrew Ganzi. I have to duck when Pasternak swings a phone at me, the cord whipping through the air like a scythe.

The fuck aren't we wireless yet, who knows? "I'm busy."

He only blinks once. "Sounds urgent."

"Pasternak." I turn to look at him but keep clicking with my little stylus on my little hand-held screen, so he doesn't think I've dropped everything to address him. "Hang up the fucking phone."

"It's John Paxson."

It's like he's hit an enormous bell with a sledgehammer. The trading pit falls silent. You could have heard a pin drop—it's why they invented the cliché. For moments like this.

"With Deng out, he wants you to suit up tonight."

It's an ongoing joke between Pasternak and me. He says somebody famous is calling, and everybody has a laugh at my expense. I figure I'm such a prick otherwise, it's okay to let this slide.

"Give it to me," I tell him.

"Line seven."

This industry is full of pranksters. There's a guy on the board of the Chicago Board Options Exchange, sends out homemade calendars each year with pictures of himself in various ridiculous scenarios—all nude, but with props staged so you can't see his junk. This guy, he's in his sixties. Worth twenty million, easy.

I grab the receiver, press the blinking orange button. I blow a long breath into the mouthpiece. "How's it going fuckface?"

What my guys don't realize, of course, is that no matter who Pasternak invents—the GM of the Chicago Bulls, John Belushi, Saul Bellow—it's always the same voice on the other end, small and far away, sounding as if she's calling me from a tin can tied to a string.

"Hey Dad," my daughter, Jeanie, says.

"Why you calling me at work?"

She sighs. "I have a favor to ask."

Somebody in the pit reaches up and tries to tweak my nipple. No respect. I wave him off, then extend my middle finger.

"Listen, can I call you back? This isn't a great time for me."

"Oh." She seems to consider. "Sure. Or..."

A buzzer goes off, announcing the close of markets in London. I hear it in the telephone, too. And then I realize she's not far away at all: she's here. Not in the trading pit, but somewhere nearby. I turn and scan the mezzanine, where packs of Asian bankers, financial tourists, are pressing their noses against the glass. And I see my girl among them, a fleck of white on a deer-tail, a snapshot of any seventeen-year-old private school knockout, standing on the viewing platform. Her wave is a flat palm turned out. In her other hand, a cell phone, pressed against her ear.

"Meet me under the Board of Trade," I tell her.

Then she disappears, swallowed by an ocean of blazers and ties.

Pasternak glances my way. "What's up, boss?"

"I gotta take an early lunch."

Usually, I take a late lunch in the courtyard outside the Exchange. The plaza is mostly empty then, sometimes entirely, especially if the wind's coming in off Congress. But I enjoy the breeze. Sometimes I need to air out. I'm inside too much. In the pits. Forget what the sun looks like. But on the nastiest days—stiff wind, horizontal wet shit, basically the entire month of November in Chicago—I'm out there alone.

I can be the only guy in the courtyard, minding my own business, and some asshole will decide to sit right next to me, slurp his skinny mocha no-whip, shout into his cellphone— forty benches spread over half a block and inevitably some jackass takes the seat nearest me.

Today there are about two million fucking people on their lunch break. A bunch of finance types sucking down cigarettes and yammering on their phones, nobody watching where the fuck they're going. I have never verified this with anyone, but I always assume sidewalks are two-way streets. Traffic flows both ways. You stick to the right except to pass. But mostly everyone just walks wherever they want to, including straight through me. How many assholes a day pick me out and try to walk over me, so I'm the one's gotta step aside? Every time: I'm a fucking swinging door. Pasternak explained it this way once: "You're the only guy out here who doesn't look like an asshole."

Everybody knows looks can be deceiving.

I don't look threatening. 5'6" and a beer belly. But fuck it. I bought my first seat on this exchange for $200K back in 1985: now it's worth over $2m.

Me and Jeanie's mom split when Jeanie was ten. Her mom is a professor down at University of Chicago. We make a point not to see one another; we communicate via our respective legal teams. When we divorced, my ex-wife got our brownstone on the Southside, half of everything I'd made up until then and a third of what I've made since. And she got Jeanie.

Jeanie's waiting for me in the breezeway below the Board of Trade, wearing a winter jacket the color of pink bubblegum. She looks tiny against the late-morning bustle and all the black overcoats brushing past, like a diamond on felt. She's been taller than me since she was twelve, but now with these boots she has on, I need to stand on tip-toes. She's a puff-ball beneath my hands, in that coat—nothing there. Weightless as cotton candy.

There's a gold cross around her neck, a fragile-looking thing. I run it between my fingers. It's cool and smooth. The two rectangles shine like they've just been polished. "What is this?"

"Oh." She stuffs her hands in her coat pockets. "I got confirmed."

I pat my jacket, hunting for cigarettes. "Aren't you a little old to be confirmed?"

"Well, I wasn't exactly raised religious." We briefly make eye contact. "I have some catching up to do."

I nod, plugging my mouth with a smoke. This religious stuff, it's her rebellion. It's new for everybody. I don't think we even had her baptized when she was a baby, and now she talks about books of the Bible like it's a series I'm supposed to be watching on HBO. Could it be worse? I suppose. But can't it always be worse?

I tell her, "You should be in school."

Already we've attracted the attention of half-a-dozen homeless. The country may be in a recession, but these guys have been on the streets a long time. They still remember the late nineties, when traders would leave work and pass out hundred-dollar bills. I'm in my jacket and tie, so they know exactly what I am. A hard-scrabble crew forms on our periphery. Circling like sharks. Smelling blood.

"That's why I'm here," she says. "My economics teacher wants to take a field trip."

I blow smoke in the direction of a few bums who're getting too close. "You're taking economics?"

"I guess the apple doesn't fall far from the tree."

Her voice is so flat, I can't tell whether she means it or if she's trying to be funny, maybe.

"I don't think that's how you use that phrase, exactly," I say.

She sighs. "Anyway, do you think we could bring my class down here and like, see where you work?"

I try to read her face, past the brown bangs and the square nose and slight overbite. More and more every day she reminds me of her mother. And like her mother, most of the time, she's totally full of shit.

"Why aren't you in school?"

"Dad." She rolls her eyes. "They let us leave for lunch."

"You couldn't ask me this over the phone?"

Parenthood is full of tricky decisions like this. On the one hand, there are massage parlors in Thailand where I'd be more comfortable taking my daughter for the day. On the other hand, I would fucking love for her to see where I work. There's something inside a man that wants his kid to be proud of him.

"Some afternoon, maybe," I tell her. "Not a Friday. Or a Monday. And not at the end of the month, or the beginning. But mid-week, sure."

She toes the pavement. "Ok, cool."

"What?"

"Will we need to pretend not to know each other?"

"I think that'd be best, yeah." I nod toward the Exchange. "It's just, these jokers. They don't get it. None of them have families."

She raises an eyebrow, skeptical as all hell, and I finally see some of my genetics coming through.

"Thanks," she says. "I think it'll get me some extra credit or something."

"Just have your teacher call me."

She grins. "I'll have him call Pasternak."

I point my finger like a gun and wink, and immediately hate myself for it. "Even better."

When we hug goodbye, I stuff two fifties into her hand. I think maybe she pauses for a moment to wipe her runny nose on my jacket.

"Is that everything?" I ask.

I stand there with my arms still open, wanting her to come clean. To tell me why she rode three stops on the Blue Line to talk to me in person. We are jostled closer to one another by the foot traffic. The "L" passes overhead. We wait for the rattling of the tracks, the squeal of brakes.

"I'm playing basketball," she says, walking away from me backwards, fading into the commuters and unwashed street urchins. "Home game tonight against Marshall...."

"I'll try to make it," I tell her, but I don't think she hears me. The "L" roars over us, the sucking out of wind from the breezeway and then its vicious return.

There's this city holiday, Casimir Pulaski Day, where basically, in honor of a Polish Revolutionary War hero, all the kids get to take a day off school. More than that, it's a city-wide "Bring Your Kid to Work Day." It's tradition; it's sanctioned; no one questions it. I always know when it's Casimir Pulaski Day because the "L" is twice as packed. And then I remember. Cavalry general! Pollock. Bring Your Kid to Work Day.

Except that a trading pit is about the least kid-friendly place on the planet. Between the farting and the language, nobody ever brings children down here. That, and if a guy comes in with his family, that's likely to be seen as a weakness. Something for the rest of us to exploit. A bit of advice handed down from the older guys when I first started: never leave pictures of your family lying around. There's nothing sacred in the pits. Absolutely nothing. Plus, no pictures means less shit you have to grab when you finally get fired and security comes to escort you out.

Security comes to escort all of us out eventually, one way or another.

This is what I tell the new guys, first day. About the pictures. And if you're on time, you're late. And don't watch porn on your phone. Don't share porn with one another, don't even *think* about porn while you're on the job. I've seen way too many guys who looked promising get canned because they thought it'd be funny to e-mail somebody else a GIF of some bimbo swinging her plastic boobs in opposite directions. Don't let the fact that it's mostly a bunch of swinging dicks down here lull you into a sense of security. There are women around. Some, anyway. And the fucking tech nerds upstairs are always watching.

So what the guys send me instead, especially this time of year, are pictures of their hunting trophies. Every day or so my phone goes off, and there's a picture of one of my guys or somebody I know from some other firm, squatting beside a slain buck, holding up the deer head by its antlers. Their cheese-dick grins inviting me to count the points.

"Six?" I text back.

I know that points are something people, hunters, count and that, as in basketball, the more the better.

A text comes back carrying a digital sneer. "Try ten, bro."

But I gotta have the last word. "Let that be a message to all other deer who dare venture into your woods."

This is how the males of our species bond. If you go hunting and shoot something large, you have your buddy take a picture of you, and then you text the image of yourself—soaked in blood, cheeks chapped from the cold—to all the other men you know. But mostly I find myself wondering about the moment before. What I really want to see is a video of some stock analyst slinging a 200-pound carcass into a truck bed, smearing himself with animal guts as he wrestles the corpse over the tailgate.

In the movie *Red Dawn*—the original, not that millennial remake pile of shit—there's a scene where a character, Danny, the youngest of the teenage survivors who are all out living in the woods after the Russians invade, shoots his first deer. And the oldest survivor, Jed, the leader, makes Danny drink the still-warm blood of his kill. He needs to drink the blood so the spirit of the deer will live inside him forever. And at first, he can't stand the taste, but by the end, he drains the cup, blood running from his chin and down his neck. Grinning like a mad man. "It's not so bad," he says. "It's not so bad."

I text again. "Drink the blood."

I don't hunt. I get a bit choked up if I see a dead pigeon on the street. But somewhere in the wild a beast is brought down; a picture is taken; the subject of the photograph is so impressed by how he looks that my name springs to mind. "You know who'd love this? John Ganzi."

It's something about me—a certain quality I have.

After lunch, the trading pits are calm. It's like we're all worn out from the past month, the past year. Volume is low, prices are flat. Half the monitors are turned to footage of the OJ trial, where the Pro Football Hall of Fame running back is being sentenced for armed robbery. Fourteen years ago or so there was the original OJ trial, which we all watched, it was on everywhere, it was kind of the first reality television show. And now? The sequel. We are equally rapt. Who goes on trial twice, for separate crimes, and gets both trials televised? It's a testament to his longevity, as well as, perhaps, and indictment of our criminal justice system. Also, our obsession with celebrity. As a country.

There's no sound. The camera stays on him, mostly. He doesn't look like a star anything. In the blue prison uniform, he looks like a janitor on the eve of his retirement. All the fight is gone.

"Hundred bucks says he gets ten years," one of my guys calls out.

A handful take him up on it. I pull a wad of cash from my pocket. "I say he gets fifteen."

The news footage is mesmerizing, even without the audio. I feel like he could have had a long television career: he's a natural in front of the camera. You have to be a special kind of stupid, though, to beat a murder rap and then get caught years later for armed robbery. I want to ask guys like him, "What the fuck is wrong with you?" They get busted for a crime, it's not because they need the money. There's some other reason he's in a hotel room with a gun, trying to steal some crappy sports memorabilia. Maybe hanging on to the last shred of his glory.

Either way, this trial is one helluva performance. They oughta give him an Emmy.

"Thirteen." Pasternak stuffs a couple twenties into the hand of our impromptu bookie. "There's a lot of thirteens bouncing around."

This is the kind of shit Pasternak notices. It's like he believes numbers hold some alchemy that he needs only to decode in order to cash in.

"Thirteen years to the day he beat that murder charge," he goes on, unprompted. "And the jury delivered the verdict in thirteen hours. Waiting on that third thirteen, baby."

All of us watch the ticker: without the sound, they'll have to put the sentencing up as a graphic for us to know who's walking away with a little pocket money.

"Mr. Ganzi."

Someone calls my name, somebody from the Exchange staff, sounds like, because they're the only ones who use the *mister* shit. It's one of the warehouse guys, and he's waving a Fed Ex envelope at me.

"Ezra." I step back from the crowd. "Good afternoon."

He hands over the envelope. "Two o'clock delivery."

Two o'clock guaranteed means shit. Most likely it's a board agenda, or new SEC filings the Chairman of the Exchange is up in arms about. If I'm really lucky, maybe a vendor has sent me two tickets to the fucking *Nutcracker*—something I can re-gift.

"Thanks, EZ." I take the envelope. "How's the wife?"

"Good, sir." He has the simpleton mail-clerk act down pat. As if we don't know he and the other high-school dropouts in the warehouse hate our guts and curse the gods that people with manners as bad as us make as much money as we do.

"Your anniversary is coming up."

"Yes sir," he says. "You have a good memory."

"Where you taking her?"

"Oh, I don't know. She enjoys the Maggiano's a whole lot. A whole lot. Maybe there. You know, they give you an entire second portion to take home with you."

My pit explodes, men shouting over one another. The OJ sentencing parades across half the monitors in flashing, animated, capital red letters: fifteen years in a Nevada jail. My guys boo and throw shit at the screens. An envelope stuffed with cash makes its way through the crowd and into my hands.

"Drinks on me!" I holler at my guys, and they all cheer back.

Ezra tries to take this moment to escape, but I grab his elbow. "Hang on."

I pop open the envelope, fan the bills, then decide fuck it and tuck the entire stack into the front pocket of Ezra's jacket.

"Take her somewhere nicer than Maggiano's," I tell him.

I don't stick around to hear him object. Or thank me. I plunge into the swollen mass of men, waving the Fed Ex envelope above my head like I'm afraid of it getting wet. I toss it on a pile with the incoming mail, where it teeters on a stack of magazines and letters, probably three day's worth.

"Pasternak." I only say his name, and I know he hears me. "Let's try to get through some of this mail tonight, okay?"

The markets close down 5 percent, the lowest the Dow's been since 2003.

I usually eat dinner at 4:30 or 5:00, usually takeout from the cart in the lobby, a sandwich and chips. A bottle of Bell's beer, whatever's seasonal. With the pits closed, I ascend to my keep on the twenty-third floor of Library Tower, the building next door. They're attached, in fact, so if the weather's truly shitty, I don't even need to go outside to get from the trading floor to our firm's offices.

Tie off, feet up on the desk: all the day's mail piled around me, fistfuls of envelopes and magazines. *Crain's*. Letters from the 1 million companies I get rewards from. A letter from the Standard Club reminding me my membership is due. I write a red letter *A* on the mail that needs action and set it aside for Pasternak. The firm pays for half of this shit anyway; who knows what it costs? The Chicago Club, for example. When's the last time I had lunch at the Chicago Club? When's the last time anyone did? Most of it, you just keep renewing because you're afraid of what will happen if you don't. What if you want back in next year, or the year after, and suddenly they're full up? Or *National Geographic*. I'm terrified to let my subscription expire. I've been a subscriber since I was four years old. Not because I read the fucking thing, because most of the time I can barely work up the energy to glance at the pictures, maybe if I'm taking a crap, but because I'm afraid that if I don't renew, every endangered species in the world will suddenly die off. My subscription might be the lynchpin that keeps it all together. Without it, ecosystems crumble.

"Pigs get fat!"

Pasternak bellows somewhere, engaging in a kind of call-and-response with himself. Something else I drill into my guys every day: don't get greedy. Pigs get fat; hogs get slaughtered. Today a position we'd backed away from a few weeks ago, when it looked like the only way it could go was up, tanked 60 percent. Far below what we sold it for. It's a moment of happiness in an otherwise bleak year. Sometimes seeing other people lose is better than winning something yourself.

"Hogs get slaughtered!" Pasternak sticks his head in. "Boss, okay for me to leave?"

The lights in the office are motion-sensitive, so sometimes if I sit still long enough they go out, and I gotta throw something across the room, or get up and wave my arms, to make the lights come back on. "Hey, grab a beer."

He takes a bottle from the still-cool six-pack on the desk. Moisture streaks the glass, the label peeling. I lean forward and pop the cap with my cigarette lighter.

"Happy birthday," I say, clicking my beer against his. "To me."

"Shit." He balances himself on the corner of my desk. "My bad, JAG. Happy fucking birthday."

I take a long swallow. "Mind if I ask you something?"

"Shoot," he says.

"It's personal."

He stops his bopping around, rattles his knuckles on the desktop. "Okay."

"Your old man, he worked the line at U.S. Steel what, thirty years?"

"Forty."

I make an expression like, about what I expected. "So how the fuck did you get so smart?"

"My dad, he's not dumb. You remember. He just never had enough imagination to dream up anything different for himself."

"You guys still close?"

"Nah," he grins. "He's an asshole. Just like everybody's father."

We drink to this invariable truth.

"My dad?" I wipe my mouth. "Spanked me with my communion spoon. When he died, Mom and I discovered he'd taken out credit cards in my name. Ran up tens of thousands of dollars in debt. I was thirteen."

"I remember."

"Anyway." I look him in the eye so he knows I'm just stating facts. "Today is a banner day. I'm forty-fucking-four years old. You know what that makes me?"

"Old as dirt?"

"Older than my father was when he died."

Pasternak lets that factoid settle. Takes a drink, then another. Finally, he shakes his head.

"He scared the living hell out of me." I drink. "That's the truth."

"Well," Pasternak says. "Here's to outliving our most terrifying monsters."

"Salut."

We drink in silence.

"A teacher from Jeanie's school might be giving you a call," I say.

"Already spoke to him." He drains the rest of his beer. "Tried to actually talk shop with me. As if I give a fuck. But yeah, I got 'em scheduled for next Thursday."

"Thursday works."

"Okay, goodnight then."

"Pasternak."

"Yeah?"

"You're the only one around here who knows I got a daughter."

He winks. "And when she trots down that escalator with the rest of her classmates, she'll just be another potential hottie in a training bra."

I shake my head. "You're a little bit sick, you know that?"

"She'll turn eighteen eventually."

I swipe a pen from my desktop and hurl it at him—he ducks it, easily. "Fuck you."

"Happy birthday, boss."

He gallops down the hall—"Hogs get slaughtered!"—and then he's on the elevator, and the floor is silent.

The Fed Ex delivery is on my desk. I rip open the tab. My knees are showered with flecks of cardboard. Inside is an official-looking letter from the law firm my ex-wife uses to communicate, because we can't stand to be in the same room together, and these days can't even muster the energy for a phone call. The gist of the letter is pretty straightforward. She needs me to sign off on a change to my custodial rights, because she's taken a new job and wants to move to Florida.

With Jeanie, of course.

I sit thinking about this for a long time. When my office lights go out again, I remain motionless, in the dark, with only the hum of office equipment and the emergency light around the exit sign, faintly glowing. I'm on the twenty-third floor. Forty floors total. Figure there's at least one person left on each floor, like me, chewing the last of their cold dinner in a black office. Sealed inside glass and steel. As dark inside as out. And as quiet. Forty lost souls.

There's one positive to waking up at five o'clock in the morning: my days stretch endlessly.

I leave the office and drive over in time to catch the second half of the varsity girls' basketball game. I keep an eye out for my ex-wife, but she doesn't show. It hardly matters. Immediately, I am absorbed by the very un-Ganzi like athleticism of Jeanie, the star shooting forward for Whitney M. Young Magnet High School.

She is a gazelle, gliding down the length of the court in six graceful leaps. Her arms are twice as long as anyone else's—she seems to have four arms, or eight. She's everywhere at once. If you've ever seen an octopus, on PBS or something, rise up on its legs and run along the ocean floor, it's pretty unfucking-believable, first of all, but that's what Jeanie looks like on the court—poetry underwater.

She scores sixteen points, grabs a dozen rebounds. A lot of parents, guys who work for me, secretly suspect their kid is the best player on the team at their respective schools, and if she's not, it's only because she's not getting enough playing time, or the coach is playing favorites, or other players are hogging the ball. But in Jeanie's case, there is no question who the best player is: it's right there in the numbers.

She hits the shot to tie it and gets fouled. She drains the free-throw and wins the game. Two of her more butch teammates carry her off the court on their shoulders. Raise my daughter high above their heads, parade her down one sideline and then the other. Their school colors primal, black stripes circling their bare shoulders, the crisp orange trim on their shorts. That's basketball, though. I read about in *National Geographic*. You can trace its roots back to the Aztecs, where squads faced off on a court pretty similar to what you see today and tried to boot the severed heads of their enemies into baskets lifted high on the wall.

I wait for her, after. She seems happy to see me when they come skipping out of the locker room on the heels of a hard-fought road win.

"You came," she says.

"You're good," I tell her. "I'm serious. You can play college."

She shrugs. Her coach stops to congratulate her. He's tall as fuck. He has to duck a little at each doorway.

"Coach," she says. "You remember my dad."

We shake hands. His are dry, strong.

"How long are you in town for?" he asks.

It takes me a minute. "I live here."

He folds his hands behind his back, embarrassed. "Sorry. I just assumed—"

"I work," I tell him, but my voice tumbles out like gravel. "I don't make it to as many games as I should. As I'd like to."

Jeanie rescues us. "I should get going."

"Let me give you a ride." I flash my car keys.

"Uh—" She glances longingly at her teammates clambering into the bus.

"C'mon," I say. "It's my birthday."

She blinks. "I'm sorry, Dad. I didn't get you anything."

I shrug. "Then let me drive you home. I'll make it worth your while."

We go for ice cream. I get a cone. She orders some kind of cherry slushy. We're the only customers, and we slurp at our rewards, huddled together in our winter jackets. She talks about her economics class. Each student has put together their own virtual portfolio, and they're competing for the best returns. She complains that some of the guys picked only adult entertainment companies, or casinos. But she believes in *moral investing*.

"What's that?" I ask, trying not to sound incredulous.

"Investing in companies owned by Christians, for one."

I stick the rest of the cone in my mouth, to gag myself from saying anything. I've been trying to be more supportive, even though this Christian thing is really coming out of left field.

"Mostly, anyway." She considers. "I'll also invest in a company if they demonstrate considerable charity work."

I remind myself she's seventeen. Only seventeen.

"Everyone has an investment strategy," I tell her. "I think yours can work as well as anybody else's."

"That's just it." She rams her straw up and down a few times, breaking up chunks of ice. "My stocks suck. I'm getting walloped by the heathens."

"A semester isn't really enough time for a contest like this. You need five years, minimum."

She's quiet for a moment.

"Maybe you can give us tips," she says. "When we come for our field trip."

I nod. "We don't trade stocks, we trade options. But yeah, we'll see."

The ice cream has numbed my mouth. My hands are the same temperature as the room—thoroughly chilled. It's cold outside, but this particular frozen sensation seems to be coming from inside of me, originating in my core.

Just yesterday at the Standard Club, I was doing the stationary bike. Some days I'll do weights, but only if there's nobody else in there with me, because I'm too embarrassed that I got to use the little silver weights, the ones they set aside for women in a little silver fucking pyramid.

But yesterday I was cycling on the recumbent, knees cracking like splitting timber, paging through *SI*. Old guy, really ancient, came in and sat on the bike next to me. Never seen him before. He sat down, and I knew, *I just knew*, he was going to talk to me. Nothing I could do about it.

I kept reading, trying not to make eye contact. He cleared his throat. He couldn't resist. After all, the gym was empty, other than us.

"I'm seventy-seven years old," he said.

Outside work, I try not to be a dick. "I hope I look as good as you when I'm your age."

I can't keep my mouth shut, obviously. Even though, in general, I can't stand people.

"My wife just died," he said.

I slowed down pedaling, lowered my magazine. "I'm sorry. Christ."

"We had just gotten home from a lovely dinner." His shoulders slumped, like he had no bones or muscles to support them. Like his chest was nothing but a bag of blood. "With the kids. She goes into the bathroom, comes back out. 'I'm dying,' she says." He made a flattening motion with his hand. "That was it."

He didn't cry. He seemed more baffled by it than anything. Maybe the sadness hadn't settled. Maybe he felt like if he told enough people, something about the whole thing would make sense.

"Fifty-two years," he said. "What the hell am I supposed to do now?"

But I didn't have an answer for him. Nobody does.

In the ice cream parlor with Jeanie, the windows so fogged we can't see outside, I wonder about that old guy at the gym, and his wife, and how she knew instantly that she was dying. Maybe it was a feeling like this: like she couldn't get warm.

"I heard from your mom," I tell her.

"She wants to move to Florida."

"Is that why you came to see me today?" I give her time to answer, but she doesn't say anything. "What the hell is in Gainesville?"

"It's warm there."

"It's death's waiting room. All those old people."

"Mom's set on it."

"Because of the new guy?"

"Patrick."

"I don't want to know his name." I try to wipe the sticky shit off my hands, but after crumpling through a dozen of those stiff, cocktail-sized napkins from the dispenser, they're still sticky. "I don't know what she's thinking, moving you now. You've got, what, a year left of high school? It's the worst time to move a kid."

"Then let me stay with you."

I rub my face and sit there a minute with my eyes closed. I shouldn't underestimate Jeanie anymore. She laid a trap like a punji pit and let me tumble into it.

"My condo—"

"Is huge," she says. "There's plenty of room."

"I work all the time."

She laughs. "I've got my own things going on."

"We haven't lived together since you were a kid."

"I spend weekends with you. Some, anyway. We have fun."

She blinks at me, inscrutable. Christ, she looks just like her mother, but with my talent for negotiating. We've created a monster.

She leans forward, reaches for my face, and plucks off one and then two bits of cheap napkin stuck to my chin hairs. She rubs them between her fingers, and they disappear like snowflakes. "Think how furious Mom will be."

It's the perfect thing to say, and she smiles just a little bit. She knows what I'll decide to do, even if I'm not remotely ready to admit it. Jesus. No one her age should have closing skills this polished.

"How's that slushy?" I ask.

"Not so bad."

She takes off the lid and tosses back the cup, trying to get at the last of the ice. When the cup falls away, her mouth and tongue are stained red, the sugar-blood pooling on her chin.

Chapter 2

The first couple years after high school, I was working at the Exchange and going to college part-time. I had my own place on the West Side, not far from Chicago Stadium. Back then, they were still murdering people left and right out there, every corner was dark, just a bunch of parking lots and row housing. Forget about catching a taxicab if it wasn't game day. But then they tore down the Madhouse and built the new arena, and eventually some art galleries moved in and that saved the neighborhood: now there's a Whole Foods and fucking Jills walking around everywhere, and the sidewalks are lit bright as day all the way from the river west to the United Center.

I was on my own, financially and otherwise. But I was a good son. I never forgot about my mom. Every Sunday I'd get down to South Chicago for dinner, to the house I grew up in. And for a few years there she kept my bedroom just as it'd been the whole time I was growing up. The Carlos May poster on the wall, my KISS dolls, a couple art projects I'd made coming up through the CPS. And there was always that feeling, stepping back into my old room, of time preserved. I'd open the door, see my water bed, the Lamborghini Countach stickers plastered all over my desk, and I'd be seventeen again. My mom felt it too. No matter how many years went by. We'd sit down to dinner, and all of a sudden it was 1981. I reverted into the socially awkward kid I'd been growing up. And this went on long past the time I was banking six-figures and could legally drink.

Some of it was due to all the physical shit being exactly the same, the books and posters and chairs, but also the smells, that slight dampness coming from the returns, the lingering castor oil in the downstairs bath, the one my dad had used for his last few months. The two of us in the same arrangement— my father's chair now empty, as it had been for years—brought up all the old fucking baggage like neither of us had changed a bit. Which wasn't true, not even for my mom, who hadn't worn a different hairstyle since Van Morrison was a coherent stage persona. We'd sit there making small talk, eating veal parm and tortellini beneath a cloud of sadness. Neither of us could have named what the sadness was, but I remember it distinctly—I remember wanting to run from it. Because she and I couldn't face what that sadness meant, that maybe she missed my being around. That maybe she was struggling to find her purpose with me gone. That maybe despite all that had happened since I left home, maybe we really hadn't changed. My mom and I, we were crushingly lonely. We had that in common, just as much as we shared genes.

Jeanie and I roll down Lake Shore Drive to the Southside, into Hyde Park. I pull up to the curb, kill the engine. The bushes are strung with white Christmas lights. A shovel leans against the porch steps, where I always left it. Usually, Jeanie hops out, and I drive away—I never look at the place. I found out early on that whether my ex had changed something or hadn't, it was equally depressing. Now I look, though, and see an "Under Contract" sign in the front yard. I recognize the logo of the real estate company, the same that handled the sale of my mom's house when she died.

We get out. I lock the car. We pause on the stoop.

When I'm under pressure, it always feels like someone has stuck a 2x4 in my gut. Like there's a big plank of wood lodged there, like I might hurl. It's suddenly hard to take deep breaths.

"She sold the house?" I manage to say.

I think again about the guy at the gym whose wife just died, if death is cold and short on air.

"Mom said she wanted a clean getaway," Jeanie says.

You can ignore certain truths as long as certain other truths persist. I could ignore the way I was raised, my life under my father, while my mother was still alive. Once she died, though, I had to work through some shit. Now that I'm standing here, about to see my ex-wife, outside the house we once raised our daughter in, together, but now has sold—just exactly how much I've missed over the past seven years wallops me, all at once.

Jeanie takes my hand. "It's okay, Dad."

She closes her eyes and says a quick, earnest prayer for us both—for patience, love—before opening the door.

We hear voices in the dining room, the tinkle of flatware. We move through the kitchen, past a countertop strewn with takeout boxes. My ex was never much of a cook. Early on, when we were first living together, she gave it a shot, but defrosted Steak-umm was the limit of her culinary skills. This meant we usually ordered in, which in my mind is one of the top-five best things about the modern world, just below text messaging, Netflix, and valet parking. Tied for fourth with wash 'n fold laundry service. Stepping through her kitchen now, I see some things really never do change. The stovetop still carries the gleam of the showroom. Some plastic strips remain on the burner knobs.

Jeanie leads me into the dining room. I find myself standing near the head of an oblong, black table. At the far end is Azita, picking at a bowl of noodles. Seven years have gone by, but her skin is still flawless, the color of hazelnut and indeterminate ethnicity—Iranian, it turns out, on her father's side. Just enough Arab in her to make any guy look twice.

She raises her head to greet Jeanie, and sees me.

"Jesus Christ," she says.

I offer a half-bow, arms extended. "Resurrected."

Jeanie indicates the waifish man seated near the end of the table. "You've met Patrick."

I haven't, but he and I nod to one another.

"Where on earth did she find you?" Azita wants to know.

"It's okay." Jeanie holds one of my hands with both of hers. She rubs my fingers as if to warm them. "I found him at work."

Azita gives a mean little laugh from the back of her throat. "That figures."

Patrick stands, wipes his mouth, comes around the table. He takes his time. I work with enough nerds to recognize the look of someone processing higher mathematics. He's calculating quite a few things right now, but he's only got two options. He can try to man-up, to follow Azita's strong, if off-putting, opening, and be hostile. Or he can work the other side, be a gracious host, and welcome me like family. He knows he's got a better chance of staying on Jeanie's good side if he chooses the latter. He pumps my hand with his clammy maw, offers me liquor, beer, cigars, all in the span of a minute.

"Bourbon neat," I tell him. "Thanks."

Jeanie takes my coat and scarf. She wraps the scarf twice around the hook.

"You sold the place," I say, stupidly, standing in the dining room feeling naked, suddenly, without my outerwear.

Azita shrugs. "We thought about renting it, but do we really want to be landlords?"

"I was happy with @Home, when we sold my mom's house."

She nods. "I'm sorry again."

She extends the peace offering, and I accept. So civilized: sorry and thank you. Words we could never say to each other while we were married, that's for fucking sure.

She and my mom never got along. The two of them reenacted the crusades over the holy grail of my affection for pretty much the entire span of our relationship, not longer than the actual crusades themselves, it turns out, but it sure sometimes felt like it.

"The commercial-at." I smile at Jeanie, who scoots up to the table, bows her head, crosses herself, and seems to say grace. "The Spanish used it, centuries ago, to track shipments of wheat. Commodities."

Patrick returns from the kitchen and lays a place for me. There's something almost womanly about his movements, how precisely he places the flatware, bending over at the waist.

"That's your business, isn't it?" he asks. "You speculate on stocks?"

I ignore the word *speculate*, which makes me sound like I ante up for five-card stud every day, and glance at Azita. She merely shrugs, waves her hand over the food, and tells me there's plenty.

"Now the Spanish use the at-symbol to denote gender neutrality," she says.

She smiles, more or less for real. I think about her students—her smiles have always been hard-won. I'm sure her majors clamor for her approval like light-deprived lab rats.

"We were just reading about it," Jeanie says. "Different languages give it different names."

"The Dutch refer to it as a monkey tail," Azita says. "Swedes, a cinnamon roll."

Patrick has prepared a bourbon for himself as well and winces at the first sip. "What is it your people call it?"

I raise an eyebrow, knowing full well what he means by *your people*, but Azita grew up outside Detroit, in the 'burbs, surrounded by more blue blood than an aorta.

She corrects him, in her way. "In Farsi, they refer to it as a Moon's Ear."

"I like that," I say.

I sip from my highball. My heart slows down a little. My gut doesn't feel quite so compromised. Despite the ice cream I just ate, I find I almost have an appetite.

What's left of dinner incudes an artichoke salad, wild mushroom ravioli, and a Dover sole where the artichokes return for a cameo, along with asparagus and fava beans. I can't eat asparagus without thinking about how my pee's going to smell afterward. There's really nothing else in the world that has that kind of dramatic effect. Coffee, if I drink enough. But the asparagus gets me every time.

It's quite a room. Azita agonized over its assembly; not so much the price. The chandelier incorporates four miles of delicate nickel chain and recalls something vaguely aquatic and pale and free-flowing. The chairs are comfortable but chic, framed in metal, their cushions the same color blue as the sky in late summer, just as the sun drops off.

There's over 100 thousand invested in this room alone, and that's before you account for the carpet and drapes and let's not even mention the china. I disliked the pattern when we chose it out of a Spode catalog a decade ago: I hate it now. It looks like someone dropped bone-white plates into a field of purple wildflowers and put the dishes away wet.

"Your hair has gotten long." I call to Azita down the infinite table.

She shrugs. "I haven't had time to cut it."

"It looks good."

Flattery goes a long way with her, so I sit back and wait for mine to take hold. Tossing out compliments like expeditionary scouts, like children forced to walk in front of the Libyan army, to find the landmines. She's wearing a long-sleeved thermal shirt. The neck is wide and sweeping, to show off her collarbone.

But she's damn inscrutable. Always has been. Her entire approach—it's like she can't be bothered with the rest of the world. She never lets it excite her, or frustrate her, or even, I'd argue, inspire.

"Jesus Christ," she says. "Jesus Christ."

She teaches at U of C. I never fully understood her focus, but it has to do with sex and Christianity, or gender in antiquity—maybe both. There were always a lot of fem-dom books lying around with titles like *Adam, Eve, and the Serpent: Sex and Politics in Early Christianity; She Who Is: The Mystery of God in Feminist Theological Discourse.* Shit that I sometimes used to pick up and try to read but immediately put back down. *Love Between Women: Early Christian Responses to Female Homosexuality.* The ability to incorporate two words ending in either "ism" or "ist"— and drop a colon two-thirds of the way through your impenetrable title—were the only requirements for publication, because comprehensibility sure wasn't.

Azita has settled her eyes on something just to the right of her plate, lost in thought. Patrick spears his fish with his right hand and cuts with his left, in the manner of the Europeans. Jeanie, despite the slushy and the late hour, eats like someone famished.

"So," I say. "Florida sounds nice."

All dinner sounds cease.

Azita coughs into her napkin. "I was going to call you."

"Why? Fed Ex is so reliable. They always give it that personal touch."

"University of Florida," she explains. "2/2. Fully-tenured."

"Sounds cushy."

"Sounds like the job you take right before you retire."

She's far from retirement, though, twenty years away, easy. I ask, "Then why take it at all?"

She shrugs with one shoulder. She wipes several strands of hair away from her face. Then she gestures, one hand, a turn of her wrist in the air, indicating the dining room, the house, and, I realize, the *Sold* sign in the front yard.

"I got transferred, actually, is what happened," Patrick says, quickly. "Better hours, more pay. Plus, it's where I grew up. My family's still down there. The business."

"What do you do?" I ask.

"Construction," he says.

"Is that like when the Mob says they work sanitation?"

I try to catch my ex-wife's eye to see if she's self-aware enough to find it funny she's living with someone who works construction—she, who has enough brains and good looks to marry royalty. That was our favorite fairy tale, actually, a shared joke throughout our marriage. She was the princess who kissed a frog, only the frog never turned into a prince. All she was left with then, was me.

"Not a great time to be in the home-building business," I tell him.

"We're consolidating," Patrick allows. "These things are cyclical."

"Cyclical?" I drink deeply. "Or eating its own tail?"

"This recession crushed us," he admits. "Still, there's money to be made."

I can't tell if he's just posturing. Sure, firms are making money off foreclosures and all kinds of government subsidies, but Patrick doesn't strike me as the type to swindle widows and immigrant families out of their homes. As I said though, looks can be deceiving.

"Gainesville," I muse. "Not actually on the water."

"It's perfect." His face alights in that self-satisfied way people talk about the places they're from, that they love. "We're an hour from the coasts—gulf or ocean."

"I never understood why people live in Florida without living on the water." I wipe my mouth with my napkin. "Seems to me Gainesville, or Orlando, places like that, have all the negatives of Florida—the humidity, the snowbirds—without any of the benefits."

Having set the bait, I am content to wait for someone to step into the trap. I set my knife on the side of the dinner plate. Immediately, it slides off, landing with a thud. I pick it up and set it down blade-side up where, mercifully, it rests.

I'd forgotten about this particular flatware, which we also registered for. Beautiful, satin-finished, stainless steel—and the fucking things never stay on your plate. Something about the way they're designed. I never quite figured it out. The way their weight is distributed causes them to slide and spin and fling bits of food and sauce everywhere. Our dinner parties were always punctuated by silverware slipping from our guests' china, the shrill slide of steel against enamel and then the solid drop of it against the tabletop—or floor. A ringing reverberation, deadening finally to silence, depending on how far it dropped. The mumbled apologies—our apologies in return for ever buying such stupid fucking silverware in the first place, and then continuing to live with it. If a guest rose for seconds, fucking forget about it. It was a Charlie Chaplin routine, them trying to keep their silverware on their plates long enough to get from the table to the kitchen and back again.

"I can't believe you still have these," I say.

"Take them." The one-armed shrug. "We're downsizing."

"Does that include Jeanie?"

Azita glares, poking remnants of fish carcass with her fork.

"Jeanie will be a senior next year," I say. "It seems like a brutal time to move a kid."

"I don't disagree." She leans back, folds her arms. "Jesus Christ."

Yes, I'm going to make her say it. And I want it to come from her, not from Patrick.

"What happened, Azita?"

"It started with a lay-off." She glances at Jeanie, then at me. "With my being laid-off."

"They refused her tenure," Patrick says angrily.

"It's happening everywhere," she explains, quickly. "Universities are figuring out it's more cost-efficient to use adjuncts than to tenure professors."

"That may be true," I nod. "But that doesn't make it just."

She shakes her head, laughing. "I doubt you're worrying too much about justice when you're getting fat off junk bonds and sub-prime mortgages."

"I don't happen to buy or sell either of those things," I tell her. "I'm not the bogeyman. I'm scrambling just like everyone else right now."

"Scrambling," she sneers.

Jeanie has cleaned her plate. "I still don't see why that means we have to move to Florida."

"It's where I could find work," Azita says.

"And it's where I'm from," Patrick says again.

"With what they offered, I should look at it as a blessing."

"And it's like fourteen-thousand miles away," Jeanie says, louder now.

"Don't be dramatic," Azita says.

"And the house?" I ask.

"You know what we paid for this house. Do you know what it's worth now?" Azita asks.

I shake my head. I honestly don't.

"Half, John. Half of what we bought it for ten years ago."

This may be true, although I suspect it's more like 75 percent. "But surely the mortgage is paid off, what with what I've been paying you in alimony?"

Azita shrugs. I see now they've only been paying the minimum. Where the extra money went, who knows?

"So rent it," I say. "Rent it to the next rube U of C hires to be an adjunct."

"I'm done, John," Azita says. "Done with being a homeowner. Done with Chicago. Done with the winters. Done with all of it."

"Done with being a parent?" Jeanie asks.

More silence.

"About that," I say. "I do have some rights as far as Jeanie is concerned."

Azita leans forward and sets down her wineglass. "And what are your custodial rights, exactly?"

"Mom." Jeanie cuts in.

"We don't need to get into that," I tell the table.

"No?"

"You've been more than generous, and I appreciate that."

"Only for Jeanie's sake. She still loves you, for some reason."

I know what kind of man I was, years ago, and what happened between Azita and me. I know what our inability to get along—to even be civil—has cost me, both in terms of time spent with Jeanie and financially. Emotionally too, I suppose, given that I'm about one more bad internet date away from purchasing a Real Doll© and fucking a mannequin for the rest of my life. Still, it stings.

I glance at Jeanie. Her hair hangs over her face. It's hard to imagine what she's feeling.

"Well," I say. "We shouldn't talk about Jeanie like she's not here."

"We could talk about you like you're not here," Azita says, eyes flashing, "like we have for pretty much her entire life."

"Look," I say, and everyone does, at me. It only unnerves me for a moment. "Let's just get something out of the way here. I know we're all thinking about it, so. You know. Today, it was a normal day for me right up until about lunch time, when Jeanie called. Came to see me, actually. And since then, the day has gone a whole lot differently from what I imagined."

"You thought OJ would walk?" Patrick says.

"Jesus Christ," Azita says.

I reach out and smooth the table runner in front of me, a black, lacy fabric with embroidered silver fishes and other aquatic life. "Obviously, Jeanie," I pause, to makes sure she's looking at me. She's not, but she seems to be listening. "Obviously, maybe I haven't been around as much as might be ideal—"

"Ideal?" Azita nearly howls.

I look at her, then Patrick, then Jeanie, whose hair is like this scrim that I can't quite see through. "I'm just presenting the facts."

"The facts?" Azita slams her hand on the table so hard the china leaps from the tabletop. "I'll give you some fucking facts, Johnny. Thirty-six hours. That's how long I was in labor.

Seventeen years. That's how long I've been raising Jeanie pretty much solo."

Maybe it's being seated across from Azita again. Maybe it's the way I can hear Patrick chewing the fava beans, how the legumes squeak between his teeth. But Jesus Christ, as I'm sitting here, I can feel the years peeling off. I can feel something inside me—deep fucking inside of me—start to untether itself from where I've kept it moored since the divorce. That same old familiar impatience. I suddenly have the urge to pound my fists on the table and shout myself hoarse, which is pretty much how I felt the entire last year of our marriage.

Instead, I stand, take a deep breath, fold my napkin, and drop it on the chair. "Not solo."

In the china cabinet are displayed a dozen antique place settings hand-painted with wild animals—boars and bears, antelopes and grouse. Some kind of homage to the anglophile fantasy of a sporting afternoon spent hunting with horses and dogs. They're hideous: defiantly so.

"Mom's china," I say.

"Take them." Another shrug. "We'll sell them otherwise."

Above the plates, sealed behind glass cabinet doors, are a set of wine glasses, gilded by 24-carat gold. "Those goblets."

"Were they your mother's too?" Patrick lifts his voice, trying hard to be friendly. He's so well-meaning, he doesn't even realize how much most of what he says makes him seem like a gigantic dick.

"No, actually." I shove my hands in my pockets, feel my pack of cigarettes there. "Those, Azita purchased on a trip to Oviedo. $1,700 for the set? Something like that."

"They're Moser," she explains.

"Keep in mind—and here's a bit of family history for you, Patrick—but at the time of purchase, she was a full-time graduate student at Northwestern, paying a tuition of some $45,000 a year."

"I've already thanked you, countless times, for putting me through school." She traces the hard line of the tablecloth with her finger. "I'm not obligated to do it again."

I throw open the cabinet door, and one of the little brass nobs comes off in my hand. I let it drop.

"Whew." I act impressed. "There's all kinds of stuff in here." I snatch a highball from the shelf. It's imprinted with a sterling silver cypress tree, a nod to my ex-wife's heritage. "These—I remember these. We just had to have them. $220 a glass, times twelve. $2,600. Plus, we paid to ship them home. Where we were? Bodrum?" I toss the glass in the air and catch it. I can hear my ex-wife's intake of breath. I judge the weight of the glass, adjust my grip like a pitcher on a fresh baseball, and turn again toward the table.

"Johnny," she says. "This has been pleasant. But maybe it's time to leave."

"I should leave?" I twirl the highball, guiding the glass through space like a rocket. "Point to one thing in this room I didn't pay for. Go ahead and do it."

She shrugs, obstinately calm. "You can't buy rights to our daughter."

"Point to one fucking thing." I give her time, but she can't. "Your entire professional career, I paid for. I should be getting a percentage of everything you earn. Because that's how it fucking works in the real world, when you stake someone, a start-up. You get kick-backs. Or you earn royalties. Where would you be if I hadn't funded your education? That entire year, or was it two, which you spent lying on the couch pretending to read? You'd be on the street. When we got married, I bought this house. We didn't have you sign the mortgage application because your credit was terrible. What's your credit score now?"

"I'm not doing this."

"What is it?"

"740."

"And I'm still paying you alimony? Jesus Mary mother of Christ." I step forward, lean in, fists clenched at my side. "Maybe I'll just take all of it. I'll consider it my birthday present. Which, by the way, you haven't even mentioned."

She looks toward Patrick, then down at her hands placed flat on the table. Her fingers are long and tan and sharp against the white cloth.

"Happy birthday." She raises her eyes to mine. "Now get the fuck out of my house."

Chapter 3

The next morning, I sit in my attorney's office, watching her jackhammer keys on her laptop like she, too, may have some rage issues tucked inside her suit jacket and pencil skirt.

"This is a big decision, Jonathan," she says. "Are you sure you're ready?"

I'm seated in a swivel chair, half-blinded by the wall of windows at her back, which afford a view of the South Loop and beyond that, Lake Michigan. I shift, groping for that stiff little lever to raise the seat, and when I can't find it, give up.

I needed legal advice around the time of my divorce. Penny Weil, Esquire, wasn't even a junior partner then. Now look at her: blonde hair cut sharp below her ears; fingers manicured like she dipped them in glue. I imagine her apartment is black and white—checkerboard backsplash, snow-toned sofa—her refrigerator stainless steel, the ice maker placed inside the door so as not to disrupt the aesthetic lines. She's the kind to make her bed each morning. Who eats pizza with knife and fork.

Her office is a goddamn monk's cell. Not a scrap of paper anywhere. I find this unusual for a lawyer.

"That's what paralegals are for." She shifts her weight from one foot to the other. "I can't think when there are piles of paper everywhere."

Paper, photos, chairs that don't immediately make my ass scream bloody murder—all of these are absent. She stands to work her laptop, which perches like a falcon on a raised and slanted desk, the kind architects use.

"Anyway," she says, gesturing toward South Chicago, "I'll get in touch with your ex-wife's attorney. But we have basically zero leverage."

"I want to fight for her." I poke the desk's tempered glass. "I want Jeanie to stay in Chicago, with me."

She leans forward, squinting, and rubs out my fingerprint with the cuff of her suit jacket. "Then I encourage you to have a conversation with your ex. That will be easiest."

"You don't know Azita."

"Not to be melodramatic about it, but the only way Jeanie stays with you in Chicago is if you convince your ex that it's best for everyone." She stops typing, looks at me, then begins typing again. "Everybody has a price, Jonathan. No one knows that better than you."

My attorney is the only one who calls me Jonathan. It's not my name; my birth certificate says John; but I like it, coming from her. I had a nun in six or seventh grade who called me Jonathan. She never let me forget about my Biblical namesake, some kind of B-list celebrity warrior with superior archery skills. In most cases by comparing the Old Testament Jonathan's many admirable traits—loyalty, truth—with the absence of those same traits in me.

The amount I'm paying my ex-wife in alimony could fund a small African village. She got Jeanie, of course. I have no idea what I could offer to make her say yes to this. One thing you learn in business school is that it's impossible to negotiate when you have zero leverage.

"So, how are you?" my lawyer asks.

"Peachy."

She's typing away, not looking my direction at all. "Any trips planned?"

"Since when do you make small talk?"

"I'm going to bill you the full hour regardless. We might as well enjoy ourselves."

Her wrists are poised above her keyboard. There's no ring on her left hand, and I try to remember if she's ever mentioned a husband. I haven't heard her reference any kind of significant other, male or female. No tell-tale use of the plural personal pronouns, we or us.

"I may run down to Cabo for a few days." I drop the name of a place she might have heard of, gauging her temperature, testing the waters.

She glances over. "Have you been?"

"No. I don't get away too often."

"Work?"

"I just lost my two best guys," I tell her. "I'm doing the jobs of three people right now."

She nods. "I notice you don't have a Will filed with us."

"How's that?"

"A Last Will and Testament? Is some other firm handling that?"

"There's no one else." I realize how that sounds, and suddenly I flush like I'm twelve years old again and talking to some girl I have a crush on. "There's no other firm."

"You really ought to have one." She resumes typing. "You don't want to leave anything to chance. I've seen shit go down you wouldn't believe. When there's no Will—"

"—there's no way?"

She pauses for a moment, looks at the top of my head, then down to my tie, then at my forehead again. "People lose their fucking minds."

"What do I have to do?"

She stops typing, steps away from her desk, and extends her hand. "Stop by reception on the way out. I printed some forms to get you started."

Jeanie's tenth birthday—I don't look back on that time with particular fondness. Her mom and I hadn't quite gotten up the courage to separate. We were trying to make it work, but it was a major victory if we were able to occupy the same room without scraping each other's eyes out.

I'd woken up with a headache, been out all night before, some industry party, a late dinner that turned into drinks and then wherever else, and when the alarm went off I wondered if I was still drunk. It was one of those mornings where nothing could move fast enough: the coffee dripped from the brew-basket like condensation. It was just about the worst state of mind to be in when I was supposed to be going out to chaperone a dozen pre-pubescents on the beach.

We'd secured a couple picnic tables, and Jeanie's mom was on me the whole time about what I was wearing and that I smelled like a brewery and there wasn't enough cheese fucking pizza and somehow that was my fault. I was blowing up white balloons, and they left this powdery feeling on my lips. I tethered those balloons to the table like a truce. Surrendering to Azita, saying look, *I'm here. You don't gotta ride my ass.* But the kids were all yelling and riled up and sugared up from the soda, and there were a couple parents there with nothing better to do on Saturday than hang out at a ten-year-old's birthday party, blathering on about their doctoral theses, which is just about the most boring subject in the world, I don't care if you study the deviant sexual behavior of chipmunks, I still don't want to hear about it—nobody gives a shit. And it was like I wanted to reach in there and yank the words out of their mouths they took so long to finish their thoughts. The worst part about parenting is having to deal with other parents. There are times you wake up and you're just not in the fucking mood—even for your own daughter's birthday.

We were just finishing the Lou Malnotti's pizza, which I'd driven all the way up to Skokie for, when out of nowhere this pit-mix, not one of ours, comes blasting in and buries its snout right in the birthday cake, which up until then had been immaculate—custom-designed for Jeanie, some kind of screen-printed photo of a band she was obsessed with then, the Backstreet Boys, with icing letters curling over it. Kids scatter; dog mounts that cake like he's gonna fuck it, all the while launching pop bottles and pizza boxes across the grass—everybody's shouting, Jeanie's crying, and I don't think, I just jump in there and grab the mutt from behind, drag him off the table, and wrestle him into the dirt. The dog's kicking, tearing up my arms, so I flip it over onto its stomach and drop my knee into its back. I finally get it pinned, and then I start digging my fingers into its throat.

Everything goes red.

The dog's doing this kind of shimmy, not really fighting me so much as wiggling its hips back and forth. And it's kind of comical really. It's not making much noise. It's got yellow and red icing around its lips and on its nose and smeared across its throat, right where I've got my fingernails hooked into its windpipe and my knee on its rump, deflating that beast the way you roll up an air mattress, pushing all the wind out one end.

If the kids were shouting before, they're silent now. I hear a voice—the owner standing over me, just a black smear against the sun, a vague movement of shadows and glare saying, "Please, guy. C'mon."

But he's not going to sway me—the selfishness of people like that. Letting their dogs off-leash. How inconsiderate—how dangerous for the dog. I squeeze harder and the dog stops making any noise at all. One final push: I see them, the pricks who never stop to think about the world around them even for a minute.

I could feel it, some kind of life spirit maybe, buckling beneath my thumbs. That's when I let go, and the dog took a deep breath, shook himself up on four legs, and staggered back to its owner.

I stood and brushed off my hands. I looked at each of them. It was like waking up when you hadn't even realized you'd fallen asleep. There was a breeze coming in off the water. The white balloons shivered against their ties. Rocking back and forth, a little shimmy. My ex-wife was there, picking up empty pizza boxes and plastic plates, and a whole stack of napkins that had scattered, and nobody had bothered to run after them because what was the point? Jeanie sprinted off one way and a friend of hers gave chase, and the napkins gusted in the other direction toward the skyline.

The dog owner knelt there with his face buried in the animal's coat. I wanted to tell him it would be alright if he cried—it would be appropriate.

I ended up giving him five grand. Because I felt bad. Even though his dog, in the end, was fine.

That's what Jeanie's mom doesn't get—he could have bought a dozen more dogs for that price and built them each a palace. But instead all I got from Azita was restraining order this and trying to take away my visiting rights which she couldn't do, turned out, because when we went to court the judge was a guy I'd grown up with, and he saw the situation for what it was, me bankrolling everyone, and let me keep my weekends and summers.

I just—looking back, do I wish I'd handled it differently? Of course. Sure. But on the other hand, I mean, fuck those inconsiderate assholes who let their dogs off leash. The rest of us live here too.

I leave Penny's office with a stack of forms to read later. This question about whether or not to let Jeanie stay with me and how hard I'll fight for her? It's clear which way I'm gonna go. In a little more than a year, she'll be shipping off to college. I can flatter myself about how much money I've provided to them both; I can hurl mortar shells at Azita as long as I want to; but it doesn't change the fact that I haven't been around. Not really. A weekend a month. A trip to the lake in the summer. But I wasn't the one who taught Jeanie to navigate the "L," or the one who stood outside in the snow with her for hours, rebounding free throws. It wasn't me calling the next parent on the phone tree, or chaperoning field trips, or stuffing thirty-some-odd gift bags for Valentine's Day.

But now?

I am older now than my father was when I laid him in the ground. Now I find myself presented with an opportunity to do the one thing he never could: be a Dad.

Sometimes, trading options, you're faced with a set of numbers, and all the numbers seem to be telling you the same thing. Usually, almost always, the numbers are correct. But every now and then, you'll be staring at a spreadsheet that seems to indicate some kind of truth, but for whatever reason, you can't bring yourself to believe it. Something inside tells you, fuck it, do what you feel.

After twenty-five years, I've learned to trust that feeling. I used to think it was hope, foolish hope, that wanted to ignore the math. But I've since come to realize it's nothing so positive. That desire to zig when everything is telling you to zag is straight-up cold-hearted cynicism. And nobody ever went bankrupt being a cynic.

Which is why I'm going to fight for Jeanie. Even if it sounds, on its surface, like the worst idea I've ever had.

Nobody else believes in me, that's for sure.

It's not that I think I can prove myself to be a good father. It's that I'm afraid of never having tried. There's plenty of shit I haven't tried, from snow skiing to eating monkey brains to gay sex, and I don't think I'll regret not trying any of that.

But I don't want anything more in common with my old man than I already have—fuck his liquor-laced breath, rot in peace.

Lunchtime comes each day at 11:00 am. I call Pasternak, and we meet at a little Irish place we like. Dark. Has that spilled-beer smell no matter what time of day it is. He cabs over to meet me, but after we put away fish and chips and bangers and mash, I make him walk back.

He bitches the whole way. "As if I'm not on my feet all day already."

"Think of the money we're saving the firm, not taking taxis," I tell him, but he only rolls his eyes. "Besides, I like to air out."

"What are you, laundry?" He's only wearing his clerk jacket. He's got his hands buried in his pockets, leaning into the wind. "Who needs to air out?"

"I'm going to fight for her," I say. "I've already talked to my lawyer."

I've told him all about Jeanie maybe moving to Florida. Besides my lawyer, and family, he's the only one I can bounce ideas off. Like everything, though, he takes it in stride.

Speaking of, I have to take three steps for every one of his. I'm like fucking Bugs Bunny walking next to him, my legs spinning. The nice thing about walking with Pasternak, though, is that people get out of his way. He's an imposing presence.

As my trade clerk, he's mostly my muscle. He takes care of all the little clerical shit so I don't have to. He researches positions and trades. Sometimes he recommends strategies. He doesn't trade, though. He's never asked me about it, and I'm content to let that ride. I don't know that he has the constitution for it. Generally, a trader needs a hard-to-find blend of mental sharpness and testosterone. Equal amounts of each.

Still, we've known each other so long, almost thirty years, he's basically the only guy who tells it to me straight.

"In that scenario," he asks, "the plan is for Jeanie to live with you?"

We shout at each other over the busses, and just then the Brown Line roars overhead. "She's an adult practically. It'll be more like having a roommate."

"Girls are tricky."

"What the fuck do you know about it?"

"I had sisters," he says. "Sob sessions that last an entire weekend..."

"She's too busy for boyfriends."

"This is a big change for you. You've never exactly been 'parent of the year.'"

We stop at crosswalk. I glare at him, but he's watching the light. No insult meant. And the truth is, he's right. This is why I've always believed I would have made a great paramedic. Stick 'em, stabilize 'em, drop 'em off so they're somebody else's fucking problem.

"I'll read a book or something."

We're moving again, across the street. We turn left on State. The pack of pedestrians we're caught up in dissipates, and then it's just the two of us walking the length of John Marshall, which for the record, I don't believe is a real law school; or it's the one you go to when literally every other school in the country won't admit you. I don't know a single person who got their law degree there.

Along this stretch, the Red Line runs below ground. We pass a set of stairs going down. A bit farther on is the kiosk for the elevator. Beyond that, a small, brick structure. You can't go inside, it's only about five-feet tall. Partly glassed in, some kind of utility access maybe. But as we get closer, I see there's an older Black guy in an overcoat, carrying one of those thin metal canes with the red tips, and he's tapping it on the third structure like he's trying to find a door for a Hobbit hole.

I reach into my pocket, pull out my cell phone. I check the screen and pretend like it's ringing. I make a face like I really oughta take the call.

"I'll see you back at the office," I tell Pasternak.

He barely hears me—for a Pol, he's got zero tolerance for cold. Which is lucky for me, because the last thing I fucking need is for him to see me showing compassion to somebody. He's already around the corner by the time I pocket my phone again and ask the blind guy if he needs help.

It's a delicate situation. There's pride at stake. I reach out and take him by his elbow. He looks a little surprised, but I tell him it's okay.

"It's goddamn confusing." I lead him toward the stairs. "There are three different little fucking brick huts along here. I mean, if the city wanted to design a subway entrance to be as confusing as possible, they couldn't have done it better. I think they do it on purpose, honestly, I mean, just to mess with tourists, maybe. Sometimes old-timers like us get tripped up too, though. Like when a dolphin gets caught in a lobster trap. Not the intention, right? Gotta throw it back. Anyway. Jesus, you would have been out here for hours. The fucking city makes it impossible to find the goddamn steps."

He doesn't say anything. He lets me guide him, all the while working his lips back and forth. It's pride, of course— he's not going to act grateful, and I'm not going to ask him to. We reach the top of the subway stairs, and I tell him I'm just going to help him get to the bottom. He nods. I can tell he's relieved. But again, he doesn't say so. People stream around us like a current breaking on rocks, but it's just me and him, my hand on his elbow, his cane tapping steadily along the stair rail.

"Which line?" I ask when we reach the bottom.

"I got it," he tells me, and shuffles off toward the turnstile.

Chapter 4

The mood in the pits hovers somewhere between "suicidal" and "listening to Tori Amos because it's cathartic." Things are down, generally. It's pretty quiet, trading volume at a burble. Since we hit the new low last week, nobody knows what the fuck to do. Maybe OJ has the right idea. Get sent away for a while, come back in ten years, see where we are.

"Look sharp: Kiddies are here."

The thing with Jeanie's school is this afternoon, happening right now, as a matter of fact. Pasternak announces their arrival as if it's the most boring fact he's ever been forced to recite. And then what looks to me like a hundred kids come down the escalator, heads bobbing, wide-eyed, like they're descending into the crush of hell, the din of the trading pits, the sickly fluorescent lighting, the banks of monitors, red as stop signs. The kids cluster in twos and threes as if there might be comfort in numbers. As if there ever is.

"Keep it PG," I tell my guys. "Goddammit."

"Yeah, and no nudity," someone shouts back.

Yes, dear God, no nudity.

I don't see Jeanie yet, but I know my daughter, my flesh and blood, is among those sweaty and lice-ridden tangles of pubescent heads coming down the escalator. And then I spot her. Christ: if ever there was a virgin born, it's my daughter. Khaki pants belted above her waist, green Polo shirt tucked in, carrying her puffy jacket beneath her arm. The gold cross around her neck catches and tosses back all the light reflected from the monitors.

She sees me and smiles. I give her a wink.

Her teacher is a fat guy in a sweater vest, your typical, underachieving dolt. Probably he has some unpublished sci-fi novel tucked in his desk drawer at home. It's no wonder all the kids think their teachers are losers. You suspect it while you're growing up, but then once you're out in the real world all that suspicion gets confirmed. Summers off? You're an adult: go out and make some fucking money. Don't talk to me about summers off.

"Okay boys," I clear my throat. "A warm welcome for Whitney M. Young Magnet High School."

Mutterings—and that's all they are, barely audible—speculate on the foulest things you'd never want your mother to hear.

"That's how I like 'em: Whitney M. YOUNG."

"A magnet school? What the fuck kind of school is that?"

"A school for entitled slobs like you."

The students disappear for a minute as they make their way across the trading floor, past the columns of monitors and snarls of other trading pits before gathering at the edge of ours. I'm hooked up to a microphone, which I hate, but if the kids are going to hear anything, I have to use it. I explain more or less what's happening on the banks of screens and, in a general sense, what all the numbers represent. I explain that all the guys in blue coats, they may look like they're not doing much of anything (laughs), but some of them own options that they're trying to sell, and others are trying to buy those options for a good price. Because the Chicago Board Options Exchange has the world's only hybrid trading floor, they can exchange options here in person or with people on the other end of their computer screens—on the other side of the world.

As I talk, I keep an eye on Jeanie. She's listening. She's digging it. As I hoped she might. Most of the other kids seem to be digging it too. A couple even have the courtesy to slide their headphones off their ears. Because this is some pretty cool shit. A quarter-century in the industry, and I still think so. Once you get past the noise and, yes, the smell of the trading pits, you can start to see all the appendages working in concert, how the pits are living organisms with beautiful and sometimes unlovable but always arresting parts.

Not only that, but I run this motherfucker.

"So, if you'll turn your attention to the screens," I instruct the rapt school children, "everyone has heard of Sony. Sony's stock symbol is SNE, as you can see right here. Earlier today I bought the right—but not the obligation—to sell 100 shares of Sony. Now, I'll show you how that's done."

We can all see the potential buyers on the monitors. My words come easily.

"I'm looking for a price above what I paid. I'd like to make a little money on this, after all, even if it is only a demonstration."

More laughs. And I feel myself settling in, finding the flow.

This business, it's my lifeblood, the narrative of commerce I've distilled and passed along to countless bright-eyed youths over the years. And I'm proud of the guys in my pit—they've pulled themselves together. Most of them look like they might even be working and not just checking their fantasy teams.

"By simply clicking on this icon here," I say, "I agree to sell 100 shares of SNE..."

Some of these school kids, their parents are artists. Or the guy who comes out to your house when you need an estimate for pest control. Or a deck refinished. Pulling down sixty grand a year. How the hell anybody lives on that, who knows. Or lawyers—these magnet-school kids, for sure some of their parents are barristers. Lord have mercy on their miserable souls, sucking out every miserable billable hour so they can pay off their crushing law school debt before they start making any actual money to live on, much less retire with. But not Jeanie—her dad is a Beast Master. He works in a pit, and lords over thirty other wild beasts in their own beautiful inferno. The whip is in my hand. And when Jeanie's friends ask her, "What does your daddy do?" she can tell them with a straight face that her daddy makes $480 an hour.

"Oh shit!"

One of my guys, but I don't see who.

I spin and glare down at the students. But they're looking right back at me—no, not at me, but over my shoulder. The boys are open-mouthed, slack-jawed. Some of the girls, Jeanie included, cover their eyes.

The screens.

I turn. On the wall of monitors, an entire column, eight screens floor to ceiling, is suddenly devoted to porn. And it's bad. Just about as bad as it can be. There's a Black guy in a grass skirt with tribal bands around his arms and legs, and a white little person, female. She's wearing some kind of feathery crown and tooth necklace. And the things they are doing to one another are, most likely, something the majority of normal heterosexual couples never do even once together in their lifetimes.

There's no audio, thank Christ. But I almost wish there was. Because for the first time maybe ever, I have nothing to say. No one talks. Not my guys, not the school kids. Even the phones are quiet. Respecting the horror of all this.

The microphone feeds back from where I've let it dangle. The piercing whistle yanks us into the unknowable future.

"Will somebody turn it off?" I say, quietly.

No one moves. I count to five.

"Somebody turn the goddamn televisions off!"

The floor is so quiet, my voice comes back to me. I never knew there was an echo in here.

In the control room above, I can see two yutzes scrambling to flip switches and turn knobs, banging on the console. Goddamn IT guys with their arrogant, snot-nose love of *Warcraft* and unnecessarily complicated CAPTCHAs. It goes without saying, one of them, and probably both, is out of a job. I've been around long enough to make a pretty good guess what happened. Somebody on break up there tossed some recreational viewing into the DVD, and accidentally hit the button to broadcast.

Twenty years ago, sure, you could get away with shit like that. Not now though.

Once the monitors are blank, I scan the group of school kids, looking for Jeanie. She's there. Staring back at me. Her eyes like egg yolks, ready to run.

The parents are pissed, obviously.

The next morning, Pasternak finds a dozen messages on the firm's voicemail. He plays me highlights. We listen on speakerphone and laugh our asses off.

A couple things become immediately clear. The issue of sex has clearly never been discussed. These parents still view themselves as stewards of toddlers rather than sixteen and seventeen-year-old high-school kids, who have probably already far outpaced them in worldly experience.

"Yes, well, it figures I'd go straight to voicemail," one mother sneers. "I wouldn't expect someone who'd host a field trip like this to have the courage to answer the phone. But my little Rozelda has all kinds of questions now, and I can assure you her questions have absolutely nothing to do with trading stocks—or corn, or whatever it is you do in that pit of depravity."

"This is Dr. Alfonso Alo," says the quaking voice of a man old enough to be my dad. In fact, for a moment, I think it is, come back from the grave to kick me in the nuts one last time. "You assholes better lawyer-up. Because this was one helluva stunt you pulled. One helluva stunt. These are minors, I hope you realize. You know what the sentencing is for showing pornography to a minor? Pretty goddamn stiff, I'll tell you that. I hope you enjoy being gang-raped in prison. Because by god that's where you'll end up, if I have anything to say about it."

And then there's the father who sounds like he's inhaled helium, but on replay we decide it's his real voice. "Riley has several relatives who are Little Persons and we've tried, for his entire life, to show him how they're just like anyone else. This…incident… has upset him greatly. He went to bed without any supper tonight. No supper at all. He's just sick to his stomach over what he was forced to witness. And so am I. You should be ashamed."

Parenthood, it's all about loss. We raise these kids and then slowly but surely, they leave us. This is natural. But that doesn't mean it's easy. You can fight it, and hang on tight, the way Jeanie's mom has from the very beginning, breastfeeding until Jeanie was well into her threes, old enough to ask for it—storming into our bedroom in the middle of the night demanding "Boobies!"—or chasing Jeanie around with antiseptic wipes to purify everything within a ten-foot radius. Or you can let it go. Try to arm your kid with certain tools she'll need to succeed. Accept that heartbreak is in the job description. That in fact, it's the main requirement.

Because you know how it turns out. For a few years, your kid needs you desperately. You're their entire world. And let's face it: they're yours. But with the exception of a few oddball cases—D&D bloggers and school shooters, mostly—kids do one day leave home. College, job in another town, another state. Marriage. And then you see what you're left with.

I have some sympathy for the parents of these Whitney M. Young students: it can be disconcerting to imagine your little boy, who, when you close your eyes, you picture in a jumper and cowboy hat, suddenly appreciating DDD tits and a well-aimed moneyshot. But do I personally phone back these outraged citizens and apologize? I do not. Legally, we're covered by the field-trip waiver the school made them sign. Morally, hell, these kids are from Chicago. They see worse stuff on the "L" every day.

I can't help but wonder what will become of these children, Jeanie included. I get that parents want to be involved, and now all the new tech makes it easier than ever. But it also raises children in a bubble, so when they move out of the house, they are utterly incapable of dealing with the real world. Or of making decisions on their own. I see it in our new hires, all the time. You have to tell them when to go take a piss, or they'll stand there all day under the goddamn screens, urine running down their legs. They'll ask a million and one questions, terrified of making a mistake. Make the mistake and then own it, I tell them. And don't download porn.

After the markets close, I drive to Whitney M. Young and meet Jeanie after school. To sort things out and gauge her temperature.

In the school parking lot, you can hear the Ike roar past, the blurred line of elevated highway traffic a block south. There's snow on the ground. The trees are naked and black. Architecturally, the school nods to some of Mies van der Rohe's most famous work, the low-slung black cubes that spot Chicago's innards like carcinomas.

Jeanie hoists her backpack high on her shoulders, walking with three other girls. She notices me, says something to them, and hurries over. Jeanie still lets me hug her. She's never been too cool for that.

"Are you mad?" I ask.

She isn't. The porn video is all the other kids can talk about, though.

"Those fucking guys," I say. "Hand to god, that wasn't supposed to happen."

"Dad, I don't think you made the movie play on purpose. No one's that cruel."

"They are, actually."

With my attorney's charge still ringing in my ears, I tell Jeanie I'd love to have her live with me. That I'm a crappy roommate, but if she moves in with me, at least she'll get to stay in Chicago. She throws her arms around my neck and jumps up and down.

"I'm serious," I tell her. "I don't clean up after myself. I never do dishes."

"I'll do all that." She's nearly shrieking. "This is so awesome!"

Her ride is here, her friends climbing into the back of a dark Ford Excursion. "Call Mom, okay?"

"Go," I tell her. "By the time you get home, your mom and I will have all this sorted out."

Jeanie is welcomed into the truck, and the black beast lurches away.

I somehow find Azita's phone number among the thousands of names that appear now in my contacts list, in my Blackberry. Some kind of synchronization happened when Pasternak set up the fucking thing, now I have triple entries for colleagues of mine, or e-mail addresses that aren't attached to any names. I have to use the search function to find anybody—there are simply too many goddamn contacts to scroll through. All of which drives me bat-shit insane. I don't know who half these people are. Needless to say, Jeanie's mom is not in my favorites list, and my ICE contact is Pasternak.

Azita answers in a panic but relaxes when I tell her everything's okay with Jeanie.

"Porn, Johnny?" she says. "Seriously?"

I swallow the urge to throw it back at her, and with it, my pride.

"Yeah," I say, casually. "It was an accident. Not our fault. The guys upstairs. You know how it is around here."

"Jesus Christ."

I eat crow; I restate my desire to take on Jeanie full-time until she graduates from high school.

There's a long silence during which I fear we've been disconnected.

"Well?" I venture.

"I don't have time for court," she says.

"Neither of us do." I dig in my pockets for cigarettes. "I feel like we can figure this out."

"Meet me for dinner," she says.

It's honestly the last fucking thing in the world I expected her to say. And, honestly, the last thing in the world that I want to do. My entire spirit shudders with the notion of it.

"Is that necessary?"

"I'll be up in your neck of the woods," she says. "Grand Lux. Eight o'clock."

I drive home, park, then walk the few blocks to Michigan Avenue. Once inside the restaurant, I go upstairs. Thirty-foot ceilings with chandeliers the size of riding mowers. Ornate and curving plush booths that look out over the river of shoppers below, the streetlights and some snow twirling, light classical on the stereo, the careful, appointed clinking of silver. It's Azita's kind of restaurant, through and through, characterless and gleaming.

The hostess tells me my party is already seated.

"Party?" I ask, but she ignores me and guides me to the back room, where, set against the glass wall, is a table for twelve.

Azita, at its head, is joined by ten or so other womanish types of indeterminate ages.

She waves to me, not getting up. "Johnny!"

I go to her, stoop to kiss her cheek. "You didn't tell me this was a party."

A shrug. "It's just a few friends. Take a seat."

I slink into the only open chair, stuffing my coat in my lap, at the far end of the table from Azita. I grin stupidly at the nearest guests. Names slip into my ear and leak somewhere out the other side. Across from me, a woman with hoop earrings and cropped hair speaks quietly with an older woman beside her, who wears librarian glasses and a cardigan buttoned to her chin. To my left, listening intently, is a woman in a straw fedora and bowtie.

"How do you know one another?" I ask the hipster.

When she speaks, only her mouth moves. The rest of her is preternaturally still. "We all teach at U of C."

I nod, swallowing a mix of panic and bile. My feet are still pointed at the door, my jacket bundled like a football in my lap. I could easily duck and run. Every part of me wants to. Then I remember Jeanie.

"This must be the famous department I've heard so much about," I say.

"We all teach at the Center," explains the first woman. Her cotton dress is cut low. "I teach in the Religious Studies Program, with Azita."

"How goes the world of gender and sexuality?"

I ask this in the way one might ask the score of the Bears game. Still, they all stare in a way that is both pitying and incredulous.

The hipster asks, "Who are you?"

"I'm...a friend," I say quietly.

In the center of the table are shallow, gold dishes. I decide to change the subject.

"Ashtrays?" I ask the table, handling one, smiling to show I'm only kidding.

"I don't think you can smoke in here," says the Fedora, seriously.

"I know it's gauche, but I don't know what those are either," says the Librarian.

"I sure don't," I say, and try to catch her eye, but she won't.

"I could use a smoke after the day I've had," says the first woman. "I'm defending my thesis next week. I've been working on it basically around the clock for months. I'm not sleeping at all."

"It's a very difficult thing to do," says the Librarian. "Such hard work."

"Well," I offer, "it's not like you're digging trenches in West Bengal."

The table, on our end, at least, falls silent.

Finally, the hipster asks me again, "How do you belong to Azita?"

I drum my fingers on the table. "We share custody of a seventeen-year-old heterosexual identified female."

At the table's far end, a heavyset brunette rises, taps her spoon against her wine glass, and laughs self-consciously. The others laugh too. I notice, for the first time, all the empty wine bottles, some still set in those shallow, gold dishes I was asking about. I realize these co-workers have been here all evening—maybe since lunch.

"As you all know," the speaker clears her throat, "we're here to celebrate Azita's promotion. We are not going to be sad about this. Even though we all wish she was staying. So instead, we're going to dry our eyes and grin and bear it and say, 'Azita, thank you for being the most generous, supportive colleague anyone could ask for.' Honestly girl, it's an honor having worked with you."

They offer a robust toast, a chorus of "Here, here!"

The Librarian rises. "Azita, when I hired you ten years ago, I knew you wouldn't finish your career here. You're too talented, too much a shooting star. There aren't many colleagues I can say I've learned something from, but you, my colleague, my peer, my friend, I learn something from every single day. To the future!"

They toast again. I look around lamely for a server, but the waitstaff appears to have given up on this table long ago.

There are more toasts, and speeches, and some tears shed. Each and every one of Azita's colleagues says something nice about her. More than nice: they are overly generous, and that generosity begins to spread to one another. The dinner becomes a kind of love fest, each woman professing her adoration of another, citing influences, drawing connections that are both personal and academic, both immediate and abstract. Azita presides. And it's impossible, after this goes on for a while, not to appreciate the openness with which they speak to one another, how they leave themselves vulnerable with every piece of praise, and how graciously that lavishness is accepted. How humbly.

It's the exact opposite of my own work environment, where humility is assumed to mean you were dead fucking wrong, and more often than not, gets you dead fucking fired.

Azita's friends laugh at their own expense; they laugh at one another. Someone belches, another grabs her own breasts to make a point—the hilarity of it all. But also, the honesty. Because there's no one to impress here. The enemy is somewhere else. I am forgotten, invisible, if I was ever seen. Their compliments leave them vulnerable but do not drain their power: instead, their power seems to amplify with every generous word. The tones are measured and deep. No one talks over anyone else, and soon everyone has had a chance to speak.

There's a natural silence. I have not said a word in over an hour. I consider rising to say something that would, elsewhere, be considered appropriate, but realize just as quick that here, no one wants to hear from a swinging dick. That in fact, this was the nature of the test: could John Ganzi keep his mouth shut long enough to achieve what he came here to do?

"Azita." I go to her, lean on the table, speak softly. "We should talk business."

She signs off, in the end, and agrees to move Jeanie now while the paperwork is being processed.

"Understand," she tells me, "that I am choosing the lesser of two evils. I don't love the idea of her living with you. But I like the idea of moving her out of state right now even less. Florida is nothing but convicts and kids who aren't convicts yet. Jeanie doesn't need to be around that."

"That's a funny way to talk about the place you're moving to," I say.

"We both know it's true." She sighs, and sort of fluffs her hair with both hands. "Maybe I'll get some research done. If I don't fucking melt first."

On Saturday, I go pick up my daughter.

City kids, they just don't have all that much stuff. There isn't room. She comes out with a rollaboard and two black trash bags. Her mom is taking some things with her, so Jeanie can have her own space in Gainesville, but everything Jeanie moves to my place with fits in my trunk.

I stand there, watching my daughter say goodbye. Patrick shakes her hand. This strikes me as insanely formal—even repressed. But then sometimes you get these third-generation Swedes, lived their entire life in Minnesota, beneath a canopy of Lutheranism and potato soup, where things are about as tamped down as they can be, and a handshake passes for physical intimacy, and there's only one position, missionary, saved for nine o'clock on Wednesday nights.

Of course, this makes me wonder about Jeanie's mom, and what kind of physical relationship she's having with the new guy. Especially given that Patrick appears to have all the emotional depth of a scarecrow. Do they actually bang? I can't imagine. She and I always had a pretty good time in bed. It wasn't college porno shit, and she could be cold sometimes. But I always chalked it up to the stress of her being in school, and then the stress of our raising Jeanie, and then of course the stress of our dissolution. Looking back, I wonder if she's ever been all that interested in sex—she was skilled, but in a practiced, studied, almost clinical way. But then maybe that's why Patrick-the-scarecrow is perfect: his job is to scare off other men for a woman whose career is everything, who's spent her entire professional life studying religion and gender fluidity, and who, although she isn't gay herself, as far as I know, may simply no longer be interested in having relations with men. I understand all of this at once, feel sorry for them briefly, then let it go, because it's sure as hell not doing me any good. Fuck whoever you want to—or don't. So long as you're happy.

"Dad." Jeanie throws open the passenger door and climbs in. "Ready?"

I smile much too big, like a Putt-Putt clown, and wave to my ex-wife and fucking Patrick, who, before I can seal myself inside the safety of my BMW, hurries over, one finger in the air like he's forgotten something.

"Johnny. Hang on a sec." He says this kindly, although I hate it when people call me Johnny. It's what Azita calls me, which is why he picked it up. "We wanted to mention just a couple quick things to you, before you go."

Azita comes down the walkway and joins her partner behind my car, where I guess he thinks Jeanie can't hear us.

"I'm going to be honest, Johnny," he says. "I have reservations."

I know from experience there's nothing he's about to say that is a deal breaker. The negotiations are over, the papers signed, sealed, and delivered. Instead, he's going to ask for certain concessions, which may run the gamut from simply needing his mind to be set at ease to asking for some kind of payout.

"Jeanie's already in the car," I say to them. "Her shit is already in the back."

Patrick and my ex share a quick glance. She nods, deferring to him.

"Jeanie is a special kid," he says.

"No shit."

"I know you know this."

My ex shoots me a look, and I ratchet myself down a couple notches too.

"We have a system," he explains. "She likes things a certain way. And we feel, these things help her be the best that she can be."

"I promise she'll brush her teeth every night," I say.

"Chocolate, for example," Azita says.

"Chocolate." I say back to her.

"Chocolate gives her gas. It gave me gas when I was pregnant with her."

I can't help jangling the car keys in my pocket. "Okay. No chocolate."

"We've noticed she does better if she goes to bed between 9:15 and 9:30 every night," Patrick says. "She really needs a full eight, nine hours to be her best self in the morning."

"We're talking about Jeanie, right?" I ask. "She's seventeen."

"She's a child." Azita corrects me. "Which is another thing—she still needs to get her driver's license. She needs someone to teach her to drive."

I know city kids sometimes take a while to get their license, but Jeanie not having hers strikes me as unreasonable. "We'll make it a priority."

"She's applying to colleges," her mom says. "We'll be the driving force for that, obviously, but if you could help encourage—"

I look at her, dead-eyed. "Why obviously?"

"We're not talking about Harold Washington," Patrick says, and this burns deeper, and much hotter, than it should. "Or even DePaul."

"We'd really like to see her in an Ivy," she says. "Northwestern can be a fallback, but we have higher expectations."

"She has straight A's, doesn't she?" I look at them both, gulping my pride down like a whiskey chaser. "She'll be able to go anywhere she wants."

"Has anyone in your family gone to college, Johnny?" Patrick asks.

I glare at him. Briefly, I fantasize about taking three steps across the asphalt and driving my car key into his jugular. The answer to his question is no, but I'm not going to give him the fucking satisfaction of hearing me say it.

Instead, I pretend to be distracted by a small dent on the driver's side door.

Standing there in front of Azita's house, what used to be our house, with a fucking *Sold* sign out front, I can feel the floodgates lift inside of me, the ones that keep a certain amount of rage and indignation contained. I can feel the angry waters start to flow. My heart rate picks up, and my hands get a little tingly, a little numb.

Patrick and Azita: all of their words are like little fucking birds that I can't net, suddenly. They flitter off while I trip after them.

"Maybe I wasn't goddamn fortunate enough to be raised with wealth," I tell them both, but especially Patrick. "Maybe I wasn't lucky enough to spend my entire goddamn life in an ivory tower, never holding a real job. I sure as shit didn't inherit some real estate investment company my daddy built, like you did."

"We're an REO rehab outfit."

"Nobody gives a shit." I cut him short. "But if Jeanie wants to spend her college years jerking off with a bunch of East-Coast pricks, I'll give her my blessing. I'll do everything in my power to get her there. Shit, with her basketball skills, she'd probably start as a freshman. But don't sit there and condescend to me, or tell me my life, my city, isn't good enough for my daughter. You can go fuck yourself with all of that."

I'll give Azita credit: she just stands there watching me. But behind her eyes I detect the faintest hint of amusement, as if, this far removed from our domestic entanglements, she can sort of appreciate the purity of my rage, even if it's mostly directed at her. It's a bit of an out-of-body experience for me.

I tear the real-estate sign from its place in the ground, spin twice, and hurl it like a discus toward the house. It wobbles once, that wonk-wonk sound of thin metal in the wind, and tumbles maybe fifteen feet through the air before landing.

Then I stuff my fat ass into the driver's seat and slam the door. I glance at my daughter, who stares straight ahead. I crank the ignition and stomp the gas pedal. Jeanie and I slip into the gulf-stream of Chicago traffic, and we're gone.

I don't wonder how much Azita sold the house for until I'm driving away.

Chapter 5

Monday after the markets close, Pasternak and I work through the day's mail and hammer out our schedule for the week. We've been taking applications.

"Where are we with our new hires?"

"Nowhere." He tosses the resume for a Samuel J. Dalal on my desk. MIT undergrad, fresh out of the University of Chicago School of Business. Plus, with a name like Dalal, he's probably a minority, which would be good for the firm's image.

"I wanted this guy." I scan the page. "What happened?"

"I called to schedule a time for him to come in. First question he asks is how I'm going to arrange transportation for him."

"He's handicapped?"

Pasternak pops a breath mint onto his tongue. "I asked him that. He says he's not. Says he doesn't have a car and wants to know how we're going to get him to the interview."

"What the fuck?"

"So, I tell him the City of Chicago has fairly reliable public transportation, if he hadn't heard. Or if nothing's convenient to him, he can take a fucking cab if he wants the job so bad."

"What'd he say?"

"Said he needed transportation. And that was that."

I crumple the resume into a little ball and hurl it into the hallway. The wad hits the doorframe and rebounds beneath my clerk's feet.

"It's this generation." Pasternak doesn't have to lean over: he just picks the ball off the floor, stretching his arm to incredible lengths, like Mr. Fantastic. "These fucking kids."

I loosen my tie. "Entitled pricks, no question."

"We had a few others."

He hands me a short stack of resumes. I page through. If you removed the names from the top, they'd all be pretty much the same. Top schools. Zero work experience that has anything to do with finance. The high school grads, okay, maybe true work experience is too much to ask, but college grads who did nothing with their summers but life guard and sling coffee? Give me a fucking break. Sure, they held office in every extracurricular group to which they belonged, at least in school. None of that means shit. The emphasis on quantity over quality.

"Does no one do internships anymore?" I ask.

Pasternak shrugs. "I never did an internship, and you hired me."

I stack the papers again and flip through them, reading only the names. "These are all men?"

He makes a gesture like, look around you. I throw the stack of resumes at him. He bats at them, and they scatter.

"Find me some fucking women," I tell him. "I want to interview three females before Friday."

Jeanie's reading *RedEye*, the *Trib's* alt weekly, when I get home. She's curled in the armchair, feet dangling over the side. Her toenails are painted the black and orange of the fearsome Whitney M. Young Dolphins.

"Look at you, reading an actual, physical newspaper." I drop my bag at the door, dump my moneyclip and keys in a silver dish. "How was the game?"

"Lost," she says. "Did you know there are coyotes in the Loop?"

I untie my shoes, putting a hand against the wall for support. "I did not."

"One wandered into a 7-Eleven yesterday." She flips the page. "There might be dozens living downtown. They eat out of dumpsters. And are mistaken for dogs."

I seat myself on the chair arm to read over her shoulder. She points to a black and white photograph, taken from a security camera. Sure enough, the back-end of what appears to be a coyote is disappearing through the door, half-obscured by a rack of Zingers and Honeybuns.

"So," she asks. "How was your day?"

"Fine, honey. When will dinner be ready?"

"Hilarious." She looks at me. "I'm thinking sushi."

I wander into my bedroom and pull off my jacket and tie. "I don't eat raw fish."

"They have fried stuff too."

I re-emerge, barefoot in slacks and a white T-shirt. James Dean if he'd lived long enough to let his body go to seed. "I usually order in on Mondays. Or eat leftovers."

There are certain desires I don't mention: the desire to watch ESPN, drink three beers, and fall asleep on the couch. This doesn't seem like it's going to happen, though.

Jeanie shrugs, snaps the newspaper pages. "I want sushi. We should check out Puffer. *RedEye* gave it a good review."

I plod back to the bedroom, beaten. "Let me get my shoes."

Fucking board meetings are really nothing but an excuse to eat donuts. Or they would be, except the Chairman is some kind of health nut, does triathlons and shakes your hand like he's trying to pulp it. Catering is always bringing up platters of crudité and chutney and pretzels and mixed nuts and there's coffee of course, thank Christ, but forget about pop—even diet, because as bad as sugar is for you, the shit they put in diet soda is worse. So he says. None of us argue. We dutifully take our plastic plates of baby carrots and sliced radish and wish silently for bacon-wrapped scallops and Diet Coke.

"That's why they call it heart-attack season." He makes the rounds, juicing hands. There's floor directors like me who he sees almost every day, but we do have some board members who fly in from New York and other places, and he's gotta put in the face-time. "December is the worst. Party after party. It's easy to put on the pounds."

Our Chairman, Dicky Sar, is about my height, but built like a fucking ninja. He doesn't curse as much as I do but talks just as quickly—raised in New York, rising through the ranks at the AMEX before taking over the reins here.

"Don't get up." His hand clamps around my shoulder and forces me back into my chair. "Did I see you in the gym last week?"

I wipe broccoli sprouts from my lips. "I like the recumbent bike."

"Do your knees bother you? I have knee trouble. I finished a three-hour run on Sunday and felt like my knees were gonna explode. Getting older, right?"

"It's a bitch."

He fake-punches my belly. "Tough time of year to try and keep the weight off."

All of us here make a cool eight grand just for sitting around this table for a few hours, plotting the future of the Exchange, weighing risks, projecting how seriously to take our competition. None of us needs the money. In fact, each and every one of us could retire today and live like a king for the rest of his life. But ego keeps us glued to the board room. That, and the need to feel we're still doing something important with our lives—something more important than making rich guys like us even richer. You get to be my age, or older, like most of these trustees, and you start worrying about your legacy.

We're facing some challenges from upstarts. We're still the largest options exchange in terms of volume, by far. But one exchange has us spooked: ISE, the world's only all-electronic options exchange.

Ten years ago, you had to be physically present, in a trading pit, in order to trade, or you had to trade through a broker who had purchased a seat on the Exchange. Now, you can sit on your couch and manage a hedge fund, save yourself the inconvenience of the commute. We offer classes, teaching would-be traders how to use our own patented electronic trading platform. But we've got different challenges than ISE does—for example, we still have trading pits, and Open Outcry, and a whole lot of folks who've been around a very long time, who are worth a very large amount of money, who want to see traditions persist. These traders spent a lot of money purchasing seats on the Exchange, to own the right to trade, and hate the idea that just anybody can roll through: they worry about losing commissions. They also have a certain inflated idea of what their seats are actually worth to the public. But the reality is, ISE is the future. To satisfy both camps, and not be out of business in twenty years, we've got to go electronic. Hence our hybrid trading platform, which, privately, I kind of view as strapping rocket boosters to a steam-engine and calling it a time machine. But they don't pay me to think about these larger issues. As far as the board is concerned, I represent the actual physical traders.

All the strategic-planning stuff? We approve the salaries of the people hired to take care of that.

Swear to Christ though, I'm in business with actual giants. Every fucking chair I sit in is so goddamn low to the floor I have to yank the little lever a dozen times to crank the seat high enough for me to be sitting level with everyone else—and everyone watches me do it. I think they wait for it. Like a judge's gavel kicking off court proceedings, watching JAG try to claim his seat at the big-boy table heralds the start of every board meeting.

When Jeanie's lights go out, and her door shuts, I wash dishes. I let the water run over my hands until it turns my flesh pink. The apartment is quiet, otherwise. I rinse and stack dishes in the drying rack in orderly rows. When my kid is resting quietly, and the house is clean, I understand the world and my role in it. I get to feel like all my shit is together.

It's the same feeling I had pushing her in the swing when she was a toddler. Because she loved the swing—it was where she wanted to be. On the playground, she was happy. So, I didn't have to worry. I could stand behind her and push, and I knew exactly what to do. One of the few times I ever had that kind of confidence as a parent.

"Pump," I'd tell her. "Kick."

But she never would. She'd just let me push her. Demanding higher, asking to slow down. Pealing laughter and singing; playground dust on my fingertips; that warmed-over smell of hot chain.

"This is your space," I told her the first night she moved in. "You want to hang something on the walls, fine by me."

Her blinds were open. A thick, amber, late-afternoon light calcified on the floor. She went to the window, craned her neck. From there she could see a sliver of water in the distance, off to the left, a mile or so away. Her room at my place is considerably smaller than the one she left behind.

"Lake view," she deadpanned.

She slipped to the floor, to her knees, and bowed her head in prayer, resting her elbows on the bed. This is something we never did when she was a child. Mostly, we just told her to go to bed, turned off the light, and left the room. Now, I pulled the door closed behind me, to give her privacy.

I've spent our first days together observing her like a gorilla at the zoo. Wondering what she might do next; if her actions are representative of her species; trying to anticipate her every whim, and failing.

Observe the *teenager feminine* in her natural habitat: shoes off, feet up, headphones on. The headphones, in fact, are never removed—if she's not listening to them, they are draped around her neck, at the ready. There is a phone, of course, which she doesn't once raise to her ear. Instead, her thumbs wallop relentlessly at the screen, her face an ever-evolving mask of amusement, peevishness, disbelief, and envy. I have heard it said that thumbs separate humans from animals; that dogs would rule the world if only they had opposable digits. With the advent of smartphones and touchscreens, thumbs seem poised to take yet another evolutionary leap, leaving the canines even farther behind.

She hangs a few things. A vintage black and white poster of a mushroom cloud, which I recognize from the 1964 film *Dr. Strangelove*. She hangs a long and narrow framed poster, on which is written that incredibly fucking cheesy "Footprints" poem, the one about how there are two sets of footprints on the beach blah, blah, blah, and how the times when there was one footprint, Jesus carried you. The third thing to go up is a kind of mobile, lit from within, displaying paper cutouts of circus animals. I remember it, vaguely, from when she was a baby. Once her door is shut and the lights are off, I watch soft pink and orange lights run along the crack beneath her door.

I offer this creature sustenance and watch it eat. Capri Sun—her bursting the seal with the pointed end of the straw, but then instead of using the straw to drink, sucking the juice directly from the foil pack. Hot Pockets, the fucking things always blazing when they come out of the microwave, it takes fifteen minutes for them to cool. The way she arrives home from school carrying a large soda from McDonald's and tells me she ate two hamburgers and fries but don't worry, she'll definitely be hungry for dinner. I mentally catalog these things and wonder at their meaning, even as I find myself remembering, with no small amount of jealousy, when I too once had the metabolism of a hummingbird.

Alone, I buy a six-pack of two-ply toilet paper every three months or so. It's a surprise when I get home one night and she has lined empty toilet paper rolls across the kitchen counter, like an accusation, with a note: *Need more!* My having only just purchased a six-pack in anticipation of her arrival. I go out and buy a dozen rolls, figuring that should last us to the weekend, when I can take the car out and load the trunk with more. I don't think too hard about it, but for the love of Christ, what could she be doing with all that bath tissue?

"Want to see a trick?" she asks me. She sits on her knees, on the couch. She takes a deep breath. She clamps one hand over her mouth and pinches her nose. Then she throws herself backward onto the cushions, and for more than a minute she lies limp, unconscious. I rush to her side, panicked.

Suddenly she wakes. "I totally made myself black out!"

"Don't ever fucking do that again," I tell her.

After a week, she decides my language is creating a stressful home environment. She creates a scorecard and posts it on the kitchen wall. She buys gold star stickers and stickers of a cartoon bomb, the kind Wile E. Coyote might throw, rounded, with the short fuse on top. Every time I curse, she puts a bomb sticker in the "Curse" column. Every time I tell her I love her, she puts a gold sticker in the "Love" column. After twenty-four hours, curses outpace love forty-seven to three. Finally, I tear the poster from the wall and set my lighter to it, dropping the flaming, curling paper in the sink, where it becomes ashes.

"I fucking love you," I tell her.

Pasternak manages to scrounge up two new candidates. One is a charity case from Fenger High School. Uses *no* instead of *any*. Braids in her hair. Typos in her resume, which otherwise looks pretty good for an eighteen-year-old, she was active in high school anyway, but Jesus, she's got tattoo sleeves up both arms that look like they were done with an ink pen and sewing needle. She's a walking case of Hep-C. This, I assume, is Fenger's best and brightest.

I'd love to hire a minority. I want to hire a minority more than I want 7 percent growth this year. And yet. When measuring one candidate against another, how much am I obligated to overlook in order to hire someone who might have a prayer of checking a census box other than "Caucasian: White"?

"What achievements are you most proud of?" I ask her.

She does this thing where she rolls her eyes up in the back of her head and her lids flutter. "I wrote all that on my resume. Under *Awards and Honors.*"

"Yes, I see that." I hold her resume close to my face. "I was just wondering, you know, which of these you're most proud of."

"All of them." She grins, and something about it seems a bit too slick, like a used car salesman. My antennae are up, suddenly. I have a passing thought her entire resume might be fiction. I realize just as quickly it doesn't matter. The reason to hire an eighteen-year-old instead of a college kid is so that you can groom them without their having developed any bad habits or pre-conceived ideas about what finance is. Trust has to be part of that though. It's a substantial investment for the firm, hiring someone new. This girl isn't it.

I pretend to write something in the margins. "Where did the Dow Industrial Average and the S&P 500 close yesterday?"

"The Dow closed down, about .21 percent, something like that."

At least she bothered to glance at CNBC before she came in. "And the S&P?"

"About the same?" She bursts out laughing, covers her mouth with her hand. "I'm not really sure."

"That's okay." I look her in the eye so she knows I'm telling the truth. "Here's some friendly advice, though. If you want a job in finance, you gotta start following these things. Every day. Up or down. Follow the market like you follow the Bulls. Know all the stats. Does that make sense?"

"Yes, sir," she says. "Sorry."

"Don't apologize." I consider for a moment. Fuck it: time for the knockout blow. "Tell me what goodwill is, and how it's accounted for?"

The eye-roll thing again. Watching her eyeballs flitter beneath her lids makes me think of baby hamsters, moving under wood chips. I feel a little sick to my stomach. When I was six, my hamster had babies and two days later, ate them all.

"Goodwill is a place you go to buy clothes that you can, you know, actually afford. Clothes and furniture, stuff like that." She looks at me. My face is smooth and expressionless as caulk. "I think maybe people donate stuff, so in terms of how you asked me, how it's accounted for, maybe it's a tax write-off, something like that? I seen people drop stuff off and they get handed some kind of sheet of paper, a receipt or something."

I watch a piece of chewing gum slip from where this girl must have had it lodged in her cheek. The chiclet, pale as dead skin, slides across her bottom lip, swings out for a moment, glistening with saliva, before being sucked back inside her mouth.

I smile, reach for my bottle of water, take a long drink. "Write this down."

"Okay." She gropes the desk, doesn't find a pen or anything to write on, so she pulls her phone from her pocket. She laughs at something in her messages, then poises her thumbs. "Sorry. I'm ready."

"Goodwill, in our business, is the excess value of the purchase price over the fair market price of whatever it is you purchase. So, say I'm going to buy McDonald's. And the book value of McDonald's is five dollars. And I pay seven dollars. The goodwill is, what?"

"Seven?"

"No," I say, and that's a wrap.

I dismiss her, and she thanks me, sort of, too young to realize what a fucking opportunity she's pissed away. Once she's gone, I slide her resume beneath all the others, thinking how, longterm, maybe a generation or two, this will level out. She graduates high school, gets a job in the CBOE warehouse, pulls down a solid middle-class salary. Has a couple kids who go to college, they wind up making six figures in banking or insurance. And their kids? Sky's the limit. But I feel no obligation to be a Human Resources pioneer. All I'm looking for in a potential hire is someone as greedy as I am, who'll shut the fuck up and listen, get to work on time (early, actually), and doesn't need me to tell them when to take a leak.

The first candidate utterly fails to meet my fairly straight-forward criteria.

"The next one better be a home run," I tell Pasternak.

"It's the end of the year. No one's looking for work, because no one but us is hiring."

"That's why we're hiring," I tell him. "When's the next interview?"

Turns out it's Monday. And just like that, it's the weekend.

Chapter 6

Saturdays, I like to sleep in. At some point, I get up and eat a little something. Then I go back to sleep. Rinse, wash, repeat.

My workweek is so long, the hours so absurd, I need the weekend to recover. To rejuvenate. It's about all I can do to muster the energy to call for delivery from my favorite Mexican place, or go pick up a burger somewhere. Weekends turn me into an infant.

This morning, the television wakes me up. The clock says eight.

"Seriously?" I pad barefoot out of my cave. "It's a little early for FOX News."

Jeanie's sitting cross-legged in my recliner. "I don't get a chance to watch it during the week. They re-run all the important shows on Saturday."

I stand there for a few minutes, scratching my stubble, watching her watch Hannity and Colmes. The television hosts' mouths are moving, and there are words coming out, but it doesn't sound like English. I listen a bit longer, trying to figure out what the fuck they're talking about, but I have no idea.

Jeanie feels me watching her. "What?"

"Aren't you…" I remind myself to step lightly. "What's it like to be the only conservative in the entire city of Chicago?"

"I'm socially liberal but fiscally conservative," she says, in the manner of a practiced news anchor. "I made coffee."

I go and get some. The coffee is strong, the way I like it. It smells like pumpkin.

"What time did you get home last night?" I come back into the living room. I figure she's old enough, our time together so short, I'm not going to impose a curfew.

"Midnight or so. I could hear you snoring from the hall."

I collapse on the couch. "Have fun?"

She shrugs—just like her mother. That one-shoulder thing she does. "Do you ever go out?"

"You mean at night?"

"I mean to hang out with people. People not from work."

I slurp my coffee, loudly. "I'm usually so beat by Friday, I can't see straight."

She finds the remote, clicks it. The anchors' voices disappear, and I decide I like them better this way, their bright-red faces yapping, but no words coming out.

She turns her body to face me. "Are you dating anyone?"

"Dating anyone..." I make a face. "You mean, is there some other human I allow myself to be seen with in public? Regularly?"

"When two people are interested in one another, they sometimes go to restaurants or to the movies..."

"Yeah, I've never heard of anything like that."

She sits up suddenly, energized by the realization that I am someone who needs to be fixed. "You have to meet people!"

I slap my forehead. "Shit. So that's how it works?"

Already she has her phone out, thumbs smashing against the keypad. "Are we Facebook friends?" Before I can answer, she's pulled up my profile. "Dad, you absolutely cannot have this as your profile pic."

I lean over to look—I can't remember what I put on there. It's the photo they took of me when they were taking photos of all the board members, a year or two ago. "What's wrong with it? My tie's on straight."

She squints. "This pic might be fine for LinkedIn or something, but you look like a real douchebag."

"Thank you."

"You need something more casual for Facebook. More fun."

It's my turn to narrow my eyes. "I don't do fun."

"I know." She looks at me seriously. "But as soon as you meet some chick, she's going to Google you. And one of the first things she's going to find is your Facebook page. You can't be on there looking like some deranged banker who's like, three seconds from throwing himself off a bridge."

"Truth in advertising."

She jumps up from the chair. She takes a quick walk through the room. She disappears into my bedroom and returns.

"There aren't any pictures of you," she says. "Anywhere."

"Nope."

"Come to think of it, there aren't any pictures of me, either."

I hold the mug close to my chest, hunker down. "Your mom kept everything."

"Don't you think that's a little strange?"

"I think it would be more strange if there were photographs of me everywhere. Inside an apartment where I live. Alone."

She stands over me. She puts her hands on her hips and tucks her chin. I know that look—I remember that look. Not on her, but on her mother. Azita would get that same expression right before she told me to take out the trash.

"Go put some clothes on," she says. "Nice clothes."

I slurp the dregs. "I stay in on Saturdays."

She makes a pouty face. "'I stay in on Saturdays.' Poor baby." She kicks me in the shin. "Get up. We're going out."

"What for?"

She claps her hands. "Photo shoot."

I wear a Brooks Brothers shirt and jeans. My topsiders. Jeanie packs a small bag with a couple more shirts so that when we take the photos, it will look like I've been out of the house on different days, or don't always wear the same thing, both of which will stretch the truth to the outer limits of credibility.

We plunge ourselves, arm in arm, into the bosom of downtown. Great thing about the City of Big Shoulders is that before lunch, on a Saturday, you have it almost entirely to yourself.

We take a photo of me against the windows at the bar atop the Holiday Inn, overlooking the river. I enjoy a Jameson neat, the water curling below me. A few blocks away, she yanks a Chelsea jersey from her bag and makes me put it on. She photographs me cheering my head off inside an Irish bar, Fado. I enjoy another Jameson, neat. It seems rude to just rush inside these establishments and take a photo: I feel obligated to spend. I buy Jeanie a diet and grenadine.

At Rainforest Café I dry-hump every enamel frog, gorilla, and parakeet in the place. She takes a million photos. Me against the mist; me uplit by red and blue spotlights; me pretending to goose an elephant. We eat some kind of chocolate and vanilla ice cream volcano cake, and I have another Jameson, neat.

She produces a long coat. I button it to my chin. She photographs me at Watertower place; in a horse-drawn carriage; ordering a Jameson, neat, at the Drake Hotel. We take a taxicab back west and eat lunch at Le Colonial. A photograph of me fumbling with chopsticks; using my fingers to dip shrimp and pork spring rolls into chili lime sauce; slurping stray ends of cellophane noodles; staging a light skirmish between my stir-fried shrimp and calamari. Another Jameson for me, and a bubble tea for my lovely guest, thank you. We take a selfie of ourselves in the bamboo stand out front. She kisses me on the cheek and snaps the picture. It's a keeper—there's ginger broth on my chin.

Even as we're cabbing home, my only thought is that I do not want this day to end.

And then a slightly darker thought follows: that if this were the last day of my life, I'd die happy. That I had just experienced one of those days that would let me leave the Earth content.

This, of course, makes me imagine Jeanie's wedding without me there to walk her down the aisle. Once we're home, I'm overcome with so much grief, I rush straight to my bedroom and weep for twenty minutes, out of view of my daughter. I blame the Jameson. I blame the wind—it always makes my eyes water. When I finally re-emerge, Jeanie's asleep on the couch, Bulls game on but muted. I slide in beside her, covering us both with a Sox blanket, watching the sky get a little bit darker as the afternoon slips away.

On Monday, Stefany Marie Vázquez arrives fifteen minutes early for her interview. Pasternak paints the scene for me later. She arrives, checks in, asks to use the washroom. Professional as hell—just what I'm always advising candidates to be. Get there early, and even if you don't have to piss, go to the wash-room. Check yourself in the mirror. Make sure you don't have spinach in your teeth. The fifteen-minutes early thing makes me want to hire her on the spot.

She's dressed smartly, in a metallic-blue blouse and suit. She's short, round, Latina. She's eased off the makeup, and her nails are short enough they don't immediately make me suspect a cocaine habit.

She brings an extra copy of her resume. She's a little older than the other candidates. She has two years at Harold Washington, my alma mater. She worked as a bank teller for two summers; she won an ¡Adelante! Fund MillerCoors Brewing Company Scholarship as a high-school senior. GPA over 3. After about five minutes, I lay her resume aside.

"Look," I say. "Your resume—you're more qualified than anyone else we've brought in. So. It's really just a matter of whether you and I get along, and whether or not you think you can handle the trading pit."

She smiles, but her eye contact never wavers. "I get along with pretty much everybody."

"That's not always a good thing."

"Because I listen," she continues, confidently. "Because I know when not to talk. And because I watch everyone else, I can help them out when they need it."

I nod. "You'll be the only female. A couple clerks are women, but you'll be the only female trader."

"I have seven brothers," she tells me.

"Catholic?"

"Venezuelan."

"Where'd you grow up?"

She gives me the abridged version, no sob story. Northwest Chicago, worked since she was thirteen while still going to school, her mom and dad both held down two jobs and that's how they made it, the siblings looking after one another. It sounds like the ideal upbringing, she puts such a positive spin on it.

"It's not only that you're female," I tell her. "Trading platforms, we're going digital faster than most of the guys in my firm can keep up. I need someone in here who's younger than thirty, who doesn't comment on the 'miracle of technology' every time they use a phone that's not connected to the wall."

"I got you," she says. "Don't worry. I'm good with computers, and all that stuff."

"Where'd Apple close yesterday?"

"Down .41 percent."

"A bondholder and a stockholder walk into a bar. Who's the more senior creditor?"

"The bondholder."

"Why?"

"They get paid first, if there's a bankruptcy or something. Stockholders gotta chill out and wait their turn."

I have to laugh. There's a way she handles the lingo—expertly, but also casually, with just a little bit of street tough in her voice—that I can't help but love. It reminds me a little bit of the old neighborhood, I guess.

I thank her, shake her hand like I mean it, and tell her we'll be in touch. Once she's gone, I call Pasternak in.

"Wait forty-eight hours," I tell him. "As soon as you get her thank-you note, hire her."

"How do you know she's sending a thank-you note?"

"It'll be handwritten, so remember to check the fucking mail for once."

He doesn't go away, though. Instead, he buzzes at the door like a toddler about to wet himself. He's been working for me long enough that I know he's getting himself primed to ask me something he thinks is important—for a vacation day, or to leave early, something that will require my kindness and/or leniency, which these days I'm finding in pretty short supply.

"Jesus Christ, DIP. What?"

"Uh." He leans one hand on the door frame. "We got one more interview."

"I thought you said three."

"Well, there's three."

I straighten my tie, clear my throat, rifle through the papers on my desk, my inbox, but I don't see a fourth resume. "Who?"

Pasternak stands at attention. I forget how tall he is sometimes. Static electricity draws stray hairs from his crown to the doorframe, wavering like anemones.

"Me, boss." He blinks. "I want to interview."

I bury my head in my hands. "Goddammit."

"I want a shot, JAG."

"Ok, ok." I try to rally, like shaking off a hangover. I didn't see this coming, not at all. "Ok. Let's do it."

"Right now?"

"Yes, right fucking now."

He gestures toward his work station. "Should I print out my—"

"No. Sit the fuck down." I glower at him while he takes a seat, straightens his jacket. He has to push back a little from the desk, his legs jumbled beneath him. "I can't believe you're goddamn doing this to me."

"I've been with you a long time, and—"

"Did Robin put you up to this?"

Robin is his wife. They've been married since they were twelve years old or something fucking insane like that. But if you've ever seen the movie *The Untouchables*, that scene where Al Capone is gripping the Tommy Gun with two hands and laughing his ass off, firing round after round and spinning the barrel in a great giant circle through the air, that's Robin. Machine gun and fucking laugh that'll make your skin crawl, both. Pretty, brunette, petite, mouth like she grew up in Canaryville.

"Ten years." Pasternak is eerily calm. "That's how long I've been working for you. We're the same age, JAG. Time for me is running out."

I shrug with one shoulder, a trick I picked up from somebody I was close to once.

"I know I'll never get where you are." He leans forward. He's got a piece of spittle clinging to the corner of his mouth. It makes him seem hungry. Rabid. I kind of like it. "But I deserve a shot."

I laugh in his face. "You don't deserve shit."

"Loyalty counts for nothing?"

"No, loyalty counts for something," I say. "But don't tell me you fucking deserve something. Because no one deserves shit."

I've never known Pasternak to act entitled, but it's a real pet peeve of mine. Some people go their entire lives believing they're special, that things should be handed to them, that their ascension should be painless and quick. They've got this fairytale fucking idea of how the world works—every kid these days is a Disney princess or Batman—and I take perverse pleasure in being the one to grind their enchanted castles to dust.

We sit for a while in silence. He's patient with me and waits. It's our typical afternoon after the markets close, but instead of reviewing our action list for tomorrow, Pasternak is asking me for a job. A different job than the one he currently has.

It's not that he can't handle it. Hell, he might even deserve it. The issue is resource allocation.

If I hire two new college graduates, or a kid right out of high school, I can set them loose, analyzing, running trades—they can be up to speed on the technology in six weeks, trading on their own by the time the ivy's green at Wrigley. If I hire Pasternak, though, that means I have to train a new clerk as well, and who knows how long that will take or what business it might disrupt. Traders are a dime a dozen. A good clerk? Shit, you see Executive Assistants spend their entire careers with their CEOs, because a good assistant is fucking irreplaceable. You literally cannot pay them enough.

There's that old adage about the boss not being the most powerful man at the company, that the boss' assistant is the one you really need to kiss up to, because he or she is the one who holds all the keys, who keeps the calendar, who makes sure your name stays high on the "To Call" list and doesn't get buried on page three. To guys like that, like me, the calendar is king. In the schedule is freedom. And the keepers of the schedules are our assistants, who after ten, fifteen, twenty years becomes more like extended family. Intricately wrapped up in one another's lives.

"It's not the right time," I tell him.

"John."

"We just lost Hauser and Strike. You know this. Our two best guys. If I boost you up to trader, I gotta train you—"

"Not as much as you'll have to train a new hire. I've spent a decade down there already."

"—and then I gotta train someone to do your job, or you do, which sounds like even more of a clusterfuck."

I'm sympathetic. I know Pasternak didn't grow up dreaming of being a clerk. It's gotta bother him a little bit that he's working under me, he who had much better grades than me growing up, who the parents trusted more, who was the better athlete, all that. I promote him to trader, suddenly he's not just doubling his salary, potentially, but tripling it. That's just out of the gate. Down the road, five, ten years? He can buy everyone in his family a house.

He looks down at his hands, folds them. "I got other offers."

"From fucking who?"

He leans back, crosses his legs, feeling pretty confident about this Ace he's been hiding up his sleeve. "I can't say. But there are a couple."

"You strong-arming me?"

He gives me the shittiest-eatin' grin, which I probably deserve. "I learned from the best."

I smile—I can't help it. I like it when Pasternak shows some spine. It doesn't happen nearly enough.

In the gym, I find the old guy whose wife has just died. He's lying smack in the middle of the workout room in the exact position of a chalk outline. I step over him, wipe off a machine as if I might use it, then step over him again. I pause, bend, listening, observing his chest. His eyes are closed. His white T-shirt is twisted, thin enough to see the outline of his ribs, his left nipple. I hear a soft whistling through his nostril hairs. When his heart leaps out at me like a punch through a curtain, I go wipe down a different machine and lean against it.

These older guys—I feel like anyone over sixty just wanders around the workout room swinging their leg up on whatever they can find just so they can stretch their hammy. A weight bench. The arm of a treadmill. The water fountain— one of at least fifteen reasons I never use the water fountain in the gym. Then the boomers sprawl across the floor for a little cat nap.

Working out with rich fucks twenty years older than me has some advantages: nobody's on the Hercules machine crushing deadlifts and grunting like they're passing a kidney stone. Also, despite my forty extra pounds, I'm the fastest pedaler on the recumbent. The downside is that none of these old-timers can hear a fucking thing, so they crank the overhead television to unexplored decibels. Inevitably, to FOX News.

I can't tell a single one of the anchors apart from one another. They're like these yipping fucking gerbils, slurping sugar water from the feeder spout. But like all things small and adorable, I can't turn away.

The great state of Illinois has made national news. Our governor, Rod Blagojevich, speaks to reporters. "There's nothing but sunshine hanging over me," he tells the press.

As a Chicagoan—hell, as an American—my heart is with Blago. A true rags-to-riches story. The son of Bosnian and Serbian immigrants, Blago was a boxer first, then a state prosecutor, then governor—but you don't move to Springfield without selling off all the pieces of yourself one by one. The newest thing—and I'm not talking about the fact that he'll probably be impeached, because the press won't let him forget it—this pressure he's putting on Bank of America to honor loans to Chicago-based businesses, it's got all the elements of Chicago politics. Blago siding with the striking workers at Republic Windows and Doors and pressuring other state businesses to cease relationships with BOA—this is the kind of thing that drives the free-market GOP bat-shit insane.

"Fucking golden," Blago called Obama's senate seat. The feds got a recording of him telling someone over the telephone that he wasn't going to give the vacant seat away for nothing. Trading senate seats for favors is not, apparently, legal, but personally, I don't see what all the outrage is about. Nothing's for free. No city on Earth runs without a healthy amount of graft, and most Chicagoans are masters of the trade.

I've spent about three minutes on the recumbent, and already I'm wheezing. Also, the bottom of my left foot feels like someone is slowly tightening its ligaments with a winch.

I punch the big square STOP button and allow my feet to churn to a standstill. I rise, wipe down my machine, and then, for good measure, stretch. Doing so, I manage to position myself beneath the television. I take the remote from where the oldest of the old ones has it perched on his treadmill dashboard. I click a couple buttons, and MSNBC pops on, featuring every conservative's new worst nightmare, Rachel Maddow. I raise the volume four or five clicks, then leave the remote high on the television shelf, well out of reach for anyone doing cardio.

I'm half-undressed when the old guy whose wife died comes storming into locker room.

"What's the big idea?" He charges right at me, glaring through sports goggles.

I stand there holding up my shorts with both hands. "The big idea? Every day I gotta endure the banalities that you fuckers call television."

"Watch your mouth." He's right up in my face. I turn my head away from his breath, but I don't give ground. "You watch your mouth or I'll kick your ass right here."

"You oughta get some goddamn hearing aids," I tell him, nice and slow, mocking him. "The rest of us don't want to hear all that bullshit."

I'm not taking off my shorts—not now. Instead, I hitch them back up and knot the tie-string. I'll shower later.

"You know what you are?" I feel his spit hit my cheek. "A fucking pussy."

And then he slaps me on the side of the head.

It doesn't hurt. It's more like in a black and white movie, when Curly slaps Mo. Still, inside, that familiar rendering, that untethering of all reason from all future action.

The old guy has six inches on me, easy. But I outweigh him. I grab the collar of his cotton gym shirt; I slam him against the wall and then shove his head into the row of lockers. The flat of my hand against his scalp is slick. I feel stubble. The locker room shakes with the sound his head makes on impact, the harsh, shuddering reverb of aluminum. When we are pulled apart by two younger members, I am surprised to discover that I'm bleeding from a cut above my nose. Either he bit me, or my schnozz made incidental contact with his teeth. I honestly don't remember. I wasn't in my body. Like so many times before, I was a vessel through which a spontaneous and entirely stunning rage poured forth. My entire person transformed into a pillar of flame, of pure release.

I get home late, but Jeanie's out. A note on the fridge says *Studying*.

Fine by me—I grab a Bell's Winter Ale and drop onto the couch like a fat lady crash-landing in an old timey fireman's net. I hold the bottle against my nose, which is bruised and yellow. The beer's pretty warm by the time I take a sip.

I flip on the tube. Winter is a dark time of year, television-wise. In summer, you can at least rely on there being a ballgame, something to put on, to have playing in the background while you decompress. Winter though, despite it being in-season for both basketball and hockey, those games are too spread out to ever bank on catching one.

Hockey. I've never been able to figure out the schedule. That, and the fact I can never follow the little fucking puck on the little fucking television screen, has kept me from ever being a fan. The city is ape-shit these days over the prospects of the Blackhawks, the Baby Hawks, the news calls them, but you can't tell me even half the city is able to follow the puck either, or knows icing from spearing. Sometimes I'll be standing there, in a bar or something, with a bunch of guys watching hockey on the television. And I take a moment to watch the guys watching the game. I can't see the puck. No way in hell they can either. And yet we're all standing there rapt, like children watching a flea circus at some traveling carnival. There were never any fleas. For all I know, there's no puck either.

I find *The First 48*. This true-crime show follows real-life homicide detectives during the first two days after a murder. They rotate cities; tonight is Detroit. I don't know that there's enough money in the world to make me live in Detroit, much less be a cop there. It'd be like policing the world through that video game *Doom*.

Eventually the detectives bring a suspect down to the station and let him sweat it out in the interrogation room. As viewers, we're treated to a black and white camera shot, from a high corner. It's very dramatic. And the questioning goes on and on and pretty soon, the suspect confesses without ever once asking for a lawyer. Guys start fessing up to all sorts of heinous crimes, and he's completely, utterly, waived his right to an attorney, at least in all the ones I've seen. What I can't figure out is, is the criminals really that dumb that he doesn't know he's constitutionally guaranteed access to a lawyer, or is all this shit just made for television?

It's made me skeptical. How much of anything of what we see on television is true? Pays well, though. I heard somewhere Blago's wife is going to make a million dollars for being on *Survivor* or some shit.

You know you have a better chance of going to prison if you're governor of Illinois than if you murder someone? This is the shit that keeps me up at night.

That, and my tendency to replay the day's events over and over again in my mind. Dissecting every conversation.

Each sound bite. Tonight, I'm flushed with shame over my behavior in the gym. Blame the testosterone. That common sense some people have, that internal governor that stops them from acting out every violent impulse is something I was born without. I don't even know that guy. His wife is dead. What the fuck do I do now? he asked me, the first time he struck up a conversation with me. That same predilection toward rage that compelled him to follow me into the locker room. The moral high ground. The world's fucking policeman. I'm not gonna stand there and let him slap me. Regardless of age.

I watch television until my eyes are so heavy they feel like they're going to tumble out of my skull. Sometimes, going to bed feels like admitting defeat. I reach for the controller, but only succeed in knocking it down between the seat cushion and the arm of the couch. I plunge my hand down there and find the controller, but also a soft and crumpled cloth. It takes me a moment to smooth it out and hold it up to the light: it's a bra. Black, lacey. Definitely not something I misplaced.

"Hey," I tell Jeanie at breakfast, tossing the undergarment to her. "I'm glad you're feeling comfortable here. But let's not start leaving our dirty laundry around."

The next morning, I again tell Pasternak to hire Vázquez.

"It's like Al fucking Gore." He shakes his head. "Ruling objections out of order at his own senate hearing."

"Don't be dramatic." I pull him aside, talk to him straight. "Hire Vázquez. Let's get through the January bump, whatever fucking shit the market's pulling right now. Once she's up to speed, that still leaves us short one guy. This summer, we'll train you on the terminals."

"Okay." His cheeks quiver—with gratitude? Anger? It's hard to tell. "Thank you."

Mid-day, Chairman Sar drops by. He walks the trading floor like General fucking Patton reviewing troops in the North Africa desert.

"Everything in order here?" he asks.

"Little bounce this morning," I tell him. "VIX is still through the roof."

He has his hands clasped behind his back—it's his thing. Napoleon hid his hand inside his jacket; Mussolini tucked his fists into his hips. Sar folds his hands behind his back and leans forward, his cranium like a battering ram.

"How's next week looking?" he asks.

"Normal. Fine."

He gestures, and his assistant rushes forward. She's one of those twenty-year vets, came over with Sar from the last place she worked for him. Two things are remarkable about his assistant: her hair—huge, curly, impossibly coiffed—and that every jacket she wears has shoulder pads. But we get along fine; I make sure we do. She's clutching a bound stack of papers three-inches thick.

"Have you ever seen one of these?" Sar grins like a kid showing off his new BB gun. "It's a bill making its way through Congress. Seven-hundred pages. Six-hundred of which are the bill itself—something about extending existing immigration programs. But tucked in the back, page 643, is an amendment that would repeal the capital gains treatment for options and commodities traders."

I make a face like I'm impressed. "That's how it works, right? Politics?"

"A 700-page document, and they hide this shit in the back."

I flip through the bound stack, but honestly, there are so many pages I don't even see the bill he's talking about.

"Well," he answers his own rant, "it's why we have lobby-ists. Still, a few of us need to fly to DC this week, meet with our people there. You in?"

"Sure."

"Set it up with Charlene," he tells me, and I glance at his assistant to let her know I'll give her a call.

My pit erupts. I spin to see the same blood-red sea of numbers roiling across the terminals that I feel like I've been swimming in for months now. When I turn back, Sar is gone.

Hell, getting out of town might do me some good.

Jeanie uploads some of my photos to Facebook. The one of me in the Chelsea jersey becomes my profile pic. I'm screaming my head off, or pretending to, veins bulging out of my skull. It's how I look 90 percent of the time anyway, so I applaud the realism, even if it was staged. She does other quasi-ethical things too, like back-date the photos to make them seem as if they were taken at different times of year, like I'm trying to establish a history for me and some Taiwanese mistress I want to naturalize.

"Hey," I ask Jeanie, whose fingers hammer away at the keys. "You can search for people on here, right?"

She looks at me like I've just asked if she's heard of this awesome thing called cable television. "Someone in particular?"

"Yeah." I think a moment, and then decide, fuck it. "Penny Weil."

She types the name in the search box, shakes her head. "Penny, what's that short for? Penelope?" She types again and is presented with a drop-down menu.

"That's her." I point to a profile: Penelope Weil, Esquire.

Jeanie brings up her page. "She's hot."

"Yeah." Her profile pic shows her behind a microphone, maybe at a stand-up comedy show or something like that. You never know what people do in their spare time.

"She's a friend?" Jeanie asks.

"She's my attorney."

Jeanie clicks around, so quickly I can't tell what she's even looking at before she moves on. Her navigation creates a blurring, rapid-fire reel of photos, maps, and personal information. "I think she's single. You should ask her out."

"I should, should I?" I reach past and click on Penny's photo albums. There are plenty of pictures with girlfriends and a few more shots of her on a stage somewhere, performing solo. The last time I saw her, she tried to make small talk. Asked about vacation plans. She may well have been flirting with me, testing the waters.

"I'll think about it." I reach over and shut the computer. Jeanie looks at me like she can't figure out why I'm being such a dick, then slinks off to her favorite spot in the E-Z chair to do some reading. Her English class is working their way through *Heart of Darkness*.

Chapter 7

Jeanie perches on the kitchen countertop, ankles crossed, balancing her laptop. She wears leggings and a long-sleeve shirt that covers most of her hands, which she sticks her thumbs through. Her thumbs and cheeks are the only patches of skin showing.

"Guess how many cattle are lost to coyotes every year?" she asks.

It's the kind of thing she knows I'll enjoy, the practical application of mathematics to real-world issues.

"As an actual number? I have no idea."

"As a percentage."

Dinner tonight is Pigs in a Blanket. This meal was a luxury for me, growing up. My father cooked it on special occasions that coincided with the first of the month, when we were flush from payday. Having Pigs in a Blanket on a regular-old Tuesday—for dinner—feels like a real indulgence. Jeanie and I will top them with grape jelly, powdered sugar, syrup, and butter. She wanted me to cook something. This is all I got.

The pancakes begin to bubble, and I flip them. "There are probably forty million cows in the U.S., counting both dairy and beef cows. The dairy cows will never be eaten by coyotes because they're tucked away safe in barns and dairies. So that's a quarter of the population, right off the bat, that won't be eaten by coyotes." I slide the spatula beneath the first pancake. Jeanie swings a plate over the stove and catches the flapjack as it tumbles. Then we do it again. I dip my measuring cup into the batter, pour a perfect circle on the griddle. "Of the 30 million beef cows, figure 90 or 95 percent of those will never be vulnerable to a coyote attack, which leaves about 5 percent, we're talking the free-range beef cows, organic, exposed to the elements. Probably 2 percent of those actually share habitat with coyotes, so I'll guess 20 percent of the organic beef cows are slaughtered by coyotes each year, so about 0.20 percent of all cattle in the U.S."

She makes no expression, just swings the plate over the stovetop and catches two more pancakes. She's reading with her other hand, sitting on the counter. "That's it exactly. Well, 0.23 percent, but still, well done."

This is the problem with numbers, though: coyotes kill less than a quarter of 1 percent of cattle in the U.S. each year. Phrase it like that, people shrug and figure, no big deal. Four percent of cattle die just because that's what cattle do. But suppose instead you tell someone that predators kill 220,000 cows a year, and that more than half of those deaths are caused by coyotes. Then suddenly people take notice. A couple hundred thousand seems like a lot; over a hundred thousand done in by coyotes alone. A population roughly the size of Ann Arbor, Michigan, murdered by coyotes each year—you can work up some indignation that way.

They're the exact same sets of numbers, of course.

By the time I'm through explaining this, Jeanie is yanking the spatula from my hand because the kitchen is filled with smoke. A smell like the dirty underside of a grill grate. Also, our smoke alarm is going off, blasting a rapid, stuttering pitch unattainable by humans. I lift Jeanie up, all hundred pounds of her, by the waist, and she reaches to hit the "reset" button. In the kitchen again, I wave away the dark clouds. On the griddle are two charred circles, now stiff and carbonized, lighter than air, what were supposed to be the final two flapjacks, incinerated.

Mid-morning, Chairman Sar struts through the trading pits like he just muff-dived Keira Knightley and pulled a black pearl out of her vagina with his teeth. I spot him in the neighboring pit, hand on someone's shoulder, shouting one conquest story or another into the other man's ear. Sar is so short, even average-height guys have to stoop a little bit to hear him. I turn back to the screens, but I know he's coming for me. He makes motions with his hands like he's pulling pins from grenades and lobbing them. Everybody laughs.

"Gentlemen," Pasternak addresses our guys. "Don your shit-eating grins."

On cue, Sar beelines and hops up on the platform with me, throwing his arms around me like we're war buddies.

He shouts down my ear canal. "You will not believe where I was this weekend."

"Tell me," I say, mustering 57 percent enthusiasm.

"First, some backstory. Out west, where I was, in South Dakota, they have so many coyotes, they don't know what to do with them."

"We were just talking about this."

"It's a real problem. The coyote kill cattle. Rip apart people's pets. Fucking labradoodles torn into cottony shreds."

I wince. It's something I've noticed about our chairman: he only curses when he's talking to me. Something he picked up, no doubt, in the newest edition of *How to Win Friends and Influence People*.

I always preferred *The Art of War*.

I want to tell him, look, I can appreciate your desire, as a guy worth 50 million, to relate to the worker-bees sweating in the pits below. But also, you don't brag about your jumpshot when Michael Jordan's around. Air Jordan is an artist. In that same way, don't bother dropping F-bombs around me. I'm fucking Michelangelo when it comes to deploying this word in all its tenses and iterations. I deploy foul language like military drones.

"So," Sar goes on—I catch Pasternak watching me out of the corner of his eye, listening— "this time of year is basically open season on those fuckers. I mean, you're allowed to hunt them."

"Coyotes?"

"Damn right. Out west, they hunt coyotes like we hunt deer."

Markets are almost closed, guys positioning themselves for the overnight. VIX is still through the roof, no end in sight, already the news is filled with stories of Americans who've worked their whole lives saving for retirement and cashed out when the markets hit bottom and so, have nothing but twenty more years of work ahead of them. Our days here are long periods of solemn quiet punctuated by swells of deafening panic and fury. As pit-master, I can watch these swells start to build like waves in the ocean. There's one building now, a little eddy, a swirl around some of my senior traders, as they try to make some moves before end of day. Four guys are waving their hands and practically leaping out of their purple jackets, trying to nail down prices.

Sar reaches up, puts pressure on my shoulder, pulls my ear closer. "Except they hunt these beasts from fucking aircraft."

Shaking my head. "No shit?"

"Imagine a med-vac chopper, stripped to the studs. Two jumpseats in back. A pilot. For fifteen grand, they'll take you up and fly you out to the plateaus, the black hills, and they bring the chopper in low, and you're hooked into these grommets that are big as scythes, and they swoop in, and you're holding the semi-automatic rifle, and down below, the coyotes are running, these streaks of burnt red against the black ground, running like rain drops down a windshield, that's all they appear to be at first, streaks of water, of fucking blood, but then you're suddenly low enough to see them, their snouts, and the guide, he just sort of leans over and gives you a thumbs up, because you can't hear anything, the wind is so loud, the motor—and you lean out with your rifle and make it rain. For real, make it rain. Those coyotes, when you hit them, leap three feet into the air and do this kind of corkscrew. That's how you know."

My pit explodes and then quiets again, the break of the waves against the sand.

"Do you get to keep the meat?"

He looks at me, pulling away a bit, like he just smelled my SBD. "When's the last time you ate fucking coyote?"

On a smoke break, I get a call from Jeanie's school. They're sending her home for the day.

I answer my phone in the courtyard outside the Exchange. Congress is all buses and dump trucks—deafening. It's unseasonably sunny. Every bench is taken. Women unwrap sandwiches with stiff fingers. People hover their lips over to-go coffee from Krispy Kreme, hoping to absorb some of the caffeine through their noses, until the coffee is cool enough to drink. I stand at the far wall, which is only about four-feet high, overlooking the road. A million pigeons mill about underfoot, like the Piazza San Marco, which is no doubt why I have this little corner to myself. For the moment, anyway.

I ask if Jeanie's running a fever.

The high-school principal, the one I happen to know the students refer to as Old Deuteronomy, after some character in the musical *Cats*, is no less than 700 years old. I've met her: she has white chin whiskers. Her voice is like the crank of a plastic jack-in-the-box that's been sitting too long on the shelf. You wish it would somehow speed up but also lower an octave or two and not sound so goddamn irritating.

"Well, I'm sorry to say, Mr. Ganzi, but Jeanie was found with some contraband during an impromptu locker inspection."

A bus honks, the wind picks up. I kick at a pigeon and send it flapping off. "I'm sorry. We didn't know rubberbands were illegal."

"Contraband, Mr. Ganzi," she says again. "Cigarettes. Pall Mall. Unfiltered. The worst kind. The most unhealthy."

I turn and stare out over the South Loop. "Jeanie had cigarettes?"

"Unfiltered. The kind my husband smoked for fifty years. Before they finally killed him, that S.O.B."

I accept this bit of personal history and move on. "I'm sorry?"

My daughter isn't a saint, but I also knew girls like her, growing up, and they weren't into anything, even back then when pretty much everybody smoked.

"Will someone be able to pick her up?"

It takes me a moment to realize she's talking about me. "No. Just send her home."

"We need to release her into the custody of a parent or legal guardian."

"Then call her mother," I flick my own cigarette into the street below. "Oh wait, she's in fucking Florida."

"You can talk ugly all you want, Mr. Ganzi." Old Deuteronomy shows no signs of being ruffled. "When should we expect you?"

"It'll be a few hours."

"We'll be keeping her in study hall until then."

I snap my phone shut and turn back toward the courtyard. I take two steps, expecting the gaggle of pigeons at my feet to do what pigeons do best and scatter. Instead, a shadow flashes in my periphery. I duck, covering my head with my arms, before I register a gigantic bird of prey, some kind of fucking hawk or goddamn pterodactyl, swooping in from my blind side. It buzzes close enough for me to hear the wind through its feathers. It dive-bombs the cluster of pigeons, snaps one up in its beak, and ascends again toward the skyscraper peaks, all in the time it takes me to utter a single expletive.

Jeanie's standing by herself in the bus circle when I pick her up—late. It's already dark, a few lights still on inside the school.

I get out before the car is parked. Catch her before she opens the door. "You're driving."

"I don't have my license." She looks at me. "I don't even have my permit."

I point, open the door, climb into the passenger seat. She slinks around to the driver's side and shuts herself in.

"Your hands are blue," I tell her. "Don't you have gloves?"

She moves the seat back, raises the steering wheel. In a car, it's hard not to notice the way another person smells. In our shared space, the recirculated air, there's a hint of tobacco on her, maybe, or I could be smelling my own leftover scent. It's not so easy for smokers to recognize one another by smell—it's not like dogs. We're wrapped up in our own nicotine fumes, and plus, our sense of smell is basically shot. That sense comes back eventually, they say, when you quit. Suddenly you notice the way everything smells in this ultra-intense way, an olfactory heightening.

"Your mom said you don't know how to drive."

"I don't."

"Turn the key." I wait until she does, and the lights and then the engine hum on. "There are two pedals near your feet. Under your right foot, that pedal makes the car go. To the left, that makes the car stop. Got it?"

"No—"

I tell her to press the brake and put the car in drive. She does so. This part is no different from go-carts.

"Now press the right pedal."

We lurch forward. Stop. Lurch again. Halt, tires complaining. I pretend not to notice, instead fussing with the air vents, holding my hands up like casting a spell to convince them to warm.

"Turn right," I say, once she's hop-scotched us to the first stop sign.

"Dad, that's Jackson."

"Do you have something against our seventh president?"

"That's like, a real road."

"And you're in a real car. Now punch it."

She swings into traffic, not too bad for Chicago. Most cars are heading out of the city, and we're heading in. Jeanie keeps her hands at ten and two. The color on her knuckles has changed from blue to frost. She keeps her eyes straight ahead.

"Check your mirrors." I fold my arms, settle in, satisfied with the warm air now pouring from the vents. "It's just like basketball. You watch the mirrors. You watch the road ahead of you. You keep track of where everybody is at all times. Court sense, right? It's what makes you a great basketball player. It'll make you a good driver, too. That, and patience. Somebody does something nuts behind you? Just let them. Stay to the right. Somebody honks, just give them the wave." I demonstrate, raising my hand palm-out and twisting it slightly, from the elbow, like royalty. "The wave is open to interpretation, but also unthreatening. Or at least, no one's going to shoot you for it. Turn left at the light."

The City of Chicago is woefully short on left-hand turn arrows. Which means cars stack up, waiting to turn left, and then the light turns yellow, then red, and four or five cars leap from their place in line and try to slip through before the cross-traffic light turns green. It's a skill you eventually master, how to make lights without interfering too much with anybody else. The trick is to ride on the back left-corner bumper of the car ahead of you, so, in effect, you both turn left at the same time. You just take the slightly inside track. When it works, it's a thing of beauty.

Traffic is heavier now around Greektown, a mix of commuters heading home and suburbanites dining out. Trucks, buses, plenty of SUVs, all hulking masses with fiery red eyes. Jeanie checks her mirrors. She flinches when a bus passes on the left, close enough to shake our car.

"So," I begin. She looks at me, but brake lights on the road ahead snap her attention forward. She slams the brakes, we curl against our restraints, we stop safely. "They found cigarettes on you?"

We're stopped at a red. She's breathing pretty fast, eyes wide like she's shooting a foul shot.

"In my locker," she clarifies.

"Possession is two-thirds of the law," I tell her, not exactly sure I quoted that particular cliché accurately. "I thought you were a super-jock."

We move forward. I tell her to turn left and position the right corner of her front bumper against the back left-corner bumper of the car ahead.

"I play basketball," she says. "That's all."

"Yeah, smoking doesn't exactly help with that."

"They weren't even mine!"

She looks at me, the light turns yellow, I tell her to floor it. Two cars go, then it's our turn. We're late—the crossing light has already turned green—and as we pass through the intersection, the area around our car is lit up by a white strobe, our transgression captured by a traffic camera.

"That's a ticket," I tell her.

"What?"

"You owe me $85."

"You told me—"

"Jeanie," I say, "not even I'm that oblivious."

"Dad, they weren't mine." We're stopped again, and she looks at me, performing her best, innocent act. "I'm holding them for a friend. I swear. Look, you know I have Bible Study friends. And one of them smokes. He's trying to quit, so he has me hold his cigarettes, and if he wants one, he has to pay me a dollar."

The cars ahead of us move, and then there are five car lengths between us. I gesture toward the road and tell her to get moving too.

"A dollar a smoke?"

"Yes."

"That's a good deal for you."

"Especially since I don't have any outlay." She checks her mirrors. "Plus, I'm doing a good deed by helping a friend quit something that is bad for him. I tried to explain all this to Dr. Bennett but she didn't believe me—"

"I'm not saying I believe you."

"Well that's just so typical. I mean, adults never believe kids. Or trust us. But it's me, you know? Your straight-A, star-athlete daughter who studies the Bible in her spare time? In some cultures, I'd already be married, with kids."

"Cultures like the Mormons."

"Dad, I'm almost an adult. I'm nearly self-sufficient. And I think that's part of the problem, you know? That adults don't trust kids. So they always think they're doing something wrong. But maybe adults have it backwards. Like, if adults just laid off and trusted us, maybe we'd prove how trustworthy we are—"

"Brakes."

"—then we wouldn't have to like, rebel, you know?"

"Red light, Jeanie."

"Because it's like a self-fulfilling prophecy, you know? Adults expect us to do bad things and so we do them, when maybe if the expectation was that we'd do good—"

"Red fucking light."

She slams on the brakes, and we slide so long I swear I have time to count to ten. But we stop—just short of a young woman crossing the street. The pedestrian stops in front of our grill, gives us the meanest stare maybe I've ever seen, then sticks out her pudgy middle finger and scowls.

Totally deserved.

"Switch with me," I tell my daughter. "C'mon. I got it from here."

Jeanie is shaking as she gathers her coat around her and then crawls over the arm rest into the passenger seat. As she does, one of her gloves falls out of her pocket. It's knitted, blue and white. I pick it up and hold the glove to my nose. My sense of smell welcomes the stale, smoky flavor of fingers that have held countless cigarettes, the way my own gloves always smell this time of year.

Despite my delinquency and borderline failing grades, and okay, my anger issues, I was only ever sent home once from school, for an altercation in eighth grade. I got into a scrap. My mother came and picked me up. She had few words for me—there was silence during the car ride home and a sort of sucking out of the air, like the tide peeling back before a hurricane arrives. There was nothing the school could dish out and nothing my mother could say that would match my father's fury once he got off work. Hurricane Enzo.

That afternoon, I sat on my bed, knees shaking. The moment the clock struck three, when I knew Pasternak would be getting off the bus, I climbed out my bedroom window and beelined for his house.

"You need to hide me," I told him, when I showed up on his front stoop, breathless.

I didn't need to say anything else. Pasternak knew how my dad could get. Those days Pasternak would knock on my door, looking for a ballgame or bike ride, and my mom would have to tell him no, not today—my father, he was in his cups.

That's what my mother called it. "In his cups." What a euphemism. What a way to wallpaper over how whenever my dad was drinking, I'd push all the furniture in my room against the door, just in case he decided to come barging in. It was like being trapped in an outhouse with a polar bear, the only kind of bear that hunts humans.

It was dusk when we heard the car door slam. I remember looking out Pasternak's window. There was this black gum tree that turned burnt rust in fall. Beneath the branches, my father climbed out of his Oldsmobile. We watched him stagger, support himself for a moment against the hood, and swig one more time from a bottle of Old English. I knew it was Old English, even though it was wrapped in a paper bag. I knew how that beer tasted, how my father's breath carried the cheap malt. We watched him try and shut his car door, miss, then succeed, then shuffle across the walk to the front door.

"You'd better go," Pasternak whispered, as if my father might hear.

"Fuck that," I said. "Lock the door."

When my father beat against the door with his fists, the whole house shook. That's how poor Pasternak was back then—how poor we all were. Shoddy construction; tiny houses. We locked the door and sat on the couch and turned up the volume on the television. Batman, I think it was.

My father yelled my name, and he yelled other things. We just turned up the volume louder. Where were Mr. and Mrs. Pasternak? They were never around. His dad was a functioning alcoholic like mine, labored at U.S. Steel until he finally died on the line; his mom worked nights as a housekeeper in a motel. She always smelled like vinegar.

The banging stopped. My father grumbled to himself. He crossed the yard, came around back of the house. We ran into the kitchen. There too, the door was locked. We watched the back door kick against its chain. And hold.

My father's face then at the window, my heart plunging through my belly when we made eye contact. His face flushed red as those black gum leaves. He tried the window, shouting, but couldn't open the sash through the black iron bars.

And then he was gone. I peeked outside—his car still idled in the street. We listened, not daring to breathe. There was a shuffling sound, a kind of knocking then, within the walls, like when a shower shuts off. The plaster shuddered.

Pasternak's house had hardwood floors. In places, the boards weren't flush. Sometimes there'd be gaps of an inch or two, maybe three, and you could see the joists below. The insulation, where there was any.

We heard a slow scratching begin near the back door and circle into the kitchen. Pasternak and I watched the floorboards, which seemed to move.

Maybe it was our imagination.

Pasternak shouted: suddenly my father's face, his pink flesh, was leering up at us from beneath the floor, from between our feet.

"John." He pressed one bloodshot eyeball to the gap. "It's time to go."

My father's voice called to me from below, his grub-like face, one arm, his fingers, nails bitten raw, reaching for me through the space between the boards.

"John," he said. "Don't be afraid."

Pasternak puked into the kitchen sink.

I watched the shadow of my father pass beneath the kitchen. Puffs of insulation rose between the seams. He was on his back, shimmying through the crawlspace. The shadow moved to the far end of the kitchen. For a time, there was nothing. And then my father appeared, coming up out of the basement, through the basement door, which had no lock.

He didn't wait to get me home. He dragged me into the living room, drove me face-down on the couch. He turned the volume on the television as high as it would go. With one hand he beat me until I lost all feeling below my waist. His other hand forced me to eat cushion. I bit that corduroy to keep from screaming, and even now, when I think of where Pasternak grew up, I have a kind of gag reflex, tasting that fabric on the back of my tongue.

Did Pasternak watch? Did he run upstairs and hide? I have no idea. We have never, to this day, ever talked about it.

The principal of Whitney M. Young doles out Jeanie's punishment: one week of after-school detention, which Old Deuteronomy tells me is lenient because Jeanie was only caught with cigarettes, not actually smoking them, plus her basketball stardom and overall good grades allowed the principal to show mercy.

The basketball coach comes down harder, though, and suspends Jeanie for the rest of the season.

I visit the man on a Wednesday morning, between blocks of P.E. His office is tucked past the locker rooms, the weight room, around the corner, under the stairs, basically in a closet—an administrative armpit. My only thought, noticing the lack of overhead lights on this far end of the hall, is that the basketball coach could die at his desk and, assuming no students came down here to get high or make out, wouldn't be found for days.

His door is open. A fluorescent lamp, without a shade, fills the room with a pale, grow-house quality light. I drum my fingernails on the door in what I hope is a friendly way. "Coach?"

He looks up from where he has a magazine flattened on his desk. He slides his reading glasses off his nose. He's younger than me, still with a full head of hair. He wriggles free of his chair, rises, extends his hand, like a hermit crab emerging from a seashell. He's tall. Once he's standing, I don't see how he can fit beneath that desk. The physics seem impossible. He's like a marionette pulled from a suitcase, shaken free, sorted out, loose and long. His white sweatshirt says *West Chester*.

"John Ganzi." I shake his hand. "Jeanie's Dad."

"Sure." He begins to tuck all of himself below the desk again, ass first, then legs, then arms, one elbow at a time. "We spoke on the phone."

During our brief conversation, he told me he was obligated to inform me of his decision "in person." I managed to contain my rage then only because Jeanie was there in the apartment with me, and my blowing up at her coach wouldn't have done her any good. Plus, kids, they watch how you treat people.

Now, finally in-person, with my having ventured into this dark cave to confront him in his lair, the Creature Below the Stairs, I have no qualms about doing whatever it takes to get what I've come here for, a battle to the death, Odysseus and the Minotaur.

He indicates I should sit, so I do. He slouches deep into his chair, and again I wonder where his legs go. I want to get on my hands and knees and look.

"I appreciate your coming to see me," Coach says. "I feel really bad about the whole thing. Having to suspend Jeanie. She's one of our best players."

"She's your best player," I tell him, point of fact, like a hard pass that hits you square in the chest and takes your breath away.

He turns up his palms, equivocating. "We have many excellent players. And we're a team."

I cross my legs. This looks funny whenever I do it, because of my belly and stumpy legs, but I want him to see I'm comfortable here. "One thing that wasn't clear to me over the phone: as far as the school is concerned, she's served her time. One week's detention after school, no mark on her record. Case closed. Does the athletic department have its own disciplinary system?"

"Well, sure." He laughs, then sees I'm not smiling. "If a player blows a called play, she has to run a suicide. If a player is late to practice, she has to run a mile. The school, well, the school's got nothing to do with what happens on my court."

My hands are starting to go numb—always a sign that I might have trouble keeping my anger in check. My heart feels like a flywheel spinning, and there's a little sweat behind my knees. I want to punch something really, really hard.

"Those consequences make sense." I use my most soothing, reasonable voice. "They fit the crimes. What I'm asking, though, is that if a player gets suspended for the rest of the season for being caught with cigarettes in her locker—not smoking cigarettes, mind you, simply caught in possession of them—what happens when a player is caught drinking? Or caught with drugs? How can you escalate from a season-long suspension?"

"It's all the same to me."

I raise an eyebrow. I lean forward, elbows on knees, inviting him to tell me more. To over-share. "Cigarettes, beer, crank: you see them as being one and the same?"

"That's right." He leans back, locking his fingers behind his head and stretching. "Substance abuse indicates a certain character type, or lack of character, if you want to know the truth, and I don't want those kinds of players on my team."

It's some kind of special bulb he's got in his custom lamp. The bulb is shaped like the eye of a needle, a half-circle curling up from the base. And the light it puts out is bright as hell. Maybe 100, 120 watts? Double whatever you'd put in your home. And that seems to be its only purpose, to be bright as hell. The light is garish. The base of the lamp reads *Full Spectrum Sunlight*.

I indicate the fixture. "That sucker really puts out some light."

"Sun therapy." He glances over at it, then back at me. "Winters are so dark here, plus there are no lights in my office, as you can see. This lamp is supposed to reproduce the qualities of the sun. Improve your mood."

I nod. "There are days during the winter I don't see the sun once."

"You should think about getting one. I've noticed a big difference in my energy level since I started using the lamp. It'll set you back, though."

"What's something like that run?"

"I think I paid about $200 for this. 10,000 lux, though, which you gotta have."

I've always hated talking to athletes. Mostly because, let's face it, the majority were given one gift and one gift only. Blessed with physical skills that exceed mere mortals, nature always seeks balance: most athletes are pretty dull to talk to. Part of this is necessity. You want them to run the plays, react, let their super-human physical instincts guide every decision. You don't want them thinking too much—you don't want the brain getting in the way. Which works perfectly in sports. A lot of failed athletes become insurance salesmen or P.E. teachers. Physically, they're goddamn Jaguar C-Type British Racing Cars. Mentally? They can toast a piece of bread—lightly.

And what drives a grown man to coach high school girls' basketball?

"The law makes a distinction," I say, quietly. He cocks his ear slightly, so I don't think he hears me. I say it again. "The law makes a distinction. In the matter of crime. There is different sentencing for minors. There is different sentencing for being caught with marijuana, coke, or meth. Our government doesn't consider them the same things. Not at all. Why should you?"

Coach blinks, leans forward, beckons me with one finger like he's going to tell me the biggest secret in the world. "Why should I? Because brother, out there, on the basketball court? I am the motherfucking King, and my word is Law."

I knew guys like this, growing up; I know guys like this now. Some of them work for me. Finance is overrun by these high-school and college athletes, who knew the roar of a crowd before they were old enough to vote, who sometimes played before tens of thousands of fans on blustery, autumnal Saturdays. Guys who, in the end, weren't quite good enough to go pro.

The smaller the territory, the larger the pissing match. The smaller the parcel they want to protect, the more viciously people dig in.

Then again, I always say, "Be king of your castle." Recognize your limitations, and what you've been granted. Does it seem like only fat girls with straight-brown hair fall for you? Then fuck the living shit out of every chubby brunette you can find.

I don't know if it's the short memory they all share, the way they exude such confidence, or that fact that what they're best at—building muscle mass—is something I never had the opportunity to learn. Or the way someone who focuses on athletics at a young age seems to develop a way of looking at the world, to develop a hardened sense of a "right way" to do things, leaving no room for alternative points of view. Which, as athletes, is of course exactly what's drilled into them: the correct overhand serve, the proper form for breaststroke. This black and white worldview follows them into adulthood, trails them long after they've hung up their cleats. Faced with a situation as nuanced as Jeanie's, often they find themselves unable to wrap their minds around it, or to see both sides.

Still, as I take in this leviathan, whose attention seems already to have wandered, like a pot of water set to a low simmer, I know that even men with morals as infallible as his have a price. I just have to find it.

I indicate his white sweatshirt, a relic from the 1990s, tight elastic around the cuffs: *West Chester.* "Is that your alma mater?"

He laughs despite himself. "Yeah. Ever heard of it?"

"Sure." I fold my hands, look up, as if recalling all the excellent times I spent there myself. "Outside Philly. Every now and then you guys put together a basketball team."

He grins, accepting the compliment. "Well, we used to."

"Did you play?"

"All four years."

"Ever drink in college?"

He shakes his head, his grin just a shade thinner. "This isn't about me."

I stand up. On the wall are the coach's college diploma and a couple photographs of a long and lanky basketball player, cut from the newspaper. In one, the coach drives to the hoop, the ball rolling off his outstretched fingers, arcing toward the rim. In the other, he stands with feet apart, hands out, a fierce look in his eyes, as if he has sworn on his life to protect the basket.

"You never played pro?" I touch one of the photographs.

He shrugs. "One year in Europe."

"Why only one year?"

"Why do all dreams fall to shit? There was a girl."

I nod, noticing how, in every photograph, the coach's shorts ride high. That hemline is now illegal in thirty states.

"Jeanie's always complaining about her uniform," I say. "That fabric is rough. What is it, 100 percent polyester? Brutal."

"Uniforms are always an issue," the coach concedes. "I remember when I was playing, nobody had a uniform that actually fit. You just wore whatever size fit well enough."

"What if I bought the team new uniforms? Maybe with the numbers on the chest and the shorts? Get some with that special wicking material? Maybe uniforms that are actually made for women instead of these hand-me-downs from the boys' teams?"

The coach nods, engaged in something on his laptop. He won't grant me his full attention, or act like it, but I know he's listening. "That'd be nice, absolutely."

I take a stroll around the office, which is really just a pivot, two steps toward the door, another pivot, and then I lean on the back of the lone chair. I look at him for a good long time, but he doesn't look at me. I've opened with what I feel is a very generous offer. New uniforms? His players will love him. They'll do whatever he asks of them from now on. And it's going to set me back a few thousand, for sure.

"Maybe the girls could use some basketballs," I offer. "Hell, I'll throw in some new scoots too. Nike, whatever they want. Just give me their sizes, I'll have the shoes shipped here."

"Shoes are important," he agrees.

I shake my head. He's got me pinned down. I've got zero leverage.

"Look," I say. "I'm offering new uniforms, new shoes. Top-of-the-line. I'll throw in some basketballs, a new whistle for you, a new whiteboard for you to draw up plays. I'm offering everything, here. What's it going to take to get Jeanie back on the team?"

He finally looks at me. The glare from the spectrum lamp obscures his eyes, behind his glasses. He turns his laptop so I can see it.

It's an article on the website of Northwestern University. Men's athletics. The headline announces the current Wildcat coach is stepping down for personal reasons. It's a big deal, his resignation coming mid-season. NU may not be a powerhouse; it may rarely sniff the NCAA tournament; but it's still a Big 10 team.

I'm pretty quick at connecting dots, parsing out people's needs, but in this case, the big picture hasn't come together for me yet.

"I didn't go to Northwestern," I tell the coach. "I don't have all that many contacts there, really. Harold Washington, U of C maybe—"

"I know you didn't go to Northwestern," he says, leaning back again, locking his fingers behind his head. "But your chairman did."

I swallow, blink, wondering if I heard him right.

"Who, Sar?"

"I can start right away," the coach tells me with a completely straight face, without hint of irony. "Just let me know."

Chapter 8

"Suspended?" Azita calls me when I'm on my way to work.

I've got the Bluetooth hooked up, so her voice fills the cabin of my SUV, coming from nowhere and everywhere all at once. It's unnerving.

"Not suspended." I've got one hand on the steering wheel, the other holding my thermos, moving lane to lane through traffic. "After-school detention."

Her voice cracks. "She's kicked off the basketball team?"

"I'm going to sort that out."

"How, exactly?"

I grind my teeth, remind myself to breathe. She's putting the nails to me. Maybe I deserve it. But it's important, above all, to remain calm.

"I talked to the coach. I'm sure we'll sort something out."

I swing past the library, ease my way below the Brown Line tracks, following them toward the Exchange. Near CBOT, some yahoo is riding a Segway back and forth in the plaza. A crowd has gathered. The wheels spin, the rider rocks back slightly, then lurches forward. I haven't actually seen one of these things live. This guy's probably got some kind of stake, showing it off here as a publicity stunt. On the wheels, he's a foot and half taller than everyone else and twice as wide. A

Segway might just be the solution to all my problems, what with everybody treating me like a door all the time, walking right through me on the street. I wonder how much they run, then just as quickly decide they'll be good for law enforcement and that's about it.

"This is not a good start, Johnny," she tells me. For a moment her voice sounds like it's coming from over my shoulder. Instinctively I swat at it, like a fly. "Jeanie is applying for college."

"Don't you think I know that?" I shout. "Look, like Obama, I am not responsible for the shit I inherit upon taking the reins. If she's smoking, she's been smoking long before she started living with me. If there are other things to be concerned about, then we're both to blame. So watch where you point that finger of yours."

I realize, as I say it, that this is the crux of the issue. I don't particularly buy the excuse that Jeanie was holding the smokes for a friend, so if the cigarettes are hers, are they the tip of the iceberg or simply her small, isolated way of rebelling? She's a good kid otherwise. No signs of trouble anywhere else in her life.

"She needs to be on the basketball team," my ex says.

"I know."

"It's her best chance of going to an Ivy."

"I know, dammit."

"If she doesn't get reinstated, then she's getting a job. She's not going to spend her afternoons drifting. I'd rather her scoop fro-yo than be some kind of derelict."

"Jeanie isn't going to become a derelict."

"She better not."

I pull into the small garage and park beneath the Exchange. Even twenty feet below street level, the wind whips through the concrete cavern, the kind of cold that causes inanimate objects, walls and mailboxes, to seem about to shatter. Everything seems fragile, or so full they shimmer. You don't want to touch anything because it might break. And even the smallest scrape, the back of your hand along a brick wall, bleeds.

With my prime parking space, I need only climb the stairs and sprint across the courtyard to the relative warmth and safety of the breezeway and beyond it, the double doors. But I sit a moment in the driver's seat, waiting for my ex-wife to say something. For now, all I can hear is her breathing.

"You sound stuffed-up," I tell her. "You should take something."

"I'm sure I caught it from a student."

"It's going to be okay." I clear my throat. "Jeanie's going to be okay."

"Keep me posted."

I nod, then realize she can't see me. "I'm teaching her to drive. Did she tell you that?"

"No passengers for at least a year," she says. "Those are my rules."

It's the noise that hits you first: a distant rumble that sharpens as you cross the mezzanine to the top of the escalator. You realize, putting your toe on the treaded belt, that what you are hearing is not one sound but the tremor of hundreds of men shouting over one another. Like the roar of a jet engine somewhere above the clouds, except that this originates below ground, in the bowels of the Exchange. Descending, their voices surround you, enter you, make your balls scamper up inside your gut. Deafening, solid as something you step through, relentless but unintelligible, a sonic layer so primal in its bloodthirstiness, in its fear, in its desire above all to live, that it never becomes white noise. I suspect a battlefield is like this. Prison, too.

Stefany Maria Vázquez spends her first week like a new arrival at Cook County Jail. Every time someone shouts an order, she jumps. She apologizes, squeezing past one beefcake or another. She even raises her hand, polite as an honor-roll student, whenever she wants to execute a trade. Five days pass; she buys nothing. Her workweek muscled out by traders in her own firm.

"Vázquez!" Pasternak glowers at her from his place on the desk. "Are you going to fucking get some action this week or did you just come here hoping to get gang-banged?"

"I could use a tug," one of our guys says.

"Me too," another says.

"Hell, give all of us a tug."

"Are you assholes trying to get us sued?" I shout at them. "Bring it down a level. Several levels."

Still, I think, here it is: her first test.

"It'd be a better goddamn use of your time," Pasternak says, quieter, but loud enough so she hears.

"Fuck off," she says.

Her nose is buried in her tablet.

"Millennials," the first trader sneers. "If they can't hide behind their screens, they're fucking useless."

"Quota." The second trader cat-calls. "Hey! El Quota."

It's what they've named her: El Quota. Because she's Latina; because she's a woman. Two birds with one stone. An indictment of my hiring practices, as much as anything.

"There it is, El Quota," the first trader shouts. "A hundred shares of Taco Bell."

The second trader hoots. "That's what you were looking for, right?"

"Buy that shit."

"You better buy that shit, El Quota!"

"I'm trying—" she says, meekly.

"Do or do not," the first trader says, and then a dozen guys finish the quote for him, "There is no try."

"Suck on these coconuts," the second trader says. "*Señorita.*"

He has bought Taco Bell for $17.57 a share.

"I bet he'll sell 'em to you though," the first trader says.

"Sure thing," says the second trader. "I was just messing with you, El Quota. I'll sell 'em all to you right now."

"At $18.05?" Finally, she looks up. "Fuck you."

"No," the first trader says. "Fuck you."

"Hang in there," I tell her, later. "Things will start to slow down for you."

She doesn't look at me, just taps steadily on her screen. "Sometimes when you're working here, do you ever feel like you want to throw up?"

"Nope."

Then I pull a handful of ginger candies from my coat and stuff them into her jacket pocket.

You reach a certain age, you think nothing in the world can surprise you anymore. There are professions that are a young man's game—athlete, praise and worship leader, hair stylist—and then you pass forty or so and you realize you've aged out. Other jobs—author, investment banker—are actually better served by aging fucks like me. We've been around. We've seen recessions and bubbles. We've seen dead cats bounce and P/Es that make us want to lick the assholes of every guy in our firm. Have a billion dollars you want to preserve? You're much better off handing it to someone like me, with all the wisdom of my experience, than to some fresh-faced twenty-three-year-old who thinks whatever climate he graduated college in is the environment he will always find himself in. The twenty-three-year-olds lost everyone's retirement funds this fall. The old guys like me were the ones who were already just about all in cash before the bottom fell out.

That said, I am amazed by the fucking balls on Jeanie's basketball coach. It's one thing asking me to call in a favor with someone I might have pull with. I could have gotten him Bulls tickets, for example, even season tickets. But asking me to ask someone else for a favor like this—Division I men's basketball coach—Jesus.

Talk about the power of positive thinking.

I could certainly use some of that myself, though, now, slouched in an arm chair outside Chairman Sar's office. Breathing in the rarified air of the Executive Wing on the third floor of the Exchange. It's an awkward set-up. Visitors have no choice but to stare at the four desks of secretaries just across the hall. Executive Assistants, or whatever they call them now: they're still all women.

Sar's assistant is a big-boned man-eater who grew up in northern Mississippi some-goddamn place, skin hard and dark as walnut. She's built like a linebacker: broad shoulders, mammoth hands, a way of looking at you like you've just exhausted the last bit of energy she has to offer. I admire her professionally, and sort of wish I had her myself, even as I hate having to go through her to talk to Sar.

"Water?" she asks me, not for the first time. She wears a headset and covers the mic. I shake my head. Before long she's speaking again to someone on the line, outlining travel accommodations in low tones.

Behind her, another assistant hammers on a word processor. She's listening to a Dictaphone through an earpiece.

Occasionally she pauses the machine, rewinds, then her fingers bash away again like hail against a tin roof.

Behind her are floor-to-ceiling windows that look down on a sea of cubicles below. All the IT and accounting guys, the nerdiest of the nerds, have cubicles on the second floor, which is wide open, with forty-foot ceilings, about the width of a professional basketball court. And just as long. It provides no small amount of satisfaction to gaze down on these worker bees from behind a wall of windows on the third floor, like some robber baron lording over his factory floor in a Dickensian novel.

I'm feeling a little "Food, Glorious Food" myself, hat in hand, waiting outside the boss' office.

Azita would say I never allow myself to enjoy things. Those moments in life that you're supposed to bask in: buying a home, launching a firm. For me, every purchase, every ladder in the rung of life, my first thought is always that someone else has done this exact same thing before—and more. Even when my net worth surpassed $1 million, a long time ago now, I recognized the achievement, but the feeling of success passed as quickly as a burp. I had the thought, "Holy shit, I'm a millionaire." But directly on its heels came the thought, "So what? There are guys worth a hundred times that."

But then I'll watch how Jeanie, she'll go to Macy's to buy a pair of jeans, and via social media, she involves no less than fifteen, twenty people in her decision-making process. She'll take photos of the jeans, and her friends will comment, then she'll photograph herself in a pair, and all her friends will comment, suggest, advise. Me, say I go to the store and buy a pair of slacks. It's highly unusual for me to even try them on before I take them home because A) I've been the same goddamn size since I was seventeen, and B) I know I can always return them. Jeanie involves her entire friendship group in the purchase of a pair of jeans: what will she do when it comes time to buy a house? She may shut down the city. Take an ad on the back page of the *Trib*. But then, as her mother would remind me, at least Jeanie will enjoy the milestones, whereas I just blaze right through them.

Along with not feeling like I need proclaim my not-so-singular accomplishments like bumper-stickers on social media comes a determination to be self-sufficient, to not ask for favors. An island unto myself. I do favors for others, of course, because I want something in return—like Blago with Obama's senate seat. But throwing myself on the mercy of others, imposing myself on others—it's something I've worked hard in my life not to do. And yeah, sitting on this leather couch, watching the secretaries, smelling the bowl of peanuts and chutney and ubiquitous crudité set out on the coffee table at my feet, makes me feel like a schmuck. It makes me feel like my dad. When I'd go with him to my uncle's house in Arlington Heights and wait in the car while my dad went inside. We always drove away with an envelope of cash. It was a handout, plain and simple, and I always swore, I could be starving on the street, but I would never, *ever* ask anyone for money.

"Okay." Sar's assistant covers her mouthpiece again. "He'll see you now."

Not bad. I only waited forty minutes. I thank her, compliment her charcoal suit jacket, and slip into his office.

He's coming out of his private bathroom, drying his hair with a towel. He's otherwise dressed.

"JAG, sit down," he tells me, taking his own spot behind his desk.

We're about the same height, but Sar's got a three-inch platform under his chair so he can look down on whoever he's talking to.

"Did you just get back from the gym?" I ask.

"Squash," he says, giving his full head of hair one more vigorous rub and then tossing the balled-up towel toward the restroom. "Do you play?"

"Nah, that's kind of an East Coast thing."

He smirks, like he's already forgiven what a hick I am for being raised in Chicago. "It's a good game. Great workout. Keeps your reflexes quick. So, what can I do for you?"

"I've been giving a lot of thought to this issue of CBOE going public. I know we're pretty far apart on some of these ongoing litigations."

"You know that?" He looks me straight in the eye. He's not admitting anything, but he is challenging me to fucking prove it.

CBOE is the only remaining private exchange in the entire world. Not because it's good for business. But because a few of the dinosaurs who were around when CBOE was first founded believe they're entitled to a larger percentage of whatever potential shares and dividends there are once we finally do go public. That, and current seat holders think their seats are worth a good bit more to the public than what our proposed IPO of $27-$29 would value them at.

Sar's made it his life mission to take CBOE public. We're mired in lawsuits, though, all of which need to be resolved before he does.

"You don't have the votes yet," I concede. "Traders are holding out. They don't see those founding CBOT guys as being entitled to shit. I'm not saying I agree with them, but I'm telling you how they see it."

He leans back. "What do you propose?"

"I can get you the votes you need. I'll address the floor guys at our next meeting, try to throw as much support behind you as I can. Maybe with that, we can work out a deal, get out from under these lawsuits."

"That'd be good." I can almost hear the gears crunching behind his eyes. He's wondering why I'm coming to him with this now, laying down my arms, waving the peace flag. "The guys trust you. You've been here a long time. What else?"

I shrug like, why would there be anything else? "That's it. That's all. I just wanted to tell you in person. I recognize that growth can be painful."

He nods, slowly at first, then more quickly. "This is good, John. This is really great news."

"That's all." I stand up. "I won't keep you."

We shake hands, I go to the door. I turn the handle but don't open it fully. I toss the next question over my shoulder, not quite addressing him, as if it's just something I thought of, that I may as well ask, while I'm here.

"I saw Kevin Boyd resigned."

"Believe that? And in mid-season. Totally screwed us. It'll be a totally lost season."

"I got a guy, might be great. If I send you his info, you'll make the introduction?"

I don't know if the request is so far off Sar's radar that he doesn't give it a second thought, or if he's too absorbed in watching the ticker on C-SPAN to really hear me. Either way, he says, "Sure. Set up a meeting with me, your guy, and the athletic director. Charlene will take care of it."

"Thanks, Dicky."

I let myself out, leaving the door cracked behind me, the way I've been instructed to since Sar came on as chairman. I pause at Charlene's desk, wait until she's finished with her call.

"He asked me to have you set up a meeting. My contact, here's his info, and Mindy Pagano, the athletic director at NU. Sooner the better, I think."

She takes the coach's card, sets it on her keyboard. "Not a problem, Mr. Ganzi. Morning or afternoon work better for you?"

After markets close, the way we do every day, Pasternak and I go through the mail and review our action list. Something's off with him today, though. He reads the call list in monotone. When one item gets crossed off, he strikes a line through it and moves on to the next. No chit-chat. No expression.

"The fuck?" I finally ask him.

"Huh?"

"You're pouting. You're a grown man, for Christ sake."

"I'm not pouting."

"Then who the fuck died?"

He doesn't answer. I turn my attention to the television, watch the ticker.

"I told you," I say finally. "Summer comes, we'll get you on the terminals. Find somebody to replace you."

"I know." He flicks a junk mailer into the trash. "It's not that."

"Then what?" I lean back, fed up. "You're like my goddamn ex. How many times you gonna make me ask?"

"It's nothing, JAG."

I shuffle papers on my desk. The end-of-month report, which I slide into my legal folder and then into my briefcase. I decide to let it go.

"I'm leaving town tomorrow," I tell him.

"Yes." He hands me a thick, manila folder. Inside, my plane ticket, itinerary, agendas, hotel reservation. "The bill is in there too, at least the part that's relevant to us."

"Great," I say. "Homework."

"I printed some news articles, for you to look at on the plane. You're meeting Sar at O'Hare."

I take the plane tickets out of the file and put them in my briefcase, in the same pocket where I keep my wallet. There's literally nowhere I hate more than Washington, DC.

"I don't know how I got roped into this shit." I start shutting down my computer. "I oughta quit the Board. Let someone else represent the unwashed masses."

"The traders trust you," Pasternak says. "I hear it all the time. Something comes up, they ask if JAG's involved. If yes, then it's okay by them. Long as JAG's in there, we're aces."

"They don't even know." I've got a copper taste in my mouth. "Their asses are this fucking close to being replaced by fucking robots. I'm the last one in the boardroom, the last human standing between them and full fucking automation. You want a job so bad? Get out of this industry entirely. That's my advice."

He says nothing. We watch television. Finally, it's time for me to go.

"How's Robin?" I ask.

"Good."

"When you gonna make me a godfather?"

He scowls at me, then smiles for the first time in a week. "We're fucking trying, okay?"

I pull my coat on, button it, tie the belt around my waist. "You know what I hear works sometimes, is jerking off right before. Then when you blow your load a second time, inside her, you're shooting fresh fucking healthy sperm. Swim twice as fast. Fucking, boom. Pregnant."

He lifts an eyebrow. "I'll keep that in mind."

I put a hand on his shoulder. "You sure you're okay?"

"Absolutely."

"We've been friends for seven centuries. I can tell when you're fucking lying."

Jeanie's next game back is on the road. I drive to North Lawndale in time for tip-off. Jeanie's teammates are pumped. There's a lot of high-fiving and butt slapping and a lot of applauding every little correctly executed play. Some people would call that "teamwork." Jeanie's return seems to have galvanized her peers and brought them closer together. The coach, for his part, still paces the sideline, but he notices me in the crowd and gives me a nod. He's got that meeting with Northwestern in a couple days. I did my part, and Coach came through.

"Set it up," he yells at his Dolphins. "Run the play."

Girls' basketball is a different sport entirely from its male counterpart. Unfortunately, you typically hear women's basketball defined in opposition to men's, by what it's not, instead of defined by what it offers players and spectators alike: not speed, but precision. Not physicality, but brains. Casual fans can recognize a slam dunk, or a fadeaway swish from the top of the key. It takes more concentration to appreciate the girls' game, the passing and the re-arranging, the set-up and then the execution. It's jazz instead of pop; scotch instead of Southern Comfort. The girls are physical of course—they seem to bleed and bruise and scamper for loose balls much more readily than the boys. They're also quick, Jeanie especially. Sometimes it seems as if she shoots the ball and has positioned herself for the rebound before the opposing players have even turned to track the shot. While the pace of the game is slower than men's basketball, and perhaps not as t.v.-ready, I've come to prefer the female brand. Anything that honors order and intelligence over brute strength, well, that's always been right up my alley.

The Whitney M. Young parents are sitting together mid-court, close to the floor on the visitor's side. But we are surrounded by North Lawndale fans, a thick pool of black tar with silver trim. The bleachers shake. Crowd noise reverberates from the I-beams above. The gymnasium is packed.

No one recognizes me or says hello. I sit down, pulling my coat around me, allowing the warmth from the gymnasium to thaw my frozen joints. I can't feel my hands when I tuck them into my pockets. All gymnasiums smell a little bit like sweat. Trading pits, too. It's good. It means people are working hard.

We fall behind early, then tie it. Two minutes from the half, we're up three. Jeanie looks more or less like herself—except for a blown play, an intercepted pass, which show some rust—but she's scored ten points and grabbed three rebounds, and took a charge from the opposing team's point guard, whose build could only generously be described as circular, as in, when she runs down the court, it looks for all the world like someone has rolled a bowling ball from foul line to foul line. With her long shorts, it's unclear where her body ends and her legs begin: her arms are beefy as tootsie rolls. Still, she's surprisingly fast. Arguably the fastest player on her team. And when Jeanie stands her ground along the baseline, and the roly poly guard crashes into her, Jeanie keeps her knees bent and her heels on the ground and flies back like a target at a carnival shoot-em game. She bounces back up in time to see the ref call a charge. Her teammates lose their minds. The coach gives $10 iTunes gift cards to any girl who takes a charge. I admire this and appreciate its inevitable trickle-down effect. Who doesn't want to raise a tough girl?

"I thought she was suspended," a mother says. She's sitting two rows down, to my left, beside another mom. Both of them wear puffy vests and ear warmers. I can't see, but I'd put money on them both sporting black yoga pants tucked into fur-trimmed boots.

"The coach let her come back," the other says.

"Do we know what it was about?"

"Some kind of contraband."

"Like drugs?"

The second mom looks over her shoulders, left, then right, scanning, no doubt, for Azita, who is not here. She looks through me, huddled as I am beneath my shabby coat, looking for all the world like a homeless guy who sprang for the $5 admission ticket to get warm.

"I heard," the second mom says, "she had joints in her locker."

"It wasn't pot." Another mom steps down three or four rows, using my shoulder to balance herself, smiling an apology, before sliding in beside the first two. "Angie said it was a crack pipe."

I burst out laughing, then cover it with a fake coughing fit, behind my fist, blowing into it. My noise barely registers with the moms.

"I tell you," one of them says. "Crack is such a problem. And it just destroys you. That would be such a shame."

"She's got a real chance for a scholarship," says the first mom. "I mean, she's clearly the best player out there."

My ears perk up at this, and I find myself flushing with pride, warm for the first time in hours.

"And doesn't she know it?" the third mother says, sneering.

What the fuck is that supposed to mean? I lean forward a little, to hear better.

"Oh come on," the second mom says, spritzing some kind of lotion or perfume or some mystical spray from Mt. Olympus along her wrists and behind her neck. I catch a whiff of dank rose petals and rubbing alcohol, and honey and nectar, and sneeze. "Nobody buys the Little Miss Goodie Two-Shoes bit."

"You mean the whole Christian thing?" The third mom laughs. "I know. Give me a break, right?"

"Doesn't she lead the Young Life group?" The first mom says, and I wonder, briefly, if she loves Jeanie as much as I do, possibly, and if she's single, or almost. "I don't think she's a bad kid."

The other two are quick to agree, raining down no, no, of course not, I'd never say that, as if blanketing their gossiping consciences.

"She just lays it on a little bit thick," the third says. "No one's that virginal."

The second mom mimics smoking a joint. "Clearly not."

They all laugh, and snort, and I'm working my jaw back and forth, wondering if I should say something, when the buzzer goes off, and the half ends. Jeanie and her teammates gather at center court, as is their ritual, in a kind of group hug, then charge off the hardwood toward the locker room, Coach trailing behind. We're up eleven now, carrying all the momentum going into the half.

I leave after watching the halftime band, a seven-piece brass ensemble that lays down some pretty funky covers of popular songs, including "Jet Airliner" by the Steve Miller Band and "Crank That" by Soldier Boy, or whatever that kid's name is. I've got a 6:00 a.m. flight tomorrow morning into Reagan. I need to get home and try to sleep.

Overhearing the conversation among the moms—that's a microcosm of parenting. On the one hand, they casually threw around words like "best" and "scholarship" and treated them as fact. On the other hand, they also cast some serious shade on my daughter's character. Not that I believe she is destined for sainthood, or even completely buy her "I'm holding these cigarettes for someone else" excuse, but there's a big difference between getting busted with smokes and being "pretty far from virginal." I drive home, through horizontal sleet that rattles my windshield and roof, marveling at how parenthood requires one to live at the extremes, rubbing your toddler's back with one hand while yelling at them to go to sleep, goddammit. Pride over her athletic accomplishments, and possible future, and despair over how little I might understand what's really going on behind the gold-cross chain and the jeans pulled up to her boobs.

I stop by a CVS and buy an Elf on the Shelf. It's some hot new parental tool some of my guys have been talking about. Basically, it's a posable eight-inch elf, garbed head to toe in Santa red, with a dunce cap. Positioned as Santa's "scout," you're supposed to place this Elf on the Shelf in different places around the home—somewhere new every morning, apparently—to remind your children that "Santa is watching" and that he's making a list of kids who are naughty or nice. And that the kids better be nice, or the Elf will report back that the children in question are to receive nothing but coal for Christmas.

I hate the entire idea, for two reasons: first, your kids shouldn't behave just because it's Christmas and "Santa is watching." What do you do, as parents, then, for the other eleven months out of the year? Second, this particular parental crutch requires way too much participation on my end, requiring me to make up a backstory for the elf, move it every night, and dress it in different outfits etc., which actually makes my life much more complicated than if I just disciplined my kid for her transgression(s) like they used to do way back in 2005.

But tonight I cruise the fluorescent-lit aisles of CVS and put my hands on the last Elf on the Shelf in stock. I take it home and set it up on my wet bar so it holds a handwritten note:

Jeanie,

Jesus may have turned water into wine, but you're still four years away from being of legal age to drink. Not only is Jesus watching: Santa is too.

Love,
Dad

I'll be gone fifty-two hours at most. I remind myself that, despite the recent disciplinary actions, my child is a straight-A student who leads weekly Bible study and is a star athlete in the City of Chicago, population 3 million. Somehow, the elf's flushed cheeks, his lack of a nose, his Nazi-blue eyes make me feel just a little bit more secure about leaving my million-dollar condo in the hands of my seventeen-year-old daughter.

Roommates need to trust one another. And haven't I always said, you don't raise your kids to do right or wrong, you just try to equip them with the tools to make good decisions when the time comes?

This self-assurance doesn't stop my hands from trembling as I pack my rollaboard and lay out my suit for tomorrow. I fall asleep before Jeanie gets home, peripherally aware that she is out awfully late for a school night, even given that she had a game in Lawndale.

Chapter 9

December.

Touching down at O'Hare is like landing in the middle of fucking Siberia—that cheery. You come in over the lake, bank left at Irving, then it's just miles of white flatland cut by the long, straight black lines of roads. The plains are a grid builder's paradise: no natural boundaries. Asphalt hashtags go on forever like some borderless game of tic-tac-toe.

On the tarmac, airport personnel stalk around like Michelin men, bundled up, stiff-armed, hurrying behind little puffs of breath. Baggage trucks are coated in salt up to their windows. The snow has been shoveled into eight-foot volcanic mounds, the tallest hills south of Madison. Come in at dusk, back early from DC, and it's even worse—it's like those far-flung Icelandic towns where it's dark twenty hours a day and suicide is as natural as hanging a *closed* sign in the window. Nobody blinks. All the airport lights are muted and dim-seeming behind the flurries. The hazards of living in Central Standard Time: I've forgotten what the sun looks like. I wake up and it's dark; drive downtown and it's dark; take lunch at my desk to catch up on e-mails and if, at the end of the day, I get plowed under by a conference call with the West Coast, I miss the sun entirely.

Talk about needing to air out though: after a flight, all that recirculated air inside the plane and the heat going full blast inside the terminals makes me want to stand outside in gale-force winds and gain some new perspective on the world. I don't even mind when I push through the baggage-claim doors to find the line at the taxi stand is about fifty-people long. I close my eyes and let myself be shuffled along by the slogging forward motion of the queue, enjoying the burning cold inside my nose, the wind against my cheeks, like the cool side of the pillow.

Eventually, I hand a cab driver my carry-on, and he dumps it in his deep, square trunk where it sits upright against a spare tire, a gasoline can, a bag of sand. Six o'clock on a Sunday, and the Dan Ryan is a parking lot. At least the cabbie's been in Chicago long enough to know to creep along the right-hand lane and use the merge lane to pass, so we make up a bit of time.

"What's that I'm smelling?" I ask him.

"Oh man," he says. "I had this young lady in here."

He's Jamaican or pretending to be. His dreads are bunched in a kind of bonnet knitted with island colors.

I breathe deep and smell perfume, like somebody emptied the bottle in the backseat.

"Young lady?" I wipe my nose. "Smells like she was about eighty."

"No man." I catch one of his eyes in the rearview mirror, bloodshot to hell. "I'd say twenty or twenty-five. Got in the taxi, man, and she be crying. Says she just broke up with her boyfriend. Says she heading out of town, and he broke up with her just as she'd stopped by his place to say goodbye. So I give her some Kleenex. She talks about him some more. She really loves him, this guy. But we get to the airport. I say, 'What airline?' She tells me no. She says, pull over in the cell-phone lot.

So I do. And sure enough man, she sucks me off right here in the taxicab. Then I drive her to her gate."

There are some things you know to be true the moment they're said out loud. You hear the words, and there's a factual aura to them. I don't want to believe this guy. The story is fucking improbable at best. But as soon the words come out of his chapped lips, I know he's telling the truth. Because of the heavy perfume smell. Because there's no reason to lie to me, a stranger. That in fact, there's incentive not to offend me, given that he's hoping I tip him at the end of the ride.

In the backseat, huddled beneath a hircine cloud, I realize it's not just perfume I smell. The floral nose is undercut with something heavier, muskier. Something not quite as bad as ass, but in the same family of smells that are unpleasant unless you participate directly in their production. The overall fragrance is strawberry rubbing alcohol with a base-note of revenge sex. Once I put my finger on it, it's goddamn hard to breathe. I roll down the window as far as it will go and try to gulp relief through the narrow triangle of fresh air.

"How about that man?" The cabbie laughs. "Today was a good day."

Poor girl. I'm sure it went down just as he described—no worse, no better. That for her, it felt like a way to reclaim something that had just been stolen. I can't imagine what bottomless pool of insecurity could make blowing a taxi driver seem like a good idea, even in your early twenties, when you'll strip off your clothes just because.

I text Jeanie that I'm on the way home.

"K!" She types back. "At Bible Study til 10."

I breathe deep one more time, to store the bouquet of that sordid taxicab in my memory forever. There's a cliché that says all a father wants to do is keep his daughter off the pole.

I think all I want to do is make sure Jeanie doesn't grow up to be the type of girl who'll blow a stranger in the cell-phone lot at ORD, no matter who just broke up with her.

When I unlock my apartment door, I think we've had an intruder. The action is so routine, insert the key and twist, that it takes a moment to realize I don't turn the key at all before the door swings open. I stand at the threshold, listening.

Flip the light on. Come inside. Close the door. I feel the energy of something that has been here but has recently gone, like sun spots on my eyelids, or the sloughing wake of a jet-ski after it's buzzed past. But nothing's out of place.

I move through my apartment and catalog my possessions, straining to hear any difference in the familiar sounds—ice tumbling in the icemaker; three clicks before the heat kicks on. Considering the many presences we feel long after the moment has passed, how our smells and gasses, our memories and fears, mingle in the spaces we leave behind. There are moments and then the far-reaching effects of those moments, a residue that can turn out to last the rest of your life.

The smell of a young woman's vindication in the backseat of a Chicago taxi.

When my ex-wife and I were in counseling, trying to save our marriage, the shrink talked about how if we didn't deal with our shit, our shit would one day deal with us. This was one of her favorite points, and she must have made it every time we met. That the more we try to bury things inside, the more forcefully those things will one day return to exert themselves upon our lives.

The way my dad dealt with pain—excruciating back pain, apparently. And it must have always been simmering somewhere beneath his everyday, commanding at least part of his attention. And my dad, he had this thing he enjoyed, which was to lick ketchup—suck it, really—off the mouth of the bottle. He poured ketchup on just about everything. Eggs or steak. He'd do it when we were home, and then he'd grin at me and Mom, and there'd be clumps of ketchup on his teeth, and we'd laugh.

One Sunday after Mass, we went to brunch with the priest and a couple of deacons, at Perkins or somewhere. I was seven or eight. I always got the western-style omelet with bell peppers and ham and some hash browns scattered over top. When my dad passed me the ketchup bottle, I shook tomato sauce all over my potatoes and eggs. The ketchup came in one of those glass bottles with the rounded lip. Once my meal was properly sauced, I stuck out my tongue and licked the rim of that ketchup bottle clean.

I did it to be funny. I was bored stiff in my Sunday suit, with three men old enough to be my grandpa plus my boring-as-hell parents, and this was in the days before hand-held electronic devices, so there wasn't shit to do but color with some crappy crayons that snapped at the slightest pressure, on an even crappier child's placemat, which I was already too old for. But I remember, my dad was mid-sentence, laying it on thick, as he always did with people in positions of power, trying to prove himself their equal, even though he was asking them for money. My tongue was still exploring the ribbed contours of the bottle neck when my dad's hand shot out from across the table and snatched the bottle away—yanked it from my mouth, from between my lips, so the glass rattled my teeth. My tongue swelled up against the taste of iron. I gagged, eyes watering like I'd been punched in the nose. The only smell was the smell of cheap ketchup, then, the way it can linger on your fingers for hours. I felt it burn behind my nose. My father slammed the bottle against the table and then released it and in the same motion hauled me out of the booth, dragging me kicking across my mother's lap, trailing blood and enamel across her Sunday dress and her plate of cottage cheese and wheat toast—rolled me to the men's room and beat my ass numb.

He was embarrassed. I realize this now, looking back. Not because I licked the ketchup bottle—although that was part of it. I suppose he probably wanted to believe he raised me with better manners. But mostly he was embarrassed because he was afraid my tonguing that bottle revealed to the priest that my father liked to lick ketchup bottles too, in the privacy of his home. And nothing would have been more shameful. The priest couldn't have known that, of course. But my father was terrified that my misbehavior, if you want to call it that, reflected poorly on him and marked us clearly for what we were: charity.

My marriage counselor latched onto this. She and my ex-wife seemed to agree that I hadn't properly dealt with that morning with my father at Perkins. Whatever that meant—"to deal with it." Emotionally speaking, I guess. But I wasn't in denial about what happened. I can remember the way the bottle spattered ketchup across my mother's cheek. I understand it as part of my history. But then, as now, I didn't see any particular reason to dwell on it.

"You don't know when," the counselor said, "but this event is going to come back and bite you someday."

I figure it will or it won't. It's not like I'm sleeping with one eye open, just in case.

But it's that leftover sense of something, a kind of vapor trail, which gets my attention when I walk in the door. Despite everything being in its place, something feels off. It looks like my condo, but there's a different energy. A lingering smell like burnt leaves. I'm sure the burglar is still inside: I can feel the presence.

"Jeanie?" I speak at the dim living room, lit only by the city lights reflecting off the whirling snow outside.

Television, receiver, Blu-ray. It's all there. The driftwood sofa. The carbon dining set. The bottom hem of a curtain flutters up from the hardwood like someone's left the window open.

On the eighteenth floor, my windows don't open the way they would, say, on a two-story house. You turn a little silver crank, and the windows tilt in about thirty degrees. I find the far-left window open, just a slit. It always sticks: you have to lean against it to get it to close tight. The air slipping through causes the sheer drapes to sweep out slightly and ripple along the window wall. Like aftershocks, or like a little fucking mouse is back there doing laps.

I sweep aside the curtain. There, teetering on the edge of the windowsill, where someone had obviously hidden it, is a short marijuana pipe and a blue mini BIC. I pick up the bowl. It's nice-looking, white swirls through red glass. There's nothing in it, but I hold it to my nose anyway. I'm relieved to just catch the afterburn of bud and nothing stronger. I whack the bowl against my palm. Nothing falls out. I slip the lighter into my pocket, admiring the view, thinking about how whoever got high right here picked a fucking fantastic place to do it. When it's dark like this, and the roofs are snow-covered, all you can see are colored lights moving way down on street-level. Cars and buses, reduced to headlights and wet reflections, are tea candles on black water. Whoever got stoned at my window probably felt pretty fucking connected to the big world out there, and for a moment I envy that fucking guy, or gal.

Back in my living room I turn the lights up full. I check the trash and find a brand-new bag, only the straw wrapper for one of those juice boxes Jeanie is so nuts about. Something about the empty trashcan strikes me as suspicious though. Not even a good Christian girl like her is so well-mannered she takes out the trash. Not without a pretty damn good reason.

Correlation is not causation, but I get on my knees and run my hands under the couch. I come away with an Old Style bottle cap. In the bedroom, everything's tidy, apparently how I left it. I go down the hall to Jeanie's room, reach in and turn on the light. I stop myself at her door, head on the frame. There is an unspoken agreement between roommates—even father and daughter. I've never eavesdropped on her phone calls. I've never read her diary. I think kids should have a bit of something that's their own, anyway, because so little is. I consider the evidence. I consider what I think I know about my daughter. No—I'm not going into her room. Not yet, anyway.

I flip off her light and as I do, catch sight of her laundry basket, overflowing in the corner. I remember the bra I found in the couch. Reminding myself, correlation is not causation, that's what I'm always telling my guys, but I wonder if that bra is a piece of evidence too.

I lay it all out on my bed and sit down. I consider the black brassiere, the open window, the sticky residue inside the bowl. I hold my daughter up against these things. Jeanie: recently confirmed, achiever of straight A's, athletic star. Also recently suspended for possession of cigarettes. Could the marijuana pipe, the beer cap, belong to her? They could. At the very least, they belong to someone she knows, and that doesn't make me feel too great. I wonder about Azita, what she's keyed into, if anything. I again weigh the facts against the evidence, marveling at how much gray area there is in parenting.

By the time I go into the bathroom to take a piss, I've just about decided to ignore it all. Bending down to toss the evidence in the trash, I kick the little white trashcan by accident and overturn it. My usual assortment of snotty tissues and dull razor blades. I'm scooping everything back in the trash when a certain shade of blue catches my eye, just the slightest corner sticking out from some balled-up toilet paper. I'd know that azure color anywhere, of course, because it's my brand.

I tug the corner of that blue triangle and come away with an opened single-pack of Trojan premium-quality Latex condom, with spermicide, ribbed for her pleasure. Electronically tested to help ensure reliability. I can't swear to changing my trash out that often, although I'm pretty sure my cleaning lady, Rosie, takes care of it each time she comes in. But I know for a damn fact I haven't been laid in at least six months, and the last time I got laid in my own apartment, I can't even remember. I'm wondering if Rosie really could have forgotten to take my trash out for over half a year when I unfurl the rest of the tissue ball and there, like a coiled snake, is a deflated condom.

I shove it all back in the trash: bowl, lighter, bottle cap, condom, wrapper. I cover it with about two inches of fresh toilet paper. I check my watch: 6:45 p.m. Jeanie won't be home for a few hours yet.

By the time I've changed into jeans and sneakers, I've already made the call.

The heavy wooden doors of Holy Trinity Lutheran Church, in the heart of Boystown, are locked. A rainbow flag hangs above a stone sign that says *Everyone Welcome.* On the east side of the chapel is an herb garden, but it's frozen, a bare fig tree standing lonesome as a hooker in the wind. I turn the corner and find the side entrance locked as well, and a small window, behind which is a yellowish light.

"I'm here," I text Jeanie.

The reply seems to come before I even hit send. She's got the fastest thumbs in Chicago.

"Here where?" Then, a few beats later, "Home?"

"Nope." I pause. "Outside. It's time to leave."

I pocket the phone as Lucas pulls up. He brought the squad car, which he didn't have to do. But when he gets out, I see he's still in uniform, the baton and pistol heavy on his hip.

We do the man-hug thing and slap each other on the back a few times.

He indicates his ride. "You want sirens for this?"

"Sirens? Yeah, sure."

"'Cause I'm not really supposed to do sirens unless there's an emergency."

We stand side by side and examine the vehicle like it's a beater that we can't get to start. Hands on our chins, humming to ourselves.

"How about the lights?" I ask.

He shrugs. "Yeah, ok."

He knocks on the passenger window, and I see there's another cop in there. Lucas makes a swirling motion with his finger. His partner reaches over and hits a button, and the lights on top of the car start throwing red and blue strobe against the stone walls of the church.

"His name is Steve," Lucas says.

"He ever get out of the car?"

"Not until there's action."

I hired Lucas right out of high school. Started him off as a clerk. He'd gone to Walter Payton on some kind of academic scholarship for poor Black kids and just that slight change, just humping it every day to a school that valued brains, that fed him square meals, made all the difference. Most of his friends from the old neighborhood are dead. The rest are in jail. Along with just about every male family member. I don't know who he had as a role model or who he tried to emulate. But he figured it out somehow. I hired him at eighteen, nineteen, and he did a helluva job for us.

Lucas though, because you run into these people eventually, these fucking good souls—his soul was too pure for finance. He's one of those guys you can't out-nice. You can bend over backwards, try to act like Cardinal Francis fucking Eugene George, but you'll never be as generous or as sensitive to other people's needs as Lucas. Turns out, these *simpatico* skills of his are absolutely worthless on the trading floor, but they're his strengths, and I imagine, they make him a pretty good cop, that even the guys he arrests end up kind of liking him. He's an undiluted soul. And at least with the police gig, he can feel like he's doing right by the world, for his old neighborhood especially, working the Southside. One day, after three or four years with us, he walked away from a six-figure salary to pull down a quarter of what he was making, with shittier hours. One of the good ones, as they say.

I briefed him on the phone. Now I pass along the pipe and bottle cap. "Jeanie will be right out."

Lucas shakes his head. "Last time I saw Jeanie she was like some super Christian."

"Yeah well, I guess that's all bullshit." The lights are flashing, and every few seconds the stained-glass windows of the church light up signal-blue and rose. "You look good."

"Thanks." He stretches, flexes his pecs. "You look good too."

There's a moment when I look at him, and he looks at me. Then we both burst out laughing.

"I taught you to lie better than that."

"I'm sorry." He can't catch his breath. "I couldn't keep a straight face."

"I look like shit."

"Yeah, you do."

"Dammit."

There's a sound at the door, and we turn. Jeanie comes out, hurrying, clasping her shoulder bag. Behind her, one or two of her Bible Study fuck-buddies. She's laughing about something, and then she pushes open the door, and her laughter sticks in her throat. She shields her eyes against the police lights.

"Dad?" she says.

The buddy cop Lucas had been keeping in reserve is out of the car faster than I register the sound of his door being thrown open. "Jeanie Ganzi?"

"Yeah?" She looks at me like she expects me to fucking answer for her, like she's a toddler and somebody's asked how old she is.

"Come with me, please." The second cop has both hands on his belt, feet spread, like a tackling dummy.

I point to the two douchebags behind her. "You. Fucking Tweedle-Dee and Tweedle-Dum. Beat it."

They do what Jesus would do and take off running.

"Dad—"

The second officer flicks on his flashlight and briefly blinds her. "Stand here."

Lucas steps away to hide in the shadows, near the car. Jeanie can't see him or the church; she can't see me. When a cop has his light in your face, everything else disappears. That light, and the cop's breath, are your entire world.

This second cop is Filipino, fists like blocks of ice. He's not much taller than me, but he grabs her wrist. For a moment my paternal instinct kicks in, and I want to snag her other arm, her free arm, and pull her away. To save her. But then I catch myself, bury my hands in my pockets. Even as my heart leaps into my throat.

"You can't do this." Jeanie is being led to the squad car. "I haven't done anything. I was in church. Am I being arrested?"

Her voice shakes and flirts with hysteria quicker than I thought it would. I remind myself she's seventeen. The arresting officer pushes her against the squad car, pats her down. Rougher than I would have preferred, but he's a gentleman about it—he doesn't abuse his access. By the time he slaps the cuffs on her she's blubbering and wheezing.

I have to turn away finally. It's too much. I hear her calling for me, then the car door opens, and shuts, and her cries are muffled, like she's calling to me from inside a sealed jar. Me, Lucas, and the third officer stand together with our backs to her, giving her time to stew.

"How's your mom?" I ask Lucas, after a while, because I am compelled to fill the silence, even with my daughter in handcuffs.

He shakes his head. "The same, man. Still the same. So deaf, she goes around yelling at everybody."

"She ask about me?"

He shrugs.

"Come on." I give him an elbow. "Remember I trained you, motherfucker. I'm inside your head."

"Yeah, she asks about you." I can't help but laugh when he says it. "Sometimes."

Behind us, Jeanie puts a shoulder to the door, a couple times. Her cries have dropped several octaves. The sounds she's making are primal, like a warthog snuffling in mud.

"She can't hurt herself in there?" I ask the other cop.

He shakes his head. "You're doing the right thing."

"Couple more minutes," Lucas says. "Then we'll talk to her."

The second cop pulls an apple out of his pocket, rubs it on his shirt. Then he snaps it in half with two hands.

"Shit." He looks at us, then at the two half-moons.

"It's ok." I say. "You guys enjoy."

Funny how the smell of fruit, an apple or an orange, overpowers everything. Smokey bar, back when you could smoke in bars, somebody peels an orange, to make a cocktail, say, and that's all you can smell. It's the same way with the apple. A little syrupy. A little sweet.

"Finally bought my own place." Lucas chews. "Me and my girl."

"You mean your baby's mama," Steve says.

"Where at?" I glance at my watch. I've lost track of how long this has been going on. When she was little we used to give Jeanie timeouts. One minute for every year she'd been alive. It was effective up until she was six or so. Then she just found something else to fucking do in her room. She'd stay there all day if we let her, just to prove some kind of point.

"Up in Edison Park."

"Give me a break." I shake my head. "Is that even still Chicago?"

"Barely," the other cop says. "Fucking barely."

"Lot of cops live up there, for the cheap housing," Lucas says.

"Everybody thinks the neighborhood is going to shit now that a couple of Blacks moved in."

We laugh about that. "You neighbors are shitting themselves right now," I tell him. "You know they are."

"Okay," the second cop says, suddenly serious. "Shall we bring her out?"

He flips his flashlight back on and brings Jeanie out of the backseat. Lit like that, she's the brightest thing on the block. Thick straws of snot drain from her nose. She can't keep her chin from quivering. Won't look any of us in the eye. Her body shakes, and not because it's December. Her hands are cuffed behind her.

"Jeanie." Lucas steps forward. "Are these yours?"

Relief washes over her face when she recognizes him. She has the audacity to smile. My head floods with rage, wondering if we're letting her off too easy. I want to rip that grin off her face.

"You're aware that smoking marijuana is still a crime in the state of Illinois?" Lucas presses.

"Yes," she says.

"As is underage drinking." The second cop throws this like a grenade.

She's quiet for a while. The police are good at what they do—this isn't their first rodeo. They wait until she says something.

"You're arresting me?" she finally says.

Lucas glances at me, and I tell him to go ahead. He reaches out and unlocks the cuffs.

"You get one get-out-of-jail free card," he says. "Because we know your dad."

They turn toward the street, giving Jeanie time to pull herself together, to wipe her nose. I follow them to the car and thank them.

"Don't mention it." Lucas picks lint off my shoulder. "Hell, this is probably the best thing that's going to happen to us tonight."

"No question." The action is over, so his partner is already halfway back in the car. "But she's a good kid. Stay on top of her. She'll be alright."

I give them both $300. They cut the siren lights and rumble off down an alley. Then it's just me and Jeanie on the street.

"Where are you parked?" she asks, trembling in the cold.

"Parked?" I look at her, hard. "I'm not parked anywhere."

"Let's head toward Clark then. That's the best place to catch a cab."

"Oh no, darling." I grab her arm. "We're taking the 'L.'"

She looks at me like she hates me, and probably at that moment she really does. "It's late. I have school tomorrow."

"Well you should have fucking thought about that before you invited people over to smoke pot and fuck in my fucking bed, Jeanie. What the fuck were you thinking?"

She backs away. She looks up at the stained-glass windows, dim and salt-laced. She wipes her nose with the back of her wrist.

"Well," she says. "Now at least we know we're both completely full of shit."

The "L" can be kind of peaceful at night. People coming home from the late shift. Twenty-somethings out late, just trying to get back to their apartments and pass out. Other folks on their way to work the early shift. It's not a bad time to ride public transportation. Everybody has a seat.

Jeanie rubs one finger on the greasy window, clearing away the effects of her breath on the glass. Everything on the "L" is slick. The floors are covered in a thin, dark film of snow and street grime.

"See anything?" I ask.

She rests her forehead on the window. "Just looking."

"See any coyotes?"

I lean against her, then harder, and finally she collapses. She lets me lean my chin on her shoulder. Together we watch the city roll by. First beneath us, then above us as the "L" tracks dip below ground. We re-emerge eye-level with streetlamps and empty offices and graffiti so expertly placed the city can't get to it to wash it off.

"That was shitty of you," she says. "That was unfair to put me through that."

It's my turn to shrug. "There's no such thing as fair or unfair, Jeanie. There's just shit that people do to one another."

"Like calling the cops on your daughter?"

"Like manipulating your estranged parents. Like pretending to be someone you're not."

I reach over and unzip her coat. Then I fish her silver cross from beneath the jacket folds.

"This fucking thing." I shake my head. "You had me convinced."

I release the necklace. She tucks it back into her jacket. She zips up to her neck and tucks her mouth behind the collar. She glances out the window, but we're rolling into a station— the last one before ours.

"Chicago." The automated voice speaks. "Doors open on the right at Chicago."

When we're moving again, Jeanie asks, "Did you know coyotes mate for life?"

"I did not."

"Not many animals do." She looks at me. "Swans. Prairie voles. Some kind of parasitic worm."

"Not humans."

She shrugs. "Not most, anyway."

The next morning, I text Pasternak and tell him I'll be late.

It's a balmy 38 degrees and sunny. Jeanie and I walk. I've decided that walking, and public transportation, are going to be part of Jeanie's punishment. Maybe if I had a yard, I'd make her lay mulch, pull bushes, something physical, to make her hurt. As it is, walking's all I got.

"So." We lean into each other, making headway against the twenty mile-an-hour gusts. "You had people over."

"A few." She corrects herself. "Nine or ten."

"For the record, it's fine to have people over. Just give me some heads up."

"Sorry."

"Some of these people you had over, they were drinking?"

"Yes."

"Including you?"

"Including me."

"How much do you drink?" But I immediately think better of it. "Never mind. Don't answer that."

We're walking faster than the bus we could have taken, which I always enjoy. Just as the bus catches up to us, the light turns red, we cross, and maintain our lead. Those passengers might be warmer, but goddamn it, we're getting there faster.

"Imagine you're a drug dealer," she says. "I've never understood, if you're a drug dealer, why you would drive around in some jacked-up Chevrolet Caprice with customized rims, crack smoke pouring out, bass turned up so loud it shakes your windows. A cop doesn't have to be a genius to take one look at that car and think, 'You know what? That there just might be a drug dealer.'"

"It's a status thing." I try to explain, like I'm some fucking expert.

"If I was a drug dealer, I'd drive a ten-year-old Honda." She considers. "Tan or gray. Wear a sports coat. Comb my hair."

Her knack for description—I flatter myself by believing those are my genes coming through. Somehow, she manages to paint a picture without using all the f-bombs, which I know from experience takes a lot of thought.

Still, I ask the obvious question. "Are you a drug dealer?"

"Dad." She punches my arm. Our jackets are so thick, neither of us feels it. Come to think of it, I can't feel my face either. The wind-chill makes it closer to ten degrees out here. Snot turns to crystal inside my nose. "But if I was, I'd dress pretty much exactly the way I am now."

We dodge a woman walking with her head down. We split her and converge like rapids. "So the whole Christian thing is just an act."

She leans toward me, conspiratorially, "I'm undercover."

"You got confirmed, for Chrissake."

She throws her head back and laughs so hard her scarf comes unknotted. She snags it before the wind carries it away. "Isn't it perfect? All I had to do was memorize the books of the Bible and stand through some ceremony."

"But Jeanie, shit, I mean, all that matters to some people."

We turn left. The clinic is just ahead. I hold the door for her. We wait for the elevator. It's one of those ancient contraptions with an accordion metal screen. We huddle in the lift, thankful for no other passengers. In our winter coats, we fill the space. The elevator clatters skyward.

In every negotiation, there are paths that lead to your intended result. Some paths peter out. Others are abandoned for any number or reasons. With Jeanie, my angles are few. Bringing in Lucas and Steve and letting them do their CPD thing hopefully drove home the legal concerns. As for my daughter pretending she's somebody she isn't—well, what she's doing isn't all that different from a kid who decides to dress

Goth, or punk, or delve into Wicca. It's an identity like any other, although in her case, perhaps a bit more duplicitous than most. There is, of course, the issue of trust—if her entire outer shell is a lie, what can I believe?

We're quiet as the door opens. I pull back the screen. We step into the lobby of the clinic.

I don't know what it is about fucking doctor offices in Chicago, but they all seem like they're being used during off-hours to illegally extract people's fucking kidneys for sale on the black market—one step away from off-the-books sex change operations for Polish immigrants and no-questions-asked workers comp claims. This is true of doctors' offices from Wrigleyville to the Loop. I've tried them all. Terrified, apparently, to paint their walls, every office presents the same off-white haze. The receptionist glares at you like you might be police, even if you've been there a hundred times; the medical devices are so antiquated you'd date them to the nineteenth century if they weren't made of steel, if they didn't gleam—menacingly. And don't even get me started on the dentists in this fucking city. I've started going out to the 'burbs. At least in Skokie it doesn't feel like you're going to round a corner and find fourteen Chechneyan orphans waiting to be smuggled to undisclosed locations west.

"Ganzi," I tell the receptionist, who taps her front teeth three times before turning to her computer.

"Jeanie?" she says.

"That's me." My daughter steps forward, hands on the counter.

"I need you to fill this out." The receptionist passes us a clipboard, and I manage to extract the pen from her inch-long, pink fluorescent fingernails.

"We're just here to pick up a prescription," I tell her. "For birth control."

"Dad." Jeanie swipes the clipboard and pen. "I got it. If I need any information from you, I'll ask."

I'm not allowed to say the word *birth control*, apparently, at least in public. We take our seats among last year's magazines. Jeanie asks me a couple questions. I answer from my insurance card. The nurse comes out and calls her name. I get up too, but Jeanie pushes me back down.

"Are you sure?" I ask.

"Dad." She gives me a dead-serious look. "I'm sure."

Then she's gone.

Faced now with time to kill, I scan the magazines fanned on the coffee table. A variety of what I'd call "celebrity" and "women's" magazines—none of them are for me. There's a wall of informational brochures with terrifying titles about STDs and unwanted pregnancies. I take one of each. I find myself clearing my throat constantly.

"You're a good dad," the receptionist says.

I look over at her. I hadn't expected conversation. But I should have. We're the only ones in the waiting area.

"All this," I say, indicating the wall of health pamphlets, "I thought was her mom's jurisdiction. Turns out her mom wasn't paying attention at all. So here we are."

"Not too many dads would put their daughters on the pill." She has a slight accent, which I assume is African, but I'm so geographically illiterate I have no idea if it's South African or from someplace else—I can't name three countries on that continent. "When I was young like her, my mom let me get the pill, but we never told my dad."

"She's having sex," I say, compelled to speak. Because of the quiet, maybe. And it'd be rude not to. Because I'm holding a pamphlet with a photograph of some guy's mouth herpes.

"I'm not going to change that reality. But I can at least try to prevent the negative outcomes of her behavior."

She laughs, gently. "You sound like a shrink."

I shrug. "I trade options."

I spare Jeanie the birds and bees talk. At seventeen, I'm assuming she knows how it all works anyway. She's seen porn, I'm sure, and not just on my trading floor.

Instead, I take her to an Asian restaurant beneath the Peninsula Hotel. We're seated in the corner, behind a potted plant. Screened and semi-private. It's always too bright, but the food's pretty good. Better than fucking PF Chang's or whatever. Anyway, Jeanie's a pro with the chopsticks. I still use a fork. I end up splattering orange chicken sauce all over the front of my shirt, and my left arm, somehow, when a piece of battered poultry bites back.

What I tell her is this: as her father, I don't have to like the idea of her having sex. I'm not required to give my approval. But also, I can't stop her. So I ask her to take her pills. I remind her a baby would really fuck up her life's aspirations. I remind her of the picture of the guy with mouth herpes. All of which makes for pleasant dinner conversation.

I also tell her that I love her. And that more than likely, she will have sex with several people before she gets married— if she ever does. That the ideal number is more than one and less than ten—that when she meets someone she really cares about one day, and they ask about her sexual history, that eight-partner spread walks the fine line between worldly and whorish. Anything less than one or more than ten will make it seem like something's the fuck wrong with you.

I let her sip my sake, then we try one warmed.

I remind her there are a lot of men out there. They'll all bring different things to the table. But the one thing they all should have in common, the ones she chooses to bang, anyway, should be that they treat her with respect. That no means no, and all that shit. It doesn't have to be love, but it must be consensual, a meeting of equals.

"That's how we raised you," I say. "Those are our expectations. And any man who doesn't give you that, can go fuck himself."

I ask her who's the guy. The one she's sleeping with.

"From church." She's picking up stray pieces of fried rice with her fingertip. We've absolutely demolished the meal.

"Does he know about, you know, your bullshit alias?"

She rolls her eyes. "Dad, we have sex, and we smoke pot. I think the cat's out of the bag."

I look around for the server. I wouldn't mind one more sake for the road.

"What's a bag cost these days, anyway?"

She shrugs. "For a quarter? Forty."

"Forty bucks?" I lean back and smile. "That's fantastic. That's what it cost when I was your age. I love that. Some things never change."

Chapter 10

The next day, Pasternak and I grab lunch from a little Jewish deli we like, where they still zip orders from the register to the counter on an overhead string. Best matzo ball soup in the city. The turkey on rye isn't too bad, either. Instead of heading back to the pit, though, we take our food up to the office. We've been meaning to review the year-end numbers, and with everything relatively quiet, today seems as good a day as any.

The downturn, the recession, has forced our retreat into more cash than any trading firm should legitimately carry. So many commodities are at near-historic lows, part of me struggles not to buy pretty much fucking everything, since everything looks priced to buy. On the other hand, we're still very much on the edge of getting our asses handed to us. Pasternak preaches caution.

"Let's step back," he says. "Big picture. What does the trading floor look like in ten years?"

A decade in the future: Jeanie a working professional, Obama out of office, me still forty pounds overweight and hammering away with my little stylus trying to beat the automated traders to market.

"Think bigger," Pasternak says. "Darker."

"Less trading pits?" I venture.

He shakes his head. "No trading pits at all."

I slurp one last spoonful of soup and lean back in my chair. Trying to imagine all that real estate. What will the Exchange use all that space for, if not terminals? You could install an indoor lap pool; two full basketball courts; a goddamn dressage arena.

"Cushions." Pasternak muses. "A foosball table. You ever been to Bloomberg? An open space like that. That's the future. Fucking ergonomic chairs and programmers as far as the eye can see."

I understand this vision. That as things continue to automate, human traders will become irrelevant, and the firms that are ahead of the curve, at the industry's razor's edge, will be the firms who convert almost entirely to tech. And fast.

"Okay," I say, wiping my mouth, my fingers. "Okay. Let's get together with somebody who's already doing this. Somebody who understands the tech. We've got cash lying around. Let's make it work."

We click around some more on our computers. I open my calendar but shit, who am I kidding? I haven't kept my own calendar since Pasternak started as clerk. He'll find a time, and then he'll schedule it.

"Hey, who'd you use to sell your mom's place?" Pasternak asks me. He asks it casually, like it's something that just occurred to him as he's picking through the day's mail.

"@Home. Azita used them too, when she sold our place. Don't give me that look. Her place."

"Liked 'em okay?"

"Sure."

I've been trying to avoid the stock ticker, but I finally cave and check the feed. Everything down, as always. Depressing as hell.

I give up, push back from the screens. "You guys moving?"

"No, no," he says. It's his turn to pretend to be distracted by his laptop. "I just got, you know, some property I want to shift around."

I cross my arms. I stare at him across the desk. Pasternak. Who I've known since before I grew pubic hair. Who I've never known to speak, or ask a question, unless he has a pretty good reason. Unlike yours truly, none of his words are extra. So, I weigh what he's just said against what I know about him and Robin, against his recent behavior.

"I hear some people are in deep shit," I say, casually, careful not to sound probing. "They've borrowed against their equity, once, twice, four times. Now their property is worth less than they paid for it."

I'm just throwing darts, in the dark. I could see a scenario like this. Robin has a big appetite for nice things. Pasternak gets paid handsomely, but maybe not handsomely enough for her.

"You know what I've heard?" Pasternak says, after a while. "Life insurance pays out for suicide after you own the policy for a year."

For a moment, it feels like our conversation might actually be penetrating some sacred space, the trust we share, the way he and I rely on one another.

"Sure it does," I tell him. "Hell, I've thought about it. There've been times I've been worth more dead than alive. Plenty of times. That's the nature of this job."

Pasternak finally looks at me. The light of the computer screen is pale on his face, like he's been out in the cold too long. The screen wavers, casting blue undulations across his eyes and lips.

"You've thought about offing yourself?" he asks.

"Sure," I tell him. "Who the fuck hasn't?"

He goes back to typing. "You oughta get some help, John. I worry about you."

Negotiators pray to the god Janus, the lord of moonlight, the many-faced god. Successful parlay requires a nuanced performance over a string of days or months. You show the other party different sides of your personality, to keep them in suspense, scare them, or, like this thing with Jeanie, lull them into a false sense of security. I've lured my daughter into the honeytrap. I've played my role as understanding father. From now on, though, shit begins to get real.

Because she played me. I went to bat for her, and she fucked me. It's all I can think about, sitting in a conference room on the Executive level of the CBOE. It's me, and Sar, and Jeanie's basketball coach—wearing a floral tie, which on him looks long enough to swing from tree to tree—and Northwestern's athletic director, Mindy Pagano. The conference room is small, designed more for impromptu moments when a standing meeting in the hall takes a turn and you decide hey, let's duck into this room for a minute and shut the door, little pitchers and big ears, all that. It's still got one glass wall overlooking the cobblers on the floor below; one conference phone like a beached starfish on the center of the table. We've been offered water, which no one but the athletic director took. I watch with no small amount of horror as she raises the glass to her lips. Little known fact: those same tallboys make an appearance at all the one-off meetings like this. I've found Sar's assistant washing them with hand soap in the boardroom kitchen. The corporate world is filled with germ traps. That open bowl of jelly beans set out on an assistant's desk, which people claw through on their way from one office to another;

elevator buttons and copy machines and all the shared equipment that is really nothing more than a swap-meet for viruses and germs—what I do is go to Home Depot once a month and buy one of those industrial-sized bottles of hand sanitizer. I pump compulsively. The amount of handshaking alone that goes on here, day-to-day, would kill an elderly person in a matter of hours.

"Head coach?" Mindy has only just realized what Sar is asking her, that she give the recently vacated men's basketball coaching job—head coach—to Jeanie's high school basketball coach. "That's not even my decision."

"You're the athletic director," Sar reminds her.

"I know my job title, Mr. Sar."

She flushes. Despite her physical build, which seems suited for hand-to-hand combat, she's out of her element here, on the third floor, the Executive floor, with the three of us. She's in a tight space. Trapped in a cage with a bear, a bull, and a giraffe. "A hiring committee well, does the hiring, ultimately."

"But your recommendation would go a long way," Sar says.

She scoffs. She's got a double chin that waggles whenever she opens her mouth. I don't know what sport she used to play—field hockey, maybe.

"I'm sorry," she says. "If that's the reason you brought me here, I don't know that I can really help."

Sar leans back and his chair squeaks. He stretches his arms above his head, cracks both wrists, then each knuckle in turn. He grunts, drops his arms, shakes them out.

"I've started kickboxing," he says. "Do any of you fight?"

"I hit the bag occasionally," the coach admits.

"Strictly Pilates for me," Mindy says, then laughs loudly at her own joke.

Sar doesn't bother waiting for me to respond, as obviously, the answer is no. "It's given me great range of motion. But in the morning, I wake up feeling like I've absolutely been run over by a train."

It's not even so much that Jeanie betrayed my trust and lied to my face, more than once—although those things make me incensed. It's that I used her trust as collateral to swing a *quid pro quo* with Sar. In a few days' time, I'm going to have to stand up in front of every guy in my pit, and all the other traders, and explain why I believe selling now, probably for less than they think their seats are worth, and going public, is a good thing—that the future, in fact, relies on our closing as many terminals as we can—because my opinion goes a long way, and the guys will swallow it a whole lot better coming from me than from some other guy. Sar for example. I've cashed in all my self-respect, so that this brachiosaurus she calls Coach can fail up and land himself a job at a Big 10 school. And now that I've met the athletic director of said school, she strikes me more like a bus driver, or a customer service rep, someone used to carrying the jocks of others but without much nerve of her own.

It's like meeting my executioners, only to discover they're not so scary after all, which leaves me wondering how I got myself squeezed into this situation in the first place. Then I remember: Jeanie.

"You know, I graduated from Northwestern," Sar says.

"Yes sir," she says.

"There's an entire wing of the business school that has my name on it."

"Yes."

"There are two fully-funded scholarships for Indian-Americans that have my wife's name on them."

"Mr. Sar—"

"I sit on the recruitment council, and my wife sits on the Board of Regents and the theatre board at Northwestern."

She's blubbering, she's so apologetic. "If there was anything I could do, I would. It's a national search. It's not—"

Jeanie's coach pipes up. "How about assistant coach?"

His voice takes all of us by surprise. His hands are flat on the table, his great tangle of limbs tucked neatly beneath. He tells her he understands he's not remotely qualified to be head coach of a Division I men's basketball team. He says all he wants is a job where he can learn from the best. He'll be the third coach on the bench, handling towels and water bottles and picking up all the basketballs at the end of practice. He'll be the one to make sure all players keep curfew. He'll be the first one at the gym and the last one to go home. He understands the situation. All he ever wanted was the chance to make an appeal to her in person. He says he'll do whatever it takes. That he can't spend another season coaching high school girls' basketball. That if he does, he knows everything he values will collapse—his career, his marriage. That if they let him in the door at Northwestern, let him shine shoes, wax the hardwood, let him shoot foul shots with the walk-ons until they are chanting the rhythm in their sleep, he'll never ask for another thing again, and die happy. That's all we want, isn't it? To die happy?

In reply, we are silent. All of us simply look at the coach, who hasn't moved anything but his mouth during the entire appeal. But Sar can't stand silences, even more than me. He views them like a gaping abyss he must heroically span.

"So, can you send her your resume?" he asks him.

"Fuck the resume," Mindy says. "You're hired. Assistant coach, starting in August."

I think about the coach's lamp, in his office beneath the stairs, generating brilliant light so he doesn't get depressed. I think about rats raised in laboratories that never see the sun. Below us, a square-acre of cubicles arranged in precise grids. I'm inside so much, more and more I'm finding sunlight hard to tolerate. When I do go outside, I hardly recognize it, and then find myself wishing it away.

The athletic director and Jeanie's basketball coach say their goodbyes. Sar asks if I can hang around to talk about a separate matter. Once they're gone and the door is shut, he grins.

"Satisfied?"

I bob my head up and down, servile. "I really appreciate this, Dick."

He waves at my gratitude like a foul smell he's only just noticed. "We give them so much money, it's the least they can do."

He updates me on the passage of the bill, the one we flew to D.C. to meet with our lobbyists about. He says the bill is D.O.A., which means the capital gains repeal is too.

"Congratulations," I tell him.

"About that other thing." Sar leans way back in his chair again, bouncing a little, so the chair again lodges its complaints. "I think we'll wait until after Christmas. It's been a helluva quarter. I think guys will be a little more receptive after the holidays."

"I think that's the right move," I tell him.

"Good, then." He sits upright, slapping his hands on the table. "You'll be all set to stand up there with me, convince the guys that this is the right thing, not only for CBOE, but for their own livelihoods as well?"

"Wherever you need me," I tell him. "Tit for tat."

Sar rises, shakes my hand. I tell him I'm going to hang out for a minute, make a couple calls here, if he doesn't mind.

He says of course not, to let Charlene know if I need anything, and then he leaves me alone in the conference room.

I dig my phone out of my pocket and flip it open. I'm just about to dial when something catches my eye. I turn toward the windows. A small gathering of employees near the center of the maze seem to be laughing together and pointing toward the ceiling. I lean closer to the glass and look out. A pink Mylar balloon has untethered and now floats peaceably above the desks. There's plenty of flight space. The ceiling is more than three-stories high. The balloon shimmies in the recirculated air. Someone's birthday, or a new baby. I can't read it. It passes my window trailing a twirling, silver ribbon. It floats, sinks, then rises up and out over the floor.

It is the highlight of the day for those workers below, the balloon the only mark of color among the gray cubicle walls, the beige carpet.

It seems then like an accident, a child's spill. Jeanie, if she were here, would say the balloon is brave, alone among the office clones, among the day-to-day drudgery—flying proudly, solo. With that bravery, though, comes the understanding that it cannot last. A bright flower in a plowed-over patch of dirt. The lone protestor on Tiananmen Square. It's fleetingness intrinsic to its beauty.

Darwinists are big on *survival of the fittest*. But I have another motto, which I believe trumps even that.

Adapt or die.

Chapter 11

If there are 14,000 museums in Chicagoland, I've eaten a company dinner at every one. I've dined beneath North America's oldest telescope at the Adler Planetarium and under the golden arches at the McDonald's museum in Des Plaines. I've slurped lukewarm buffets overlooking the river, on the river, in the middle of the fucking lake—and the amazing thing is, the food all tastes the same, as if this city nourishes itself on the teats of a singular, behemoth catering company.

End of year, I'm expected to host a shindig for my employees, something they can bring their significant others to and stand around drinking at on someone else's dime—my dime—but unless you're Sam Zell, bussing a thousand people out to a big tent in an undisclosed location for a circus-themed party headlined by Don Henley and the fucking Eagles—you do the museum circuit.

This year, we've got the Chicago Stock Exchange Trading Room at the Art Institute. It's cozy and familiar. When the city tore down the original Stock Exchange back in the seventies, they took some of the frescoes and columns and rebuilt the room as an event space, here, resurrecting the original, elaborate stenciling that fits together like an Escher print translated into Baroque: the pale greens, the lacey gold curlicues near the ceiling, the fluorescents shining through the old windows like daylight. It's a magnificent room that makes me realize two things: one, that nothing I occupy today will ever be preserved in a museum, and two, that in an industry as transient as ours, where you're only as good as your last quarterly report, it's nice to step into the CSE Trading Room and think about the year it was built, 1894, and just how fucking long ago that actually was. It makes the current downturn seem, not insignificant, but it puts recent events in perspective. For more than a century the markets have persisted. Ours is an old profession. Ancient Greece was nothing but stock brokers and hookers.

Fifteen round-tops are set along the lower level, on what was once the actual trading floor. Bars run the length of the mezzanine, two or three steps above. We're all comfortable here. It feels like home. In general, traders are in our element when we're standing a touch below ground, suckers for sunken living rooms and Japanese terraced gardens, or chorales—anywhere men stand shoulder-to-shoulder, behind and above other men. Say one of us, one day, happened to find ourselves in Chicago circa 1894, we could stride into this very room in its original location and, after mastering certain gestures and profanities particular to the era, hold our own. Imagine Cubs first baseman Derrek Lee time-traveling back to hit against Old Hoss Radbourn. There'd be some nuances he'd have to get used to, sure, but it would all still be recognizable as baseball.

The center table features me, flying solo; Pasternak and his wife, Robin; two of my senior traders and their escort-service dates, both of whom speak with just a trace of foreign accent, adding just the right amount of international intrigue, and who are absolutely too gorgeous and articulate to actually be in a relationship with either of my guys; plus the man all of us refer to as our silent partner, Eugene O'Connor. He staked me umpteen years ago when I was just starting out and keeps a tidy, more or less passive, 15 percent working interest in our little shop. He's 170 years old—he knew Old Hoss Radbourn personally—and lost his wife in 1982. Since then he's done his best to keep up with Chicago's original hustler, Hugh Hefner, including the blue velvet blazer he's chosen to appear in tonight. Pasternak had him down as a "plus-one," which makes sense when I see who he's got hanging from his arm: Ms. Penelope Weil, Esquire.

She's exquisite in a floor-length emerald dress, a mother-of-pearl clip in her hair. For someone usually so buttoned up, the expanse of her bare shoulders seems a dangerous and exciting thing. I knew she was Gene's attorney, but haven't seen them together. I wonder briefly if they're banging, then just as quickly put the thought of Gene and his old-man balls out of my mind.

There's no time to say hello. I catch Penny's eye, and she smiles before I return my attention to the twenty or so traders and their dates—plus a dozen clerks—all queuing up to kiss the ring.

"Everybody calm down," I laugh. "Bonuses have already been handed out."

The young ones, like Stefany Vázquez, the lowest of the low on our greasy totem pole, have maybe only been to one or two events like this in their entire lives, if any. They've never experienced an open bar stocked with primo shit. She, like the rest of her generation, are reckless. Every last one of them gets too drunk too early, may have even arrived drunk, and winds up leaning in too close to shout exuberant but ultimately banal things in my face. "Do you know what I mean? Do you know *what I mean?*" These types, including Ms. Vázquez, who's lovely, but still, very new, have me looking for an escape route ten minutes after I arrive.

The musicians we've hired make for a good distraction. When I've had enough of a conversation, I point to the three borderline homeless people playing light jazz in the corner and suggest my younger employees give them a closer listen. *Borderline homeless* is maybe too strong. There's a dude my age with a closely cropped white beard and Andy Warhol shades manning a keyboard; a heavy-set hipster draws a bow across a cello or some kind of wide, stringed instrument; and a homely woman sporting tattoo sleeves and not enough dress alternately scats, hums, or sings vaguely recognizable lyrics from popular songs while rattling various handheld percussion instruments. Their style lies somewhere between classical and jazz, and during cocktail hour I catch phrases of Nirvana's "Smells like Teen Spirit."

"They say you stop listening to new music after you turn thirty-six." A small group of familiar faces has gathered around me, including Pasternak and his wife. "Where did you find this band?"

"Someone recommended them." Pasternak grips a full cocktail like brass knuckles. "Columbia College."

"The string player is out of tune," Robin remarks.

We all listen, and it's true. I'm no musician—hell, I stopped listening to new music when I was *twenty-six*, probably. My iPod is crammed with eighties bands like R.E.M and Jane's Addiction, and nineties emo shit my ex-wife was into— but the keyboard player is definitely plunking out one melody that the singer seems to be following, while the cellist or bassist or whatever he is, whatever he thinks is coming out of his instrument is about two or three sour notes away from what his bandmates are playing.

"Jesus." One of my guys shakes his head. "Can I fucking shoot that fatty and put him out of his misery?"

His escort date comments in a vaguely Slavic accent. "Can he not hear himself? Is he crippled?"

"Hey!" Pasternak shouts loud enough for most of the room to hear. He shouts again, and the musicians finally notice. He walks toward the band, waving his arms. The music stutters to a stop, like a horse and cart tumbling off a cliff.

"You." He points to the fat guy. "I have a request."

The cellist blinks. "Okay."

"There's this ancient fucking Chinese song that I really love. Do you know it?"

"Chinese?"

"Tune-ing."

The cellist stares at him a moment, then glances at his bandmates.

"Tune-ing, motherfucker." Pasternak slaps his own head. "Tune your goddamn cello. It's like a couple of cats up here fucking each other to death."

The musicians confer. The soloist then steps forward to announce they're taking a short break. The room bursts into applause. The little group I'm standing with turns back to one another, huddles closer, congratulating Pasternak—thanking him, really—as we welcome him into our fold.

Pasternak and most of my senior guys have been with me long enough where they need to decide if they're in for life or if they need to start looking for work someplace else. They're doing the holiday rounds just about every night, like I am, double-booked in all the fancy locations all across Chicago. For them, it's just beginning to sink in that they can either go on like this, turning slowly through their lives, making just the faintest hiss, like a record that's come to the end but no one's thought to lift the turntable arm, or take a risk for once in their lives and strike out on their own.

"It's enough to make you hate the holidays," Robin whispers to me when, inexplicably, things dissipate, and we find ourselves standing next to one another. "And I used to love Christmas."

"Heart-attack season." I toss back the last of my Jack and Ginger, my favorite couple, until the ice knocks against my teeth. "One party after another."

"And they're all the goddamn same," she says. "No offense."

"None taken." I step forward and drill Pasternak in the shoulder. He's been talking to a guy we recently promoted, a full glass of clear liquid in his fist. He's a wet fucking noodle. "Nice job handling the band. Is that your first drink?"

He looks baffled. "What?"

"Or did you quit drinking?"

He flushes, red as Santa's tights. "I thought—"

"What, are you twenty?" People around us laugh. "Drink. You've earned that right, at least. Now come on, down the hatch."

Pasternak offers a half-toast and drains his highball. He wipes his mouth, gives me a wink, and asks if I want another.

He doesn't have to ask.

You see it all the time in new hires. Social situations, the smart ones do nothing until someone else does it first. Eat, or take a drink of alcohol. Because cultures differ in various workplaces, you may not know what does or doesn't fly. It's a smart strategy. One I wish more of our new hires followed. Stefany Vázquez, for example, is at this moment, showing a couple of her colleagues a tattoo she has on the back of her thigh. But Christ: Pasternak, I expect to drink. Maybe I'm feeling mean-spirited—every Christmas party needs a Grinch—but that's really my entire issue with him. I want him to own his seniority. I want him to unzip his eight-inch cock and let it thud on the table every now and then. Unless he really did quit drinking, in which case, I feel sorry for him.

Robin slides in closer, once he's gone. She holds her wine glass to her lips as if she doesn't want anyone else to see her mouth moving.

"He admires you so much," she says.

I raise an eyebrow. "Well, he shouldn't."

"That's what I told him." She smiles so I know she's only half-joking. "No offense."

"None taken."

"I told him, find a new job. Where they pay you more. Where they respect you."

"We respect him."

"You don't make fun of people you respect."

I wonder where the hell he's gone off to, because now would be the perfect time to take a long drink and change the fucking conversation.

"Have you checked out the band?" I ask her. "Sounds like fatty finally got in tune."

"Don't worry." She licks her teeth with her lips closed. "He won't leave. He's too loyal. I tell him, you know what else is loyal? Dogs. And people who belong to cults."

And then Eugene and his date, our mutual attorney, Penny, swing past. He points to my empty maws.

"I hate seeing anybody without a drink in their hand," he says.

I wave, vaguely. "Pasternak is somewhere."

Gene's been to so many of these, he can't even tell you what venue he's standing in. It could be 2008 or 1978—he's wearing the tie to prove it, wide enough to park a golf cart on. When he and his date saddle up, Robin slinks off.

"When the fuck are we going to eat?" Gene wants to know. Despite his age, the guy still has a full head of hair, white as cotton. "I believe you know Ms. Weil."

I wait until she offers me her hand, and then I take it. "Penny."

"Merry Christmas, Jonathan."

"Happy Hanukah to you," I tell her.

"Rule breakers." Gene grips our arms. "It's happy holidays now. For everyone. Carte blanche. Can't fuck it up that way."

"Did you quit drinking?" Penny asks.

"No, Pasternak—"

"Let me ask you something." Gene puts his face in mine. He applies pressure to my neck, so I have to bend down and wallow in the smell of shrimp cocktail on his breath. "Rumor has it, the CBOT guys are ready to settle. A public offering can't be far behind."

He's fishing, and he knows I know this. I smile the kind of smile that says I wish I could help you. "Now Gene, you want that kind of information, you need to ask for your board seat back."

"How many guys are going to lose their jobs?"

"Even if what you're asking is true, I am not at liberty to say."

"Customers don't want to trade with computers. This is a human business. A customer-oriented business." He's opening and clenching his free hand—he doesn't have a drink either. "A customer wants to trade, they dial the phone, they goddamn well better get a voice on the other end—and one that speaks English."

"Okay, Eugene."

"That guy, Sar." Eugene shakes his head. "There's rumors. I hear them. He wants to automate every fucking thing. That guy, he'd automate his jerk-off time if it'd save him a million."

I put my hand on his shoulder, so then we're standing there, arms locked. I shake him a little, give his arm a squeeze.

"Okay, Eugene. Okay." I'm also looking over my shoulder to make sure the Chairman isn't actually here. We invite him every year, and he never comes—but it'd be my luck for him to decide to make an appearance tonight. "I feel like it's my duty to remind you, this is a party. No work talk at a party."

"I know, I know." He releases me, then crushes his hands together like he's loosening up for a bout. "But CBOE goes public, the barbarians won't just be at the gates, they'll be god-damn over them."

"They already are, Gene."

"There's no goddamn dignity in that." He wags his finger. "No goddamn pride."

I look at him, then at Penny, who shakes her head.

"Tell me something." He whispers now, leans in close. "How's my namesake?"

He means Jeanie. "She's good. I'll tell her you said hello."

He chortles, and raises a finger to his lips, as if encouraging me to keep quiet, reminding me that we share a secret. As if he'd ever let me forget.

"Come on, Gene." Penny offers her arm, and he takes it. "Let's find our seats."

When they saunter off, I release the breath I've been holding. There are three people in the room, besides myself, who know about Jeanie—four if you count Robin, and that's at least three too many people for me to feel comfortable. I wonder briefly if I've been getting sloppy, then decide no, it's just a coincidence—Pasternak and Penny know all my secrets, per their job descriptions. Robin and Eugene probably have better things to do than out me.

Pasternak returns with fresh drinks. When he does, Robin circles back like a fucking piranha and is suddenly standing right fucking next to me again. I actually startle a little.

"How's Eugene?" My clerk asks.

I taste my cocktail, then stir it with my finger. "Is there actually ginger ale in this?"

"Did you know that's where we get the word, *cocktail?*" Pasternak sips from his own, Rum and Coke if it's anything. "Way back when, in George Washington times, when a guy wanted to sell another guy a horse, he'd shove a piece of ginger up that horse's ass, to make the horse strut in a certain, perky way that buyers liked."

"Cocktails?" This story has that air of truth to it, so unlikely it may be true.

"They perk you up."

"You're so smart." Robin strokes his arm, and they kiss.

"Okay, break it up," I say. "I want a godchild, but not right here."

Robin blushes, wipes her mouth. "Sorry."

"Anyway," I say, "I think Gene's losing it."

"Really?"

"A little."

"Not a chance." Robin leans against her husband, and he drapes an arm around her. "He's just taken more drugs tonight than the rest of us."

We've broken a cardinal rule of seated dinners and spent cocktail hour chatting mainly with those we'll be seated with. It's a faux pas that would have driven my ex-wife insane. No one here gives a shit—most of us, by the time we sit down, are swimming in our plates. Finally, the catering staff rings the little bell, and all of us stumble to our tables, many of us double-fisting, as if we expect the bar to close, which it won't, not for another three hours. With my vision slightly blurred by whiskey, the walls are a swirl of chartreuse and gold, the chandeliers stuffed with fifty bulbs or a hundred, all sparkling and watery, reflected infinitely in the mirrors high on the walls. I pass Stefany en route to our respective places. She hoists a bottle of Disaronno and gestures with it, at me, in a happy way, a kind of toast, as we come together and part.

I make a speech. I thank everyone for coming. I acknowledge how utterly shitty the markets have been since August. I admit some humble uncertainty about the future. But one thing I am certain of, I tell them, is that I'm certain of the courage and passion of everyone on staff. This is our ship, I say. We are all on it together, this giant fucking pirate ship. A seaworthy vessel if ever there was one. And some of us, our job is to swab the deck. And some of us, we climb the jib and hoist the sails and scamper around up on all that rigging. Others cook, or keep watch, or mind the cannons, or read the fucking maps so we know where we're going—and some of us sail the ship. And sometimes, we find ourselves in the middle of a big fucking storm. We got waves coming over the sides. The ship's heaving and we're all of us hanging on for dear life, praying to God or Vishnu or whoever the fuck, and we look to one another and think, Shit. I don't know if we're going to make it.

I pause for a moment to let those last words sink in. Everyone is watching, listening. I point to one of our senior traders, across from me. "You," I tell him, "you don't know if we're going to make it." I point toward a table in the back, where Stefany sits. "You, Ms. Vázquez, don't know if we're going to make it. But we're on this ship, and we close our eyes, we hold hands, and batten down the fucking hatches and wait for the storm to pass."

The storm, I tell them—the storm was this fall.

The dining room is silent. Even the catering staff has stopped bussing our salads. No one so much as sips from their glasses.

"But, my friends, storms end." I pause. "Clouds clear. We see some fucking sun for a change. And when we do, when the mist is gone and the sky returns, we spy an island, out there on the horizon. Pasternak calls out, 'Land Ho!' And we sail to it. And when we get there, we drop anchor. On this island, we find the most delicious fruit. The cleanest water. Booze that goes down smooth and gets us insanely drunk with no hangover the next morning. And we find beautiful women. And beautiful men. And it's good to have the sand under our feet again. To feel the earth under our feet again. To feel the sand between our toes. To have steady legs. The streets are spotless, the beds are warm, it's fucking paradise. So, what do we do?"

"Burn!" Stefany calls out from across the rehabilitated Chicago Stock Exchange trading floor. "Loot!"

"Yes!" I climb onto my chair and raise my arms. "We have swords. And firearms. And fucking cannons. And they have shit we want. So, what do we do?"

A few more answer. "Burn and loot?"

"What is it we do?"

"Pillage!" A dozen now. "Loot and pillage!"

"Burn and pillage!"

"Loot, burn, and pillage! Burn and pillage!"

Soon the entire room is chanting. Pasternak claps his hands, keeping time. He stands, and others stand as well. Then someone gets up on a chair, and then everyone else is standing on their chairs, all the while chanting, "Burn and pillage!"

Someone tries to hop up onto a table. The table flips—or almost. Other guests catch it while the trader pitches headfirst to the floor. We lose a glass, maybe a plate or two. Things get shuffled around. No harm done. It sends my guys into frenzy. We're screaming our heads off, wobbling on four chair legs, each of us giants.

People talk about team-building exercises, ropes courses or wine tastings. But nothing beats eighty people in a fancy room shouting "burn and pillage" together. By the time we sit back down again, sweating and out of breath, I'm so in love with each and every one of my guys it feels like my heart's gonna explode.

Salad arrives: a crisp blend of edamame and mandarin oranges, arugula and walnuts. A chili-lime dressing. Bread is passed. I stuff half a sesame bun into my mouth, hoping to soak up some alcohol. A server is suddenly tableside offering us red wine or white.

"To a better tomorrow," Eugene toasts.

"What's so bad about right now?" I ask, innocently, and the table laughs.

"Well," Robin says, "it could have been a lot worse, that's for sure."

We all look at Pasternak's wife. Not because she's spoken out of turn, exactly, but because we're surprised she's weighing in on this particular conversation, the state of the markets.

"I mean, thank God you went to 30 percent cash just before the bottom fell out," she says. The rest of us, we all look at our plates. "If you'd been all in, would we even be sitting here?"

I finish the food in my mouth. "It's not a good thing, being in cash, because then we're not making any money."

"At the time though, it saved our asses."

I shrug, conceding, and turn my attention back to my plate.

"And whose idea was it, to go to cash?" She looks around the table, presumably expecting one of us to answer.

"Robin," Pasternak says.

I smile—I can't help myself. I know what she's driving at. Pasternak pushed me hard last summer. I wouldn't say it was his idea, per se, but he deserves some credit for making me see reason, convincing me we were better off playing defense in Q4.

"Here's to you, bub," I tell my clerk, and he toasts back, and everyone else takes a swallow.

But Robin won't let it lie.

"Don't forget the work he did on that little bird strategy you guys put in place last winter," she says.

Eugene gives me a look. "Little bird?"

"The falcon thingy?" She wants someone to name it for her.

Eugene appears concerned. "That's not some kind of sex thing, is it?"

"That's the *baby bird.*" One of my traders corrects him, flapping his elbows and forming his mouth into a beak, straining his neck like he's hungry for cock. Rightfully, the Asian mail-order bride he's brought with him slugs him on the shoulder, and he knocks it off.

I stare at Robin. "You're talking about the Iron Condor."

"Ah!" Eugene claps his hands, once. "My favorite."

"Condor, falcon, whatever." Robin's wrist flaps back and forth like a dead fish. "It was my husband's idea."

The Iron Condor is an advanced strategy for trading options. We started pushing them on our guys earlier in the year. Basically, Pasternak and I took a look at the markets, figured we were either flying so high we were never coming down, or we were at the bursting point of one helluva bubble, so we took short and long positions well below and above the current market prices of several assets. It's a risky bet. Your potential loss is much greater than your potential gain. But as the year progressed, it was pretty clear we'd made the right choice, which we knew we had more than an 80 percent chance of making anyway. We did pretty good as the year wore on, taking little credits here and there, but once the housing market collapsed, we exited the short side a lot richer than we'd entered it in January.

I remind the table that the Iron Condor is a classic strategy.

"Classic, but very complicated." She nods her head, emphatically. "Only someone as good at math as my husband could have pulled it off."

"Pasternak also convinced me we had enough money to throw this party, in this venue," I tell the table. "I wasn't sure we could, or how it would look, after how things went this year."

"And thank God he did." Robin's right on top of me, her tunnel vision so narrow she can't see I'm being gracious. "You were about to hold it where, the Rainforest Café?"

The table laughs, and I correct her. "The House of Blues."

"That place is a dump," Eugene grunts.

"It's not that bad."

"No, it is," Robin says. "Thank God one of you has taste."

"Pasternak." Gene shouts at him because he can barely hear himself. "I didn't know you'd hired your own PR gal."

Robin slips her arm around her husband, her eyes lit with wine, reflecting back the sconces and artificial skylights. "I'm proud of him. Why shouldn't I be?"

My clerk scrambles to establish some kind of foothold. "No, he's right. I really don't need you bragging for me."

"Well, somebody needs to." She looks around the table, waiting for us to agree.

When no one does, Pasternak pushes back, stands, and drops his napkin on the chair. "Excuse me." Right on cue, running from the fight, like he always does, Pasternak, who I love in some kind of twisted brother-son-best-friend-from-childhood hybrid way, crosses the dining room and takes the mezzanine steps in two long strides. He disappears around the corner, heading to the men's room.

"Am I wrong?" Robin's looking at me.

"Time and place, honey," Penny stage whispers.

The conversation shifts. Eugene recounts a recent trip to the Galapagos. The untamed wild, he says. Turtles the size of cathedral bells.

"It's the place that inspired Darwin, after all," he says. "The cradle of evolutionary thought. On those islands, we see where we, mankind, raised ourselves out of the muck and mire to live as kings among the beasts."

It's a narrative that appeals to me as well, and I say as much. But no one else at the table has been, so Gene monologues about the virtues of indigenous people, how nice it was to get away from all the modern distractions, the way most bullshit vacation stories go. This one ends with an image of a shirtless Eugene, on the beach, around a fire one night, sharing some hallucinogenic drink out of a coconut shell. Does it pass the truth sniff test? I'm so blotto, I don't even know. I don't care. I'm watching Robin, whose wine glass is empty.

"Robin," I say. "Another?"

She glances at her wine glass, then at me. "I didn't realize I was empty."

I lean out of the conversation and snap my fingers. The catering staff knows who the host is, and they spring-to. A server is at our table in the time it takes me to drain the last few drops of whiskey and ask if anyone else needs more.

"What is that, Robin? The pinot grigio?"

"Chardonnay, actually," she says.

With her accent, *chardonnay* comes out sounding more like a bray than something you might cultivate and cellar or charge $40 a bottle for.

When the server is gone, I ask her, "Enjoying the wine?"

"I'm more of a beer drinker," she admits. "But I like this chardonnay. It tastes like butter."

"They might have a keg of Natural Light or something in the back."

She's not sure whether I'm being funny or if I'm insulting her, so she settles in her chair and tries to decide.

"Pasternak picked the wine list," I say. "I don't know much about it."

"Not surprised." She blows a strand of hair from her face. She's got that look like if she slows down drinking for too long, she may just fall asleep. "Like I said. At least one of you has taste."

"He's a smart guy," I agree. "Probably oughta be paying him twice what he's making."

"You're damn right." Her attention seems to focus now. She stops looking around the room like she's hunting for someone more interesting to talk to. When she steadies her eyes, they're on me. "Twice what he's making, at least."

"We'd be lost without him."

"I know that." She blinks. "You know that. This entire table knows that. Hell, the whole fucking room."

Our table stops talking to one another, or Eugene wraps up his catalogue of Southeast Indian hallucinogens.

"How long has he worked for us?" I ask.

"Ten goddamn years," she says. "A whole decade."

Drunk as she is, her accent is coming through, so thick it's comical. She's just a broad from Bridgeport, in the end. But she's tried hard to distance herself from that place.

"And you don't appreciate it," she says. "You never have. You take him for granted. You treat him like an old, smelly sweatshirt."

I raise my hands, innocent. "I just agreed he was indispensable."

"Then where's the money?" She raises her voice so the table next to ours stops their conversation. "What's that movie, with the Black guy, Cuba Gooding, Jr.? 'Show me the money.'"

"Tom Cruise," Penny offers.

"Show me the money!" Robin pounds the table, and her plate jumps. "Show us the money, JAG."

Sometimes, you start messing with something just to see what happens. A blackhead, say. Or a cat at a friend's house, when the friend leaves the two of you alone for a moment. Seeing if you can make it bite its own tail, just because it's there. But this has gone better than I hoped. I've wound her up, and now she's off, like a pull-back toy racecar.

"You don't appreciate him," she says. "You don't pay him what he's worth. You're so cheap, it's amazing anybody works for you. This fall, he saved your asses. All of your asses." She stands, gestures with her wine glass, sweepingly, to indicate the others in the room who are listening, which is everyone. "And what kind of thanks does he get? You hire some Mexican teeny bopper instead of promoting my husband and paying him what he's worth."

"I'm Puerto Rican." Stefany calls out from across the room, but everyone at her table is already laughing, including her.

"El Quota!" some of the guys shout to her, but it's all love now, nothing but love.

"So, all the good ideas are your husband's?" I ask.

"That's right."

"And all the shitty ideas are whose...mine?"

She pokes the table for emphasis. "All of you, you'd be jobless, out on the street, if it wasn't for Pasternak. You owe him your livelihoods. The fucking food you eat. Each time you stuff a hundred up some stripper's crotch, you should be thanking my husband you're not out looking for a job. And you—" she indicates me, "Mr. High and Mighty. Mr. Big Shot. Strutting around. Your ideas are shit. I know that. My husband knows that. Everyone in this room knows that all you do is take all the good ideas that everyone else has and keep them for yourself. Face it: you made your fortune in the nineties, when any monkey with a dartboard could have picked stocks and made money. How's it been since, huh? Pretty shitty, right? I know, because Pasternak shows me the books. And what kind of thanks does he get? Not a one. *Nada*. Not even a fucking raise. Sure, we get a bonus, sure. But no raise. No promotion. You're so greedy—you know what you are? You're just like this little leprechaun, hording his little pot of gold, bopping around and pretending to be friends with everyone. Pretending we're family. Fucking...pirates. You can't sweet talk your way into convincing the leprechaun to show you where that pot of gold is hidden. You have to snatch that little fucking leprechaun and string him up by his toes and beat it out of him!"

I think for a moment she might leap across the table and try to do just that. But then it's like she sobers up, suddenly, and realizes the room has fallen stone-dead fucking silent, and everyone is watching her. Sure, she slurred her words so badly only half of what she said was even fucking intelligible, but I think most people got the drift.

I gesture toward Robin, for the benefit of the room, a gesture that says, *And there you have it.* In this gesture is the entirety of my friendship with Pasternak and the differences between us. He has never been able to separate himself from the neighborhood we grew up in. On some fucked up, subconscious level, Robin is part of that. In case anyone was wondering whether Mr. and Mrs. Pasternak had found some class, some decency, some notion of how to comport oneself, the answer is they haven't. And in this gesture, she understands how much of her husband's professional stagnation can be traced directly back to her.

We hear a door open and close out in the hall. Moments later, Pasternak strides into the dining room. He bounds down the steps and is halfway to his chair before he stops and notices no one is saying anything—that in fact, all eyes are on him. He checks his fly, wipes his mouth, glances at his wife, who sits there, leaning her full weight on the back of the chair next to her, glaring at him. Then he completes what he set out to do, takes his napkin off his place setting, where a server has charmingly folded it in his absence, and sits.

"Great dinner." He pulls himself closer to the table. "What'd I miss?"

It's a funny thing about marriage, or the people we end up married to. How we know one another's liabilities from the very start. Robin, for example. She's always had a mouth. And very little social etiquette. She just wasn't raised with any. Objectively, she's actually come a long way. But each of us, we're so blinded by love, or sex, that we decide the steep downside in our partner simply isn't important. Or we believe it can be overcome. Or we tell ourselves one day our partner will change. Just as Pasternak has chosen to overlook the fact that Robin's a social ticking time bomb, we move forward, and are surprised when our partner does not, in fact, change. That instead they seem to become even more set in their ways. And then those liabilities, which we've been aware of from the start, begin costing us things like promotions and invitations and friends and extra income—like fissures in the earth, those liabilities widen until one day they split, rupture, and sink our entire operation.

I pick something out of my teeth and set my napkin beside my plate.

I turn to Penny. "I hear this museum has special windows, designed by Chagall. Do you know Chagall?"

She nods, a bit afraid to look at me, it seems, or embarrassed for me—or Robin. The situation's awkward as hell. I don't blame her.

"They're supposed to have the gallery open for us. Would you like to wander over and take a look at them with me?"

She nods again. I rise and offer my hand. She takes it. At full height, she's a solid head taller than me. In my defense, she's wearing four-inch heels. I lead her through the round-tops, past my still-silent employees, up the stairs, and out of the room.

"At ease," I tell them all. "As you were."

There's another options strategy, pretty basic, called a Married Put. Works like an insurance policy. Say you own an asset. In a Married Put, you'll purchase a put option for an equivalent number of shares. Married Puts are good when you're really bullish on an asset, but maybe you don't entirely trust yourself, so you want to establish a floor, in case you're wrong and the asset tanks instead of flies away. We have these in real life, of course. Prenuptials, for example, which I should have fucking signed before I married my ex. Life insurance, in a kind of morbid way, works the same. You think you're going to live to a hundred, and make a million a year until you retire, but in the off-chance you don't, you have disability and life insurance.

Sometimes you're watching a sporting event and you're aware of it being something you'll never forget, even while it's happening: you know you'll watch it on *ESPN Classic* for years to come. Robin's diatribe was like that. I hope to Christ one of my millennials got the whole thing on video, because if not, what the fuck else are they good for? That's the dank shit. She created an instant classic.

I'm not bothered by it, not in the least. I know Pasternak is unhappy, thinks he's not getting recognized. And alcohol—with gals like Robin, it just opens up something they can't control. I feel worse for Pasternak. When someone finally fills him in on everything that went down, he'll choke on his goddamn honey-crusted salmon.

I know it isn't personal. Marriages have secrets. And when you have a wife who doesn't know how to keep her trap shut, those secrets, those things said in private, spill out.

What bothers me, even as I maintain hold of Penny's hand, and she lets me, and I feel the warmth of her palm in mine, and maybe a little sweat between her fingers, is that there is no one in my life who would stand up for me the way Robin did for Pasternak. Maybe there never has been. Eugene, maybe. But what's that, the affections of an eighty-five year-old tycoon who sees you as an ATM and little more? It took courage to do what Robin did, fucking courage, even if it was liquid courage. It's the purest example of devotion I've seen since *Iris*.

We hedge our bets all the time. Whoever has your back, they're your Married Put. I got no one like that.

Penny and I pass dim galleries of vaguely recognizable works of art. Growing up in Chicago, Polish or not, you come to know your Who's Who in Polish History. Kandinsky for one, his paintings splattered across the walls here like the American flag puked up forty ounces of freedom. Another canvas, by a different artist, consumes an entire wall. The image, of a park scene along a riverbank, mid-nineteenth century, is made entirely of microscopic dots of paint. The two-dimensionality of it fails to move me. As do all period pieces, if I'm being honest. The minute I see a bodice or parasol, I change the fucking channel. But I appreciate how, in this particular painting, which of course I've seen before, though I couldn't tell you what it's called, the aggregate is greater than the individual parts. Still, we walk swiftly past. Most walls are in shadow, due to our being in the museum after-hours.

"What a treasure," Penny sighs. I look behind us to see if maybe she's referring to a specific piece, but the comment seems general. "Do you collect?"

I pat my belly. "The only things I collect are pounds."

She grins. "I'd love to have enough to one day collect art. Fill entire walls with it."

"What's stopping you?"

"Oh you know," she says. "Hundreds of thousands of dollars in school loans, for one."

I tilt my head, and she follows my direction toward a sign pointing us to the Chagall Windows. "You're better off. I don't really believe in hard assets."

She says it back to me with a certain edge in her voice. "Some people refer to them as masterpieces. Impossible to value. Or put a price on."

"Yet people do."

Jeanie's art teacher, back when she was in third or fourth grade, I remember her pretty well, because it was one of the few things my ex-wife and I agreed on then. At parent-teacher night, the art teacher, this flaky, patchouli-drenched sprite with uncombed hair, welcomed us to the studio. It was an art room, like any other, but she called it a *studio*. And she showed us evaluation sheets, the criteria she would use to grade our children.

"It's art," I remember saying to her, and a few parents nodded their heads. "Isn't it, by its very definition, subjective?"

"You'll notice I'm not grading them on whether or not I like what they've created." She beamed back at me. "Or whether or not it moves me. Instead, I am looking for mastery of certain artistic skills. And if not mastery, at least an understanding."

She would grade them on things such as shading, color balance, proficiency with various tools, and of course, imagination.

But my ex-wife and I talked about her all the way home. Get over yourself, we wanted to say. You're teaching elementary art in a private school in Chicago. You've sold out. The kids you teach are future lawyers or engineers. There's no angst. There's no establishment to fight against. You *are* the establishment. Give everyone a fucking A and let's get on with our lives.

I am aware, suddenly, of Penny no longer walking beside me. I cross a kind of wooden gangplank, and then realize I'm standing right in front of them: the Chagall Windows. Penny has stopped at the foot of the walkway, to absorb the glass from the entrance. But the lights seem too bright. I was expecting something more subdued, more carefully down-lit.

"These always make me think of *Ferris Bueller*," she says.

I lift one eyebrow. "Maybe you've seen that movie in re-runs."

She folds her arms. "I'm old enough to remember watching it on Betamax."

"Bullshit."

"Never ask a woman's age, Jonathan."

The Chagall Windows are three roughly 6' x 6' glass panels, hung side by side. Each panel is itself composed of smaller squares. These are bisected by what I always think of as the stained-glass look, irregular shapes cutting across several fields, the background fragmented. There are painted scenes, homages to the benefits of public works. A very art-deco point of view, very Ayn Rand, in my opinion, despite the fact these were created in the seventies. The human forms are watery, uneven, like a child's drawing. The colors have faded over the years. There's a silver dove of peace flying high above the sky-line.

"Pretty optimistic, given the period," I say.

"How so?" She moves toward me, touching her chin in the manner of someone appreciating a piece of art they've yet to form an opinion about. She smells amazing in this closed space. Her shampoo is a wash of honeysuckle, and there's something earthy and sweet beneath that seems to be unlocking whatever synapses are connected directly to my dick.

"The seventies," I say. "There was a recession then too. Vietnam. Gas lines in some states."

"Disco."

"Yes," I laugh. "Later, but yes. Fucking disco."

"I like the fashion back then."

"I appreciate the hemlines, anyway."

She moves to the third panel. Blue light falls across her throat, her collarbone, the turn of her wrist. She points to where a ring of children hold hands. One of them seems to be placing a bet on a roulette wheel.

"You're right that this is meant to be optimistic," she says. "The seventies brought a kind of renaissance of public art in Chicago. People had this sense that art should be for the people, of the people. Accessible. The Picasso in Daley Plaza?"

I shrug. "I can picture it, I think. I didn't know it was Picasso."

"Installed around the same time." She stares at the windows, chin raised. Her eyes are the same color as the dress that one of the children wears, which matches the emerald cuts in the center of the circle. "And that's not a roulette wheel."

Busted. "I'm not judging."

"I minored in art history."

But something catches my eye in the center panel. A somewhat ghostly, female face wears a kind of Amish skull cap. She seems to be enveloped in flames, or perhaps by a rapidly growing, leafy vine. Someone off-canvas is handing this woman a thespian mask. The giver is unseen, only the person's two legs, and his or her hand, reaching with the mask. Around the central figure, the glass seems both to be moving toward her and also blowing out from her, like an eddy in a river.

"Ok, art major," I say.

"Minor."

"Why is this little person off-camera here handing this bigger person, who's obviously in distress, the kind of mask you'd wear to a party at Stanley Kubrick's house?"

Penny considers. She has this tick of pulling in her bottom lip with her teeth. "You think she's in distress?"

"She's on fire."

"I'm not sure." She points, outlining the movement in the glass, the way the outer panels are checked like white bearskin, or peacock feathers. "She may be handing the mask to the person who's falling off-camera."

"I hadn't thought of that."

"The central figure, this woman, the image speaks to me of transformation. Of some kind. Whether pleasant or painful—interpret it how you like—things are going to be different for her, moving forward."

"She's giving away her mask."

"She doesn't need it anymore."

I find myself reaching for where Penny's hair, which resembles amber in this light, has tumbled a bit from where she had it pinned. I pick it up gently, revealing a startling and tender expanse of skin—her neck, a blue vein, a diamond stud flashing on her ear. Instinctively, she reaches up, touches my hand. I freeze, then she does, and then apologizes.

"No," I take my hand away. "That was too forward."

The moment has gone. I notice she's flushed, and I don't think it's the light. I've never seen her flustered in the least, or even impatient.

She saves the moment by pointing again to the half-person on the window, below the flaming woman, who seems to be rearing away from the canvas, mask in hand. "If you've ever been on television, then you know you can never trust what's happening just off-camera."

I try to compose myself. My heart is about to leap out of my fucking chest. The way her skin looks.

"They don't put guys as ugly as me on television," I say.

She tells me the summer after she graduated college, just prior to law school, she got scouted at a Cubs game and wound up a contestant on a reality show called *ElimiDate*. I haven't heard of it, but the premise was that one guy or gal starts off on a date with three or four women or men and then eliminates one date per round until, presumably, he or she is left with the one he or she wants to go home with. Each round is a different kind of date activity, putt-putt or a fancy dinner. Penny's first round found her shoulder-to-shoulder with the other contestants in the Wrigleyville bar, Sluggers, defending why she would never sleep with a man on her first date against three slutty, overly made-up Jills, shooting So-Co and lime between turns in the slow-pitch softball batting cage upstairs.

"I was first cut," she laughs. "The guy decided I must be a virgin, and that was it."

"You're not enough of a narcissistic asshole to win a show like that," I tell her.

She admits that for all the scenes, the different date locales, the one-on-one camera confessionals, there was always a fully stocked bar just off-screen, that is, if they didn't happen to be filming in an actual bar, where their own private bartender slung drinks as quickly as they could throw them back. From eight in the morning until taping ended sometime after dinner, producers plied the contestants with liquor, swapping out empty glasses for full ones between takes. The theory being that people do some crazy-ass shit when they're drunk. Alcohol brings out all your basest, most competitive urges, and you get closer to the raw, primitive emotion that makes a person impossible to live with but makes for fucking fantastic television.

"The producers feed you lines," she says. "They ask you to say a line with one kind of emotion, and then say it again with a different emotion, and then they splice it all together back in the studio, so they can make you look however they want to make you look—like the virgin, like the girl next door, like the slut. You know, there's all these types that viewers respond to."

I look again at the Chagall Windows. I'm coming around to Penny's interpretation, the character falling away off-screen, grasping for the mask of the muse exploding in front of him.

She cocks her head, absorbing the painting one last time. We oughta be getting back, or people will talk. Not that they aren't talking already. "Your turn."

"My turn?" I try to take a sip of my drink but find it empty. Swear to God if I could have one super power, I'd be able to make any kind of drink appear in my hand the moment I wanted it—I'm always fucking dying of thirst. "My turn for what?"

She turns and moves closer to me. Our legs brush. She leans against the rail, backlit by the light through the blue windows, bursts of color erupting around her head. She has my total attention.

"Tell me a secret," she says.

She leans forward, and we kiss. I taste her breath, not only the pinot grigio, but the essence of her breath, warm and full of her spirit. I consider the flaming woman on the stained-glass window, about the mask she drops as she ascends. I consider the real possibility that these lips, pressed against mine, pliable as an offering, might be my last shot for something legitimate. That if I could toss away my own mask, my own armor, and explode into fire, what a fucking relief that would be.

Chapter 12

Monday morning, I step off the "L" with three women wearing Santa hats. They scurry across the platform and down the stairs. In the breezeway, a guy rings a bell for the Salvation Army. The worst kind of graft, if you ask me, this city-sanctioned begging, imagine if every non-profit had a permit to stand on the sidewalks with hand instruments. Inside the lobby, wrapped presents are piled beneath a Christmas tree and blue menorah. The ornaments are color Kodaks of our charity work, the families we help through United Way and Habitat, the youth leagues affiliated with the Cubs. It's good PR to remind the world we're not such greedy bastards after all, at least not all the time.

Rolling through the revolving doors, I'm feeling pretty good for once. Maybe the markets get a little bump before the New Year, and we start climbing our way out of this downturn. I mosey up the escalator to the mezzanine, then cross to the escalators that lead to the pits.

I send Penny a text. "Found ur earring on the bathroom sink."

I get her reply just as my feet hit the trading floor. "Working."

Fair enough, fair enough.

We spent the weekend together. Saturday night became Sunday morning brunch at the Sofitel, then a matinee at Chicago Shakes, something she happened to have tickets for, Pirandello's *Henry IV*, which turned out to be a lot of young men of questionable sexual orientation wearing tights and belted blouses, prancing around medieval set dressing, although I followed the story well enough. Penny finally went home about ten o'clock last night because she wanted to sleep in her own bed, alone, in order to be fresh for work this morning.

Additional weekend highlights include Jeanie being out of town at a basketball tournament in Lansing, and Robin—fucking Robin, of all people—blowing up my phone with voicemail after voicemail, none of which I listened to. I'm sure she sobered up come Sunday morning and realized the fucking horror of what she'd done, calling out her husband's boss in front of the entire firm. I'm sure she was trying to apologize. Well, fuck her. I'm not going to let her feel better by permitting her to say sorry. I'm inclined to let her stew in her own shit for a while. Once Jeanie was back midday Sunday, I turned my fucking phone off.

Penny though—you never really know someone until you kiss them for the first time. You can be physically attracted to a person, they might even make you laugh, or be your intellectual equal, but until your lips are on their lips, nothing's certain. Contained in that first kiss is the DNA for the entire relationship. If the kissing doesn't work, nothing else will either. Not only the romance, but the day-to-day logistics of being with another person all the goddamn time. A kiss is, empirically, not just a kiss, despite what the song says. I've smooched women who shoved their tongues down my throat like they were trying to taste my tonsils, swirling their tongues in my mouth like a goldfish spiraling down a toilet bowl; I've kissed women who tried to swallow my face with one bite, teeth gnashing like Audrey II from *Little Shop of Horrors*; I've kissed women so stiff it was like putting my nose against plywood. None of them worked out.

I'm no Don Juan. I get mine—less than most guys in my position, to be honest, since motivation is a major factor in how much play you get, and my motivation, in this regard, is basically nil due to hours at work, lack of sleep, a teenage daughter I'm now charged with keeping off the street, etc. But rules of civility apply.

Open your lips a little bit, because you don't kiss your boyfriend the same way you kiss your brother. Stop doing that thing with your teeth. And like many things in life, a little moisture goes a long way.

I've always considered the tongue the nuclear option. There's a place for it, sure. But the tongue should be employed diplomatically. Everyone's got one, and a happy trigger finger just makes all of us jumpy.

Penny was perfect. The smell of her shampoo was creamier, up close. As in most aspects of her life, she was neat, conscientious, and correct.

Kissing is the first hurdle. There's usually another one later, when you've got the person comfortable enough so you're eyeball to eyeball. Maybe things haven't progressed too far. Most of your clothes may even still be on. While the two of you share the same pocket of air, a little television light maybe, in the background, or streetlamps outside through the window shades, reveal your Janus Face.

This is not an expression of ecstasy, but something quieter, more still. The Janus Face reveals the side of us we keep hidden, our most vulnerable expression, the true revelation of who we are. Neither good nor bad, the Janus Face is a window. And windows are, by their nature, completely neutral.

I stopped dating a girl once because her Janus Face reminded me of a badger. Suddenly, pressed against her, that's all I could see. Her forehead too wide, her eyes dark and beady. From then on, even in daylight, all she reminded me of was a small, woodland creature. I had to cut her loose. On the other hand, my ex-wife became even more beautiful. She's gorgeous anyway, quick to smile and a bit shy about the things she finds funny, but her Janus Face was regal and serious like some kind of Persian royalty, like she should have been floating in a barge down the Karun, beneath a canopy of stars.

It floored me, every time.

Penny—she's fastidious by day. One of those perfectly pulled-together people. But in that first moment with her, our eyelashes fluttering against one another, whatever side of her personality that let her minor in art was revealed as some carnal sprite, devilish, a bit wild, totally irresistible. Needless to say, she passed the Janus Face test.

As for not sleeping with a guy on her first date, that may have been true when she was twenty-three, but she showed no such hang-up when the moment came to tear open the blue Trojan pack, unfurl the latex, and roll it onto my cock. Honestly, she slapped it on me with an alarmingly practiced hand. I thought to comment, then thought better of it. I didn't want to know, not really, and only a complete idiot would kill the moment to ask a question like that.

I'm a lot of things, but I'm no idiot.

We paid close attention to one another's bodies. Instructing, adapting, learning. This is one advantage to aging: more confidence to ask for what you want. Also, the humility to learn. This has a lot to do with me. I resolved to be more open with Penny. To adjust. I am committed to this new tact. And it went better than planned. When she finally came, thrusting her hips off the bed and grabbing her left ass cheek, I thought to myself, Jesus Christ, I might very well be in love with this woman.

The only time I ever tried cocaine was like that—I immediately swore I'd never do it again. The very moment that thirty-second high was over, I wanted another bump. Seeing Penny lose herself like that—I wanted it again too, right away. Because of the abandon. Because she crinkles her toes when something feels good. Because she tastes like an oyster.

So, I descend the escalator feeling pretty goddamn decent for once, which I know better than to trust—in fact, I should be wondering what's coming around the corner. I realize something's amiss the moment I hit the trading floor.

Pasternak has arrived before me every day for a decade. This morning, none of my guys, including my clerk, are here. Fucking pit is totally empty.

Ezra scurries by, on his way back from making a delivery. I ask him what today is.

"December 22, Mr. Ganzi."

"It's not April?"

"No sir."

"April 1?"

"Not as far as I know, sir."

"Then where the fuck are my guys?"

I log-in, check the news. I keep glancing at my watch. Plenty of absurd scenarios cross my mind: a flu outbreak, or Pasternak having unwittingly granted vacation time to our entire firm. At ten minutes until seven, I see one of my traders at the top of the escalator. I'm just as baffled as I am pissed.

I text Pasternak. "Shall I expect you at work today?"

I open my calendar, wondering if I've missed a breakfast meeting, but I got nothing. I look again. More of my guys have filed in, but no one's come down yet. They're all just waiting up there, all of them wearing shit-eatin' grins. Once my entire fucking firm is leaning over the rail, they turn and, as one, file down the escalator.

First one to hit the floor is Stefany Vázquez. She carries what appears to be a cereal box. As does the guy behind her.

"Good morning, boss." She strides right up to me and places the box on my desk. Then she hops down the steps and takes her position in the pit.

"Mornin', boss." The second trader steps up and plunks down his cereal box.

Then a third, one of my senior guys, shakes the cereal box he carries to a kind of island rhythm and dumps it in my lap.

Lucky Charms.

One by one, my guys drain into the trading pit, but not before depositing an 11.5 ounce box of Lucky Charms on my desk. The boxes keep coming. My employees set Lucky Charms at my feet, on my lap, in Pasternak's empty seat. In short order, the trading desk is overrun by that blue-eyed, red-haired Leprechaun boy, decked out in green scarf and derby hat, juggling a rainbow of marshmallow shapes: purple horseshoe, blue crescent moon, pink heart. A few of the boxes are different. On these, the same pre-pubescent Mick hurls a yellow marshmallow at the viewer, beneath the tagline, *New Hourglass!* A just-released marshmallow shape, a lemon-colored implement that has been used to mark the passage of time since Jesus was a boy. "Like sand in the hourglass" and all that existential drama—it seems appropriate.

"Very funny." I manage to look like I'm enjoying myself. "Who's the wise guy?"

The traders keep coming in, the boxes pile up. Other pits take notice and stand on the rim, laughing. Meanwhile, images of maniacal leprechauns stack up around me, the gaping smile and pitched eyebrows replicated thirty or forty times.

Growing up, the Lucky Charms mascot wasn't a leprechaun boy but a giant man-wizard in black Chuck Taylors—as a Southside kid, I sort of thought of him as one of our own. It was a big deal when they added blue diamonds. It was all over the television. Weeks of anticipation. Boxes flying off the shelves. That frosted-oat cereal was a staple at our house. For years, it's all I'd eat.

Sometimes you don't have to look too far for the root of all your troubles. Sugary blue diamonds are no doubt responsible for my borderline diabetes and my obsession with riches.

Finally, the parade ends. Everyone settles. I can't move without kicking over a box of Lucky Charms. I'm buried in cereal. And my guys, all of them, are laughing, giving each other high-fives and fist-bumps, pretty goddamn pleased with their prank. I grin, wryly, and run my finger beneath one of the cardboard flaps, the corrugated edge sharp against my knuckles, and pop open the box. I withdraw the thick, plastic bag, grab both corners, and pull open the seal. A blast of trapped air hits me, carrying with it the smell of sugar and space-food marshmallows, but damned if it doesn't speed me right back to the house I grew up in, our kitchen table, my father's voice reading betting odds to my mom and me, the way the newspaper snapped as he folded it in thirds.

I plunge my hand inside the box. I shake a fistful of cereal into my mouth. I chew, aping for my guys, and act like it's the best fucking thing I've ever tasted. They love it, of course—everyone is cheering. I play along, chewing with my mouth open, tossing marshmallows in the air and catching them with my teeth, then catching only some so the bits and pieces hit my face and scatter. Honest to god, some things don't stand the test of time—*Dukes of Hazzard* or The Outfield—but Lucky Charms still taste magically delicious.

I stand on my stool and fling handfuls of Lucky Charms across the trading pit like scattering seed. Some reach up to snag a piece or two; others try to catch the marshmallows in their mouths. I open another box and sling cereal like fertilizer. The air is filled with Lucky Charms dust: blue and pink and green. The particles drift toward the ceiling, lit by floodlights, the air infused with sugar like a psychedelic dust-storm.

All of this, of course, because of what Pasternak's wife, Robin, called me at the party on Saturday night. "You're a leprechaun," she said. "We oughta string you up."

As I said at the time, an instant classic.

When I've opened four or five boxes and sown their contents across the trading pit, I applaud my firm, their ingenuity. "If anyone wants some cereal to take home—"

They applaud me too, laughing, brushing pixie soot off their shoulders, picking hard bits of marshmallow out of their hair. Every footstep brings with it the grind and squeak of cereal being pulverized. Guys from other pits swing by and snag an unopened box on their way past.

"Thieves!" I shout at them.

They turn on me, popping open the box and tucking it under their arm. "Hey, I got kids!"

Everyone's in a good mood, buoyed by the prank and the fact that it's a short week, what with the Christmas holiday coming up. I hand out boxes of Lucky Charms to pretty much anybody who comes by. I keep an eye on my phone, but there's nothing from my clerk. I decide we must have talked about him taking the day off, and I've just forgotten about it.

I tap one of my guys on the shoulder. "No Pasternak?"

He shakes his head. "I can't believe he missed this."

It occurs to me to buy a position in GIS. With a few quick strokes of my stylus, I put in a stop-order for 3,000 shares. I purchase these as soon as the markets open, which they do, right on time, the way they do each day, reliable as gravity.

Chicago blues always catch my eye. Mid-morning, I see a familiar face on the mezzanine: Lucas.

He scans the trading pit. He gives me a little nod and heads down the escalator. It's not completely out of the ordinary for him to be here. We're on his beat. Given the hour, I figure he's come by to see if I want to grab lunch.

"Lieutenant." I offer him a box of Lucky Charms. "Had breakfast yet?"

He takes the cereal. "What is this?"

"My guys had a little fun."

You have to hand it to Chicago cops: nothing impresses them. He leans past me, takes in the mound of cereal boxes, and his expression barely changes, just a quick eyebrow-raise, and then he hands the box back to me. Guys like Lucas, they've seen fucking everything. "Got a minute?"

"Sure."

I tell somebody I'll be right back. Then Lucas and I head up the escalator to the mezzanine.

I know something's up because he won't look at me. He keeps adjusting the weights on his belt, the handcuffs and baton, the gun.

"Bring back memories?" I ask.

"What, being here?"

"You miss this place. Be honest."

He blows out a long, slow breath. "I've seen some crazy shit, doing what I do. Stuff that'd give most guys nightmares. But honestly? I have a nightmare now? Say I have one of my stress dreams? I'm right back here. Stuff like, you know, the markets are open, but I can't find my pit. Or I'm in the pit, but I'm being suffocated by beefy white guys in trader jackets. I wake up gasping for air, sweating through my shirt. Trying to trade but none of the numbers make sense, and all the little digits are flying across the screens—off the screens, sometimes. Like lemmings over a cliff. You know that story?"

"Lemmings, sure."

"Anyway, stuff I do now, as a cop? It's fine. It's not always pretty, but it's fine. This place, though? Man. You couldn't pay me enough to come back and work here."

We reach the top. There's a small cafeteria. It's quiet, pre-lunch. Dim.

"Coffee?" I ask.

"No, I'm good. Let's sit."

There are a couple traders I don't know, reading the paper or staring off into space, their days already cooked. A wall of block windows lets in some fucking daylight occasionally, and Lucas and I take a table beneath it. I don't usually eat here. Food's ok, but the place reminds me of an airport lounge, that same cold transience. Like all of us might be here now, but we've got one eye on the clock. Soon as that sand fills up the bottom of the hourglass, we're gone.

"What's up?" I ask once we're seated.

He places his hands on the table, leans forward. "How you doing, JAG?"

"You're freaking me out, man. I gotta tell you."

He swallows, seems about ready to say something, then looks away.

"Jesus, Lucas. What? Is it Jeanie?"

He looks surprised, then shakes his head. "No, no. Jean's fine. This isn't about Jeanie."

I collapse, hand on my heart, waiting for it to slow the fuck down, the rhythm. Anything else seems manageable, so long as she's ok.

"It's DIP," Lucas says.

It takes me a minute. "Pasternak?"

"We found him this morning."

I'm imagining a strip club, him passed out in a booth when the lights come on. "Found him where?"

"No." He looks me straight in the eyes for the first time. "One of our guys. A couple guys, actually. They dragged him out of the river this morning."

His words eventually parse themselves out inside my brain, so I understand their meaning. "What the fuck was he doing in the river?"

I have a sensation like there's this Ferris wheel inside me. And one of the cars, it's filled with panic. Another car is filled with dread. There are more cars: sorrow, regret. And as the Ferris wheel turns, the cars make a slow, merciless arc from my bowels to the base of my throat. I recognize panic at the apex of the wheel, then sorrow—so much I choke back a sob. Then sorrow drops through my stomach, launching dread up through my rib cage. The sensation nearly pitches me off the chair.

"We don't know," Lucas says. "We don't know if maybe he fell—"

"Is he okay?"

Lucas shakes his head. "No, JAG. That's what I'm telling you. The medics, they went through the drill, on the spot. But by the time they arrived—there was nothing to do."

"Nothing to do," I repeat.

"He's gone, John. Dead."

I jump to my feet. I pat down my pockets like I'm looking for my keys. "Fuck."

I can't find my phone. I must have left it in the pit. "Fuck."

I take three steps toward the escalator, then return to the table and sit down. Then I'm up again, but Lucas reaches out, puts two hands on my shoulders, and steadies me into the chair.

"Breathe," he tells me.

Time takes on a stuttering quality. I hear his words, but I process images as still-shots. Across the lounge, a worker in a hairnet empties the trash, spinning the bag twice before knotting it. Two traders pass, one showing the other his BlackBerry, both of them laughing. Lucas has a circular BAND-AID on the back of his hand, like he's had a wart removed.

"It's lucky in some ways," the cop is saying. "Somebody saw him go in. We knew where to search. With the water as cold as it is, say he goes in by himself, he may not turn up again for a month, if ever."

I swallow, looking at my one-time progeny, wondering if this fucking guy has lost all sense of humanity. "Who saw him go in?"

"Some kid. Just happened to be on the bridge with his girlfriend. Saw a dude acting strange, next thing he knew, DIP was in the water."

I study each of his words: body, river, strange. I try to pin these words on Pasternak.

"That's all off-record," Lucas says. "Nobody's supposed to know that yet."

"We were together on Saturday," I say. "Our holiday party."

He takes out a little spiral notebook and pen. "The whole firm?"

"Are you writing this down?"

"I need a statement from you, if that's okay."

I touch my forehead to the table briefly—cool, slick—then sit up again. "Yes, whole firm. At the Art Institute."

"He seem okay to you?"

He seemed like Pasternak. "Robin was there. Everyone had fun."

"He didn't say anything to you? Anything unusual?"

"No."

"Anything happen that night, that you're aware of?"

Images erupt like gunfire on the backs of my eyes: a cocktail glass, sloshing its brown contents over the side; Robin standing at our table, pointing; Pasternak strolling in moments after like he was the only animate being in a roomful of wax dummies.

"No," I say. "Nothing I can remember."

Lucas nods. "You—everyone—was pretty lit."

It strikes me suddenly that this man, who I plucked out of the ghetto and heaped riches upon, only to have him reject the majesty I handed him, not that I was expecting to be thanked, but still, is now really and truly a Chicago cop. He has not come to my place of employment as a friend—not strictly. He's a police officer first. Maybe, I think, only.

Those calls yesterday—Robin wasn't calling to apologize. She was looking for her husband.

"Does Robin know?" I ask.

"I just came from there."

"I appreciate you giving this the, your, personal touch. Seeing it gets done. It means a lot that all this, it's coming from you. Someone who knew him."

"Ain't no thing."

We sit for a moment. Nothing is said. He's waiting for me, and I'm waiting for him.

"Unless...?"

"Hmmm?" he asks.

"Unless I'm under investigation—"

"No." He tucks his notebook back into his vest, his pen. "I just wanted to come down here, let you know."

He stands, then I stand, and we shake hands.

"He asked me for a raise," I tell him. "A promotion."

"Did you give it to him?"

"No." The wheel turns faster now, so I can't distinguish all the shitty things I'm feeling. "I told him wait until the summer, then we'll see."

His walkie-talkie makes a noise. He peers down at it like it's an insolent child that won't stop squawking and switches it off.

"Long night," he says. Then, "You know, when I was working here, there'd be mornings I'd be walking in, I'd feel physically ill. Sick to my stomach, man, about what the day would bring. It started in the lobby. Up the escalator, across this cafeteria, the whole time like I was walking into a gale-force wind. Feeling sicker and sicker, the closer I got to the pits. That was pressure, JAG. Pushing against me. By the time I hit the floor, it was like I was walking with twenty-pound weights on my shoes. I could never catch my breath. I always had the feeling like I was watching myself work this job, going through the motions, not keyed in at all."

"You were a good trader." I shake my head. "I never would have guessed."

"Friday nights I'd get home so wired, I'd shut my door and collapse. I'd do nothing all weekend, just so I'd be ready to roll again Monday morning."

Despite the circumstances that have brought him here, I feel a kind of fatigue. If he couldn't hack it, he couldn't hack it. "Being a cop is different?"

"Honest to God, John, I sleep like a baby." He smiles sadly, then turns. He gets halfway to the escalator. "Except when I'm dreaming about this place."

People smarter than me claim there are six stages of grief. That may well be true. But for the rest of the day, interacting with my guys, braving an interminable floor director meeting after the closing bell, walking home in some kind of stormy, wintry mix because I desperately need to air out, I combat a maelstrom of clichéd and overwrought emotions.

The idea that I will live differently now, in his honor, occurs to me a dozen times over the course of the day. I have a vivid daydream, utterly ridiculous, of taking Robin in and providing for her, as he would have. I jot notes for the founding of a suicide prevention education program for grades 9-12. I resolve to crack down on our behavior in the pit, to build a culture of support instead of whatever spiral of psychosis we exist in now.

None of these, of course, will ever happen.

Those moments your life resembles something out of a movie, when there's true drama, your subconscious searches its memory bank for the appropriate response. But the difficult times, the heretofore never experienced, leave little for our subconscious to draw from, other than what we've seen in films. There's no precedent. No previous experience to serve as a roadmap or provide a clue for how we're supposed to behave. So, we lean on what we've witnessed on the silver screen and turn our grief into a commodity, exchanging the humanity of our sadness for something celluloid.

On my way out the door, I pass Charlene, Sar's Executive Assistant, wearing a rain jacket and white tennis shoes. She opens her umbrella against the sleet. A gust of wind turns the fucking thing inside out. She doesn't hesitate: she hammers the umbrella on the sidewalk, cursing, and then hurls it into the street, her face a twisted mask of anger and frustration, her hair a frizzy, fucking mess.

I've been there. We all have. People have off-days. Hell, I've had off-years. That's the thing about living in a city. Everything is public. You throw a fit, 9,000 people notice, but they don't let it slow them down.

Most days, I'd stop to give her a hand. But not today.

I said nothing to my guys. Tomorrow, maybe. But not today. Because me getting up there, telling everyone to quiet down, all of them listening, waiting, in a vacuum of apprehension, would all be so much cliché. And Pasternak deserved—deserves, dammit—better.

Tomorrow, I'll say something. When I've had time to process. When the three-inch silt of Lucky Charms has been cleared away. Without that maniacal leprechaun staring at me, that nimble figure from Irish folklore who I've always viewed as a kind of evil spirit, as a harbinger of mischief, and of doom.

Chapter 13

Jeanie asks what's wrong as soon as I walk through the door. She's flopped sideways in the armchair, in what's become her favorite spot in the house, her nest. I slide off my shoes and come into the living room. She removes her headphones and asks if I'm okay.

I go to her, touch her socked foot, which is on the back of the chair. I think about when she was a girl, how warm her feet were. I'd take off her shoes, and her feet would be these little hot bricks.

I slide to the floor, to my knees. She swings around as if to catch me. I reach for her, and she brings me in. I bury my face in my daughter's lap. And weep.

The first apartment Azita and I shared was way up north, near the Green Mill. Back when that area was absolute sketch, beggars and prostitutes waiting for the rich, white concertgoers to get off the train at Lawrence, because the Avalon is up there too. Now, of course, the lesbians have moved in and turned the neighborhood around, but back then, you hustled from doorway to doorway, swept along by the cold.

I was taking the train each day to save money. One night, Northbound at Jackson, we sat for thirty minutes and didn't move. Finally, the doors opened again, that fresh tunnel air. Some passengers got off. Finally, I did too. Up on street level, all of us who'd been underground were trying desperately to hail cabs. But there were none, so we rushed below ground again, or tried to pack ourselves on busses that were already overflowing. Every sense heightened, all of us amped up with the anxiety of having our routine disrupted. That little bit of doubt, that uncertainty, caused our hearts to beat faster and to be impatient with one another. I walked about a mile and a half to Grand before finally catching a taxi north.

Turned out, someone had thrown themselves in front of a train at Irving. Shut the line down for hours while the police scraped body parts off the track, the windshield, the platform.

What struck me about that event, most of all, was how inconsiderate that was, for that person to kill themselves in a way that inconvenienced thousands of other citizens. At rush hour, no less.

If you're going to kill yourself, do it quietly. No mess.

Be a man.

Jeanie makes spaghetti with red sauce and ground beef and tendrils of onion.

"Where did you learn to cook?" I ask.

"Patrick used to work the grill at some bar downtown."

I shovel starchy noodles into my mouth, thinking that, at least, partly explains my ex-wife's attraction to him.

"I don't remember there ever not being a Pasternak," Jeanie says. "I mean, he's been around since I was little."

"He was the first one to give you a bottle, if you can believe it. Other than your mom and me."

She sets her plate aside. She digs her laptop from her backpack. She sits beside me at the counter, opens her computer, then Facebook. She searches her friends with deliberate strokes of her finger across the mousepad. She clicks on Pasternak's profile. *Dan-O*, it says.

"You two are Facebook friends?" I ask. "I don't think I'm even Facebook friends with Pasternak."

"I don't see him on here much," she says, scrolling.

And now she won't.

DIP's Facebook profile is already one long reel of RIPs and remembrances.

We lean forward together, Jeanie and I, close enough so her hair is against my cheek. We read the comments out loud. I recognize names. Co-workers and colleagues.

"So, this is what happens to your Facebook page after you die," Jeanie says. "It becomes a wailing wall."

I move her hand out of the way and take control of the mousepad. A lot of these names, I don't recognize. They're using nicknames for him I've never heard. I figure they're friends from old times—people he hasn't spoken to in a long time. Somehow Facebook makes it all seem immediate though, like you've never really lost touch. I resent their weepy posts and emoticons, as if anyone on here can come close to emoting something actually real.

"Does it ever get taken down?" she asks.

I wonder if I should post something. My fingers hover above the keys, the cursor flashing in the box with the standard prompt, *What's on Your Mind?*

Too much to list here.

I click a photo of him. He's standing on the court before a Bulls game, palming two basketballs, arms outstretched. I remember him talking about it the next day, how he sat courtside and spent the game chatting up Bill Murray, who happened to be there too. Some kind of vendor gift, VIP access.

All the photographs in the album are from that night. Maybe a few too many taken with the Luvabull girls, strictly speaking, for a married guy, but who could begrudge him some fun? There are other albums, from a ski vacation to Crested Butte, Colorado; from some kind of day-trip with his extended family, beneath blue skies on a Chicago architecture boat tour; far too many shots of him with Old Style beer, shooting hoops or throwing corn hole in his backyard. I slide so deep into the wormhole of photographs, I don't realize Jeanie's no longer paying attention.

The first time I met Pasternak, it was summer. He knocked on our door. His family was the new family on the block, the Poles. We were seven.

"Do you have any airplane parts?" he asked.

Even then, he was a giant. Taller than my mother, thick as a punching bag. His jeans had holes in the knees, and not because he thought it was cool.

"Are you building an airplane?" I asked him.

He said he was. He invited me to come see. What he'd done, in his backyard, was tape a couple of moving boxes together and scrawl *USA* in magic marker across the side. Some vinyl siding was lashed together and set apart, as the wings. But mostly, he'd been stockpiling ammunition.

He'd wrapped maybe thirty charcoal briquettes individually in newspaper and had stacked them like cannonballs, neatly, in a pyramid.

"What we'll do is," he said, "is fly over, light these on fire, and drop them on Charlie."

This was near the end of Vietnam. Everything was about the war still. His plan was to build a plane and bomb North Vietnam. With charcoal briquettes. Heaved from an airplane made of cardboard boxes.

"I can't help you build the plane," I told him. "But I have an idea about what we can do with those."

We gathered the charcoal and carried them out into the street. There was always an abandoned vehicle or two, especially in winter. A Pontiac hatchback had been parked for over a year on the corner, its tires squares, its windows covered in salt and grime. We layered briquettes below the car, then jimmied open the gas tank. We ran a rope—in our minds, a fuse—from the charcoal pile to the gas tank. I'd found a book of matches in one of my dad's old coats; we lit the charcoal pyramid and ran.

We crouched behind a mailbox, watching. The flames swelled as the briquettes lit. One after another. But just as the rope began to burn, a pair of men's shoes stepped off the sidewalk and scattered the coals, yanking the rope from the gas tank.

It was my father. We made eye contact, across our street. Once we did, I immediately knew two things. One, he was drunk. And two, we needed to run.

Pasternak and I were friends after that. Bosom buddies. All through school. Same year, moving up, playing sports, all that coming-of-age shit, double dates and sleepovers, camping trips to the Indiana Dunes, swiping beer from my old man—sometimes people called us by different names. Laurel and Hardy. Ganzi and Pasternak. We were mismatched but inseparable.

He went to work straight out of high school. The steel plant was pretty much gone at that point, so he did a lot of odd jobs. Construction. Painting barges. Physical stuff that was pretty far below his intellectual capabilities. Robin came later. She's maybe five, ten years younger. By then, I was starting my own firm. I offered him a job. He was a quick learner. Good with the money. Soon he was making more than he'd ever dreamed of making. We both were.

Now, with him dead, my parents dead, his mom long dead and his old man in a nursing home, so goes the last of the old neighborhood.

I'm the end of the line, in a manner of speaking.

No one will ever know me better.

If you were picking teams in kickball growing up, you knew if you got DIP, then you got me too. Times kids were dumb enough to put us on different squads, we threw the game into chaos, driving toward our own goals, stealing the ball from teammates.

Like losing one's shadow, Pasternak's improbable death is like a preview of my own. How easily things might have gone differently, in a slightly altered universe. It could have been me being pulled out of the river this morning. No question.

Police know they're dealing with a drowning by the position of the victim's hands. Most of us, when drowning, will grab for anything we can, hoping whatever we catch onto next will yank us to safety. When a body is pulled from the water, the police pry open the fists. Inside are usually mossy wisps from the river bottom, or trash, or sand, whatever was within reach while the victim was thrashing for life. Sometimes, the drowned will strain muscles in their backs and necks, or break ribs. The physical reaction to drowning is so strong, the body will sacrifice its non-essential parts in order to live. It clutches at empty sea. Sometimes, the hands are cut and bruised, or there are fingernails missing, from where the victim clawed at a pier or a retaining wall. Those last movements, arms flailing while the legs cycle, seeking purchase in an attempt to propel the body toward breathable air: are they the pro-active movements of someone who wants to live, or simply the reactions of someone trying to fend off the inevitable future?

I dial Robin. It goes straight to voicemail. I call every half-hour throughout the night. I don't reach her, and I don't leave a message.

Before things went south with Azita and me, the two of us, and Jeanie, we'd sometimes go to this Indian restaurant in Evanston, after Azita was done with classes. And instead of taking Lake Shore home, we'd take Clark. We enjoyed seeing the city that way, stop sign by stop sign.

One night, where Clark splits with Ashland, there were two cop cars blocking one lane, lights flashing. Lying in the middle of the street was a man about my age, in a coat and tie. He lay on his side, head resting on his arm. Blood on the ground. Lit by the cruisers and the streetlights.

"Is he dead?" Jeanie asked from the backseat.

I honestly didn't know.

"Don't say that word," I told her.

"What Daddy is trying to say," my ex-wife said, "is that you need to be sure what a word means before you use it."

Silence. Then, "Okay."

"So." Azita has always been an excellent teacher. "What does *dead* mean?"

More silence. Then, "It means you disappear."

I've thought about how I'd do it, of course. Struck by a terminal illness. Or facing life in prison.

A gun would be too gruesome. My family—nobody—should have to clean that up. Not to mention inexact. You hear all the time about people pulling the trigger, but their aim is off, so now instead of being dead they wind up blowing off half their face, and just like that, they're a vegetable for the rest of their goddamn life.

Truth is, anything that involves someone I know being the first to find my body is out, which eliminates hanging, pills, asphyxiation, and the classic bathtub wrist-slit. By these exacting standards, though, anything that inconveniences others is also off the table, such as the aforementioned hurling oneself in front of public transportation, or jumping from a great height, or death by police.

Pasternak, for all his flaws, did it close to perfect. Whether he considered it or not, drowning inconveniences only a few people who are paid to be inconvenienced by such things, and gives the person who initially discovers the body one helluva story to tell at dinner parties.

When my time comes, I'll drive somewhere east, up into Michigan. Plenty of forested land there, wild and untouched. I'll park my car off the road, away from traffic. I'll leave the keys in the ignition, with a close-to-full tank of gas. I'll carry with me a burlap sack, and a loaded pistol, and I'll walk naked into those woods. Once I disappear, I'll never be seen again.

Sometime in the night, I get up and turn on my desk lamp. I root through the piles and put my hands on the forms Penny gave me to write my Last Will & Testament.

There's a questionnaire. Do I want heroic measures taken in order to prolong my life? In the event of complete incapacitation, do I want to authorize someone to pull the plug? Do I have an heir in mind? No, yes, and yes.

I need an Executor, someone to oversee the business side of my passing, to make sure the money goes where it's supposed to and that my wishes are carried out. I start to write

Pasternak's name and reach the letter T before dropping the pen. The T ends in a curlicue, a bit of moon's ear trailing off down the page.

I also need someone to make my end-of-life decisions. Like my Executor, this position requires an ability to compartmentalize, to set aside one's personal feelings and do what they think I would have wanted, or have explicitly, legally outlined. I find myself wondering if Azita hates me enough to purposely prolong my life in a vegetative state just to fuck with me.

Finally, I write Penny's name down for both. It's either she or Eugene, and Jesus, if I don't outlive Eugene, who's got forty years on me at least, I've definitely fucked my Karma up something fierce and deserve whatever's coming. Regardless of whether Penny and I keep up our romantic explorations, she's the right cold bitch for the job.

I go into the living room. Thinking, hoping, Jeanie might still be awake. But it's dark.

I stand outside her bedroom, listening. I knock. I barely breathe. When she doesn't answer, I try the knob. It turns. She's asleep in her bed, giving herself over to slumber with the same abandon she's had since she was a toddler, head thrown back, arms splayed, one leg dangling over the side. The sheets are twisted and rolled.

She uses the same nightlight she's had since she was small. Silhouettes of circus animals revolve around a set of lights that change color every few seconds, casting pink tigers and green giraffes, purple elephants and blue lions, parading across the ceiling and wall.

I sit on the edge of the bed. The mattress sags. She continues to snore. When she was an infant, her mother and I were so terrified that she'd stop breathing because they drill that SIDS shit into you at the hospital before you take the kid home, we must have checked on Jeanie every ten minutes. Holding my finger below her nose until I felt her exhale. Placing the flat of my hand on her chest until I felt the inhale.

"Jeanie," I say. "Jeans."

As a child, she demanded to sleep with her door open. Not because she was afraid of the dark, but so that she could see us passing in the hall after we tucked her in. Knowing we were still awake was comforting to her somehow. It made her feel secure. Or she hated being alone even then, the way she'd sit outside the bathroom door whenever I took a shit, waiting for me to reemerge. "You're taking a long time," she'd say through the door.

Finally, she sits up. It takes a moment for her to untangle herself from the bedding.

A white lie: "I thought maybe you were awake."

"It's okay." She draws her knees to her chin, wipes sleep from her eyes.

"I wanted to show you something I'm working on."

I hand her the Last Will & Testament. She flips on the beside lamp. She has covered it in a scarf so the room is infused with rose and lavender light. The big-top animals scurry off, but there's a trace of them, still, washed by the brighter orb, like ghosts turning through the room.

"I was thinking, you know, if I die. You get everything," I tell her.

She grips my arm with both hands, hugs my shoulder. "You're not going anywhere."

"I was thinking maybe putting a provision in there, maybe you don't get all the money right away. I was thinking, maybe when you're twenty-five?"

"Better make it thirty."

I nod again. "That economics class of yours is doing some good."

When we were all still living together, there'd be times, maybe I was getting dressed for work, when I could hear Jeanie and her mom downstairs at the breakfast table, giggling over one of the inside jokes they shared, the way a quick glance between them could explode into snorting laughter. I'd pause, halfway through buttoning my shirt, and listen. I'd close my eyes, and it was like I wasn't there. I imagined then I wasn't, that I had died, and this was the two of them in the months and years after my passing. Eating breakfast together on a school day.

This used to depress the hell out of me, imagining myself as a kind of stalker-specter. I suppose no one really likes the idea that the world will go on just as before, with or without us. But after a while, I came to look forward to these moments. Precisely because they proved to me that life goes on, that Azita and Jeanie would get on just fine without me, world without end, amen.

I wake up to a dozen new text messages and several missed calls. No one leaves voicemails anymore, because no one checks them, but my caller ID shows my guys have been blowing me up. They've all seen the paper or have by now caught the news on one social media feed or another.

I sit for a long time in my kitchen, in my underwear, staring at a bowl of Lucky Charms until the cereal turns soggy and falls apart. I'll go into work, sure.

After Jeanie leaves for school, I call one of my senior guys.

"You see the news?" he asks as soon as he picks up.

"I did, yeah." I rub my eyes, trying to find energy after only a couple hours' sleep. "That's why Lucas came by yesterday. I just didn't—he asked me to hold off saying anything."

"I can't believe DIP fucking killed himself."

There's a long pause. My instinct is to defend my clerk, but then, why pretend it was anything else?

"What a pussy," he says.

I feel a kind of tugging on my cheeks, like biting into a lemon. "I'm going to be a little late today. If anybody asks, just tell them: business as usual. I'll be around at lunch, if anyone wants to talk."

Once we're done, I dial Robin. Straight to voicemail.

Then I dial Pasternak. It doesn't ring. Just a pause, then his voice, "Speak!" Then a beep.

I hang up. I dial again. Listen. Hang up. Dial again. "Speak!" Some kind of charge to the listener. "Speak!"

Beep.

"Speak!"

Beep.

For a while there, after the divorce, I spent most of my free time playing video games. Avoidance. Depression. Coping mechanism: call it what you want. I was deep into *Grand Theft Auto*. Played the shit out of the Seattle version, where you're this Black gangster dude from the ghetto. It has a kickass soundtrack. The game lets you move so independently, you can grab yourself an automatic weapon and just go shoot up a dance club if you want to, for no reason, which I sometimes did because to be honest, it relieved stress.

The last time I played, though, my character was outside City Hall, somewhere downtown where there were a lot of people. I was carrying a gun, it was lunchtime, and I was taking pot shots at civilians. When you do that, there's generalized screaming, and all the little avatars run off in different directions. I chose a spunky brunette in gray workout clothes and decided to chase her. I ran after her, staying a dozen yards back. Who knows why. Just to torment something. I remember, as we ran, through the downtown and then into a park, that a light rain began to fall. We crossed jogging paths and playgrounds. We reached the sea wall. And instead of stopping at the water's edge, she ran into the water and drowned. I stood on the beach watching, and after a moment or two she bobbed to the surface, face-down, limbs dangling in the classic pose, unmoving except for the little current that made her dip and then re-emerge.

My first thought posed itself as a question: how terrified would someone have to be to choose suicide over trying to escape?

My second thought, more of a realization really, was that this was a totally fucked up game. Her death was somehow different from the mass carnage I'd inflicted up until then. Because the developers had deliberately installed that feature, where background characters could commit suicide. Her death wasn't accidental, or a design flaw. She fucking ran into the water and died.

I never played again.

In the paper is a short article about how the police pulled a body out of the river. The article says what Lucas told me, that it was lucky someone saw him go in, otherwise the chances for recovery, with the water as cold as it was, were slim. The man, the paper says, was identified as Daniel Ilan Pasternak of Lisle, IL, a trader at the Chicago Board Options Exchange.

Posthumously—and incorrectly—granting him the promotion he was looking for.

Jeans,

If you're reading this, it means I'm not going to be there for certain events in your life that I was really looking forward to. Think of me at these times, but don't let missing me stop you from rightfully enjoying all the good things that are coming your way.

The only thing I've really wanted in this life was to be a good father to the most beautiful, wonderful human being I've ever met.

That's you, Jeans.

Who cares why I'm gone—no matter how it happened, it wasn't my intention. If I could have my way, I'd still be here. So, you can be angry, and feel hurt, and you should feel all those things, and more. But know that there was nothing I wanted in this world more than to be with you always.

If you can forgive my early exit, allow me to offer a few takeaways. Wisdom gleaned from more than forty-four years on this earth. Some of what I'm about to say might not make sense now, but maybe someday you'll face a situation and think, "You know, Dad mentioned this in that letter he wrote." And then maybe I'll have helped you out a little bit.

First, there are two kinds of people in this world: circles and squares. Strive to be a circle, and have patience with the squares.

If you're on time, you're late.

Court-sense is undervalued. You have it. Most people do not. Again, have patience.

People are dicks when they're afraid of something. Figure out the fear, you figure out how to get along with people.

Sex isn't love. And if you end up spending too much time and effort staying with the first person you have sex with, well, you won't be the first, but let yourself move on eventually. Sex isn't love, and honestly, love isn't sex.

Sex is great, though.

Doing what you're asked to do, at work, does not mean you are an achiever. It simply means you're doing the minimum.

Instead, make yourself indispensable. It should take your employer three new hires to replace you, when you finally move on to greener pastures.

It doesn't matter what you say, so long as you say it with confidence. Most people will be so relieved someone else has something to talk about, they'll join right in, even after the most banal or absurd remarks. Before you know it, you're having a perfectly lovely conversation.

Which supports what is perhaps the greatest truth: people are sheep.

Decide for yourself on whether or not there's a god, or gods, but remember that anyone who gets too worked up about the situation either way probably deep down believes exactly the opposite of whatever it is they're screaming about.

You'll outgrow it eventually, but never forget where you came from.

Travel.

Save your money until it hurts.

Don't trust men with big asses.

Don't trust women who wear chokers.

Don't ingest—or inject—anything made in a lab. (I'm talking about drugs.)

Stereotypes exist for a reason. Still, don't be a dick, and never judge anyone.

Make your own money, so you never have to rely on a man to take care of you.

Run fast, jump high, shoot every time you touch the ball.

Don't take shit from anybody.

Love,
Dad

Chapter 14

On Christmas Eve, Jeanie and I go to the candlelight service at Holy Trinity, because it doesn't feel like Christmas without the opportunity to belt some carols and light a flame, spread holiday good cheer. Here, we don't have to think about Pasternak if we don't want to. We can take a break from it. Call timeout. We breath the redolence of the resin and the piney smoke the priest waves over us as he comes down the center aisle with one arm swinging the censer at the end of a gold chain. We take Eucharist, kneeling at the altar, watching others tilt back their heads and drink the wine and cross themselves, until it comes around the circle, and it's my turn. I drink and hold the liquid in my mouth until it burns, until my body begins to notice it hasn't breathed in thirty seconds, a minute. Jeanie crosses herself and returns to her seat; around the altar, people take turns, the next congregants awaiting their blessing. In ninety seconds, my eyes water. All I can think about is how badly I want to breathe. All I can think about is how deeply the cheap wine burns my gums. Until I finally swallow, my entire universe becomes the inside of my mouth, the vaporous crushed grapes, the back of my tongue. We soak in the vibe of the church and stay until it is only us and the acolytes cleaning up. Not wanting to leave; feeling insulated, in the sanctuary, from grief. It is as close to a Christmas miracle as we are likely to receive.

The next morning, we open presents and make breakfast. By nine, I've opened a Barbaresco. I let Jeanie have a glass. If she's going to be drinking, she may as well know what the good shit tastes like.

The next morning, we attend the funeral of Daniel Ilan Pasternak.

Across the snow, against the sky that is the same color as the snow, headstones are black smears on the ridge. We approach, Jeanie and I, staggering through drifts, our breath warm and wet behind our scarves. Already I've lost feeling in the pinkie on my right hand, and in my left heel. Circulation issues. Thirty-three years a smoker.

We make fists inside our coat pockets and lean into the wind, into one another, keeping to the cemetery's careful grid. Up a soft incline, we're near enough to hear the Rite of Committal. We're late. Traffic on the Ike. The mourners bend toward the priest like sad crows.

This impulse we have to bury our dead in straight lines: man's best attempt to impose order on something inherently messy, a right-angled approach to a decidedly non-linear event. But grids make it easy to find your loved ones. The cemetery at Saints Peter and Paul provides maps at no charge.

Pasternak's commendation is a grim, plodding affair. As it should be. He died too young. It's fucking tragic. I overhear a woman whisper, "At least there aren't any children." As if Robin, who's been baby-crazy since I've known her, takes any comfort in that.

My slacks flutter, my overcoat clings. All of us squint against the kind of gusts that can unravel scarves. Even our clothes want to be free of the sound of it, the droning air. The priest talks not over it, but through. I can't make out too much of what he says. I turn my back for a moment and wipe my eyes. Down the hill, the way we came, gravestones fan like pinball gates. Behind me, the procession sniffles against the cold. My own nose so frozen, I don't feel any sensation there at all. A chilled, hollowed-out smell. The grave marker Robin chose is pink-granite, hewn with a rounded top. His name in block lettering across the front, above the relevant dates.

I take Jeanie's hand. "You're not wearing your cross."

Strands of her maple hair twirl around her face. She swipes at them, to tuck them behind her ears. "It started to feel hypocritical."

"At what point, exactly?"

The priest finishes whatever he's saying and gestures for the coffin, redwood with brass trim, to be lowered into the ground. The hole welcomes the box with its beveled edges, the brass handles gleaming. The casket lowers—eight grand it cost—and when the box has vanished, and the dirt fills in around it, I imagine how quiet that would be. The finality of it brings tears to my eyes. I actually stagger a bit. Jeanie grabs my elbow and asks if I'm okay. I tell her I'm fine. I didn't eat enough breakfast, is all.

A hymn starts up, but I tell Jeanie, "Let's head to the car." Thinking that when I die, I want to be buried someplace like New Orleans, with a fucking parade and a brass band escorting me down Esplanade. Or Vietnam, where at least the cemeteries have some goddamn color, the coffins designed as dragons or birds or prescription bottles—whatever you were into in life, they'll make whatever you want.

I'd request a war elephant. Ride that sonuvabitch into the afterlife, scattering demons before me.

I make Jeanie drive from the cemetery to the wake. I slide a flask from my coat, which I've filled with Balvenie, 17-year, Double-wood.

"I thought only alcoholics drink in the morning." Jeanie eyes me, then the road.

"Leave it alone," I grumble. "This is not standard operating procedure. Trust me."

Chicago traffic: one of the truly random patterns of the universe. Bad as it was earlier, there's no one out now. It's a crapshoot anyway, driving to the western 'burbs. You just never know.

We reach the subdivision, but I wave Jeanie on. We're ahead of the mourners. I tell her to keep driving. Everything is a blur of trees and powerlines and asphalt. We sit for a while in a Target parking lot. Jeanie is patient. Take me outside the city, away from the grid, and I have no idea where the fuck I am.

I drain the flask. "I'm ready."

By the time we arrive, cars are parked down the block. So many people, you'd think someone famous has died. Many more than were at the cemetery. The walks are mostly shoveled. We shuffle past identical townhomes, painted slate or sage, with black trim, and white garage doors. There are wreaths on lampposts, a smell like a dryer vent. A neighbor is taking down Christmas lights from his eaves. Occasionally, a car passes, the hush of its wheels kicking up salt and wetness.

A couple of my guys smoke on the front stoop. I nod, grimly. Inside, the house is quiet. Jeanie stays close. Coats are piled in a reading nook off to the left, but we keep ours with us.

"Hey." She pulls me aside, under the stairs, against a book-case. "Are there people from your work here?"

I shrug. "A few. Most of the firm is working today. Markets are open."

We find Robin in the kitchen. Her hair is pulled back. She wears a black dress and choker, like Chekov's seagull, in mourning for her life. A smell like pasta water has overflowed on the stove.

I take her arms. "I've left messages."

"I know." She dabs her eyes with her pinky. "I kept meaning to call you. There's just so much."

"Even if you had been prepared," I say, "it would be overwhelming."

She sees Jeanie and pulls her in. "Darling girl."

"It's been a long time," Jeanie says.

"Tragedy brings people together."

Jeanie nods. "I guess that's why they call it a silver lining."

The widow sobs once, before covering it with her hand. "I'm sorry. Thank you for being here."

A sister, or some kind of relation, comes over. Jeanie and I excuse ourselves. We owe the family a few more minutes. We cruise the buffet. Potato salad, a Jell-O mold, some stray buns, a cold, picked-over ham. The carcass of one smoked fish or another. We don't touch any of it. I tell Jeanie we'll go someplace nice for dinner.

"I feel like an intruder," she says. "Like any minute, I'll be found out."

"It's good that you're here," I tell her. "It's not the most pleasant thing, but it's gotta be done."

We get sodas and try to make ourselves small in a corner. Not much has changed since the last time I was here. Their tastes run decidedly Nordic and child-free. The living room floor is covered by a white, bearskin rug, like a polar bear has passed out drunk in front of the television. The couches and chairs are low-slung, black leather. A chic beige disc, about the size of a Roman shield, stands sentinel in the corner—the entire speaker system, operated by swift swipes of the hand, which Pasternak cranked to painful decibels at their house-warming party a few years back.

He and Robin were full of plans, then, for how they were going to fix up their new home. Shale tiles for the backsplash, finish the basement, build out the back deck. Twenty people or so, mostly family, everybody related to somebody else in the typical Chicago way, cousins of cousins, all of us spilling out from the garage into the driveway, lounging on deck chairs, tossing corn hole, sipping rosé, scarfing down a spread that Robin must have spent a week preparing: everything on sticks. Beef, chicken, and pepper kebabs; corn; cubes of melon and pepperoni; pretzels dipped in chocolate and swirled with white icing. The kids dug it, and the adults enjoyed the way it all tasted like summer. We set off a few poppers and Roman candles, leftover from the Fourth of July.

That night, as drinks took hold and people began to talk louder and tell more and more stories that pushed the boundaries of good taste, Pasternak and I found ourselves in the kitchen, away from the guests. One of his brothers, he said, was opening up a Jamaican chicken joint on the Southside. Pasternak was thinking of investing. Wanted to know what I thought.

"Restaurants are risky," I said. "And more work than anyone imagines."

"But purely from an investment standpoint?"

"Look," I said. "I'm not telling you what to do with your money. But if it were my hard-earned fortune, there's no way I'd invest in a restaurant. Chances are 80 percent the place goes belly-up within a year. Plus, there are more effective vehicles for putting your cash to work."

"It's my brother," he said.

"All the more reason to say no," I told him.

I have no idea whether he invested in that place, or what became of the restaurant idea, or to be honest, what the fuck Jamaican chicken even is. But I'd tell him the same thing if he were standing here now, blue from hypothermia, river muck caked in his ears.

"It's not as sad as I thought it would be," Jeanie says. "Being here."

I am hustled back to the present. "It's a party like any other. Be pleasant. Drink your drink. Make small talk."

"I'm terrible at small talk."

"We don't have the natural talent for it," I tell her. "But you can learn. Just like I did."

We sip our drinks. We nod at people we don't know, and they pass by. Neither of us remove our coats. It doesn't feel like the kind of situation to get too cozy in. It's mostly family. I always feel, when it's mostly family, and I'm not part of said family, it's easy to overstay my welcome.

One of my traders comes in from outside, grabs himself a plateful from the buffet, and waddles over to us. With his back turned, he whispers. "Who's this?"

"Who's who?"

"The brunette you walked in with."

"This is my daughter, asshole."

The trader wipes his hand on his pants and shakes hers. "Nice to meet you."

Which, of course, is when it hits me.

Sweat breaks out across my back, under my arms, and in a beaded circle around my bald spot. Also, behind my knees, the way I always feel before I hurl.

What Jeanie asked when we were coming in, about my guys being here, and later, about being discovered—now she merely shrugs and sips her diet 7UP. The trader turns from her and talks to me through a mouth stuffed with whitefish.

"I didn't know you had a daughter," he says.

"Right," I say. "Well, I do."

"I've worked with you seven years, JAG," he says. "How the fuck can I work for you seven years and not know you have a daughter?"

"You never asked."

The front door opens, and a blast of cigarette smoke comes in with the cold, sweeping in another one of my guys.

The first trader calls to him. "Marc. Come here. This is Jeanie. Ganzi's daughter."

Marc juggles his lighter and a pack of Newports, manages to extend his hand. "No shit?"

"No shit," Jeanie says, returning the handshake.

"Where you been keeping her?" he asks me.

The truth is, I have no goddamn idea. Part of me is still trying to figure out how I could have exposed her to these savages and not even realized it until right now. What's the phrase? Blinded by grief.

A few more of my guys wander over, and then it's like a conversational gang-bang with Jeanie in the middle. They ask about high school. Basketball. She mentions her economics class. The field trip to our trading floor. Everyone howls, slapping one another on the back. Then they shush themselves, remembering where we are. She mentions her mock portfolio and moral investing. Nobody snickers. They nod and consider. They love talking about this shit almost as much as they love talking about tits—maybe more. They review her portfolio. A couple of my guys give her pointers. They're amused by her plan to invest in only humane and moral companies, but also they agree it's a golden idea that, as a book, would probably sell a million copies. Liberty University, or someplace like Oral Roberts, would probably make it required reading for incoming freshmen.

One of my traders says, "Situation like that, a one-semester class? What'd I'd do is buy up the riskiest stocks I could and hope they take off. It's a competition, right? One semester, it's not long enough to reward a long-term investment strategy."

"That's what I've been telling her," I say.

"Shoot for the moon," he says. "It's the only way to win."

"Like what?" she asks.

They give her pointers. Tech. Sectors with high volume, high volatility. They encourage her to buy and sell as much as the rules will allow. To be, as one of them eloquently puts it, a beehive of fucking trading activity.

And they're all laughing, even Jeanie, who maybe seems to be enjoying the attention from a bunch of older guys. I'm proud of her, holding her own, full of confidence and poise that she definitely got from her mother. We stand around talking about the Bears, the Bulls, the goddamn White Sox—with baseball season still four months away. I say general stuff about the recession, the wristwatch Jeanie gave me for Christmas. They ask if she's looking at colleges, if she wants to play basketball. She's neutral on both counts.

We talk news and sports and food and state politics. We talk about everything but Pasternak.

"You oughta see this girl play basketball," I tell them. "You oughta see her drive the lane. Unfuckingbelievable."

The conversation devolves, quickly, into war stories from my guys' glory days playing high school and intramural collegiate sports. I take the opportunity to say we should probably be going. Mostly because, as boss, I don't like to be anywhere too long with a bunch of my employees, outside work.

I believe in keeping a certain amount of distance. This day has already mixed my personal and professional life more than I'd ever meant to, frankly.

We find Robin at the foot of the stairs. She takes my arms.

"Thank you for coming." She pulls herself close enough for me to smell the Chardonnay.

"All my guys wanted to be here," I say. "But with the short week, half of them are on vacation."

"I know how it is," she says. Then, "Do you have a minute?"

I tell Jeanie to wait for me, then follow Robin up the stairs. We enter a dark room. When she turns on the lights, we're standing in Pasternak's office. It smells like him, his essence locked inside like a fart-in-a-bottle.

"We're starting a fund." Robin goes to his desk and returns with a business card. "For his high school. Your high school. A small, yearly scholarship that we'll give to a student who shows interest in economics. I don't know if you're much of a philanthropist, but if you'd consider it—"

"You don't even have to ask." I take the card and put it in my shirt pocket.

"I just want his death to mean something," she says. "Silly as that is."

I wait. She didn't bring me up here to tell me about the goddamn scholarship.

"Can I ask you a question?" she asks.

"Shoot."

"The police, they never said either way. But I can't let it go." She wipes her face dry with quick passes of her finger. "I keep asking myself, what was he doing in the river? Because he knew how to swim, you know? He was a good swimmer."

"It was cold," I say. "He was drunk."

I have questions too, questions that demand answers. Such as, why weren't you with him? How could you leave him alone in the city after a night like that, after all the alcohol and the stunt you pulled?

I say nothing, though.

"We had a fight," she says. "I took a fucking taxi home, almost $200. And I keep thinking, if we hadn't fought..."

"Don't do that to yourself."

"You don't think he—"

I reach for her, draw her in. I hold her and let her weep.

"Don't let yourself think that," I tell her. "Don't let yourself go anywhere close to there."

When she pulls away, she's caught her breath. "He wanted you to have this."

She goes behind the desk. Usually when somebody says something like that, they hand you a broken watch, worthless but for the sentimentality of it. Or five mounted coins from a collection that aren't really worth much, not without the rest of the seventy coins they were originally sold with. A guy I grew up with gave me his one-hitter, along with a pocket-sized carrying case he'd carved himself out of wood. He was going into the Navy and had to quit. I still have it somewhere, tucked into my storage unit in a blue duffle bag I've had since high school.

But what she reveals is a basketball—red, white, and blue. It's signed by all the members of the 1993 Chicago Bulls. Everybody's on there: Jordan, Pippin, Paxson—who hit the game-winner with three seconds left in Game 6 against the Suns, for the championship.

"This is too much." I turn the ball in my hands, admiring the signatures. "You should sell it, at least."

"No," she says. "It was his prized possession."

We say our goodbyes. This time she weeps openly. I let her lean into me once more. I can feel her shaking. I can feel her bones, she's so thin.

"You're allowed to be sad about this," I say. "It's fucking tragic."

"It's not only that." She pulls away a little, but I still have my arms around her. "Our accountant—there's no money. None at all."

"Robin, that's impossible."

"Our home, he took out a second mortgage for some kind of investment. Our accountant is trying to figure out where the money went. Maybe multiple investments. Or multiple loans? I'm still not clear on that."

I let her pause, to dab the corner of each eye.

She continues. "On top of that, the market—we bought this place for a price, and then the second mortgage was for almost twice that, and here we were this whole time thinking we'd made a killing, you know, everything's—your house is supposed to be this big investment in your future. But now the accountant says our house might not even be worth what we bought it for initially, much less what we took out on it."

"Hush." I pull her in again.

"I'm scared, John," she says. "You hear terrible stories. People being so underwater they can't—"

She pauses, swallows, pulls away from me, or tries to, but I keep her close. It's an unfortunate turn of phrase. It's too soon for either of us to consider anything, or anyone, being underwater. The word hangs in the air between us, makes the hairs on the back of my neck stand up. It feels like Pasternak is watching us, that he's here. I can smell him. A leathery kind of scent: Newman's Own ginger mints and Drakkar Noir.

"People owing more on their houses than their houses are even worth," she finishes, "and I don't really understand any of it."

I'm not going to tell her things are going to be okay. Because they probably aren't, not in the short-term. She's looking at several unpleasant possible scenarios, the most likely of which involves her moving back in with her parents in Bridgeport with whatever severely depreciated nest egg her accountant is able to salvage.

"This accountant of yours," I say, "sounds like he's got things under control. Listen to him. Do what he tells you."

"I trust him," she says. "It's just that…"

"Tell me."

"He's not family."

I hug her once more, as firmly as I can. "You have any questions, something doesn't make sense to you, or if you just want a second opinion, you call me, okay? Any time of day or night."

She says her mom's going to stay with her a while, until things settle down. We make our way to the office door. At the top of the stairs, we pause. We can hear the voices below, a bit louder than before, after a couple beers, a few glasses of wine, the cheap shit always packs the hardest punch. The collective sadness not so much forgotten as tabled, because dammit, Pasternak was a helluva guy, wasn't he? Never let things get him down. A goddamn optimist, is what he was, a real bull, and wouldn't he be pissed to see us all moping around his living room, nobody drinking, nobody laughing, all of us sour pusses and not even sports on the television. Robin and I eavesdrop shamelessly.

I reach into my coat pocket and hand her an envelope. She accepts. She doesn't open it, but says thank you, and bows her head, unable, suddenly, to look me in the eye.

"It's not fucking charity." I lift her chin, forcing her to see me. "Something this fucking tragic happens, money gets tight for a bit. It's the same for everyone. This can tide you over until all the shit gets worked out."

At the bottom of the stairs, I put my arm around my daughter, and we depart. We are gone: out the front door, down the salted walk, and into the street. The cold against our cheeks reminds us we're alive. I have to stop myself from sprinting to the car, from howling.

"How much did you give her?" Jeanie asks once we're out of sight.

I keep my arm around her, and she allows it. "Just enough to get her through this stretch."

"C'mon." She elbows me, sharply. "I want a number."

"More than your economics teacher makes in a year."

Driving east, returning to the city, there are long stretches of strip malls and highway ramps and then the low brownstones around Midway. There is a factory yard for fixed-trunnion bascule bridges, known as "Chicago" bascules, and not far from where Robin grew up, abandoned grain silos along the South fork of the river.

All at once Chicago appears: a glittering, silver tangle at the edge of a dun-colored expanse of warehouses and train yards. The city looms and grows larger as I-55 loops toward it, bisected by arteries running north and south, by the Metra, the skyscrapers gleaming and monstrous as we sail beneath them.

I know a hedge fund manager who writes a monthly circular. He sends it around to colleagues and posts it online for free. A lot of guys read him because he's that rare blend of entertaining and occasionally right once in a blue fucking moon. He makes predictions. He'll spout off a lot of different formulas and theorems, when pressed, about how he makes them. But in the end, it comes down to one thing.

His office sits on the thirty-second floor of the Merc. When it's time to write his monthly flyer, he opens his window shades. If he sees construction cranes, he writes something bullish. If not, he closes his blinds and panders to the bears.

That's what it boils down to: new construction. The thought being, if companies are building, then they're feeling pretty good about the economy.

There was a time, even six months ago, when every corner was being renovated or rebuilt. Spaces in locations where nobody in their right minds would want to live were suddenly stuffed with move-in-ready lofts. I'd look out my apartment windows and see the bob and sway of construction cranes, their heads slowly swinging, bent against their loads, like industrial, pre-historic beasts. Buildings covered in scaffolds like exoskeletons. At night, the evening sky was spotted by their leaning silhouettes.

Now, driving toward the lake, with Jeanie behind the wheel, the skyline is quiet. No cranes or scaffolding. Only a sensation like something recently extinct. As if all life has been suddenly, unexpectedly snuffed out.

Nothing moves at all.

I make Jeanie drive us to Volare, under Michigan Avenue, for the best Italian food in the city, a place as easy to miss as a freckle. In nicer weather, the patio offers a view of the valet parking lot and above it, rusted I-beams and ghostly, concrete supports. Tonight, or rather, this afternoon, we're inside with one other couple, retired, silent. I order a Campari and soda. Volare serves Campari with olives. No other place does that.

"I'm going to ingest about 4,000 calories," I tell Jeanie. "I'm just warning you."

"Stress eating," she sighs. "We learned about it in health class. I'm right there with you, don't worry."

I ask Jeanie what she's doing for New Year's Eve. She's non-committal. She asks if I have any plans, and I explain how

I stopped going out on New Year's back in 1997, after Azita and I couldn't catch a cab downtown after midnight. Had to take the "L" back up north, ass-cheek to ass-cheek with a thousand drunken children, until, mysteriously, the "L" stopped at Belmont and a tired voice came over the speaker announcing the end of the line. Azita and I lived still north of there, so we had to hoof the last two miles in the bitter cold. Poor woman walked sixteen blocks barefoot, the frozen concrete better than the blisters on her feet—a relief, even. Carrying her high-heels over her shoulder. Me bitching the entire way, drunkenly, exhausted, feeling thoroughly defeated by the city, about how only people with no class walked barefoot, streetwalkers and the like, and pointing out all the other shod women we passed. Anyway, that was it for me and NYE. And eventually, for me and Azita.

"You want to have friends over?" I ask.

The arancini balls arrive, wafting in on a garlic and herbal breeze. Technically an African dish, the Italians have co-opted it. One of the perks of ruling the world for 800 years. We level our forks at them, and they crumble into fried bits of risotto and molten mozzarella.

"How many friends?" she asks, dipping her toe in the water of my sudden, inexplicable permissiveness.

"How many friends do you have?" I ask. "Because if I had friends over, it'd be Penny, Eugene, and Pasternak." His name hangs there, above the table, like some chandelier adorned in spider webs. "It's part of why I'm afraid to die. I'm afraid nobody will show up."

She sulks, stabbing at the appetizer plate. "Ten or twelve."

"How about six or eight?"

We settle on ten. "Can we drink?"

I lean back, finish the food in my mouth. "Beer and wine. That's it. No shooters, no punch. None of that shit. And everyone spends the night."

"No one's driving anyway."

"And no one is going to be the legal drinking age either, are they? If you want booze, then you play by my rules."

The server, a tall, rugged wop with an accent straight out of Sicily, brings the wine, a dolcetto from the Piedmont. I chat him up, and he admits to basically just having stepped off the boat. He loves Italy, but the economy is so bad....

"Out of the frying pan into the fire," I commiserate. "Some timing, your arriving here just as our economy turned to shit."

"Well, there are no jobs in Italy neither," he says. Then, "How many glasses?"

"Two," I tell him, and he fills 'em up.

When he's gone, I push one glass toward Jeanie.

"Are you sure?" she asks.

"After the day we've had?" She holds my gaze. "Yeah, absolutely."

Jeanie raises her goblet. "To the land of opportunity."

We toast. We drink. The first sip is so dry it makes me cough. The second is better. I swirl the glass with vigor.

"It needs air," I say.

Don't we all?

Jeanie asks, "Are you going to be there?"

"On New Year's?" I clear my throat, look her in the eye. "You bet your ass."

Volare hand-makes their pasta. All of it excellent—the gnocchi, the tortellini—but the pappardelle is the star, mostly because you don't see pappardelle on too many menus. Long, wide ribbons of dough, bathed in the sauce of your choice—Alfredo for me, with a couple broccoli heads swimming in all that white, creamy goodness that together tastes like Neptune's splooge. The broccoli stops me from feeling guilty.

Jeanie orders broiled fish because she's a high-school girl perpetually worried about her weight, but she empties her side plate of ziti. We consume two days' worth of calories in about twenty minutes.

"Zeppole." I hold up one of the fried, still-warm rolls. "Nobody serves zeppole."

"Why did you give Robin money?" she asks.

I thrust the roll back in its basket, and cover it with the towel. "I see you have your mother's fearlessness when it comes to making inappropriate dinner conversation."

"Are you sleeping with her?"

"Jesus, Jeans, no. Not everything's straight out of some goddamn celebrity magazine." I wipe my mouth and stuff my napkin into my lap, shaking almost, anger building, reminding myself it's just a question from a seventeen-year-old girl. "Pasternak was an employee. I gave Robin his last month's salary."

She seems to accept this answer and returns to sopping up bits of sauce with her bread. "I just keep thinking about how awful it would be to drown."

"Jeans—"

"Is that wrong of me? More than the fact that, he's, gone...I just keep trying to imagine, you know, drowning."

I stir my drink, withdraw the toothpick, and pop an olive into my mouth, hoping she'll change the conversation. But no luck: this is one of those times as a parent when you just have to roll with it and be there, because your child needs to be heard. And sure, I'd rather be sitting on a beach, sucking down a Mai Tai beneath the hot sunrays of Martinique or Aruba, talking about baseball or reality television, but instead it's five fucking thirty, dark as my asshole outside already, a true Chicago winter night, my belly so full I feel like I could puke up my entire meal if I just lean a little bit to the left, and all my daughter wants to do is talk about death.

"I don't think I'd like to go that way," she says. "Drowning."

"Why not?" I decide to play along, let her talk it out. "How do you want to go?"

Jeanie seems startled by the question. She fumbles her fork, puts it down. She places both palms on the tablecloth. "Not like that."

"How do you want to die?" I ask again. "Shot from a cannon? Stabbed through the heart? In the hospital, strung up like a marionette with cords and tubes?"

"I don't know."

"What do you want to die from?"

This she can answer. "Old age, I guess."

"We all die from old age." I shove my empty glass to the edge of the table, hoping our server will notice and bring me a fresh one, like, ten minutes ago. "Death is a sexually transmitted disease that all of us end up catching, one way or another."

The server notices my drink and retrieves it. He asks if I want another, and I nod. I don't say anything, and he doesn't force me to. He disappears through the restaurant doors. I made a mistake when we sat down, got too personal with him, asked about his life. Put myself at a disadvantage, immediately, because it levels the playing field then. Surrendered my power. Not speaking helps gain some of it back.

"So." I turn again to Jeanie. "What's it going to be?"

"In bed." She takes a deep breath. "Asleep."

"You're going to sleep through the most dramatic moment of your life?"

She considers. "I'm too afraid to be awake for it."

"How old?"

"Ninety-two."

"Alone?"

"With...my husband."

"Your husband?" I gesture at the older couple sitting on the other end of the patio. They're probably seventy, seventy-five, the peak of their September years. "You want your husband to wake up in the morning, expecting breakfast, only to find you dead?"

She shivers. "Together then."

"A ritual suicide?"

"No. Naturally."

"You're banking on an awful lot of good luck." I drum the table. "Ain't nobody that lucky."

A cow kicks over a lantern in some old lady's barn: an entire city burns. Most, if not all, massive fucking disasters originate with something that, on any other day, might not have made the slightest bit of difference.

All great conflagrations start small.

God's honest, I don't drink and drive, especially not with Jeanie in the car. But Jeanie has had one or three glasses of wine. I'm not putting her behind the wheel. And sure, I live close enough that we could walk home in twenty minutes, half-hour tops, but that means coming back tomorrow to get the car and all that shit so, as we egress, I take the car keys out of Jeanie's hand and lead the way to my vehicle. I hold the door for her as she gets in. And then I climb into the driver's seat.

If you ever plop down behind the steering column and ask yourself, "Wow, am I okay to drive?" The answer is definitely not—no, you're not okay to drive. Get out of the car and call a fucking cab.

But when do I ever take my own advice?

It'll be seven minutes to home. Five if we time the lights.

Two blocks from my place, a squad car takes a right off a side-street and comes up behind me. I'm not worried. River

North on a Friday, we're hardly moving. Ten miles an hour, tops. You could make better time walking. It's the kind of environment in which you get a DUI only if you pass out in the middle of the road with your engine still running.

Or if the cop just feels like being a dick. Because sure enough, the police cruiser flips on its lights and squawks, once.

"Do you have any goddamn bubblegum?" I ask Jeanie. It looks like only one cop, and he takes his time, door open, before getting out of the car.

"I have Altoids," she says. "Shit, they're in my bag."

Her bag is in the trunk. No getting to them now.

"Thanks for nothing," I tell her.

"Who the fuck calls it 'bubblegum'?" she says.

I roll down the window as the cop approaches. I keep my hands on the steering wheel.

"Can I help you?" I ask him, courteously going on the offensive.

He glances in the car, at Jeanie, then at me. "You know your city sticker is expired."

It takes me a minute to figure out what the fuck he's talking about. The fucking city makes all vehicle owners renew these tiny fucking stickers that we're all supposed to adhere to our license plates—seventy-five bucks a year. You don't have to renew, of course, but the fine is about $500 for driving with an expired sticker, and sure, chances are you won't get caught, but you hear stories of cops patrolling parking lots, even residential garages, looking for delinquents, so you're better off just coughing up the registration fee and getting left the fuck alone.

A few weeks ago, I'd given a fairly simple set of instructions to Pasternak. I asked him to take my vehicle registration and seventy-five dollars cash to the little check-cashing place under the Board of Trade. This dimly-lit counter shop renews license plate stickers, among other quasi-legal government-reg-ulated commercial services. I don't know if it just takes this long to process or if Pasternak figured they would just mail me my new sticker or what, but obviously he never went back to pick it up.

I try to explain this. I have Jeanie open the glove com-partment and find my registration and the little index card that shows I've paid for a new sticker, even if it hasn't yet been put on my car.

The officer makes an unpleasant face and looks at my li-cense. "Have you been drinking?"

I drop my hands into my lap, sweat dampening the reg-istration, the index card.

"We were at a wake all afternoon," I tell him. "Bunch of Poles. They drink Vodka for breakfast, these guys. So, I had a beer or two. Nothing major."

I gamble that no is more suspicious than borderline truth. Plus, there's the possibility he is sympathetic to my loss. Death makes everyone charitable.

He peers inside the car again. Jeanie sits in the passenger seat, arms folded, watching us both with teenage contempt.

"This your daughter?" he asks.

"I have a name," she says. "It's Jeanie. What's yours?"

He rolls my license through his fingers like a magician with a playing card. One way, then the other.

"Say the alphabet for me backwards," he says. "Starting with P. Ending with F."

I do.

There is a long beat as I measure him and him, me.

Finally, the police officer says, "Step out of the car for me, sir."

"M," Jeanie says as I open the door. "You forgot M."

"Goddammit."

The cop hooks his thumb through his belt. Soon we are joined by two plainclothes cops in a sedan. Followed by a second squad car, lights twirling. Suddenly, there are four policemen on the scene and three vehicles, all of whom have come down to watch some short, rich fat guy try and wriggle his way out of a DUI.

The first cop makes me walk a white parking space line. He waves a penlight in front of my nose and tells me to follow it using only my eyes. He gets pissed off when I turn my head, and he has to tell me twice.

This is where, Clark and Grand? Chads and Jills walking to their favorite tapas restaurants; college kids humping backpacks the size of VW Bugs; old people dressed to the nines, trying to make the late seating at Howl at the Moon. Every cab that weaves past our blocked lane feels obligated to blow its horn.

What I feel is not shame, exactly: the present becomes all. I try to do whatever the officer asks me to do, as well and as soberly as I am able. I recognize it for what it is, a game, where I'm the dancing monkey. Still, I feel hope, that if I balance on the line long enough, or follow the pen with my eyes in exactly the way he asks, maybe—just maybe—he'll let me walk.

This'd be better if I was blotto. At least the whole episode would be hazy in my memory. But at this rate, I'll remember it all. I'm too dumb, or too insulated by my station in life, or just a bit too far this side of sober, to be afraid. You always hear, there's a thin line between courage and stupidity.

Once it's obvious shit isn't going my way, one of the cops gets Jeanie out of my truck and puts her in the back of his squad car. The police lights spin. They have me up on the sidewalk, middle of Clark. Jeanie watching it all. The flashing lights, cops barking orders. Other cops standing on the periphery of the lit space, just watching, like they might learn something, or like they think I might run.

"You know Lucas?" I ask at one point. We're waiting for my BAC reading on the little blow-tube device.

"Who?"

"Officer Hart. Used to work for me. Godfather to my daughter."

The device beeps. The cop reads it, shows it to me. Legal limit: I'm fucked.

"Man, I don't care if her Godfather is Mayor Daley himself." The cop shoves the breathalyzer into his back pocket. "You get caught driving under the influence with a minor in the car? You're going downtown, brother."

Your brain does funny things, situations like this. Starts to conjure what you believe are reasonable arguments, like trying to gain purchase on a muddy bank. Your feet keep sliding against what you know is inevitable. But that doesn't stop you from trying. I chase fleeting escape routes, perform mental acrobatics, wondering if maybe I just let them take my car, they'll let me go. Thoughts like, if this was Mexico, I'd just slip these guys a hundred bucks and be on my way. Thoughts like, I really hope none of my guys are having dinner downtown tonight.

They allow me one phone call, for Jeanie. No way in fuck am I calling her mom. Jeanie keeps her mouth shut, Azita may never find out.

Instead, I call Penny.

"Are you sober?" I ask as soon as she picks up.

"Mostly," she says.

"I'm getting a DUI," I tell her. "I need you to come to where I am, pick up my daughter. Take her home."

There's a long pause. She asks where I am, and I tell her.

"Okay," she says. "I'm coming."

"You can't miss us."

As if on cue, two trannies in knee-length, brown-leather coats stop and wave their cigarettes.

"Goddamn," one of them says. "It can't be eight o'clock yet. Homeboy here was hitting the booze early."

"Such a nice car to be driving intoxicated," the other cackles. "Hey officer, excuse me, sir? Can I have his car after you take him to jail?"

The cop and I make eye contact, and for the briefest moment we're just two guys from the Southside who can't fucking believe the shit people do nowadays. How different the city is from the one we grew up in. Then just as quick, he becomes a cop again, and I the perp. He tells me to put out the cigarette and holds the back of his squad car door open for me as I duck in.

Penny drives a Toyota FJ Cruiser, which barely fits down the street with the cop cars everywhere and the pedestrians. She swings open the door, climbs down, gives me a nod from across the street. That's as close as they let her get. The cops bring Jeanie out of the backseat of the police vehicle. She stands alone, briefly, in the naked spotlight of the unmarked car. Tears pour out of her. Down the front of her is puke, down her dress, her hair and in her hands.

Poor girl is so terrified, she's thrown-up all over herself, and the cops have been letting her sit in it for who knows how long.

In the drunk-tank, I pass out cigarettes like dealing blackjack, hoping to appease anyone with even mildly violent impulses. Eventually, they leave me alone and harass the next newbie. I lay down on a bench, my ass so fat only half of me fits, but I'm able to kind of wedge myself up the wall a bit and shut my eyes.

It smells like vomit here, too. And aftershave. And man-stench. Far off is a metallic kind of rhythm, like a loose dryer belt.

I can taste a little bit of the olive juice still, from the Campari. Tonight has ruined that drink for me, forever. Pressure above my eyes indicates that I am approaching sobriety. I should be figuring out what to tell Jeanie. I should be plotting the most expedient route through what's sure to be a legal morass. But all I can think about is Pasternak.

The narrative I settle on is this: sometime after Penny and I make our exit from the Art Institute, as the party is winding down, Mr. and Mrs. Pasternak have a fight. He feels like she humiliated him. She calls him a coward—all the same old shit. Their fight escalates and extends. They stumble toward the parking garage. Finally, hysterical and sensing an opportunity for drama, Robin hails a cab, jumps in, speeds off, taking the car keys with her, leaving Pasternak in Millennium Park without a ride home.

Maybe he tries to find a cab, too. But there are none to be had, coming up on midnight in the deadest part of downtown. He makes a decision, heads north on Michigan, figuring he'll either find a taxi at Wacker or at one of the hotel stands along the way.

He walks however many blocks to the river. God knows there is nothing more beautiful to a drunk guy than water at night. All the lights reflected in it. There are steps down to the riverwalk below Michigan Avenue. He takes them. He stumbles along. There's an almost European feel, being that close to the water, below street level, with the closed-up coffee shack and empty bike racks, and if he strains, he can see the locks and beyond them the flashing lights of the pumping stations out in the lake. He bums a smoke from a couple of punks and, after a drag or two, flicks it into the current.

He's thinking of Robin. The stunt she pulled at dinner, while he had excused himself to the men's room. About what, as a man, he is obligated to do. Maybe Robin is even blowing up his BlackBerry—maybe he wants to call her, but his battery is dead. Either way, he's disgusted. He throws the phone into the river. Only it doesn't sink. It tumbles and sticks among some rocks, or on an exposed step of the retaining wall. How lucky, he thinks—he can save it. He finds a place to anchor himself and lies down on his stomach. He pushes some trash out of the way, a Fritos bag, some bottle caps. His knees and elbows are wet, and the river smells like dead fish. He thinks the water is a little less nice, up close. He looks and sees the phone again. He braces himself and finds that if he leans out far enough, if he stretches his fingers, and closes his eyes—concentrating, straining, and spinning faster now that his eyes are closed—and reaches for the phone, if he sees it in his mind's eye and makes himself long enough, and sets his jaw, and tries, really tries, he just might grasp it.

Chapter 15

Pasternak's desk is as he left it the Friday before he died: chair askew, headset draped across the telephone, a Joakim Noah bobblehead stuck with post-its.

His workspace is a moment in time, arrested, but for the mail that has continued to arrive since his passing. His inbox is filled. The tilting mound spills across the blotter. The mailman began a second pile, and a third, beside the overflowing, wire-mesh tray. The stacks lean into one another, envelopes and circulars and magazines co-mingling like leaf piles. In the same way our hair and nails keep growing long after we have, ourselves, expired, the mail arrives, regular, 10:30 and 3:30 weekdays.

Somebody should tell the fucking postman that Pasternak is dead. Somebody should go through the firm's mail. It takes me a week to realize that somebody is me.

On Thursday before the New Year, I sit in his chair. The leather arms are worn and flaking. Flecks of white underside run the lengths of the chair arms like caps of waves, the incoming tide. I ease into the seat and find myself chin-level with the desk. I stand, reach beneath to find the lever, and pull, raising the seat to full height. I climb up, able still to cross my legs. I reach for a short stack of mail, the most recent, stamped with today's date.

It's all bullshit. Promotions for discounted subscriptions to *The Economist, The Wall Street Journal, Crain's*. Holiday cards from other firms. In the desk drawer, I find a letter opener, double-bladed and monogrammed with Pasternak's call-sign: DIP. I open the holiday notes, all of them single 4" x 5" cards with the firm's name and some standard platitude stenciled across the top. All personally signed, not by the senders, but by their assistants, forging their boss' John Hancocks. I open a dozen or more, the card stock so stiff I can barely fold them into gliders, which I send skyrocketing down the hall, toward my office, toward the exit. There's no one else around. The airplanes pile up like the most tragic day in aviation history.

I fish through the sloughing piles of mail, find the smaller envelopes, the ones with color, all the holiday cards and, once they're sorted into their own stack, arm-sweep them into the trash. I don't even know if we sent out cards this year. I don't remember signing any.

I want to be methodical about this. I try to channel Penny's efficiency. I sort the remaining mail into four piles: personal, junk, magazines, catalogs. But the longer I sit, the more I feel Pasternak—not so much feel as smell him. While searching for a staple remover, a blast of Newman's Own breath mints bursts from the open drawer, stray candies pulverized and strewn across the interior felt. The knob is slightly greasy, the way anything he handed to me always was, his glands a goddamn river of secretions and sweat. On the desk is a bottle of water. I open it, put the lip beneath my nose. His breath is there, but also his essence, from when he breathed on the bottle to take in water and returned some of that water to the bottle, the way one does. Leaving a trace of some airy, impossible-to-pin-down part of himself, which I taste when I wet my lips.

I discover a bill, then a follow-up bill charging us interest after non-payment. In the desk drawer I find a stapler, but it's empty. In the hall closet are office supplies. Tucked at the top are bulk-package staples. Two-hundred staples a box, twenty boxes. I will never use all these staples in my lifetime. They will outlast me, and either be thrown away or gifted to whatever office slob replaces me. The goddamn staples may very well outlast him, too. The books we set aside for later, the wine we collect, the stacks of letterhead and business cards and sub-scriptions and Facebook profiles, outlast us all.

My goddam action list is seven pages long; my to-call list is about half that. If I never sent or received another commu-nication, I could keep working until the ivy is green at Wrigley, at least.

Pasternak once asked me what I would do if I didn't have this. The answer seems to me now to be here among these glue sticks, the colored card stock, the three-hole punch—of which we have four—the three-ring binders, the fresh, unsharpened pencils with their rough flat-tops, the many species of folders: two-pocket, clasp, accordion. The Dictaphone and boxes of tapes, reels of typewriter ribbon from the Mesozoic Era. There was a time someone ordered these things and thought to them-selves, *I better buy in bulk, because surely we'll use it all.* Until the day came when the Dictaphone was put on the shelf and forgotten. The dinosaurs too probably had foodstuff stored away, a particularly scrumptious leaf-eater they were saving for just the right occasion, right up until the asteroid hit.

I slide a thick, staple-bound edge from under the com-posting mail. A glossy catalog from Baxter & Vadas, a luxury travel agency. On the front cover, a private jet stenciled with Pas-ternak's name—a helluva sales gimmick, and ironic too, because Pasternak came nowhere close to affording his own jet. He only received the catalogs at all because he booked travel arrangements for me. I tear the front cover down the spine, dig around for some tape, and stick the cover to the wall above the molten mail.

I flip to the back and lay the catalog flat, smooth it out. In the advertisement, two women in sparkling swimsuits recline on deck chairs. The view is from above and a little bit behind. Their bodies curve, golden, the topography of their limbs greased with sunshine. Their painted toes stretch toward a pool that reflects palm trees and sun and blue sky. An arm's reach away, an umbrella drink. Their sun hats hide their faces, but this image shatters the frozen-over feeling I've been carrying with me. I can almost taste the salt air, the syrupy coconut of the cocktails, the stiff straw cutting the roof of my mouth.

I haven't seen the sun for fucking weeks. Sunlight, and all the good that comes with it: an easing off, a deep breath, summer meaning one less thing to worry about, in terms of the bad weather, the first box-score in the morning paper a kind of promise.

I want it more than I've wanted anything, suddenly—a writhing warmth in my belly that makes my legs restless. I want to wrap my arms around the sun like a beach ball and hug it close, swallow it, choke it down.

Jeanie's basketball coach and his ridiculous, beautifully luminescent lamp: it doesn't seem so crazy anymore.

Penny was in court today. Most likely, she's wrapped up by now.

I text her. "Have you been to Cabo?"

I gotta get the fuck out of here for a while. Cabo; Puerto Vallarta; Zihuantanejo like Tim Robbins in *Shawshank*: I'll sew my own goddamn sails if I have to. Chew off my arm to free myself from the bear trap of this place. Wondering if, like Lucas, once freed, I'll finally be able to sleep.

I'm ass-deep in columns and rows, looking over last quarter's reports, when someone knocks on the door. "Enter."

It's Vázquez. She's still wearing her trader's jacket. Her hair's up, pinned to the back of her head like a Sea Cucumber. She looks like she just sustained eighty-mile-an hour winds.

"Everything alright?" I ask.

Typically, she runs her mouth a mile a minute, but now she steps into the office like a child sneaking downstairs after bedtime, a kind of shuffling, leading with her toes. She grabs her left thumb and cranks her right hand against the joint, kneading dough.

"You look like shit," I tell her.

She sits.

I slide some irrelevant papers over the worksheets on the desk. "For fuck's sake, say something."

She gives me an abridged sob story, an apartment full of younger brothers that she's responsible for. Her dad off working in Texas because that's where the jobs are. For him. He sends some money home, but he's never around. Her mom kind of comes and goes—Stefany is the steady one, the earner. It's a whole lot of pressure, she tells me, being the first to graduate high school, to earn an associate degree, to have a big job downtown.

"What's the issue?" I ask.

"I've heard stuff," she says, like she's testing out the sound of her voice.

"Stuff." I pretend to busy myself with things on the desk, in the drawers. "What kind of stuff?"

"Firms are letting people go. I heard that our firm—people are saying we have no choice but to lay some people off."

"No one's laying anyone off," I grumble, thinking the rumor mill is really working overtime.

"Because I'm getting married."

"Congratulations."

"And weddings are expensive, you know? And it's not like I have my dad to pay for it. I have to pay for it myself. Me and Taylor. That's my husband. Well, my fiancé."

"Got it."

"And we're trying to save for our first apartment. There's things we're planning to do, financially—"

I raise my hand like a traffic cop, and my gesture stops the words in her mouth. This is starting to sound to me very much like over-sharing. I don't know why she's come to me with this. It's not entirely clear what she wants me to say. But I can't listen to another goddamn word.

"Let me stop you there." I start shuffling papers, just so I have something to do. None of the papers actually go together. "When I married my ex, she was a graduate student. You've heard the tales of woe, I'm sure, of graduate students being able to differentiate between brands of instant noodles, of using coffee grounds twice, all the glamorous poverty that comes with rising through academia. Of course you've heard about it: they never let us forget it. So my wife was worse than broke, she was in debt past her eyeballs. Which meant we were going to be in debt together. Sure, I had a good salary. But we started pricing weddings, looking at ten, twenty grand to throw something downtown, plus we wanted our own place right away, to own, not rent. Plus her classes."

"See?" Stefany smiles for the first time, and wipes one eye with the back of her hand. "This is why I wanted to come talk to you. Because I knew you'd have some great advice."

"Yes, well." I turn the entire stack of pages upside down and begin shuffling them that way too. Most of these are single-sided, so I end up shuffling a lot of blanks. "We eloped.

Drove out to Union Pier, got married by a judge, with a notary present, on the back patio of a B&B. Came back to Chicago a few days later, had people over to our apartment. And that was that."

"My dad would kill me if I elope."

"You want my advice?"

"More than anything. I respect you so much. There's probably no one I respect as much as you."

I take a big breath. Maybe she was right to be hesitant, coming in here.

"It's time to put your big-girl panties on."

She blinks, rubs her ear, looks at me.

I say it again. "Put. Your. Big. Girl. Panties. On."

"I don't understand."

My brain feels hot and sloshy, like steaming cider. Overripe. With a serious bite. "Was your father born here?"

"No," she says. "He was born in Puerto Rico."

"And your mom?"

"Her too."

"And growing up, they had a lot of money?"

"No," she says. "None."

"I had a father," I tell her. "One thing about my father was that he always carried around one of those thirty-two ounce Big Gulp red fucking thermos cups."

"I can picture that."

"He never went anywhere without it. Now, I don't know when I figured it out, but when I was ten or eleven, I realized that thermos was filled with alcohol. All day long, my father would sip from that thermos, refill it who knows how many times? And one day, you know, when you're an adolescent, things are so black and white: one day before he left for work, I poured the alcohol down the sink and refilled the thermos with water. Put it right back where I found it, next to his briefcase, and he took it with him that morning when he left.

"He came home that night still carrying the thermos. We ate dinner together, and the whole time I kept expecting him to ask me about it or give some hint that he knew what I'd done. But everything was normal. He put me to bed that night, even, which was a rare thing. Tucked me in and turned the lights off. Kissed me on the forehead.

"I thought, you know, maybe I'd succeeded. Maybe I'd poured out the alcohol, and he decided never to have another drink."

"That was brave of you."

I glare at her. "The next morning, I woke up to an empty bedroom. We didn't have all that much to begin with. I had some toys. A bike. Some clothes. But I woke up, and my room was empty. All my clothes, all my toys. My basketball. My baseball cards. He'd taken all of it during the night. Cleaned me out."

"Sold it?" she asks.

"Sold it?" I laugh. "No, that might have actually made some sense. He burned it. All of it. Walk outside, big fucking charred garbage can in the street. All my shit, ashes."

"Fuck."

I shrug.

"It's terrible that happened to you," she says. "But you have a daughter. Don't you want her to have the nicest stuff?"

"When she's earned it." It comes out sharper than I intended, full of venom. Stefany startles, blinking, like a balloon's been popped.

I'm furious about a lot of things, all at once. I'm furious that I was stupid enough to take Jeanie to the wake, so everyone knows I have a daughter now, and someone as shameless as

Stefany Vázquez can try to take advantage of it. I'm furious that she's come to me with this at the end of the day, that I don't have someone else to manage her underdeveloped sense of self-worth.

Most of all, I'm furious at Pasternak.

Fuck you. Fuck you to fucking hell.

"What do you want?" I shove this question in her face, at full volume. "Do you want more of a stake?"

She looks surprised. "Sure."

"You're not getting one more red fucking cent."

"Just as long as I'm not getting fired—"

"People get fired when they make stupid fucking mistakes." I tuck my chin and glower. "Are you going to make a stupid fucking mistake?"

"No."

"Then what the fuck else do you want from me?"

She doesn't have any idea how hard it would be for me to fire her now regardless of how big a mistake she makes. A woman and a minority? Fucking forget about it. I'd have to have a file cabinet full of her fuck-ups in order to stand up in court against her inevitable wrongful termination suit.

New traders are a crapshoot. The guys at DIP's wake were correct: a semester isn't long enough to hold a stock portfolio contest. Newbies like Vázquez are the same. Virgin traders, either they get lucky right out of the gate, a couple stocks take off on them and run, and they get a reputation as knowing what the fuck they're doing; or the opposite happens, they stumble initially, hit a streak of bad luck, and fairly or not, get labeled a loser. It's one of the truly unpredictable things in life. Stefany's had some bad luck, but she's not helping herself.

"I staked you a hundred grand," I say, more gently. "That's twice what I usually stake a new hire. Please hear what I'm saying. Really listen. It's time to leave your safe space behind. Put your big-girl panties on and join the real world."

At lunch, I go down to the courtyard. I need to air out. The plaza is empty, everyone driven off by the wind and cold. I press myself against the wall, under the breezeway. I balance my phone between my shoulder and ear and hold my cigarette with one hand, switching hands every sixty seconds so only one appendage at a time is exposed to the cold.

"Weil," Penny answers, when I call.

"It's me."

"Jonathan."

A long silence.

"You didn't text me back." My fingers burn from the cold. I switch hands, keep smoking. "How's it going?"

Another long silence, or not quite—I can hear her typing.

"Are you calling to chit-chat?" she asks.

I imagine her posed at her standing desk, her back to the skyline. She faces her door, orienting toward the north rather than toward the place where I am from, the Southside. It's coincidence, of course. I gave up trying to find symbols in anything a long fucking time ago.

"I'm calling to thank you. For coming to pick up Jeanie. I really appreciate your going out of your way for me like that."

There's a long silence. Not quite silence: the click-clacking of keys.

"Anything else?" she asks.

"No," I tell her. "Talk later."

"Goodbye, Jonathan."

The dial tone comes harsh and quick.

I stamp my cigarette out against a trashcan. I check my watch. Three hours before close.

I text Pasternak. "Gone for the day."

I'm in the backseat of a taxi before I realize there was no reason to text DIP, that he can't reply, even if he wanted to.

I know guys who quit drinking entirely because they scared themselves. Maybe they got into legal trouble like I have now with this DUI; maybe they hit their wife; maybe they took stock and realized they'd had at least one drink a day for a month straight and worried about sliding into alcoholism. Whichever way it broke for them, they quit.

I am required to participate in counseling as part of my probation. The counselor is up in Lincoln Square, somewhere off the Brown Line I guess, a place I couldn't find with a map, it's so goddamn residential. The counselor is my age, tubby, with big glasses. He talks streetwise, but he's a plush doll deep down. To work with addicts every day, I imagine you'd have to be.

Most people assume, you drink every day, you've got a drinking problem. But the counselor makes the opposite argument, that slurping three drinks a day is healthier than drinking twenty-one beers on Friday and Saturday while abstaining the rest of the week.

My father with his Big Gulp thermos of vodka and ice, which he carried with him when he left the house each morning, along with his chocolate brown, Samsonite briefcase.

The counselor makes me take a multiple-choice test. It's more or less the same questions over and over, which try to ascertain whether or not I have a problem with alcohol.

"Have you ever felt guilty about drinking?"

"Have you ever woken up in the morning after a night of drinking and not been able to remember part of the evening?"

"Do you drink before noon fairly often?"

Whether or not you're an alcoholic, you don't want to spend a moment longer than you have to in substance-abuse counseling.

The counselor glances at my answer sheet. "Well, you know how to take a test, anyway."

I catch a cab over to Whitney M. Young Magnet School, where, I know, it should be final period, which for Jeanie means economics. The receptionist takes my digital photo and signs me in. I write my name on a sticker and plaster it over my left nipple. I walk through the metal detector, and the security guard tells me to have a good afternoon.

This is a nice school. Both Azita and I were relieved as hell when Jeanie got in here, after the testing she had to do and the application process. It's Chicago Public Schools, sure, but the application process weeds out the really bad apples so there's not that worry of gang violence or Jeanie getting turned onto crack during third period. Instead, it's rich-girl drama: underage drinking and sex. Even still, metal detectors at the door, our modern world.

I don't know if it's the polish they put down on the hallways or what, but the fluorescent overheads reflect in shimmering pools on the floor. Plenty of windows let in some sunlight and offer views of a courtyard and the distant city. When I pass the cafeteria, I notice the walls are decorated with punchouts of snowflakes on red, green, and white construction paper.

At Jeanie's classroom, I hover outside the door until her teacher notices me. He brightens, waves like we haven't seen each other in ages, and hurries over to shake my hand.

"Wonderful to see you," he tells me. "Thank you again for having us onto the trading floor."

I don't know whether or not he's serious, what with the way the field trip ended, when the kids were hustled out with naked boobies still on half the monitors. "Sure thing."

"I know it ended rather oddly," he says, "but right up until then it was an absolute thrill. You traders are giants! If I could do it again…"

Jeanie comes out then and rescues me. "What are you doing here?"

I ask her teacher, "Mind if I take her for a moment?"

He tells me to go right ahead and withdraws into his classroom like a turtle pulling back inside his shell. I offer Jeanie my arm, and she takes it. We walk until we are out of earshot, toward the long, enclosed skywalk that connects the main school with the gym.

"Aren't you delivering the Gettysburg Address this afternoon?" she asks me.

We pause midway across the bridge, beneath a long, handwritten banner wishing the Dolphins' girls basketball team good luck. The team has signed it, Jeanie's name scrawled brazenly across the center in orange marker.

"I've got time." I say. "And if I don't show up, will anyone really give a shit?"

She smiles quickly and shoves her hands in her armpits. It's chillier on the bridge than in the hallways. I touch the glass, and the cold burns a little. The cold makes everything so fragile. This entire walkway, I feel like I could shatter it with a flick of my finger.

She asks, "What's up, Dad?"

I shrug.

"C'mon." She stares at me in that way she has, that way her mother has. "Out with it."

"These guys, the other traders, rely on me. I'm their voice. I represent them and their livelihoods. I protect their ability to put bread on the table, to provide for their families."

"And?"

"If we go public at $27 a share, they're being short-changed. Their seats are worth more than that on an open market."

She takes my chin between her forefinger and thumb. We're more or less the same height now, all of a sudden, it seems like. She leans in, close enough for me to smell her berry-flavored lip balm. She runs the flat of her hand along my scalp. I close my eyes and shudder at the tingling down my spine. The gesture is nurturing, the way a mother might stroke her infant, to quiet him.

"Where's your courage?" she asks, quietly.

"Gone."

"I doubt it."

She rests her hand at the back of my neck. Both of us lean forward until our foreheads touch. We press together. I keep my eyes shut. My heart pounds in my chest. The force of her keeps me anchored to the floor, the walkway, the earth.

"I've always looked out for them," I say. "For the traders. It seems wrong now to lie to them."

She takes her hand away. I open my eyes. She folds her arms again.

"Let me tell you about the John Ganzi I know," she says. "Let me tell you about my dad. My dad is a motherfucking demon. When he wants something, he figures out how to get it, and then he takes it. Fuck anyone else. Fuck everyone else."

"And now?"

She pokes me in the gut. "You look like a kitten."

"Fuck off."

"You've given up everything for your job," she says. "Mom. Your health. Me—us."

I blink, then turn away. There's no use arguing about it. Still, the truth hurts. I feel suddenly like weeping; I touch the cold glass again to steady myself. "And if the vote doesn't go through?"

She does the one-shoulder shrug, that cool indifference that is part of her genetic inheritance from her mother. "A few millionaires don't get quite as rich; a few privileged white boys get to keep working. It's not really Armageddon, is it?"

The bell rings. She glances back toward the hallway and her classroom.

"Stop being such a pussy," she says.

Whenever we want to get everyone together, all the firms, we take over the cafeteria. We set up a little speaker system. Beneath the low-slung ceiling, in the dim transience of that space, the drab gray walls and tile floor, the smell of burnt coffee and crusted baking pans, we hash shit out like men. It's the only room big enough to hold us all.

It's well into the afternoon by the time I arrive. The cafeteria is packed. I say a few hellos and make my way to the front. There's a buzz in the air that reminds me of a locker room, the pent-up energy, all that testosterone, secreted through skin. Eugene is here, blessing this historic occasion with his presence. He tosses me a silver button. I turn it over. The pin reads *Sar* in black letters, and the letters are crossed out with one red slash line diagonally through it. *No Sar.* I laugh, and Eugene winks. I notice a few other guys wearing the pins. Sar has always had detractors, who view him as being out of touch with the day-to-day slog of the pits, which might not be fair but is probably, at this point, at least partly based in fact. He spent hardly any time in a pit—he's a suit through and through.

Sar's assistant, Charlene, finds me. She's changed her hair. Short, golden knots pepper her scalp. She wears a burgundy pant-suit, her shoulders wide enough to block doors. She hands me a green slip of paper and a red slip of paper. This is how the future will be decided, by lot. Each man will approach the ballot box and cast his vote: green for yes, red for no.

"Can I have that button?" she asks.

I hand it over.

"He'll want it for his scrapbook," she tells me.

Sar himself is on top of me then, pumping my hand. "Ready for your big moment?"

"Ready as I'll ever be," I say.

This is what I committed to when I secured a sit-down with Northwestern for Jeanie's basketball coach, when I got Jeanie back on the team. Bills come due. Nothing for free. When I stand before the majority of options traders in the City of Chicago, I'll be obligated to tell it to them straight: change is coming. Electronic trading platforms are the future. Human capital is antiquated, inefficient, and not cost-effective. They need to open up their members-only boys club and become a publicly traded company or risk losing this beautiful industry entirely.

The Chief Operating Officer, an oversized, jolly Irishman whose jacket hasn't fit since 1983, taps twice on the microphone and gets everyone's attention. He cracks a few jokes. The guys laugh. Everybody loves him. He rose from nothing, like me, the whole time working his way up through the Exchange, and made it all the way to the Executive suites. He introduces me, and I'm surprised at how relaxed I feel, how calm. I've known the guys in this crowd my entire life, seems like. More than my co-workers, it's like addressing my brothers—something deeper than brotherhood, really—my comrades.

I finally take the mic. The room seems dim. Traders slouch against tables and walls like sacks of grain. A few yawn. I get it:

our day starts early. Most of them are here because attendance is mandatory. Because we need a quorum to vote. Few probably realize how their asses are on the line. The last ones on the boat, so to speak, the low guys on the totem pole.

"Most of you know who I am." The mic feeds back a little. I step away and clear the cable out from under my feet. "Those who do know me know that I don't sugarcoat anything. I'm not going to stand up here and blow smoke up your ass. I've never cared for politics. And those who know me, you know that's not what I'm about."

I swig from an Evian bottle. I tell them, I may not be about politics, but I am about the future. Specifically, I'm about how to make money in the future. Because I'm sure as hell not out here humping every day for my health.

We don't know much about the future, I tell them. All we know for sure is that the future is going to come.

Not for Pasternak, I think, but do not say.

There is total silence now. Everybody, whether they're for Sar nor not, wants to hear what's next. Hell, so do I.

"Adapt or die," I tell them. "That's the rule we live by. As traders—as human beings. It's what I want to remind you of now. Adapt or die."

I pause to drink more water, glance at Sar. He stands with his hands folded behind him, as stiff and unmoving as Grant's statue. He's expecting from me the speech to end all speeches, win one for the Gipper and four-score and twenty. I've prepared nothing, though. I usually don't, on occasions such as these. Blessed with the gift of gab. But as I stand in front of these guys, even with all that's on the line—the future of the Exchange in the balance—my thoughts turn to Jeanie. What we do for our children. Remembering my own father yanking the ketchup bottle from my mouth, throwing blood-red sauce across my mother, my priest. How the first time I tasted beer, a Coors Light, which Pasternak and I swiped from the fridge and shared in the alleyway behind his house, I liked the taste far more than he did.

At the end of the day, I tell those gathered, we're here to put bread on the table. That's all, and everything. They closed the original Chicago Stock Exchange too. They moved it into a museum. Is that the future we want for ourselves as well? To be museum pieces? To be artifacts?

"My daughter," I say to the beautiful, unshaven faces before me, "she's been following this story in the news, about how there are coyotes living in the Loop. They scavenge from trash cans and dumpsters. One entered a 7-Eleven recently, bought a forty and a pack of menthols. But seriously, to me, this is amazing stuff. Coyotes in downtown Chicago."

Most traders, we're not dumb. We are not easily charmed. You'd never select a trader to participate in a hypnosis, or a magic show. Those that aren't school-smart have something else, a kind of street toughness. We call bullshit on you real quick. The guys are listening to me now, but all of them sense a kind of build-up. They're waiting for the turn.

"Coyotes were here first," I continue. "When Illinois was being settled in the eighteenth century. Homesteaders would hear coyotes howling in the night. The coyotes couldn't have envisioned Chicago from their place on the prairie in 1750. But it came. It happened. It was built. And those glorious beasts had a choice: adapt or die."

The overhead lights blur briefly; seven or eight bulbs become eighteen or twenty. I wipe my eyes and blink several times at the men looking back at me. I see Pasternak in every face. His ugly mug floating between shoulders, above other heads—poor Yorick.

I look at my shoes. I try to pull myself together, wondering if I'm stroking out, or if DIP has come back to haunt me like Jacob Marley. I raise my eyes again, and Pasternak has settled in a high corner toward the back of the assembly. I clear my throat, dig in my pocket for loose change, an old tic. Reminding myself to focus.

I don't want to come off like I'm telling these guys what to do. I don't want to be their executioner. Because for me, personally, it doesn't matter what happens. I'm covered. Retire tomorrow, somewhere real South like Tampa. And the truth is, I'm on-board with the idea that what's best for the Exchange in the long-term might be hard on some firms in the short-term. Markets are good at a lot of things. Predictions. Forming majority opinion. Demanding profitability and sniffing out inefficiencies. Human beings are inefficient. But it may be beyond our capacity, above where we find ourselves on the evolutionary ladder, to recognize that about ourselves.

"We have two choices," I tell them. "We can cling to the way we've always done things, all of us chicken littles with our heads in the sand, and pretend electronic trading platforms aren't coming. Or we can get out in front, embrace the future, try to position ourselves on the cutting edge and make damn sure that we're the world's largest options exchange for the next thirty-five years as well."

The guys burst into conversations then, some outraged, some basically just expressing some combination of surprise and exhaustion with the entire business. I raise one hand and mostly quiet them.

"Are some pits going to close?" I ask. "Yes." More complaints from the crowd, expletives, displeasure directed mostly at me. "Are there going to be lay-offs? Almost certainly. But those closures and lay-offs are coming regardless. Wall Street has been cut in half this year. But in the end, those jobs you're going to lose, those firms that are going to merge? They're not the point. The point, friends, is that when you go home at night and look in the mirror, do you see someone who will seize the next opportunity, learn new skills, and thrive? Or are you someone who's going to go down with the ship?

"I tell you who I see when I look in the mirror. A fucking coyote. That's right. And here's why: coyotes adapt to their environment. City, country, woods—they don't give a fuck. And a hundred years from now when this glorious city has become something we can't even imagine from our place here in 2008, I plan to be able to still stroll into 7-Eleven and buy myself a motherfucking Honeybun."

The crowd erupts. Chants of "Sar, Sar, Sar" and "Ganzi! Ganzi!" mixed with the outrage you'd expect, a few "Fuck you, JAG," and a few less-than-politically-sensitive riffs on my call-sign. But plenty of others nod at me in solidarity or offer low-key applause, below the belt and out of sight. Eugene glowers, arms folded, but whatever, fuck him.

"Be a coyote," I shout at them. "I want to hear you howl."

Sar's on me then, slapping my back and taking the microphone.

"Knocked it out of the park," he says.

I stand aside and watch the traders make their way up front, one by one. Some avoid eye contact, palming their ballots and slipping their papers unseen into the box. Others make sure I see which way they're voting. They present their green slip of paper in solidarity, or gesture with a red scrap as a rebuke. After every vote is cast, including mine, the COO opens the box. So much green paper spills out that the votes are not worth counting. The Exchange has voted overwhelmingly to settle the various pending lawsuits, which means we'll go public, this decade, most likely, at a cost per share well below what most of these traders deserve. But sometimes, it's in your best interest to let yourself be fucked. That's something they don't teach you in business school. We take a hit on the share cost here, now, we make it up with volume in the years and decades to follow.

I check the corner again, but Pasternak is gone, his celestial form having no doubt cast a vote that is in lockstep with the rest of our firm. That fucking guy never had an original thought.

Home, bottle of Bell's Winter White in-hand, I try to dig up something for dinner. Jeanie is on Christmas Break and out with friends. I've given her a midnight curfew. We'll see if she meets it.

In the bottom drawer of the fridge, in the crisper, I find a head of broccoli, the kernels a brown, off-yellow color that looks like diarrhea. Water has collected in a corner of the produce bag. Deeper in, I find a single hamburger bun and leftovers from two weeks ago—guacamole, the top lacquered with a hard, white crust.

Fucking death throws everything off. It leaves no dark corner unexplored. I take everything out of the fridge and throw it in the trash, then drag the bag into the hall and send it tumbling down the shoot. Someone else's problem. The garbage men. Scavenger homeless not afraid of a little scrim on their guacamole. A coyote, perhaps.

I text Penny. "Dinner?"

I catch up to her at Zebra Lounge, this little hole in the wall off Rush and Division, where she's ridden Happy Hour straight deep into evening. The last of her co-workers say goodbye;

I order a double shot of Jameson. I'm way behind. Penny's groping me beneath the table as soon as I sit down, a public display of affection I'm not nearly intoxicated enough to enjoy.

I guide her to the bar stools at the upright piano. We page through a three-inch binder of sheet music. We make the piano player crank out every song we can sing along to. Elton John's "Your Song." Toto's "Africa." Bon Jovi's "Living on a Prayer." If you want to make a Chicago bar come to a screeching halt, play "Living on a Prayer." Without fail, at any drinking establishment in the City of Big Shoulders, every conversation pauses at the appropriate moment long enough for the patrons to pump their hands in the air and belt the call-and-response chorus. Penny and I howl right along with them, sloshing our drinks across the ancient upright and the laminated pages of music, christening them.

Eventually, we make our way to a restaurant, a Michelin-starred place with long, wooden tables and black and white napkins the maître d changes out depending on what the diners are wearing. The sommelier recommends a Bourgogne. We order that and a champagne toast. He brings a complimentary amuse bouche—a mint and cantaloupe jelly, served with water crackers. Sitting elbow-to-elbow with strangers, Penny and I lean across the table to whisper to one another. I tell her I'd like to lick the jelly from between her toes; she admits to sometimes fantasizing about fucking in the bathroom of a restaurant as fine as this, how the rhythm she'd pound against the wall would rattle serving stations on the other side, the rows of empty glasses, dirty dish tubs, and flatware bins.

We scoop warm marrow from cow bone. We slurp fresh oysters from the half-shell, with a dash of Tabasco, as all around us other Midwesterners gape in horror. No one understands oysters out here on the prairie. We chew marinated curled dock the server claims were harvested not fifty yards from the restaurant, soaked in olive oil and sea salt and charred over an open flame. We do not let the name of this weed go unremarked upon, musing on its proximity to a part of the male anatomy; nor do I ponder how many homeless have pissed on this weed, as within a fifty-yard radius of this restaurant there are only dumpsters and empty brownstones and crumbling, asphalt slabs. I dissect squab; she eats pumpkin ravioli that tastes like a crisp fall night and a fire pit. We finish one bottle of wine and then drink absinthe poured over an upturned spoon, diluted by a sugar cube. We exhale liquid fire into one another's mouths, when we lean across the table and kiss.

"Cabo will be great," I tell her.

"I don't want to go to Cabo." She says this with plenty of sugar. "Let's do Belize, somewhere we can be active."

"I want to sit on a beach somewhere I need only raise a little flag on my plastic fucking chair for some oppressed, indigenous server to come hustling over to bring me a fresh coconut drink."

"That's anywhere for you, Jonathan," she says. "You're rich."

"They're not always indigenous," I say without humor. "That makes all the difference."

"You know," she slurs, "that when Captain Cook landed in New Zealand, the natives brought out young boys as gifts?"

"The fuck?"

"The natives thought the crew were all gay. Because there weren't any women on the ship."

I stare at her, blankly.

"There weren't any chicks," she says.

"I got it," I tell her, more harshly than I mean it. But sometimes something comes out a certain way, out of your mouth, and you're surprised by its tone, its passion or anger, and then you realize how you really feel about a given topic, that your voice, your physical response, was ahead of your conscious thoughts or recognizable feelings.

"It's kind of like the first time I was on an Exchange floor," she tells me. "We toured the Board of Trade, in middle school. I thought, here is the beefiest gay club in Chicago."

I toss back my drink. The ice knocks against my teeth. Maybe it's the booze, or my level of satiation, the weird-ass food we just inhaled, or maybe it's just that I haven't admitted to myself yet what a shitty day this has been. The fuck does she know about it anyway, what it's like toiling side by side with other men? I look around for the server, but he's nowhere. I twist my napkin into a rope.

There is a mathematical equation, a direct correlation, between the quality of a restaurant and the fight you can get into with your date there. I've never confirmed this with a server, but I suspect that when you wait tables at a Michelin-starred restaurant, you see the mother of all fights between couples. It's as if we save our resentments, our pitiful tally of wrongs, our benchmarks for who is sacrificing more for the relationship at any given moment, until we find ourselves someplace a dinner for two sets you back $500. Because no one wants to get into a knock-down, drag-out fight in fucking Bennigan's. With goddamn Monte Cristo grease running down our thumbs. Instead, we wait for an establishment that changes its menu nightly, where the servers are sweepingly invisible, who ask your water preference upon being seated. There, huddling below globules of light, a half-bottle of wine and countless cocktails sloshing in your belly, the experience begins to reveal your relationship for what it truly is. Fine dining as truth serum. Being waited upon like that, impeccably, can make you look across the table at the person you're sharing this fantastic meal with and realize that your feelings toward the other person don't merit a dinner as exquisite as this; that your feelings toward one another hardly justify the truffle shavings on your fried egg and frisée salad; the endless parade of dish-appropriate utensils; the unpronounceable liqueurs in your post-dinner drinks. Like turning light on a dark corner, an excellent restaurant can—instead of heighten the romance, as intended—prove your relationship void of any romance whatsoever. And that's the worst sensation in the world. Both of you sitting there feeling like phonies, sure that all the other patrons can see your evening for the sham that it is, and you haven't even gotten to the main course.

So you pick a fight. Something small at first. How all great conflagrations begin. A cow kicks over a lantern. The pressure of the night begins to be too much. A crackling of small flames scattered in the conversation, in the corner of a barn, until the entire fucking city is burning down.

Penny comments on the tie I'm wearing. My style has never wavered. If it can be called anything, it can be called an absolute lack of style. The tie in question is woven with seafoam and purple argyle. She wonders, do I ever wear it properly knotted at the neck, or do I always let it dangle like a carnival sideman?

I know exactly what she's driving at. Azita, too, was always after me about my hygiene. My grooming. How I ought to shave more, use hair gel, not cut my toenails in bed. Like I was a fucking labradoodle. It was one of our ongoing arguments, spanning years. Couples, when they've been together long enough, have these. The things you hope will one day change about the person you've committed to spending the rest of your life with, but that, of course, never do.

"I enjoy the way it feels like a noose," I tell Penny. "Maybe one day I'll fucking hang myself with it."

She leans back in her chair, hand still palming her cocktail glass. "Do it then, if you're so miserable."

I think of Pasternak. "Too soon."

"Or find a hobby. Collect something."

"What, like art?" I can't help the cynicism in my voice. I see her expression and know that I've cut her. "I can't imagine a bigger waste of time. Or money."

I can feel the alcohol turning mean. I concentrate on my lips and over-pronounce.

"I wouldn't expect a plebe such as yourself to collect anything but Type II diabetes, frankly," she says.

To be honest, I don't even know what the fuck that means. "Is that a knock on where I went to school?"

Nearby tables have noticed our spat but are politely ignoring it. I can't help thinking about how things look to other people. I try to steer back to calm water.

"How was your crème brûlée?" I ask.

She wipes her mouth with her napkin, black so as not to leave noticeable fuzzies on her skin-tight, knee-length skirt, and tosses it on the table. "You know what? I don't think this is working out."

I put down my fork. "Oh, but we're having so much fun…."

She shakes her head. "I drank too much. Get the check."

"Well I certainly wouldn't expect you to pick it up," I scowl. "I'd hate to break with precedent."

By now, those seated nearest us have completely stopped talking and are, in fact, blatantly listening to our escalating row. This could be big, they think. Really big. Tell our friends later about it, big. A week from now they'll have forgotten the fried frog legs with fennel and corn dashi, but they'll remember the argument between that dwarfish-man in the bad tie and the drop-dead gorgeous date he obviously hired off the back page of *The Reader*.

I level my eyes. "You'll give Eugene a wank for a ticket to our Christmas party, but you won't finish a second date with me?"

Her eyes blaze. Maybe it's the torches on the wall.

"You're a pig," she says, and I can't help but hear Pasternak's voice, *Pigs get fat.*

"Can he even still get it up?"

"Stop it, Jonathan."

"My name's not fucking Jonathan." I slur my name so badly, it sounds like a dishwasher cycle. "It's John. Just John."

She leans forward. "Well, just John? You're just a fucking asshole. And this date is over."

And she is gone.

I sit alone at our table for twenty minutes, until our server decides Penny really isn't coming back and offers to bring me the check. As I sit there, swirling the remnants of my ice, feeling much too drunk for a restaurant as nice as this, feeling every eye upon me, knowing everyone saw her walk out, I still feel a need to keep a pleasant expression on my face, what might almost be a smile, projecting benevolent assurance that yes, yes, all will be well—the lady just needed some fresh air, and we're so sorry to have disturbed your dinner.

It's moments like this that make me feel like a fraud. Despite what I pull down each year, despite the position of respect I've attained in the incubator of the Exchange, I still believe, deep down, that at any moment, everyone around me, these blue-bloods who were raised frequenting restaurants as nice as this, who grew up with house staff and weekends in Steamboat, will eventually sniff me out—my working class upbringing, my lack of proper etiquette—and turn me back to the streets, back to South Chicago, back to my leaky water bed and the tiny house with no yard and no A.C. and a basement that floods each time it rains. That all this, the high-thread-count table linens, the electronic jazz on the stereo, isn't really built for someone like me.

It's as I've always feared: I really don't belong, after all.

Chapter 16

I wouldn't call security in my apartment air-tight, but the doormen do notice who comes and goes. I slip Ralphie, the night guy, a $50 bill, along with a list of ten kids he can let upstairs for Jeanie's New Year's Eve party.

"That's just for you," I tell him, because I've already contributed to the holiday pot the building collects for the staff.

"Many happy returns," he grins, palming the bill into his coat pocket.

Jeanie and her best girlfriend, Ella or Emma, I can never remember, have been cooking all day. There are creamy dips in bread bowls; baked nachos with sour cream and shredded pork; chopped vegetables. There is kale, fried on the stalk and set up-right in a vase. There is potato salad, ham salad, and curried deviled eggs. I'm impressed as hell.

"Did you learn all this from Patrick?" I ask.

Jeanie shrugs. "The guy can cook."

She's assigned me grill duty. Chicken tenderloins marinate in orange juice and onions. I've pounded out two-dozen hamburger patties. Jeanie found corn on the cob somewhere and has asked me to throw them on the grill for a minute or two after they're boiled, for a little char. I go out to the porch, zip my coat to my ears, brush snow off the handrail, and light the grill. The cold sharpens the senses, turns brake lights of cars below into laserpoints. Each sound amplified: the echoing meditation of a furnace exhaust. Something shuffling on the rooftop, a pigeon or hawk. The impatient traffic sounds, everyone trying to leave work and beat the rush home. I hustle back inside, my earlobes burning from the cold.

Jeanie's bathtub is filled with iced beer. I lean against the sink, considering this boozy grotto. This has been her bathroom since she was ten. She's sat on the tub edge while I pulled splinters from the heel of her hand; stuck her busted knee beneath the faucet while I wiped with an antiseptic cloth; made faces at herself in the mirror while I taught her how to put rubberbands on her braces. Now her bathtub is stuffed with beer cans like dyed Easter eggs, nestled in icy, cellophane shred. I feel a sadness settle. It all feels very final, her being so grown-up.

Emerging, I find my living room transformed. The chairs and couch have been arranged in a U. There is an indoor putting green, an eight-inch strip of AstroTurf about four-feet long, with a little flag and cup. There is a baseball video playing on the television, highlights from the 2005 White Sox Championship season. On the stereo, I recognize songs by the Beach Boys, and Jimmy Buffett, and old-school tracks by Gloria Estefan and the Miami Sound Machine, Belle Biv Devoe, and Boys II Men. My apartment feels warm as summer: the thermostat is cranked to 85.

"Yo!" I wave down Jeanie. "What's with the heat?"

"Dad." Hands on her hips, she rolls her eyes. "We can't have a Fuck the Winter New Year's Party and have it be all freezing cold in here."

I go back outside to flip burgers.

My first drink of alcohol was a half-can of Coors in the alley with Pasternak. My second was the dregs of a bottle of

Cutty Sark, New Year's Eve, 1975. Dad had passed out before the fireworks. I tipped the glass bottle with both hands and drank the rest. Oh, it burned—Jesus Christ, it felt like dragon fire all the way down. My eyes swelled with peat and bog. It was terrible, and I immediately wanted more.

Jeanie's first drink, I suspect, was under more controlled circumstances. Half a glass of red wine at one of Azita's dinner parties, sometime in her early teens. Given that my father died of liver cancer brought about, almost certainly, by years of unrepentant drinking; given my own proclivities; what are the chances Jeanie will have an alcohol problem? Very high. One might even question the wisdom of my allowing minors, Jeanie in particular, to consume booze under my roof, under my watch. I'd like to believe my perspective is realistic: the kids are going to find a way. I'd prefer they do it while I'm home, so that if there's an issue, I'm here.

Who knows? Maybe I would have felt differently two weeks ago, before Pasternak died. And all that counseling I've gone too since, on account of my DUI—it's proved nothing other than that no one knows didly shit about addiction, certainly not how to prevent it. Or even define it: I almost feel like the definition is in the outcome. Do you have a DUI? You may have a problem. If not, move along.

I'm carrying a platter of grilled meat into the kitchen as Jeanie's friends arrive. It's a shocking thing when they step out of their boots, shrug off their overcoats, and reveal safari-print shorts and bikini tops, summer dresses and linen skirts. One girl sprouts fairy wings. A boy goes shirtless. He wears a necklace strung with Smarties. All of them enter my apartment like shedding chrysalises. They cross the room fluttering with color and light. In two corners, Jeanie has positioned the same kind of sun lamp her coach uses. The condo windows glow, trembling, like Tinkerbell. Here, I think, the drafts and darkness cannot penetrate.

In my room, I remove my shoes and change into a T-shirt. Already, I'm sweating. I rest for a moment on the bed and text Penny.

After our fight at the restaurant, I let things cool down overnight and called her first-thing the next morning. We were both apologetic, both more embarrassed for the way we behaved than out of any concern that we'd hurt the other person. Whether that was because we recognize our own toughness in one another, or whether it was because neither of us can really bring ourselves to give a shit about anyone else, other than ourselves, I can't say. Our conversation was polite, reserved, accommodating. Very adult. She mentioned she was triple-booked for New Year's, and I told her to add another invite to her list, if she'd consider joining me as a chaperone for Jeanie's church friends.

"Plans?" I text.

There's only a short pause before her reply. "Def going out. But where?!?"

"10 high school kids and a bottle of Veuve. My invite stands."

"Tempting…"

"Keep me posted."

I take my Sox cap off the closet hook and tug it over my head. Nothing says summer, to me, more than this.

I turn off the grill and bring the meat into the kitchen. I scan the beverages. A couple bottles of wine and soda. One of Jeanie's male friends, also bare-chested and wearing a glittering grass skirt, slips past and opens the freezer. He reaches in and comes away with three red popsicles. The dessert is deep purple with shreds of fruit skin in the ice: merlot and cherries. My contribution to the party.

"Take it easy on those," I tell him.

He hee-haws, mouth gaping. "Yes sir! It's a marathon, not a sprint."

I suck down a popsicle myself. It's not too bad. Edible, anyway, and almost good for you. One's enough though. I pour myself a double Lagavulin. A nod to my father, who saved a little of his paycheck each month so he could buy an expensive Scotch to ring in the New Year. I toast him silently and swallow the burn.

My mother, her one New Year's Eve tradition, was to force our entire family outside to make a shit-ton of noise. At the stroke of midnight, we banged through the screen door to blow air horns, blast cheering trumpets, and smack tambourines against our knees until we bruised, hollering at the sky, cheering the crackle of unseen fireworks, our voices echoing back to us from the many alleyways and side-streets. After so many years of this, our neighbors joined in. By the time I was in high school, whenever the clock struck twelve on January 1, our street burst with celebrations. We'd light sparklers and run with one in each hand, arms out, so the flames trailed behind us like thrusters. I lobbed mine in the air to watch the arc of light through the sky. Or wrote my name, the tracers shaping letters, briefly buffeted by the wind, before blinking out. The smell of gunpowder from the snappers; the charred, carbon stench of Black Cats.

Back in my room, I settle in bed, feet up, and flip channels on the flat screen. Now, at age forty-four, New Year's Eve is something to be endured, to wake up on the other side of, relieved not to have to do it again for another 364 days. I usually spend it alone, like any other night. Which works fine up until midnight, when people throw open their windows, up and down the street, and shout "Happy New Year" into the blackness. My apartment is high enough that I can see ambient, strobing light from fireworks in distant towns in the greater Chicagoland area. That's a lonely feeling, absorbing all that light and color, resenting it.

I watch a movie, *Knight's Tale*, about a peasant who becomes a knight through pluck and courage. An underrated movie that happens to be fucking hysterical, one, with a memorable performance by Paul Bettany as Chaucer. Two, they swap-in modern rock songs during the jousting and sword fights, to give the viewer a taste of what it would have been like back then in the arena. That charged atmosphere, everyone stomping their feet, that swirling energy.

What happens is, the protagonist, William, is serving as a squire to a knight who dies in a joust. He and the other squires seize the opportunity, dress William as the dead knight, and enter him in competitions across the kingdom. He skyrockets to the top of the standings, winning the hearts of fans. There's a love story with a princess, of course, and an exploration of William's humble origins as son to a poor, half-blind thatcher.

There's a lot about the movie I relate to.

William is navigating the narrow streets of the slum he grew up in when my phone buzzes. It's the front desk.

"Mr. Ganzi," Ralphie, the doorman says. "Someone to see you—"

"I'll be right down."

I assume it's Penny downstairs and hang up. I'm thinking this is real progress. I grab my smokes and slide on my shoes. Look at us being two grown-ass adults. Thinking she's come to bury the hatchet. Marveling that two people can get too drunk and shout at each other in public and no harm done. That hell, this might even make our relationship stronger.

I duck my head into the party—low lights, thrashing bodies dancing, the smell of hops and fermented grapes—and head downstairs.

But I find no sign of Penny. I give Ralphie a look like what the fuck?

"This gentleman," he says, gesturing toward the waiting area.

There's a potted plant with leaves as big as elephant ears. From behind this *colocasia*, like some mutant arachnid from a sci-fi flick, Jeanie's basketball coach appears. I didn't see him sitting there, context being everything, and all that.

"Mr. Ganzi." He is deferential and does his best to bow when he offers his hand.

"Happy New Year," I tell him.

"Sorry to bother you on New Year's Eve," he says.

I pop an unlit cigarette into my mouth. "I never have plans on New Year's."

He nods toward the smoke. "I see where Jeanie gets her proclivities."

"Alleged proclivities."

"Alleged." He grins. "Listen, I know I should have called, but I was so excited. Karyn Bass came by my office today. I literally just put her in a cab."

"Who?"

"Bass? Head coach at Georgetown?"

"Basketball?"

"You're really not a sports guy."

I pat my belly. "Step outside with me."

The drop-off circle of my apartment building is arguably the goddamn windiest place on the planet, the air swooping from rooftops and plastering empty to-go platters against the lobby's glass walls. Dark has fallen.

Huddling against the concrete wall, I manage to light the smoke. "This is the women's basketball coach?"

"She's very interested in Jeanie. Your Jeanie. Our Jeanie."

I nod, thoughtfully. "What's that mean, she's interested?"

He tells me they're recruiting, gives me a short commercial—Big East school, storied program, excellent academics. Then he offers his studied opinion: it's a program that's seen better days, but they've had a successful recruiting class the last couple seasons, the coach is still relatively new, but that the tournament—the NCAA bracket thing, I'm assuming—should be no problem next season, and after that, sky's the limit.

"This is huge, Mr. Ganzi. Just huge."

A tumbleweed of loose-leaf paper and plastic bags bounds toward us from across the street. It passes ghostly below the streetlamps.

"Scholarship huge?"

"I'd say so." He bobs his chin. "Jeanie's good, Mr. Ganzi. She can play a lot of places."

I tell him her mom and I figured she'd have to go somewhere smaller, so that she could play. He says not necessarily, she fills out a little bit over the off-season, gains some strength, hones that quickness. He says it again: sky's the limit.

"This is just the beginning," he tells me. "Bass has to fly home Friday, but she's hoping tomorrow, even though it's a holiday, she's hoping maybe Jeanie could meet her at the school, at Whitney Young, maybe shoot around a bit."

"That legal?"

"Sure," he says. "I mean, it's not like she's offering a sports car. It's just a game of H.O.R.S.E."

"Ok," I tell him, stamping my cigarette against the brick wall. "Let me know when."

He pumps my hand. "I'll text you."

"Happy New Year," I say again.

Then he's gone, collapsing himself into one of the cabs that has been waiting in the traffic circle.

I light another smoke, considering. Georgetown: even Azita would have to be on-board with that, Jeanie playing hoops in our nation's capital. And sure, I hate Washington D.C., but with Georgetown, you fly into Dulles, you can pretty much skip the swamp entirely.

Fuckin' see you later, 2008. The Ganzis are moving on up.

I watch the numbers above the elevator doors ascend, skipping thirteen. Stepping off on the eighteenth floor, I am met by my neighbor, a spinster who doesn't seem to work but who seems to possess limitless resources. She's wrapped in a blanket so large it must be a floor rug. It trails behind her like a barbaric and royal train.

"Mr. Ganzi!" She waves at me from outside my own apartment door at the end of the hall. I can hear the thrum of bass from my unit. I know what she's pointing at before she speaks. "This music is too loud. Too loud!"

"Mrs. Xiang." I walk toward her, palms out, peaceably. "It's New Year's Eve. My daughter has friends over."

"I can hear your music in my apartment! With the television on!"

I nod, check my watch.

"Listen," I say. "I promise we won't go all night. Let the kids ring in the New Year, and that'll be it."

Already, I've got my keys out, swinging them on my index finger in what I hope looks like a happy-go-lucky way, then working the lock, the welcoming jangle and clack of coming home.

"It's not New Year's for all of us," she scolds.

I raise my hands, guilty as charged. Then the door opens, and I slip through.

Now this is a party: the kids have capitalized on my absence— when the cat's away, and what have you. My surround-sound speakers test unexplored decibels. The guests seem to somehow be wearing even less clothing than before. Every boy is shirtless, their young nipples like plunger heads. The girls wear glitter and bikini tops or sheer bathing-suit covers and little else. The smell of a locker room—sweat soaks my ballcap. I won't check the thermostat. I'm like that little trio of fucking monkeys: see no evil, hear no evil, speak no evil.

I return to my bedroom cave and close the door.

I turn channels, deliberately avoiding the New Year's countdown. Improbably, *Knight's Tale* is playing on a different channel. I watch the middle part again, where Chaucer makes a terrific speech, "to better understand the sound...of a whisper." I laugh, as always.

Maybe because it's New Year's, or maybe it's the frame of mind I'm in given the status of the Exchange, but all I can think about, watching this film for the second time in three hours, a few Scotches and one merlot popsicle into the evening, is that this movie isn't how real life works at all. Even if you had the courage and intelligence to seize the moment when it came, opportunities such as the one William and his friends are gifted when their knight dies—that shit never happens. Look, I get it: movies are an escape. They don't mimic real life, or even mirror it. Maybe, I ask too much from them. But I can't shake the feeling that my own life has been less about seizing opportunities and more like water following the path of least resistance downhill. I wonder, as I watch the credits roll, if I ever made a career choice, really. Or did Eugene just owe my dad a favor, hire me out of high school to carry his shit around, and now, twenty-five years later, I've accumulated more wealth than my own father could have ever imagined?

Jeanie knocks on the door. I roll off the bed to greet her. Her eyes are lit with a kind of shimmering mercury. She wags a red solo cup at me. She is unsteady on her feet and slurs her words "There's someone at the front door."

"Who?"

"I've already talked to Mrs. Xiang twice." Wag, wag, sip. "It's your turn."

"I've spoken to her already too," I grumble, but of course I flip off the television and head toward the door. On my way, I snag her solo cup and toss the wine down the sink. "Slow down a bit."

I'll tell her about Georgetown in the morning. I want her to appreciate the news, to make it a special moment. For her to understand what an opportunity it is, so that she seizes it. She's too blotto right now to care. I fill her red solo cup with water and give it back to her.

I find at my threshold not Mrs. Xiang but Ralphie, our doorman, and one of Chicago's finest—no one I know. I usher them into the hall, closing the door behind me.

"I'm sorry, Mr. Ganzi." Ralphie sweeps his black bangs. "But we got a noise complaint."

He tilts his head toward Mrs. Xiang's door, which I swear is cracked for a moment and then quickly shuts.

"Jeanie has some friends over," I explain.

"I know," Ralphie says, "and we appreciate your giving us a guest list." He glances at the cop, and it's like what he says next is for his benefit. "You're the ideal tenant. This is just a requirement of the job, unfortunately."

"I'll get them to turn it down," I say.

"I don't want to spoil anyone's celebration—"

"It's almost midnight. Things will wrap up pretty quickly after that."

We stand there like men, silently, considering the situation and recognizing my HOA violation for the injustice that it is.

"Is there underage drinking happening in there?" the cop finally asks.

He keeps his hands on his belt, feet apart, eyes hidden by the brim of his hat. Briefly, I am returned to the street corner again, touching my nose with one finger and then the other, while half-a-dozen cops watch. A feeling like panic then, and sweat behind my knees.

"It's just a little sleepover," I tell them. "I'm the chaperone. These kids are Bible study kids. Athletes. Those sorts."

"It's illegal to provide alcohol to minors."

"Yes sir, I know that."

He glances left, then right, like checking his blind spots. "Lucky for you, it's New Year's Eve, so I have better things to do than break-up a bunch of high-schoolers partying with their dad."

It hurts for some reason. "Thank you."

"But turn it down."

Ralphie flashes a quick, apologetic smile and hurries after him. The elevator chimes, they step on, and are gone. I stand for a moment rubbing my face. It's quiet. I have the sensation of dust settling. Then the music inside my apartment starts up again, so loud that I can feel the front door shuddering beneath my hand.

When I grab the knob, I find it locked.

I check my pockets. No keys.

I knock, twice. I ring the buzzer. I pound on the door until the wood bends. Nothing: just the bass, which I can feel through my socked feet. How Helen Keller became a music critic, apparently—don't ask me how I know this. But she'd "listen" to the music, the concert, with her bare feet, critiquing it through the vibrations and waves.

I have no choice but to knock on Mrs. Xiang's door. She answers so fast, I'm sure she's been watching me through the peephole.

"Go away." She has the rug-blanket pulled around her head like a Habib. "Leave me alone."

"Mrs. Xiang—"

"I already call the cops. They do nothing."

"I'm glad you're man enough to admit it," I say. "Listen, I'm locked out."

She blinks. "So? Call Ralphie."

I pat myself down, turn out my pockets. "Not even a phone."

She lets me in. Eight years living in this building, I've been inside her apartment exactly once, when she needed someone to feed her turtle. There's no sign of it now. The aquarium that was its former home overflows with colored paper, an accordion desk lamp, a tangle of electrical cords.

The odor of duck cracklings with an undercurrent of marmalade; carpet, too. The hardwood floors are covered by Persian rugs and scraps of cast-off loop pile. Christmas lights twinkle around the television, which mumbles softly, broadcasting *Dick Clark's New Year's Rockin' Eve*. The apartment, a junior one-bedroom, is, by all rights, a studio with one wall running down the center.

I step through, ignoring the scattered water glasses, the forgotten bowl of popcorn. There are long spools of yarn; bags with Chinese characters; small sculptures made of sticks.

Our balconies don't connect, but they look onto one another. I open the patio door against her protestations of letting in the cold. No one is on my deck. I squint against the wind, tears welling in the corners of my eyes, then duck back inside.

"Do you have a phone?" I ask.

She points to a beige landline, stuck on the wall like a wart. I pick up the receiver, the plastic cool and slick. I wave my finger above the dial pad, admiring how worn the buttons are, some unreadable. Goddamn cellphones: it's unnecessary, now, to memorize phone numbers. I guess at Jeanie's, but it reaches the voicemail of someone named Aracely. I try again, swapping the four and five. No luck: it's an Ameritech office. I dial my own cell phone—the one number I do happen to know by heart—on the off-chance someone hears it, but of course they don't, because I left the phone on my bed. Mrs. Xiang watches me the entire time, the way a person eyeballs their neighbor chopping down several tall trees, deep interest mixed with even deeper concern for the well-being of their hearth and home. I dial Ralphie at the front desk, thinking he might have some kind of skeleton key, but it just rings and rings—he's off, no doubt, handling some other New Year's Eve crisis. Doctors and police officers have the right to bitch about working on nights like this, but doormen have it rough too, without half the attention. Or gratitude.

"What happened to your turtle?" I ask Mrs. Xiang.

She grins. "Turtle soup."

I don't ask if she means this literally. I return to the sliding door and gaze out through the frosted glass. Only about three feet separate the corner of her railing from the corner of mine. Three feet seems like thirty, though, when you're two hundred feet above street level. There is no question that someone falling from my apartment deck would die. Chance of survival: zero.

"I don't suppose you have a harness?" I ask.

"I have leash."

"That was rhetorical." I consider. "What about an old bedsheet?"

She produces a dusty bed linen from a box. It too is beige, stained and torn. I take it out to the porch, sliding the door closed behind me.

I unfold the sheet. The wind nearly yanks it out of my hands. It billows like a sail, a slow snap and the cough of the fabric letting out. I gather it in, roll the sheet into a rope. One end, I knot around the porch rail. The other I loop around my right arm. I am under no illusions. I do not expect this bedsheet to hold me, if I fall. My only hope is that if I slip, this rigging will arrest my tumble just long enough for me to gain purchase again, before plummeting to the corner of Chicago and Orleans. My toes curl in my wet socks.

Mrs. Xiang opens the door. "What the fuck you doing?"

I drag one of her patio chairs to the corner. I climb the chair and lean into the concrete wall. The wind hammers, deafening. I put one foot on the rail, and then remove it. I sit down in the chair and take off my socks, tucking them into my pockets.

Like a hobbit, my bare, hairy toes peek out from beneath my cuffs. I stand on the seat again. I brace one hand against the wall. Incredible how cold stone can be. So solid. So indifferent. I step up on the rail with one foot, then the next, until I am steady enough to balance. I don't want to stand here long. Time is my enemy. The wind is its own steady force, consistent in its velocity. But easy to compensate for. My eyes tear; I wipe them. They tear again, and again I swipe them dry.

Don't look down. Look only from Mrs. Xiang's rail, where my toes dangle off the side, to my own rail, my own patio, my chairs there, the Fire Magic grill and the fork and spatula I still need to take inside—items that seem impossibly far away, but that also offer their own kind of safety and welcome, because of their familiarity. Because they're mine. Because they're where I want, more than anything, to be.

I picture Jeanie inside the apartment. I think of George-town, and how much she needs me now: to make her drink water, and take aspirin, and prepare for tomorrow. Tomorrow is her glorious future.

The distance from Mrs. Xiang's rail to mine is one yard. The length of a coffee table. A swatch of fabric—the basic unit of measuring textiles. A yard of ale: two-and-a-half imperial pints. A yard, something that is yours, to maintain, to play in, or, if you're a prisoner in, to march.

I lean against the wall. Breathe deep. Close my eyes.

Christ, JAG. You can almost just flop down and land on your own deck. It's not that far.

The wind sounds like a hand-dryer, the roar and high-pitched whine. My clothes stick to me like cellophane. I hear one car horn far below. Followed by several more, the way strangers in Chicago wish one another Happy New Year, "Auld Lang Syne."

And then the wind stops. My clothes relax. I open my eyes. There is a snow-pile on the corner of the rail. A shadow passes in the ambient light around me. On the roof of the sky-scraper across the street, a winking cell-phone tower. A smell like iron. Like blood.

I decide not to step, but to jump.

I plant both feet, bend my knees, and launch myself into the air. Another person might choose differently, faced with an equal distance to span at such great heights. Try to step across, perhaps, or push off from the wall like a jai alai player. My legs, though, are short. I don't know if I can span the gap. And I'm not about to bounce off the wall like *The Matrix*.

It's the standing long jump or nothing.

I leap and clear my own railing easily. All too quickly, the far railing comes screaming into view. I realize, as skyscraper lights spin overhead, that I was so focused on the distance, I never considered the landing. I try to compensate mid-flight. I have time to tuck my shoulder, to cover my face with my free elbow, even as my bound arm snaps back toward my jumping-off place, still tethered to Mrs. Xiang's rail. Briefly, I am suspended mid-air like a man who's been drawn and quartered. My velocity pulls me one way, the bedsheet yanks me back from the direction I came. I turn, fully parallel now to the ground, and belly-flop onto my porch. My legs kick over a deck chair, send it clattering into my grill, rocking it up on two wheels. I smash against the cement, both arms above my head like Superman.

"Holy fucking shit." The shirtless boy with the grass skirt stands at the open patio door, an unlit cigarette stuck to his bottom lip. He has lipstick on his shoulder, his Smartie necklace now a white string with a few sugary half-crescents dangling from it. "Mr. Ganzi, are you okay?"

I manage a kind of guttural sound.

"That was fucking awesome!" The kid rushes out, untangles my right arm from the bedsheet, helps me to my feet. "You were like a kangaroo! You leapt like twenty feet!"

"Three." I stand, running internal diagnostics, prioritizing points of pain. "The height adds drama."

"Shit, man." The kid claps me on the shoulder. "Happy New Year."

One side of my face is scraped from where I hit the goddamn concrete. Also, I've fucked my knee up something fierce. It throbs and then shoots painful spurs, alternately, although there is no visible wound. I check my reflection in the patio door and pick bits of gravel and plant soil out of my cheek. The jump tonight has made me instantly sober. That slightly drunk feeling I've been savoring is gone, replaced by a cold clarity.

A girl, Jeanie's friend, Ella, rushes out then, calling for me. She sees me and recoils: I'm sure I look like Anakin fucking Skywalker when they take off the Darth Vader helmet, a pale grubby splotch of a human being, bleeding from his face.

"Mr. Ganzi," she stutters. "You might want to come check on Jeanie."

I nod, grimly, and follow her inside.

The apartment throbs with music. It is somehow much louder than one hour ago. What Jeanie would call Dub: disembodied, somewhat robotic voices proclaim banal encouragements to keep the party going, while sounds akin to the winding down of chainsaws, drowned in reverb, consume every motor function. The music is so loud, the bass so animate, that I'm overcome by the sensation of wading through sonic mud. A dweeby gal wearing several leis manipulates the dimmer in time with the beat. In the center of the room, amid the pushed-back, now very rumpled furniture, bodies sweat. Above them all, Jeanie, bouncing on the couch cushions, arms extended, naked but for a shear cut of fabric knotted like a revolutionary's belt around her waist.

Her friend shouts something into my ear, but I have no idea what she says. I feel only her breath. Her spit splashes on my eyelids. I grab the Sox blanket off the couch and squeeze through the dancers who, frankly, aren't wearing much more than my daughter. I reach up and throw the blanket around her hips.

"Come on," I tell her, swaddling her. "Let's get down."

She doesn't resist. She stumble-falls to the floor and drapes her arms around me. For a second, my heart leaps with joy, like it does each time I think Jeanie is happy to see me, like it has since the moment of her birth. But her breath smells like spoiled wine, and her eyes are burgundy clouds when she finally raises them to look at me and focuses enough to recognize who it is that supports her weight.

"Dad?" .

We sway for a moment, slow-dancing. She belches, swallows it. Cringes.

I shout into her ear. "Where the fuck are your clothes?"

She cannot, apparently, manipulate her lips. Instead, she points to a dark corner of the condo.

I release her, hoping merely to guide her, but she topples.

"Use your legs," I tell her, like she's eighteen-months old again, kicking against the air. "Walk, for fuck's sake."

But she cannot. I try to support her, one arm around her waist, hers on my shoulder, but her legs are sea grass—she can't hold herself up. We make it several steps before she collapses to her knees, the weight of her head like a one-ton anchor.

"A little help?" I shout into the void, but no one comes to my rescue. I have the thought, even as I'm positioning myself behind my daughter, wrapping my arms beneath hers to keep her head off the floor, that they have each and every one of them been where I am now. That is why her friends are not concerned. Jeanie is simply drunk again. Tonight is my turn to help her.

I support her like I'm giving her the Heimlich. She slumps, hair over her face, mixing with drool.

"Kid," I tell her, "you have got to walk. You're much too big for me to carry."

"Pelo," she sputters, a spit-string clinging to her cheek.

"What?"

"Puke," she says, clearly this time.

I spin, grab her wrists, and, leaning into it, drag her toward the bathroom like hauling a wet carpet. She is dead weight, drooling, eyes closed. The blanket unwinds, showing her breast, her thighs, her butt. I'm ashamed for her, and for me, but I don't want to stop our momentum toward the toilet.

The closest bathroom is hers. The door is locked.

"Pew," she groans.

I pound on the door—nothing. I try the knob again: locked. I have home-field advantage, though. I happen to know that the finishes in this apartment are cheap, so that one good solid thrust with a bit of weight behind it will open any locked door. I grab the handle, lower my shoulder, and the door explodes. We surprise two people on the other side. A girl is on the edge of the tub, panties around her ankles, while a boy comes up for air from between her legs.

"Get the fuck out of here," I tell them.

They see me—Scarface, dragging Jeanie—and run.

No longer certain if Jeanie is even conscious, I pull her into the bathroom, sweep her legs to the side, and shut the door. She is face-down, legs curled on the bathmat, fetal.

"C'mon, girl." I get her up, make her hands touch the toilet seat. Her eyes flutter, or I only imagine it. She can hold herself up enough to rest her face against the lip of the bowl. She spits, or makes a movement with her lips like spitting, a little taut sound—too drunk to puke.

I wipe her hair from her face, hold it back. I encourage her to throw-up, root her on, promising she'll feel better, that it'll do her good. But what I'm really doing is promising myself, and ignoring completely what's staring me in the face, hoping this all doesn't mean what I think it must, wanting to brush over it, plow through it, get back to normal. If only she pukes, I tell myself, I will put her to bed, send the friends home, get on with our lives in the morning—the workout for Georgetown. She spits; I dab her mouth with toilet paper. I'm near tears, unwilling to admit what is so clearly unraveling before me.

No—she just drank a bit too much, that's all.

A strand of off-color spittle trails from her teeth to the water. I entertain driving her to the ER, her being a minor, how I'll be liable, as host, as someone who was supposed to be responsible for these kids, who allowed a common source, who provided a common source. Who permitted illegal things to happen under his roof, and all of this on top of my DUI. Okay then: no cops.

I glance at the beer tub, now only slushy water and discarded tabs. Ashamed, turning all this over in my mind, even as Jeanie becomes a puddle in my hands. She's so loose, I could stuff all of her into an overnight bag, fold her, and zip it with the smallest effort.

She goes slack, suddenly. She cracks her head on the tile. I gather her in my arms. There is blood. I spin the toilet-paper roll and fold a pad around my fingers, pressing it against the back of her head, all the while saying her name, each time louder. No response. I grope with my free hand for my phone. My arm slips and she collapses, head lolling against my chest. Swiping and tapping with my thumb, I open a web browser and search for "Signs of Alcohol Poisoning." Finally, I pull up a list of symptoms that describe Jeanie precisely. She is awash in my arms, her skin like wax. Somewhere I read that she should be taking more than eight breaths per minute. I watch her chest. There is a barely perceptible rise and fall, so slight I might be just making it up, wishing it into existence. I adjust my hold on her, put my finger beneath her nose. When I feel air move, I look at the clock. Thirty seconds, give or take, pass before I feel her breath again. Then another. Then nothing. Another twenty seconds pass, we're beyond one minute now, four erratic breaths in eighty seconds.

First, panic. Then, a bottomless drop into despair, a cold and deep certainty that my daughter is too far-gone to fix.

I dial 9-1-1. I hold the phone to my ear, even while swaddling Jeanie in the Sox blanket. I drag a towel from the closet, thick and soft and pink, and wrap her in that too. I catch us in the mirror on the back of the bathroom door. We are like some kind of pietà, but in reverse. The holy father cradling the young, dead virgin in his arms, praying her back to life.

I stand.

"Jeans," I say softly, doubting she can even hear me. "Put your arms around me." She doesn't. I wait, watching the clock. Her eyeballs dance like hamsters behind her lids.

"9-1-1 emergency."

"757 North Orleans." My voice trembles. "At Chicago. Seventeen-year-old female. Uh. Probably alcohol poisoning? Unconscious. I'll meet the ambulance in the lobby."

And then I am hoisting my daughter in my arms, all that adrenaline from the leap earlier tonight, from this, from farther back than this—the divorce, the Recession, this recurring dream I've been having where Pasternak and I are on the beach but I keep seeing shark fins in the water and I can't convince him not to swim—have I mentioned this? He always runs and dives into the break, before I open my eyes—makes her no heavier than a pit bull in my arms, a compact and even weight. I kick open the door. I am aware of the partygoers, and they now are aware of me. Of Jeanie. That perhaps this is something different. The music has been turned down to welcome the apple dropping on Times Square. The broadcast plays on, the anchors now reporting from the street, interviewing tourists, frozen solid. I hurry through them all, taking a short-cut through the kitchen, where I see, on the counter, Jeanie's name spelled out in red-stained popsicle sticks.

"Jeans." I manage to swing open our apartment door. "How many did you eat?"

By the time I reach the elevators, I am openly weeping. My tears are for Jeanie, and for myself. For my shame and fear.

The ambulance and I hit the lobby together. Ralphie is there, waving his walkie-talkie. Residents stop to gawk, and he assures them all is well, everything is okay, somebody has just had a little too much fun.

"Alcohol," I tell the EMT. "Poisoning, I think."

He takes Jeanie from me, lays her on a stretcher, straps her down with Velcro, takes one of her eyelids between his forefinger and thumb and rolls it back.

"Any sexual assault?"

"What?" I swallow. "Why?"

He does not blink. "Because she's not wearing any clothes, bro."

Rage like a wave crashes down, swamping my fear. I brace for it, let it break over me, and breathe deep.

"No sexual assault. I'm her father."

Outside, they shove the stretcher up and into the back of the ambulance. The memory of DIP's coffin being lowered into the earth, a hole hewn at right angles, the dirt sown on top.

"You can ride along," the EMT says.

I clamber in. The doors slam behind me. Already a second paramedic has wrapped Jeanie in a blanket.

He preps an IV bag. "Any drugs?"

"No," I answer. Then, "I don't know."

"Allergies?"

"Penicillin."

He rolls Jeanie onto her side. He bags an IV, shoves the needle into her arm, for hydration, he tells me. He opens her mouth, runs his latex finger around her gums, then probes deeper. She vomits; he directs her head toward the bucket. When she finishes, he takes a small tube, like the suction thing at the dentist, and clears her mouth. The whole time he's speaking into a radio perched on his shoulder. A litany of numbers and medical acronyms. I listen, trying to grasp any word that sounds like fucking English. There isn't much. Their profession, like mine, has its own linguistics that stay mostly hidden, inaccessible and opaque, behind their own pneumonic code.

I try to look out the fogged window, to see where we're going. "Northwestern?"

"Rush." The paramedic shouts over his shoulder. "Trust me. You want her at Rush."

She comes awake for a moment, just as we're pulling into the circle. She tries to sit up, but the paramedic puts a hand on her chest and makes her lie down again.

"These nocturnal hunters," she says, "often hunt in packs...."

It takes me a while to understand her. She's quoting a PBS documentary we watched, about how coyotes are becoming the opposite of endangered. The EMTs roll her off the back of the ambulance.

"*Canis latrans impavidus*," she says. "*Incolatus. Thamnos...*"

I turn, expel a great gush of tears, and, choking, try to follow.

The driver stops me. "We'll take her from here."

"What about me?" I ask, because truthfully, I have no idea where to go.

"ED." He points vaguely west. "Waiting room."

And then they are gone, Jeanie swallowed by one set of double-doors and then another. Behind her, a parliament of white lab coats and green scrubs. Their efforts are swift, and professional, and competent, leaving me on the walk with a wretched emptiness.

She needs to be science now, to be organic matter, nothing more, so that the hospital staff can do its job. So that emotions don't get in the way. Still, it takes everything I have to not force my way through those doors, to not follow her. It feels as if something is unspooling from my insides. Whatever that something is, Jeanie holds the other end.

I feel a buzzing in my hand. I coax my phone to life by clicking a button on the back.

There's a text from Penny. "Where r u?"

The ambulance lights spin, casting shadows on the brick walls, the slick pavement, the gray snow piled knee-high on the curb. The spin of the mobile in my daughter's bedroom, that parade of circus animals; a silent carousel of emergency lights, alternately red and then blue. I click the button on the back of my phone. The screen goes dark. I trudge across the compact snow, piled like coal ash, and when I find the first garbage can, I drop the phone in.

I wait alongside a handful of people, who are, I realize—just as they were at the drunk tank—primarily people of color. Everyone, in fact, but me.

They are here for tragedies suffered by friends or loved ones. Fingers blown off by firecrackers. Accidental stabbings. Drunks like my daughter, poisoned to within inches of their life.

I sit as far away as possible from them, as if they have some kind of virus I don't want to catch. Afraid the smallest acknowledgement might drag me back to where I began, in South Chicago, might never allow me to rise above my own father, whose misplaced and inexplicable self-confidence I hear in many of the cocksure voices coming in and out of the waiting room. Bragging about how fast they were going when they trashed their car, or high how they blew on the BAC. For shady lawyers and circuit court judges, business is good.

I've never been scared enough to quit drinking. My hang-overs get worse as I age; I've been arrested for driving under the influence; I've ridden in an ambulance with my daughter who may have drank herself to death under my watch. And yet.

I know what terror is. I know the face of addiction. It is the face of my father, beneath the kitchen floorboards. Calling for me. It's the color of my father's face in his last days, overripe and cancerous, not ashen but bruised like turned fruit.

Around 2:00 am, a doctor appears. All heads turn his way, but it's me he wants.

He informs me, clearing his throat several times, that Jeanie's blood-alcohol level was 0.32. Any more, and we could have expected an entirely different outcome. As it is, she will recover. We are lucky, he says, blinking behind square eye-glasses, that I brought her in when I did. He offers additional platitudes, his script lifted from *St. Elsewhere*. He recommends counseling, not only for Jeanie, but for me. And her mother. Florida? He can recommend someone there. He'll have the desk give me a number.

I ask can I see her? He says not yet. Then his pager shakes, and he checks it, and he hurries away, lab coat flapping behind him.

I should call Azita. But it's late, even for New Year's. Sun-rise will not come for hours yet. Jeanie's going to be ok. If I call her mother now, I'll only wake her, and cause her unnecessary panic. Whereas, if I wait until morning, she'll take it better. Or at least, it won't be so dramatic, that phone call you dread in the middle of the night. There's no difference between calling them now or six hours from now, except that in waiting, I can let them sleep. I can do that much for them, at least.

Eventually, I wander from the waiting room, looking for a gift shop or newsstand. Somewhere to buy a pack of smokes. I left home without shoes or coat, without anything but my wallet, with its insurance card and a couple hundred dollars cash. I walk and feel woozy and have to lean for a moment against the wall, either from exhaustion or from where I cracked my head on the porch. My face feels tacky, the blood drying.

I find the gift shop open. It sells flowers, stuffed animals, wrapped baskets of nuts and chocolate and dried fruit. Bottled water, balloons, a few magazines, and cigarettes, not Camel Wides, but Kamel Reds, which I am glad for all the same. I ask for a pack of matches, and the woman behind the counter gives me two.

A security guard has followed me from the waiting room. I can see him in the hallway, hanging back, working hard to make it seem like he's not watching me. I nod hello as I pass, returning to my vigil. I'm barefoot, cheek oozing, looking like I haven't slept since the Reagan administration. But I also haven't been trailed by anything more than an eager sales clerk since I was in high school, back when we'd hop turnstiles at Old Comiskey and try to dodge the ushers, who, after a summer or two, came to recognize, and, I think anyway, root for us.

Through the waiting room and to the revolving doors.

"Sir," someone says with practiced authority.

I put my hand on the glass.

"Sir."

I stop, turn. The security guard approaches, his sleeves rolled to his elbows, revealing tattoos of dragons, wildebeests.

"I'm going to have to ask you to stay inside."

"Excuse me?" I've already opened the pack of smokes, the thin plastic seal sticking to my thumb as I try to flick it toward the trash.

"Can't let you leave right now."

I glance through the windows, trying to see outside, but I see only my own reflection. Behind me, the hospital lights, blurry orbs, indifferent shapes. "Are we on lockdown?"

"No, sir. We just need you to stick in here for a bit."

"I'm going outside for a smoke."

"Can't let you do that. Sir."

His arms are crossed. He's so muscular, he's got that hard, little knob right above his elbow. I don't know what the fuck that muscle even is, or what exercise you have to do to make it grow. His entire countenance, in fact, implies that if I step through the revolving doors, he'll snap me in two.

"How long?" I slide my cigarette back into the pack, which makes the cellophane bulge. They never fit back in the way they come out from the factory.

"The police are gonna want to talk to you," he says. "Busy night, though. Might be a while. So just take a seat, chill. They should be here shortly."

Pasternak once told me Robin believed in dragons until she was in her early twenties. Which sounds crazy; which sounds like an indictment of our educational system; but then, I've never seen a goddamn blue whale. I just take it on faith, from television and biology textbooks, that they exist. You grow up believing all kinds of crazy shit if no one tells you different.

I could see being raised a certain way, with artsy parents maybe, or with people who were just dumb as fuck and didn't read, where dragons are taken as historical fact, where you might imagine they still roam the wild somewhere, endangered but protected in some National Park on some other continent. Then, as now, Robin's faith in dragons strikes me as sweet. At her core, she is a good person, if overly eager to claim her place on the economic ladder several rungs above the one on which she was raised. She deserved better.

Azita too: I'll be the first to admit, I ruined what we might have had.

I've made all kinds of mistakes. Sitting in the waiting room, waiting to see my daughter, waiting for the police to find me in this purgatory, I am a prisoner. I'd pay any amount of money, make any sacrifice, pray to any god you could name, to be able to take action. Yet, here I sit. Already wondering how I'm going to fit these present circumstances into my life story, the narrative that tells me who I am, the movie that stars me as the hero. With the dog in the park at Jeanie's tenth birthday, with my DUI, I could convince myself they were outliers, weird blips that did not, in the end, define me. A blemish, perhaps, like Cindy Crawford's mole, which makes the object more beautiful. But how many outliers can you accumulate until they can no longer be ignored, until they're no longer outliers but the sum total of your life?

I must fall asleep, because in what seems like a matter of minutes, someone is saying my name. I open my eyes, rub the stiffness from my neck. Stretch my legs, wiggle my toes.

Lucas is there, in his Chicago blues, looking grumpy.

"What time is it?" I ask.

"After four. I was heading home when I heard your name pop up."

I nod, shaking away remnants of semi-drunkenness, the adrenaline having long since drained, leaving, in its place, a feeling like a dry creek bed through the center of my skull. "Happy New Year."

"Not so happy for you."

"I didn't know they'd send you."

"Cops don't like it when their C.I.s talk to other cops. We get jealous."

I grin. I flash my pack of cigarettes like a badge. "Mind if we do it outside?"

He shrugs. We head to the revolving doors. I ask him where his bulldog is, his partner Steve. He tells me he left him in the car.

"For now," he says, and I can't tell if he's joking. "How's Jeanie?"

We move through the doors, retreating into our coats, pulling our elbows in to brace ourselves for the cold, and when it doesn't come, when we find some kind of warm front out-side, or warmer, anyway, than January has any right to be, we visibly relax. In the center of the pull-around, both the U.S. and the Illinois flag slump against their poles.

"She's okay." I turn to the wall, light a match and then my cigarette with one flick of my wrist. "I still haven't seen her."

He nods, stuffs his hands in his pockets. "Helluva year."

"Helluva year," I agree.

"Fucking, see you later 2008."

"Don't let the door hit you in the ass on the way out."

I light my next cigarette with the butt of my first, trying to restore my nicotine supply to base level. Lucas watches me. It doesn't seem like he's about to arrest someone. Me, for example.

"What happened, JAG?" he asks.

"I let Jeanie have friends over." I am moved to be truthful. "I took their keys. I let them have only wine and beer. No liquor. I told them specifically: no liquor."

I describe how I found her, the last few hours. I omit the popsicles made with merlot. I don't know whether their existence could get me in more trouble than I already am. I tell myself, if it hadn't been the popsicles, it would have been something else.

"Swear to God," I tell him. "I thought I was going to lose her. I thought I was going to lose her, and I felt it all just spiraling away."

He slips a card from his shirt pocket, hands it to me.

"Rehab?" I wipe my mouth.

"This is no joke, JAG."

I shake my head. Laugh. Light another cigarette.

"She's seventeen." I wave him away with the smoke. "She doesn't need rehab."

Lucas crosses his arms. "I was thinking the two of you could go together."

As we talk, slowly and quietly, as friends, there is the sense of the city waking up, the long night letting go. It's not quite light, but rather whatever the morning equivalent of gloaming is. Lucas and I can see one another now, our clothes sharpening. Across the street, a vendor opens his cart. Vehicles disappear up parking ramps. Far off, across the highway, skyscrapers with office windows lit are slowly erased by the sun, rubbed out by the winking glare of steel and glass.

Shadows retreat.

It's a beautiful fucking city. It really is.

Growing up, I'd walk to school each morning, see the far-off skyline, and wonder about the men built those towers, those palaces of commerce and glass. Some of the kids from the neighborhood, their dads worked construction. One kid's pop had poured concrete for the American Furniture Mart. Another kid's dad spent a month on scaffolding, forty stories high. They'd point to buildings that, from our crumbling neighborhoods, looked like turrets on a play castle. They'd name them proudly, claim ownership, and by doing so, feel as if the city somehow belonged to them. For many, it was their only inheritance. Their civic birthright. But it did not belong to them in the way that it belongs to people like me.

Since its founding, Chicago has been the Wild West. A little more unbuttoned, a little more rough and tumble than cities to the east. An upstart. At heart, a blue-collar town, despite the fortunes that are made and stolen here every day. A city built on the aching shoulders of hog butchers and the price one man will pay another man for a sack of corn. The working class, the fathers of the kids I grew up with, may have built this city brick by brick, but they are not permitted in its marble halls or its shimmering, rocketing lifts. They are not afforded lake views, or river views, or views of cubicle grids below. Chicago is a working-class town, grounded in blues and some of the most optimistic people you'll meet anywhere. But its greedy heart is concrete and stone, its only morality a loose interpretation of, if not a willful disregard for, rules.

"JAG?" Lucas has been talking, but I've no idea about what.

"Sure, sure. I hear you."

"Nobody's pressing charges. You and Jeanie can go home after this."

Right now, our home is a trashed apartment full of passed-out, soon-to-be hungover high school kids. The workout tomorrow for the Georgetown basketball coach—who knows now if it will even happen?

I want to take Jeanie out of town for a few days. Catch a taxi from here to the airport. Buy fresh clothes in the terminal, fly anywhere with open seats, somewhere tropical, Mexico or the Caribbean. Fucking Fiji. No phones, no bags, just us and a beach and whatever we find along the way. Just a few days to get our bearings, to air out, to replenish our Vitamin D.

Just the beginning, her coach said. Still, it feels like an end.

Something flashes in the corner of my eye. I turn. Across the street, there is a narrow alleyway. Through it, I see, unmistakably, the hindquarters of a coyote square the corner and disappear.

I don't think, but instead bolt across the street.

"JAG?" Lucas calls to me. "John?"

Beneath the skybridge, I hook a left down the alley. Sure as shit, a coyote waits at the far end, at the foot of a dumpster. He stands profile, his head turned toward me. He is very still. His fur is full and gray, with streaks of red. His tail is down. I watch his ribcage rise and fall, his breath like wood smoke. He shakes his snout. I take a step toward him, and he jogs off down an alleyway to the right. I sprint after him, heart pounding.

My time spent on the recumbent bike pays dividends. I'm hardly winded when I clear the end of the next alley in time to see the beast cross and enter a parking garage.

I wish like hell I hadn't thrown away my phone. Jeanie will never believe this.

The coyote seems to turn back once to make sure I'm still behind him. And then he trots up the entrance ramp to the next level.

I follow.

Pasternak once asked me what I'd do if I didn't have this: the firm, the pits, the riches, the stress, each of them a kind of drug, which I don't have any problem admitting I'm addicted to. I appreciate the distance my wealth affords me from those people in the waiting room, in the drunk tank, allowing me the means to fly first-class or sit in boxes at ballgames.

That's what he meant, of course. Without those things, I am alone.

I run—more of a shuffle now, really—up one spiral ramp and then the next, my heart a burning log in my chest. My hands feel numb, the way they do sometimes when I overdo it on the treadmill. Something about the stress I hold in my upper back.

I don't see the coyote, but I smell it, a bit of tomcat and burning leaves.

I never took DIP's question seriously, because I couldn't seriously imagine myself without the job, without the action. Honestly, I've always assumed I'd stroke out one day on the trading floor. Fall backwards into the arms of my men to be passed overhead like the body of the executed Christ. I realize now, cresting the fourth parking ramp and coming out into daylight, onto the roof, thighs afire, that I never took his question seriously because those things, in the end, meant nothing. They have never been anything other than place-holders, a way to afford my life, to pass the time—a way, in the end, not to kill myself.

The only thing, I realize, which I could never do without, is Jeanie.

There is no sign of the coyote. I dry-heave, right out in the open, bent double, hands on knees.

"Jesus Christ," I say to no one. "If this is what it feels like to die—"

I walk to the rooftop edge and rest against the rail, looking out over the highway and in the distance, the city. I wait for my heart to slow down. It pounds there in my chest, insistent as a war drum.

The sun is coming up fully over Lake Michigan. This time of year, any light is blinding. I never bother with sunglasses between October and May. But this dawn is naked, no cloud cover. The water ripples, heavy and still-dark. The city is golden on the shore, reflecting so much light I can barely stand to look at it, imagine the detonation of a nuclear bomb, that all-encompassing and blinding swell of energy that you have to turn away from the moment it flashes.

I breathe in the cold smell of asphalt. I exhale exhaust from a laundromat. I inhale fresh bread from a Polish bakery.

I exhale the stench of city septic. Breathe in canned air dust, a sausage "with," the way my palm smells after holding the grab-bar on the "L." Breathing out the cartilage and wheat-flour smell of glue traps, or the white pollen shit that falls everywhere in June, of my own breath heavy in my wet scarf, tightening it again around my mouth and nose, breathing in the redolence of home.

To the beautiful skyline, I shout and holler and whoop the way I once did in my youth, each year at midnight.

There are birds above, loud and large. The wind picks up. My scalp tingles, the scabs on my cheeks. A blood smell, that iron taste on my tongue—I collapse against the rail and crane my neck toward the sky like a new-born scavenger, like a condor opening its eyes for the first time.

The city burns, illuminated. Light washes everything, shimmering like quicksilver. A transformation, a city always in the act of becoming.

Acknowledgments

Thank you to Stevan V. Nikolic and Adelaide Books.

Many thanks to the friends who read and gave feedback on early drafts, including Maggie Morgan, Meaghan Mulholland, and my invaluable first reader, who's never wrong: Heather Dewar.

Thank you to Steve Cushman, Owen Duffy, Heather Newton, and Emily Gray Tedrowe. Thanks to Betsy Thorpe for guidance; Michele T. Berger for staying on my case about finishing this thing; and the North Carolina Writers' Network for providing community.

Thanks to Francesca's Café in Durham, NC: RIP.

Thanks to Paulos Strike for insight into the finance industry; thanks to the real Chicago Board Options Exchange for hiring me way back in the early aughts and giving me so much good fodder. Not that any of what went on there made it into this book, because this book is fiction, and all resemblances to persons living or dead....

This book takes place right around the same time when it was only the Cincy 6. Love you all, and all our new additions.

To my parents, Lyle and Ro, my sister Cara, my nephews Isaac and Luca: thank you.

Thanks especially to my daughter Eloise; to my son, George; and to my wife Amelia, who'll always be the classier half of our *duprass*.

About the Author

L.C. Fiore is an award-winning novelist; a music podcast host; and baseball fan.

Before he learned to write, he spent his early childhood filling up notebooks with cartoon stories.

One of his earliest memories is of visiting a library with his father. Although L.C. couldn't yet read, he had a sense, looking up, that those impossibly high shelves held great mysteries. Even today, the world never quite opens out for him the way it does when he renews his library card—the surging sensation that suddenly, through books, anything is possible.

L.C.'s debut novel, *Green Gospel* (Livingston Press, 2011), was named First Runner-Up in the Eric Hoffer Book Awards (General Fiction); short-listed for the Balcones Fiction Prize; long-listed for the Crook's Corner Book Prize; and was a finalist for the First Horizon Award.

His second novel, *The Last Great American Magic* (Can of Corn, 2016), won Novel of the Year from *Underground Book Reviews*; was a Gold Winner in the Readers' Favorite Book Awards (Tall Tales); a Silver Winner in the IBPA Benjamin Franklin Awards (Historical Fiction); and a Finalist in the CIPA EVVY Awards (Historical Fiction).

L.C. is a Chicago ex-pat who grew up in the Midwest and now lives in Chapel Hill, North Carolina, with his wife and family. He earned his BA from Sewanee: The University of the South and his MA from Northwestern University.

In what seems like another lifetime ago, he worked as an Executive Assistant at the Chicago Board Options Exchange. Many of his experiences at CBOE inspired events and characters portrayed in *Coyote Loop*.

Since 2011, he has served as the communications director for the North Carolina Writers' Network, a 1,400-member organization that provides programming and resources for writers of all levels of skills and experiences: www.ncwriters.org.

He launched The A440 Podcast in 2019, a half-hour long weekly podcast dedicated to underexplored aspects of music and people who work with music in interesting ways: www.a440pod.com.

His fiction has appeared in *Ploughshares, Michigan Quarterly Review, New South*, and *storySouth*, among many others, and has been anthologized in *Sudden Flash Youth: 65 Short Short Stories* (Persea Books) and *Tattoos* (Main Street Rag).

His nonfiction has appeared on NPR, *TriQuarterly Review*, The Good Men Project, and in various baseball publications, including *The Love of the Game: Essays by Lifelong Fans* (McFarland & Co.) and many Bill James annuals from ACTA Sports.

L.C. Fiore considers himself a fantasy sports apologist.

His wife often makes fun of him for reading "books that are only pages and pages of numbers." But numbers tell stories too. He knows what "Shoeless" Joe Jackson hit in the 1919 World Series, for example, and, as he harbors a secret passion for statistics, he's pretty excited to have written a novel about the finance industry.

Made in the USA
Columbia, SC
09 March 2021

33589969R00202